Welcome to the
Great Mysterious

Welcome to the Great Mysterious

Lorna Landvik

For my brothers,
Wendell and Lanny
and in memory of Greg

Acknowledgments

I would like to thank Leona Nevler for her care and passion. I'm grateful to have her as an editor and to have Ballantine as a publisher. Thanks, too, go to my globetrotting agent, Betsy Nolan, and to Jenny Alperen in her office, who sends me good stuff through the mail.

I'd like to thank the Loft and the McKnight Foundation for support and checks—I appreciate both.

To all the readers who have taken time to write me—thanks! Your letters mean a lot to me.

To my friends and family; I'm lucky to have you on my side. And as always, thanks to Harleigh and Kinga for all the important things, and to Chuck—you're the man.

Welcome to the
Great Mysterious

Chapter 1

ll right, so I'm a diva. There are worse things—a mass murderer, a bigot, a telephone solicitor.

I'm surprised my sister even uses the word as an insult. Why should I be offended by the truth? My dictionary defines *diva* as "a distinguished female singer." I certainly am that. The word, however, is cross-referenced with *prima donna*, defined as "a temperamental person; a person who takes adulation and privileged treatment as a right and reacts with petulance to criticism or inconvenience."

Well, I might ask, who likes criticism or inconvenience? And why shouldn't one take privileged treatment as a right? A little self-esteem is *not* a bad thing. Ann, for instance, could use a serious infusion of it.

Throughout my life I have heard the question, "Are you *really* twins?" It's an understandable query; Ann and I are as different as the proverbial night and day. Ann once elaborated on that analogy in an interview, describing me as being night—dark and dramatic, living among stars—and herself as light and plain and about as exciting as an afternoon nap.

We're fraternal twins, obviously, and don't share that spooky, ESPy you're-my-other-half thing identical twins do. Ann and I are more like sisters who could have been born years apart if

Mom hadn't been such an industrious egg layer. We're very close and have shared everything from chicken pox to clothes to deep secrets, but when I look at Ann face-to-face, I don't see my mirror image. In fact, if I looked at Ann right now, what I'd see is a big pest.

For those of you who don't know me (where the hell have you been living, in a cave with no TV or cable access?) I am Geneva Jordan, star of stage, screen (unfortunately, my theatrical schedule hasn't allowed me to do hardly any of the movies I've been offered), and television (if you didn't see me accept my Tony award, I'm sure you've heard my voice singing the Aromati-Cat cat litter and Chef Mustachio Frozen Pizza jingles). Recently I just ended a year and a half's run in the title role of *Mona!*, a musical about DaVinci's mysterious model.

> *She's a gal with a crazy half smile, she's Mona Lisa!*
> *Oh, what I wouldn't do to get a piece a . . . that Mona Lisa!*

You'll have to trust me that the music is so catchy, the lyrics actually work.

My role as Mona Lisa brought me my second Tony, a cover story in *New York* magazine, and a relationship with Trevor Waite, my costar. My role as Mona Lisa and its resulting dividends, *especially* my relationship with Trevor Waite, is also what brought me close to mental and physical collapse. Which made my sister's request all the more preposterous.

"Please," she begged over the phone, changing her tack from insulter to supplicant. "Riley and I need this time together."

"I'm not arguing that, Ann. It's where I come in as baby-sitter that I'm objecting to."

"You're Rich's godmother."

"I'm aware of that, Ann. But godmother does not mean rescuer."

"Then what does it mean?"

I looked at my watch. I didn't have to be anywhere for another hour, but she didn't have to know that. "I have to run, Ann. I've got a hair appointment."

"What does it mean?"

"Listen, Ann, I don't—"

"Quit calling me Ann."

"That's your name, isn't it?"

"Yes, but whenever you're in one of your I'm-right-and-you're-wrong modes, you overuse my name. Like a cranky old schoolmarm or something."

"First I'm a diva and now I'm a cranky old schoolmarm. Nice talking to you too, *Ann.*"

I could hear her protests as I hung—okay, slammed—the receiver back in its cradle.

She called back immediately, not grasping the concept of a dramatic exit. I let my machine pick it up.

"Geneva," she said, "please. I'm sorry. I don't know where else to turn. Please pick up. . . . Please help me, Dee."

Oh, that was low. *Dee* was a reference to the childhood nicknames bestowed on us by our Grandma Hjordis.

"It's Tweedledee and Tweedledum!" she used to say in her Norwegian accent, "my favorite twin grandchildren in the world!"

We were her *only* twin grandchildren, but she made us feel that we couldn't have been surpassed by quintuplets.

She lived next door to us, and her home was a cinnamon-roll-smelling haven for my sister and me, a place where she played endless games of Hangman and War with us and let us upend all her furniture cushions to make elaborate igloos (when we played Roald Amundsen discovering the South Pole) or wigwams (when we played Leif Eriksson discovering America). She had a canoe in the backyard that we'd pretend was the *Kon-Tiki.*

Grandma Hjordis was a Norwegian nationalist to the core and never let an opportunity pass to indoctrinate her granddaughters in the robust history of her homeland and its explorers.

"Try not to be afraid of new things," she advised. "The world is more fun if you're not a scaredy-cat."

When she died suddenly, breaking our fourteen-year-old hearts, we buried her nicknames for us with her, and only brought them out in moments of crisis.

I picked up the phone.

"All right," I said, my voice a concentrate of exasperation. "You have a one-minute extension. Don't think I'm saying yes. I'm just saying I'll listen to you—for *one more minute.*"

"Okay," said Ann eagerly, like a game show contestant heading for the bonus round. She took a deep breath. "You know how hard Riley works—my gosh, you don't get to be chair of the English department without working hard—"

"You're not telling me anything new, Ann."

"Your interruptions don't cut into my time, do they?"

I sighed. "Get to the point, Ann."

"Okay, okay. Anyway, this is a chance for us to be together—alone—for the first time since Rich was born, Geneva. Thirteen years! And in Italy, Geneva—Italy!"

I sighed again. "Can't Mom fly up?"

"You know her hip is still bothering her. And how can she leave Dad?"

After a lifetime of good health, our parents, now living in a retirement community in Arizona, had finally drawn the sorry-you-lose cards. Mom had had hip-replacement surgery the previous summer, and Dad was recuperating from a mild stroke that affected his balance and sometimes his memory. These old-age infirmities were certainly no fun for them. Still, didn't they realize their problems were a big inconvenience for the rest of us? (Don't sic AARP on me—I'm just joking.)

"All right, all right."

"You mean all right as in you'll do it?"

I laughed—inappropriately, I suppose. "God, no. I meant all right as in don't talk anymore."

"My minute's up?" Sometimes my sister is far too literal for her own good.

"Ann, I'll get back to you by the weekend, okay?"

"With an answer?"

"No, with an Ole and Lena joke."

Ann ignored my sarcasm.

"Thanks, Geneva."

"I haven't said yes yet," I reminded her.

"I know, but thanks anyway."

I hung up quickly; her gratitude actually seemed to have heat, and my ear burned from it.

I grabbed my cashmere coat—one of the presents Trevor had given me that he hadn't repossessed. When we had broken up, I threw my engagement ring at him, never thinking for a minute that the tightwad wouldn't give it back.

I guess he wasn't really cheap—he did spend a lot of money on me—but he often tainted the gift-giving experience by telling me what wildly expensive thing he was *going* to get me before presenting me with a less expensive substitute that somehow "said Geneva louder." Cashmere said Geneva louder than mink. A picnic in Central Park said Geneva louder than lunch at the Four Seasons. Once we were browsing through a rare-book store, and the first edition of *Marjorie Morningstar* said Geneva louder than the first edition of *The Great Gatsby*.

"You're so much more Marjorie than Daisy," he had said, taking out his credit card to pay for the book, which conveniently happened to be about three hundred dollars less than the one I wanted. I suppose I sound ungrateful, but really, it hurt my feelings that everything that said Geneva was second-best.

Outside the air was brisk and everyone was moving in the usual out-of-my-way-or-I'll-trample-you pace I love so well. Autumn in New York—my favorite time of year in the city. You can see why they wrote a song about it. On that day it was as if all of Manhattan was still in the back-to-school state of mind that had begun in September, busy and energized and full of big plans and bigger ideas. A person's senses were cranked up: colors seemed sharper, noises louder, and smells from hot dog and pretzel vendors' carts positively aromatic. And yet in the midst of all this a slight melancholia seemed to filter through the city skies, making everything seem . . . I don't know, somehow _tender_.

A fan stopped me outside of Tiffany's.

"Geneva Jordan!" she said in that surprised tone that made me feel I was less a human than an apparition.

I fluttered my fingers in a wave, hoping that was enough for her. It wasn't.

"Will you sign my—" She looked at her armload of packages for something to write on. "My Tiffany's bag?"

"Only if I can keep what's inside."

She looked stricken for a moment, until I reassured her I was only joking.

I always have pens in my coat pockets; it speeds up the process. She handed me the bag, and for a minute I thought about running off with it and giving her a really good scare, but instead I politely asked her name.

"Beth," she said. "I read about you leaving _Mona!_, which, by the way, I loved you in. Not as much as I loved you in _Sunny Skies_ or

The Wench of Wellsmore, but still, those scenes between you and Trevor Waite—"

"How kind of you to say so," I said, capping my pen and giving her back her Tiffany's bag. "Now I must run—nice talking to you!"

I raced off as quickly as I could on my three-inch-heel boots. These fans will stand around and yak all day if you let them, telling you what they've liked about your career and what they haven't— as if you've been waiting all your professional life for their critique. Don't get me wrong—I'm not above my fans. I just like them a whole lot better when they stick to flattery.

"Miss Jordan!" said Wendy the receptionist, as if I'd caught her doing something she shouldn't have been doing. "We didn't expect you until two-thirty!"

"I had to get out of the house," I said, draping my coat over the faux leopard couch. "Can Benny take me early?"

"Of course I can, darling," said Benny, picking up his cue far better than some actors I've worked with.

He rushed over to me, giving me a big smooch on the lips. "I just kicked Claudette Pehl out of my chair. I told her, 'Darling, I don't care if your hair's still wet—I've got more important clients to attend to.' "

"Sure you did, Benny," I said. Claudette Pehl was only *the* fashion model of the moment, all seventeen years and sixty-eight pounds of her.

"Coffee?" he asked, taking me by the hand and leading me into the salon, "with a dash of Bailey's?"

"A *big* dash."

Lou Reed was blasting through the salon's sound system— at Hair by Benny, nothing was done in baby steps. Each chair was upholstered in some faux jungle animal skin and most often occupied by somebody recognizable. Polly York, the PBS news commentator, was getting foiled in Martin's chair, and over in André's, Gina Bell, the ice skater, was getting one of her signature pixie cuts.

After I changed into a cotton smock printed with tiger stripes (every smock matches its chair; kitschy, but what the hell, that was part of the fun of Benny's) and got shampooed by one of those sullen girls whose mental health you can't help but worry about, I sat down in Benny's chair.

"Looking at you, the word *rough* comes to mind," he said, handing me a mug that smelled more of booze than coffee.

"Oh, Benny, don't mince words with me." I took a sip of the enhanced coffee and made a face. "I said a dash, not half a bottle."

Instead of making apologies and scurrying back to the coffee machine, Benny flicked the end of his comb against my shoulder blade.

"Shut up and drink it," he said. "You know you could use it."

I could and I did.

"Ahh," I said after chugging it down. "Things are looking better already."

I knew *I* was. Benny wasn't one of the top hair stylists in Manhattan by chance; he knew how to cut hair and, most important, how to make his clients look good while he did. The lighting was warm and mellow, fading out lines and wrinkles and large pores and everything else that conspired to make you look like the wicked stepmother when you still felt like Cinderella.

I looked great . . . for forty-eight. I could easily pass for forty, which I had been doing until my sister was interviewed by a feature writer for *The New York Times* and blabbed our real age—as if she hadn't been schooled enough on this particular topic. Still, looking forty isn't exactly a plus in show business, although it is easier to age in the theater than it is in the movies, where they start casting you as the mother in *Little Women* when you feel you'd be perfect for Jo.

I do have a lovely nose (my own, thank you very much), pretty teeth (mostly my own), and good hair (the natural waves are mine, the Red Flame color—Benny's marvelous idea and for ten years my signature—is not), but I'm called gorgeous primarily because I'm a star.

It's not undue humility (in my case, all humility would be undue) that makes me say that; I turn heads, first and foremost, because of who I am and not what I look like.

"Benny, what do you think about short hair?"

We both watched in the mirror as he held out a rippled strand of my hair.

"Not for you, darling. Your hair is so dramatic . . . so free. You'd look like a computer saleswoman with short hair. Or a drill sergeant."

I laughed. Benny was one of the few people who wasn't afraid to tell me what he really thought.

"All right, then. Just take off the split ends."

As Benny snipped and sniped in his jungle lair (his gossip was almost as good as his styling), I closed my eyes and tried to think of more excuses why I couldn't possibly help my sister out.

As they say, timing is everything, and this timing was bad. I hadn't left *Mona!* just for the fun of it. I wasn't burned out on the show yet; what had made me not renew my contract was a doublehitter—heartbreak and menopause, neither of which I'd admit to the world at large. My press release merely mentioned my gratitude for being with such a fine production and my wish to explore other creative avenues.

What I really needed time for was to practice my three R's—relax, replenish, and rassle my screaming hormones to the floor. I wanted to putter around the city, have late-afternoon teas at the Carlyle or the Pierre, see the shows I hadn't been able to see because of my own, and spend my free weekends at the various country homes friends had invited me to. I needed time to spoil myself rotten.

"Earth to Geneva," whispered Benny in my ear.

I opened my eyes, startled.

"Sorry I was boring you," he said with exaggerated nonchalance. "Believe me, there are plenty of women who'd *pay* to sit where you are and listen to me."

I laughed. "I do pay you, Benny, remember?"

Benny shrugged and with his fingers fanned out my hair. It was long and wavy—"hippie hair with an uptown attitude," as Benny described it. (I follow the Dick Clark secret of youth—never change your hairstyle.)

"So how does it feel to be an out-of-work actor?"

Tears welled up in my eyes.

"Geneva, darling! I didn't mean anything by that—I was only trying to be funny."

"It's not that," I said, waving my hand. "It's my sister."

In the mirror, I saw concern pinch the features of Benny's round face.

"She's not ill, is she?"

I shook my head. "Nothing like that. She and her husband have this opportunity through the college to go to Italy."

"Hmm," said Benny, checking to see if my ends were even. "I guess I'm not quite grasping the dilemma."

"They want me to baby-sit!" I said, and seeing the ice skater look over at me with interest, I lowered my voice. "They've got a thirteen-year-old son they don't want to take out of school. Richard—Rich, that's his name. My godson."

Benny poured something delicious-smelling onto his hands and massaged it into my scalp. "And you don't want to baby-sit this Rich because . . . ?"

"Because I'm on vacation!" I said, and again my raised voice made the snoopy skater with her stupid pixie cut look over. "Because my doctor says I'm overstressed and overworked and I need to take it easy!" I whispered. "And besides, I need to get over . . . things."

"That cad," said Benny. It was his Pavlovian response; whenever I mentioned anything that might directly or indirectly have to do with Trevor, he said, "That cad." It was for this sort of thing that I tipped him so well.

"But doesn't your sister live on a pond or something in Indianapolis?"

"A lake," I said. "She lives on a lake outside Minneapolis."

Benny shrugged; to the transplanted Australian, it was all the same.

"But mightn't that be peaceful?" he suggested. "Sitting by the lake out in the middle of nowhere?"

"The lake'll probably be frozen," I said. "And even if it isn't, I'd be sitting with a thirteen-year-old."

"Right, the kid. He's that bad, huh?"

My tears, which seemed to be on double overtime, welled up again.

"Oh, Benny!" I said, and then, in a move far more fluid than any double axel Gina Bell ever performed, I swiveled my chair, shielding myself and my tears from the prying eyes of that nosy little ice nymph.

That evening I lit a fire and repaired to my many-pillowed couch with a good bottle of champagne and an even better box of chocolates. I had left the show only three days earlier, and I still felt strange and out of sorts at eight o'clock. I could imagine the cast backstage, goosing each other under their elaborate costumes or doing any of a number of childish things a cast in a long-running show does while waiting for the curtain to go up. I always loved that time, listening to the excited hum of the audience and then the collective holding of breath as the orchestra began its overture. We were the elite of the Broadway stage, ready to go on, but not before we shared a bad joke or accused each other, in indignant whispers, of farting.

What I really missed were those preshow kisses Trevor Waite and I used to share before we broke up.

Something crackled and hissed in the fireplace, a perfect accompaniment to my mood. I took a big, sparkly gulp of champagne and reminded myself not to waste time thinking about Trevor.

My reminder did no good.

"How could I have been so blind?" My only excuse, and a lame one at that, was that his charm had obscured my vision.

Trevor's great you're-the-only-one-for-me charm was practiced on everyone, from Mrs. Wang at the corner market, who always slipped a perfect peach or a basket of berries into our bag, all the while winking at Trevor, to the *New York Times* reviewer who wrote, "He's a modern version of Errol Flynn and Laurence Olivier. And then he opens his mouth and sings like Placido Domingo!"

When he focused those ice blue eyes on you, time didn't stop, but at least a couple of seconds were lost. When he smiled at you, you felt as if you were being given a present. But his biggest gift was his voice. God almighty, that upper-crust British accent (he adopted it as his own once he moved from Manchester to London) coupled with those deep, rich tones—get me the smelling salts. I know it's a cliché to say someone has such a nice voice they could read the phone book and make it sound good—but he could, and did once, accepting my challenge.

"Bradshaw," he read, after clearing his throat. "Amy, Arnold, Beverly, Bruce, Bryan." Holding the splayed directory in one hand, he raised the other. "Continuing with the Bradshaws," he intoned, "we have C. L., D. R., David, Doris, Douglas, and Grant. Harold, I. J., Jody, Julie, and Lloyd."

He read to me from other sources more poetic than the phone book, and I think that was what I missed most about him—it's tough to beat the romanticism of an English actor with a beautiful voice reading you Shakespeare on a rainy New York afternoon.

Along with our love of listening to his voice, we shared a lot— the excitement of mounting a new show, laughs, a fondness for Thai food and Alfred Hitchcock movies and late-night walks. Both actors, we understood each other and the crazy world we'd chosen to make our living in. More than anything though, we had that strong chemical charge—he was oxygen, I was hydrogen, and when we were together, sparks of some kind always flew.

I was initially so enamored of Trevor that I was willing to overlook the flirtation he shared with one of the chorus girls. By nature, performers tend to be flirts, but the flirtation escalated until I was certain he was having an affair (when I confronted them once after a show, he vehemently denied the charge; she only smiled). Seeing as I knew how to be fairly charming myself, his charm became more obvious to me, and I saw how he most often poured it on to get something in return. When he directed this charm at the new understudy of the second female lead, I finally had to face the fact that what he wanted in return at this point in his life was more women, *younger* women.

A sob I didn't even know was gathering jumped out of my throat, and I realized that darkness—not a darkness of light but a scarier, deeper one—had crawled into my arms.

I have always been a night owl, even as a little girl. Ann was one of those people who could fall asleep half a minute after she crawled into bed, leaving me to amuse myself, which I did happily—making up songs, imagining myself in various scenarios with classmates and boys I liked, practicing my imitations of TV and movie stars. But one night—I think I was about nine—my imagination was overtaken by a loneliness of such depth that my child's brain wondered if this was what it was to go crazy.

"Ann! Ann!" I had whispered, rocking her shoulder. "Ann!"

"What is it?" she had asked, sitting up, her eyes wild.

"Ann, *I'm so lonely!*"

My sister squinted at me, trying to gauge whether or not I was joking. Determining that I was not, she asked, "Why, Dee? I'm right here."

"Oh, Dum," I said, pressing my body next to hers. "Just hold me."

I couldn't articulate the feeling then, nor did it matter that I couldn't, as Ann fell immediately back asleep (the traitor).

The next night it came back again.

"Ann! Ann!" I said, shaking her shoulders as though it were part of a CPR maneuver. "My loneliness is back!"

My sister wasn't too impressed, advising me, before she rolled over, to "just tell it to go away."

I did, and it obeyed, but not permanently. It wasn't an every-night fixture, but each and every time it came, the loneliness was so deep and encompassing, I feared I wouldn't be able to get out of it. My coping mechanisms ranged from denial ("You don't exist, I feel swell") to bullying ("I'm stronger than you!") to submission ("Okay, I've given in to you, now will you leave?"). In an acting class I once took, our teacher urged us all to soften our debilitating emotions by naming them.

"Give them incongruous names that blunt their power," she advised in her perfect diction. "Call anger Fred, anxiety Myrtle, fear Lulu." I named my loneliness Petunia, and at first I think it did help to blunt its power, but after a while I realized it was still loneliness, only with a silly name.

I was never happy to experience it, but at least on this night it diverted my attention from Ann and her request. Petunia taunted and harassed me, but finally I was all cried out, and the time came to deal with my latest problem. That stupid saying "When life hands you a lemon, make lemonade" came into my head, but I'll be damned if I knew the recipe.

First of all: I am not a bad person. Maybe I'm a little self-centered, a little flamboyant, but if that were a crime, everyone in show biz would be doing hard time. I like the idea of helping people, and I'm sure if I had more time, I'd put the idea into practice. I like to think that I give so much while I'm onstage that offstage I can slack off a little.

But my damn conscience was suddenly a parrot who couldn't shut up: *She's your twin sister, she's your twin sister, she's your twin sister.*

She had certainly done big favors for me. Reliable, responsible Ann, with her steady teaching job right out of college, had always bankrolled my big dreams. She's the one who paid my bus fare to New York after I had spent all my money on clothes; she's the one who'd enclosed a five or a ten in her weekly letters to me, the one who'd helped me out with rent at least a dozen times. Because Ann was so free with her money, I thought teachers earned great salaries; it wasn't until my first Broadway play that I learned differently.

I had heard her arguing with my mother in my tiny kitchen. I couldn't exactly hear their words, but the volume was loud enough to wake me. Apparently they were not aware of the gravity of this sin.

"Do you realize," I asked in my best wounded and weary voice, "that I need rest for my voice?"

Ann, who could always be cowed by the demands of her show-biz sister, pressed her lips together and bowed her head. My mother, however, was not taking the bait.

"Well, good heavens, it's not as if you didn't sleep the better part of the day away."

"Which isn't that inappropriate when one considers I didn't get in until five A.M.," I said.

"And whose fault is that? My gosh, look at your father—he was out the door by eight." She looked at her watch. "In fact, I'm supposed to meet him at Macy's at noon."

Touching my temple to let them know I had a splitting headache but would bear it stoically, I went to the coffeepot (in some households it's the TV that's always on; in the Jordans', it's the coffeepot).

"What were you arguing about, anyway?" I asked once I had downed a cup of caffeine restorative.

"Nothing," said Ann in an abrupt, case-closed manner.

"Good gravy," scoffed Mother. She leveled her gaze at Ann. "Two minutes ago your whole life was collapsing."

"Your life's collapsing?" I asked my sister, who more than anyone I knew had the sturdiest, most impenetrable life—a veritable bunker of a life.

"No, my life's not collapsing," said Ann quietly.

Mother sighed. "It's just that she doesn't have money for airfare home *or* next month's rent."

"You don't have money for airfare or next month's rent?" I repeated like some idiot.

Ann wiped her nose with a napkin and began clearing the table. Mom fished a tube of lipstick out of her purse and added more unneeded color to her lips.

"You'll never get it out of Little Miss Proud, so I'll tell you." She gummed a paper napkin, leaving a fossil-like coral imprint on it. "Ann borrowed money to get here to see your show and now she needs to borrow money to get home, if her landlord hasn't already rented out her apartment to someone who pays her rent on time."

If I had been the twin whose secret had been divulged to the other by our mother, you can bet I would have stormed out of the room or flung something breakable against the wall. Ann, however, washed out her coffee cup. She could have armed herself with the sprayer hose and given Mother a well-deserved blast, but my sister, unlike me, was above that sort of thing.

"Ann," I said, putting my arms around her, "do you need money? If you need money, you come to me. You know that."

"But you're a poor starving artist," said Ann.

"Not anymore. I'm the star of a Broadway hit."

It was true; the reviews had been raves, and it looked like the days of slinging hash and temping in insurance offices were over.

"Oh, Geneva," said Ann. "I'm so glad." And then she laid her head against my shoulder and sobbed.

"Ann," I said softly when she calmed down a bit, "when did you start having money problems?"

"Since *you've* had them," said my mother. "Ann's money problems can be directly linked to yours. When you needed money, Ann was there to make the loan, knowing she'd probably never get paid back."

Being four minutes older than me, Ann has always taken her position as the elder seriously. She is very protective.

"Mother," she said, her voice so calm that I knew a big storm was coming, "it's a dangerous policy not to know what you're talking about."

"I know how many loans your father and I made to Geneva. And I know that she'd probably turn to you for money after we cut her off." Here she gave me a pointed look and added, "We had to, Geneva—it was for your own good." She looked back at Ann. "Now, I only mention it because Geneva herself has admitted—"

"You only mention it because you want to cause trouble," said Ann. "What I do with my money is my business. I'm sorry I made it yours by asking for a loan. It's something I'll never do again, for destitution couldn't be worse than your righteous offense."

"That's right," I said, mimicking my sister the English teacher. "Destitution couldn't be worse than your righteous offense."

Mom sighed; she had long ago learned that the firepower of allied twin daughters would eventually mow her down.

"I'm going to meet your father," she said, anchoring under her arm the pebble-grained purse that never left her side.

We offered no resistance, and after she left, I got the whole miserable story from Ann.

Over the years I wasn't the only one to have benefited from her beneficence; she'd been helping out with groceries for an elderly neighbor, paying the occasional electric and heating bill for a friend who was a single mother, and buying any number of supplies that students couldn't afford or tickets to plays ("It makes language come alive for these kids") or Modern Library novels or poetry compilations ("Some of these kids have never had a book of their own").

"I was able to get by for years," she said, shaking her head, "but then I guess . . . then I guess things just got a little out of control. I was having to borrow from my credit cards, and the debt just seemed to pile up."

My sister wasn't the only one shaking her head.

"Oh, Ann," I said. "When are you going to learn that to take care of others you have to first take care of yourself?"

I'm a big fan of the kind of philosophy that encourages the idea of me first.

"Oh, Gen," said Ann, and her voice was weighted with resignation, "what about those people who need help taking care of themselves?"

I got my purse (unlike my mother's, mine isn't a permanent accessory) and took out my checkbook.

"How much do you need?" I asked, writing her name on the pay-to-the-order-of line.

She thought for a moment and then told me, and I wrote it out for twice the amount.

Ann didn't gush, but her gratitude was evident.

"Thank you, Geneva," she said, kissing my cheek.

"Now don't cash it and dole it out to panhandlers at the airport."

"Not even the Hare Krishnas?" she said, laughing, even as tears glistened in her eyes.

"Especially not the Hare Krishnas," I said. "I will not have you supporting people whose religion requires them to do such ungodly things to their hair."

Chapter 2

I was married once, at what now seems the impossibly young age of twenty-four, after a whirlwind courtship. Although I have heard of successful marriages that come after whirlwind courtships, I personally do not recommend them. Take a little time to know the person you vow to love, honor, and cherish—or at least take longer than forty-eight hours, which is how long I'd known Jean-Paul before I said "I do." Fourteen months later he said *adieu*.

He was French in the Frenchiest sense, charming, dashing, and effortlessly stylish, and equipped with a palate sophisticated enough to tell a great bottle of wine from a really good one as well as an aged, pungent cheese from a rotten one. He was directing Genet's *The Maids* off-Broadway, which was so existential, I got a headache every time I watched it. Of course, I never confessed this to Jean-Paul, who was of the mind that Americans were *enfants* when it came to theater: "Zey want to be spoon-fed strained comedy and musical pabulum! And always, of course, ze 'appy ending!"

Apparently he was no fan of "ze 'appy ending" when it came to our marriage either, and I came to the ego-busting realization that it was not me he had wanted but the green card his marriage to an American citizen gave him.

C'est la vie, as I wrote to my sister. But blithe as I managed to appear on the outside, I was *shattered*; I had truly thought Jean-Paul and I were going to have a lifelong collaboration onstage and off. He was going to direct me in Molière and Hugo adaptations, and I would produce for him two adorable children who would call me Maman, accent on the second syllable.

The ax that split my marriage apart fell one morning after I'd asked Jean-Paul to pass me the cream and he told me he wanted a divorce.

"Okay, okay, keep the cream," I joked back, folding the Arts section of the paper to read the latest reviews.

Jean-Paul pushed aside the paper. "Geneva, I am not keeding." He cupped his hands around my face, a gesture he often used when he wanted my full attention. "I 'ave just . . . ah, *zut!* How shall I say? For me, I do not think eet is good to be married."

I remembered my mouth going completely dry as I stared into my husband's needing-a-shave face, clinging to the hope that this was all an unfunny joke (after all, Jean-Paul *was* French and humor wasn't his strong point), but if hope was my lifeline, it was a rotting, unraveling rope.

"Why . . . what?" was all I managed to say.

"I . . . I weesh I could explain eet. . . . I do love you, Geneva, you know that. Eet's just that I don't want to be married to you anymore."

I'm ashamed to say that at this point I began to grovel.

"Whatever is bothering you, Jean-Paul, I can change! I can learn how to cook—I know it's important to you that I learn how to cook—and I don't have to spend so much time at the theater, and I . . . Jean-Paul, I don't understand. Please stay married to me!"

"Oh, no, no, Geneva, please don't cry," he said, wiping my tears away with his fingertips. "I 'ate eet when you cry."

"Whayl, I 'ate eet whayn you tell me you whant a dee-vorce!"

Jean-Paul stepped back—he always took offense when I lapsed

into his accent, even though it was just the natural reaction of a mimic and I didn't mean anything by it.

"Now ees not ze time to mock me!"

"Now ees not ze time to dee-vorce me!"

He stood by the sink, his compact body tensed, and the position he stood in reminded me of a Greco-Roman wrestler ready to take down his opponent. I began to laugh. My emotional barometer was registering shock, anger, and pain, but this laughter was so unexpected that it made me laugh even more.

The look on Jean-Paul's face was one of betrayal. " 'Ow can you laugh at a time like thees?" he shouted, and charged out of the kitchen, but not before batting off the stove top the frying pan in which he'd made us omelets just a half hour earlier.

It still makes my mouth grow dry and my heart pound to think of that day—he started packing as soon as he left the kitchen—and I don't even want to describe the wreck I was, pleading, begging, sobbing. I believe at one point I was actually hanging on to his leg as he tried to walk to the door.

I was so young, so trusting, so certain that the stories he told me of growing up in Burgundy ("My family 'as farmed that area for over seex 'undred years") and the moment he knew he wanted to work in the theater ("Eet was nothing so fancy as seeing ze Folies Bergère on a trip to Paris—eet was seeing my grandfather dancing in ze barn for an audience of cows") were stories I would memorize and eventually tell to our grandchildren, the way he'd be able to relate stories of my childhood.

We hadn't even been married long enough for his bad habits to annoy me—I still thought his nonchalance toward deodorant was sort of, well, *zesty,* and why shouldn't matchbook covers be used to clean teeth at the dinner table? I was so in love. Jean-Paul liked to have his first cup of morning coffee by himself, and while he was puttering in the kitchen I would roll to his side of the bed and just inhale; I'd doodle "Mme. Jean-Paul Gatien" all over the margins of my script; so in love I actually *liked* ironing his shirts, folding his laundry. I was still naively thinking we were yet in our honeymoon stage, so when Jean-Paul left, I feared my sanity might be a casualty as well as my heart.

A week later I heard that he was living with his old French girlfriend, a magazine stylist, and then I ran into Jean-Paul's best friend, who told me that *les deux amants* had never stopped seeing each other, even while we were married. The realization that Jean-Paul had never loved me was even a bigger betrayal than his leaving the marriage. Who knows—maybe mine had been more infatuation than love, maybe we would have had children, maybe we would have grown apart (certainly most of my contemporaries who married young had), but Jean-Paul was a thief who took away my chance to experience those maybes. Even worse, he was a thief who stole something innately precious: my confidence that I was a person worthy of love. Now, you have to understand that confidence has always been my high-flying flag, but the fabric of that confidence was shredded by Jean-Paul's behavior. The pieces that remained were enough to convince me I was a spectacular actor and singer, but as far as my love life was concerned, any belief that of course I deserved love was gone.

Petunia thought she had an unrestricted visiting pass during that first year, descending upon me night after night, and it was only the show I had just been cast in that saved me—for months I focused on nothing but my professional life, since paying the slightest bit of attention to my personal life would have been deadly.

I've had several other marriage proposals since, but I only have to be burned once to know when to sidestep a blaze.

"Don't let past unhappiness imperil future happiness," coun-
seled my sister after I told her I had broken up yet again with a
man who wanted to marry me.

"What, did you just open a fortune cookie or something?" I
asked. "Come on, Ann, you're an English teacher. Who lets you
get away with saying stuff like that?"

"All right," she said. "Let me say it in the vernacular you can
better understand: Just because Jean-Paul was a shit doesn't mean
every other man is going to be."

"Ann, you said *shit*. I'm telling Mom."

Ann laughed. Ours was the kind of mother who believed soap
was the best way to expunge foul language out of a mouth. Of
course, I, as the more "expressive" twin, was the only one who
had experienced this procedure. Several times.

"Come on, Geneva, why'd you say no this time?"

"Can you relate to the words 'abject fear'?"

"Yeah, but did you love him?"

"I thought I did, but I guess I didn't. Because real love would get
me over the fear, right?"

"Maybe regular fear. I don't know about the *abject* kind."

We laughed, and then Ann said, "Oh, shoot. I've got to run. Riley's home."

"So?" Other than my sister, there weren't many people to
whom I could confess my abject fear. It has always been my tem-
perament to put on a happy face and to make jokes (regarding
Jean-Paul, I used the line about my having failed French more
times than I can count), but Ann knew how much I hurt and always offered a shoulder—even if it was over the telephone wires—
to cry on. So I did not want what was shaping up as a nice chatty
pep talk and counseling session to end just because of the appearance of her husband.

"So I'm *ovulating*," she said with an uncharacteristic giggle. "See ya."

This telephone conversation occurred when Ann and Riley, hopeful parents, were still in the at-least-we're-having-fun-trying stage. Later there would be depression and appointments with specialists. Finally, a week before they were going to meet with an adoption agency, Ann found out she was pregnant.

"The rabbit finally died!" she cried gleefully over the phone, and I, gleeful for her, just cried.

The only time I ever missed a performance was when I flew out to help Ann deliver her baby. Riley was an excited, supportive, loving husband, but also one for whom the slightest suggestion of blood sent him falling backward into unconsciousness.

I was enlisted as relief coach, the one who would assist from the sidelines until the inevitable time when the queasy Riley would have to be benched. By the time Ann was dilated to eight centimeters, he was already woozy.

"God help me!"

Up to now, Ann had been fairly stoic, issuing the occasional soft moan, but this plea was said with the passion of an actress auditioning for Joan of Arc.

"She's in transition," explained the nurse.

"What does that mean?"

"It means batten the hatches."

Ann screamed words that, considering their source, shocked me, and most of them were directed at Riley, who sat on a chair in the corner, looking as miserable as any man would whose own wife had just damned him to hell.

"I never knew things got so . . . violent," I said as my sister screamed.

"That's nothing," said the nurse. "I had one laboring mother who told her husband that if he ever touched her again, she'd take a chain saw to him."

The doctor, like a famous actor making a scene-stealing cameo, came in when Ann was pushing.

"There you go," he said soothingly, "you're doing great. Just one more big push."

Ann hollered from some deep place—really, with all my voice training, I've never been able to make a noise that powerful—and out slid the baby.

Seeing it was a boy, I said, "Little Richard!"

The joke was unintentional; I wasn't announcing the singer of "Tutti Frutti" but the tiny baby whose name (in honor of the modern lit teacher's assistant who'd introduced them) had already been decided.

"Yes, you have a son," said the doctor, holding the baby up, and Ann let out another sound I'd be hard pressed to reproduce: a combination laugh and cry that was full of mirth and joy and awe.

Riley, looking dazed, had started to stand up from his chair in the corner when all of a sudden he slipped to the floor as effortlessly as a cartoon character falls off a cliff.

"Father's down," said the nurse, going to him.

Even though they whisked the baby out too quickly for our liking, the happiness in the room seemed buoyant; really, it seemed as if all of us, including Riley when he was revived, might float to the ceiling.

When the doctor returned, we fell to the ground with a thud.

"Ann . . . Riley . . ."

Boris Karloff couldn't have said those two names more ominously.

"What's wrong?" I blurted out as Ann said, "What?" and Riley asked, "Doctor?"

"Would you mind stepping outside for a moment?" the doctor asked me.

"She's my twin sister," said Ann, practically shouting. "Whatever you have to say, you can say in front of her."

I don't know where she found the courage to speak. I know I for one was struck mute.

"Well," said the doctor, clearing his throat, "there's no easy way to tell you this, but—"

"*What?*" pleaded Ann and Riley together.

"Your son has Down syndrome."

I often think back to that moment, think of that audacious sunshine streaming through the blinds, so inappropriate, so gauche, like a mourner who'd come to a statesman's funeral in shorts and a tank top, drinking beer out of a can. I think of Ann and Riley as they listened to the doctor and of being struck by the feeling that it was the two of them who were the twins; both of their faces were identical masks of despair.

My sister's tears that day could have filled the water glass and little pitcher that sat on the bed tray on wheels, could have filled the bedpan, the wastebasket, the diaper bag she'd so happily brought along, could have filled any receptacle in that room. She cried as I've never seen a person cry.

Granted, Ann was a crier. She was the type of person who sobbed whenever *I* got hurt—when I fell off my bike, unhinging an oval of skin from each knee, and when David Corley, whom I was madly in love with in kindergarten, told me I was a pee-pee head. She was also the kind of person who cried at every Walt Disney movie we ever saw, from *Bambi* (understandable) to *The Parent Trap* (fairly understandable) to *The Love Bug* (huh?).

So I expected tears, but the unrelenting force of these worried me, and I followed the nurse out of the room.

"Do you think she needs a shot or something?" I asked. "She's going to cry herself sick."

"She doesn't need medication," said the nurse. "Those tears need to come out, and they might as well come out now."

That nurse knew her stuff; Ann let all those tears out, wailing in fear and pain and anger until she went home.

She still cries at movies and will shed tears of condolence when I tell her about my latest loss on the love battlefield, but since the day she left the hospital, she has never cried for Rich. At least publicly.

"Oh, Geneva," she said when I shared this observation with her, "of course I cry for Rich, but I try not to do it in front of him. He needs more important things from me than my tears."

And boy, has she given him those things. Riley too. I've never seen two more rational people go so completely nuts over a kid. Every one of his accomplishments is trumpeted in letters and phone calls, and Ann has kept not only a detailed baby book but a scrapbook of every year of his life.

But mostly she talks about what a joy he is, how he is "pure, undiluted, total love."

Once I tuned in to a talk show on which parents effused the same way about their Down syndrome children, and I remember being so touched by their exclamations that tears came to my eyes. Yet I couldn't deny the nagging thought that their enthusiasm, like Ann's and Riley's, was used to convince *themselves* of what they were saying.

Rich's and my physical distance, I told myself, was the reason I felt emotionally removed from my nephew, and to make up for these feelings (or lack thereof), I played the role of the excellent godmother, sending him fabulous birthday and Christmas gifts from FAO Schwarz and little surprise presents—video games, action figures, T-shirts—throughout the year. I sent him Valentines and Easter baskets and autographed eight-by-tens of my costars; Rich has a whole wall dedicated to "Aunt Gennie's show-biz friends." I'd say hello to him whenever I spoke to Ann on the phone, and I patiently sat through all of his new knock-knock jokes.

Hadn't my support in absentia been enough? Why was I being asked to participate up close and personal?

I woke up the next morning on the couch. Pleated paper chocolate wrappers lay crumpled on the floor; my empty champagne glass stood next to the nearly empty bottle, and my stomach spilled over the top of my underpants like a mud slide over a retaining wall. I got to my feet slowly, a victim of both a hangover and what felt like a five-pound weight gain. Heading toward my bedroom and a few more hours' sleep on something more comfortable than the couch, I stopped to pick up the ringing phone. I wasn't going to bother hearing who it was; my intent was to merely slam down the receiver so I would stop its incessant clanging, but then I heard my agent yell, "Geneva!"

I sighed. My head throbbed. I held the receiver to my ear.

"Yes?" I said, as put out as a teenager asked to put the milk away.

"Well, I'm fine, thanks for asking," said Claire in that breezy manner of hers. "I was just confirming the time, because I know details like that sometimes escape you. One o'clock, right?"

"Claire," I said, my voice gravelly, "what the—"

"See you then!"

I looked down at my calendar and saw a bunch of scribbles (my overall penmanship has suffered from years of dashing off autographs) which I deciphered as "Russian Tea Room—Claire, 1:00."

It was ten after twelve now.

"Great," I said out loud, figuring that minus travel time, I had about twenty minutes to pull myself together, a feat that in my condition would daunt even Houdini.

"*D*arling, you look . . . interesting," said Claire as I sat down at her table. "I'd offer you a drink, but it looks as if you've already taken someone up on the offer."

"Hey, there's Zach Bloome," I said, waving to the famous cellist, who was in town for a Carnegie Hall engagement. The restaurant was abuzz, full of a mix from the entertainment and society worlds as well as wide-eyed tourists. It was our sentimental restaurant choice; our first lunch as client and agent had been there twenty-five years ago, when we were both new to the city and rather wide-eyed ourselves.

To the waiter I said, "Coffee, please. And bring it by the potful."

"Well," said my agent, "how do I look?"

Before answering, I drank an entire glass of water.

"Ah, I needed that." I peered over the top of my big black sunglasses. Claire smiled back brightly. "Okay," I said, sensing a trick question, "how are you supposed to look?"

"I'm not supposed to look older."

"None of us is," I said, nodding at the waiter as he set down my coffee. "Older-looking is not something we should aspire to."

Claire's bright smile faded. She looked down at the table, fidgeting with her napkin, straightening her silverware.

"You forgot, didn't you?" she asked softly.

"Forgot what?" I wasn't in the mood for games, not with a headache three Excedrin had failed to snuff out.

Claire's bottom lip started to quiver, and I stared at it, fascinated—not because it was slightly lopsided from the lip liner she'd probably applied without her glasses, but because Claire Schwartz is a tough-as-nails, take-no-prisoners kind of businesswoman. Why, she'd happily leg-wrestle a producer if she thought it would get her client a better deal. She'd been my agent since the beginning, and her faith in me had been a sail in what hadn't always been tranquil waters.

"It's just that . . . well, fifty's sort of a big deal."

Suddenly I felt a little sick, and it had nothing to do with my hangover.

"Oh, Claire," I said, "it's your birthday, isn't it?"

She nodded. "When I called to remind you about the time, I didn't think I had to remind you about the event." Her tough negotiator's voice had been replaced by a little girl's.

"I . . . I thought we were celebrating the reopening." The Russian Tea Room had been closed for several years for renovation (its over-the-top opulence suggested Busby Berkeley had returned from the dead in a new career as restaurant designer), and we had missed it. I shook my head. "I am so sorry, Claire. Tell you what: Let's raise your commission to fifteen percent and we'll call it your birthday present."

Something glittered in her eyes. "You mean it?"

"No. It was just a flashy gesture. Flashy . . . but empty."

Claire managed a laugh. "Another one of those, huh?"

Even though I had it coming, that comment stung, and I was happy that the waiter asked, "Have you decided?" because it allowed me to change the subject without obviously changing the subject.

"What do you recommend for me and the birthday girl?"

An hour later we had exceeded our cholesterol limit for the month (foie gras, blintzes, a duck dish, *and* dessert) and had plowed through the bottle of wine I'd ordered when I tired of the coffee.

We talked about business, about the Pulitzer prize–winning playwright who'd left his actress wife for her male costar, about how yet another musical based on an animated movie was being mounted.

I smiled at my agent, whose face was flushed and whose hair was a little mussed, as if the wine had relaxed her curls too.

"You sure don't look fifty."

Claire shrugged. "I feel it." Her finger played along the rim of her wine glass. "You really did forget, didn't you?"

Damn . . . just when I thought I'd been excused and wasn't going to get a note from the principal.

I folded my hands and looked at them because I wanted a focal point other than Claire's face. This was the wrong thing to do, because there on my right hand was the beautiful white gold filigreed ring set with a sparkling ruby that Claire had given me on my milestone birthday, my fortieth.

"It doesn't mean we're engaged or anything," she had joked. "It's just that I saw it in the antique shop and I thought, now, *that's* Geneva."

I unfolded my hands quickly and put them in my lap.

"I guess I did. I mean deep down, I *know* October fifteenth is your birthday, but my sense of time is all off since I quit the show, and I'm still reeling with all the stuff that went on with Trevor—"

The look on Claire's face told me she was both (a) bored and (b) hurt, and because I couldn't bear looking at that face, I suddenly stood up and, in front of everyone enjoying lunch, sang "Happy Birthday" to my agent. I didn't just sing the song, you understand; I *sold* it, sang it as if I were at the Pearly Gates auditioning for entrance. I scatted, I embellished, I held the last note—a high G, I might add—for what seemed like twenty minutes.

The wait staff and patrons broke into wild applause and wouldn't let me sit down without taking several bows.

"That's just the beginning," I said to Claire when I finally sat down. "The first of fifty presents for fifty years."

My agent sighed. "Oh, Geneva, a card would have been fine."

I walked on East Fifty-seventh Street toward home, squinting against the chilly wind that had whipped up. I must have been giving off my do-not-bother-me vibe, because no one approached me; I probably would have bitten their heads off—or cried in their arms—if they had.

Lousy was the pervading mood, veering toward shame. Neither is a favorite. I had waited with Claire for her cab, blathering on and on about how I was going to make it up to her.

"Why do you do this to yourself?" she asked, pushing aside hair that had blown in her face.

"What do you mean?"

"Look, I'm your agent. You pay me to advise you in your career. Now, as your friend, I'm going to give you some personal advice— for free."

Not particularly wanting to hear whatever this advice was, I prayed for the immediate approach of a cab.

"You're not a baby, Geneva. Occasionally you're going to have to remember that other people have needs too."

"Dat's no fun," I said in my best baby talk.

Claire smiled in an unamused way. "You didn't just forget my fiftieth, Geneva, although that in itself is hurtful enough. No, this is all part of a pattern, a pattern of your forgetting—or worse, not caring—what someone else needs."

"Yikes," I said, fanning my face.

"You know I love you dearly—oh, good, here's a cab—but once in a while you be the supporting player and let someone else be the star."

With that great exit line, she got into the cab and slammed the door.

The thought of firing her did occur to me—believe me, there

are plenty of top agents who would never even *consider* talking to me like that—but I haven't completely crossed into Joan Crawford country. I can stand the truth sometimes. And the sad part was that I *knew* this was the truth.

I held my collar together at my throat as the October wind blew, but even that gesture couldn't stop me from shivering.

When I called Ann to tell her that I would take care of Rich, there wasn't the scream of delight I'd expected. Instead there was absolute silence.

"Ann," I said after a moment, "are you there, and if you are, are you conscious?"

Still nothing.

"Ann, you're starting to scare me."

I heard an exhale.

"Oh, Geneva," she said finally. "Thank you."

My sister said this the way a panhandler accepts a twenty-dollar bill—with gratitude so deep that you have to make a joke or burst into tears.

"Is Rich aware, though," I asked brightly, "of my fondness for corporal punishment?"

Chapter 3

ecause I see nothing wrong with a little self-aggrandizement, I threw myself a going-away party. I wanted to spend the evening eating fancy food, drinking champagne, and having people tell me how kind, selfless, and/or devoted I was.

The party was on a Monday night, which is when theaters are dark and their employees can have some of the fun they missed over the weekend. The ivories were being tickled by our show's composer; the small catering staff I had hired served drinks and hors d'oeuvres; and that happy murmuring, clinking, laughing party sound filled the apartment. Everyone who had been associated with *Mona!* from the beginning had shown up, with the exception of Trevor Waite, whom I pointedly did not invite. Through Faith Bennet, who has the daunting job of replacing me in the role of Mona, I learned that the cad had told her to relay the message "Ellie and I send our best."

"Ellie?" I said thickly.

Faith nodded. "Ellie. As in Ellie Armstrong—the toast of Broadway?"

"I thought *I* was the toast of Broadway."

"You're the old toast—in fact, you're the crouton." Faith laughed, but I declined to join her. "Little Miss Ingenue is the new toast. *Gibson Girl* is a hit."

"I heard it stinks."

Faith smiled, appreciating the venom we actors feel free to express toward our rivals. "It doesn't stink according to the critics, and Miss Armstrong certainly doesn't stink according to Trevor."

"So they're seeing each other, huh?"

"More than *seeing*, darling." Faith, who's had some *minor* success on TV, can't quite forgive me for being the star she's supposed to replace, and she loves firing these little poison zingers at me whenever possible. Her mission completed, she held out her silk caftan as if she were trying to catch a good wind, and I watched as she set sail for a return visit to the buffet table, noticing she was a little heavy aft.

I was left to seethe over Trevor's latest romantic adventure with yet another young and dewy ingenue. All of the male midlife crisis clichés he had started to fondle during our last months together, he now fully embraced—especially the need to hold on to his youth by holding on to the nearest twenty-two-year-old. I had also heard he had traded in his old BMW for a brand-new Jaguar; it seemed in all areas of his life, Trevor had decided we older models required too much maintenance.

"Scowling doesn't become you, Gen," said Claire, whose good graces I was once again in after giving her a very pricey Steuben crystal carafe and matching wineglasses for a belated birthday present.

"Faith just filled me in on Trevor's latest conquest."

"You didn't know?"

"You *did?*"

Helping herself to the fantail shrimp, Claire nodded. "I thought everybody did."

"Out of the show, out of the loop, I guess." I didn't like this one bit—I wanted a little R and R, but not at the expense of being the last to know about what Trevor Waite was up to.

"Speaking of being out of the show," said Claire, "I had a long conversation with Mr. Powell today."

Angus Powell was the producer of *Mona!* His first reaction to my legally leaving the show had been, "I'll sue her!"

"He asked me to ask you if you didn't feel guilty for leaving the show just at the start of the busy season."

"That ingrate," I said. "I suppose it doesn't matter that I stayed on an extra six months and that my contract was up?"

"Nope, doesn't matter. All that matters to him is that the show will probably lose money without you in it." She helped herself to another shrimp. "So refresh my memory—when do you leave for Wisconsin again?" With a long red fingernail, she swiped at a drib of cocktail sauce on her lip.

"*Minnesota.* In six days. But if anything comes up, don't be afraid to call. I mean, I can always make other arrangements."

Claire's smile was almost . . . well, feral. "Oh, no," she said, "I don't care if it's Sondheim or Spielberg; I will not interrupt Geneva Jordan doing a good deed." She laughed, as if something was funny, and once again I was not sharing the joke.

"Don't eat too much of the shrimp," I said as I left in search of a more simpatico conversationalist. "You know how seafood makes you break out."

I wormed my way into a little knot of people.

"We were just talking about you, Geneva," said Lacey O'Rourke, a syndicated columnist. "And I was saying how my sister would never trust me with her kids. If my cooking didn't kill them, my taste in music would."

"Yes," said Roy Dale, the costumer for *Mona!* "Whatever are you going to do with some thirteen-year-old boy out in the sticks? Take him to barn dances, or supervise spitting contests out on the north forty?"

I have always thought the costumes for *Mona!* were the show's weakest point. Roy *thinks* he has wit and flair, but like house cats, they aren't let out much.

"Roy, have I ever——"

"Geneva," said Joe Bernardi, who's choreographed my last three shows and also serves as *Mona!*'s lead dancer and its unofficial diplomat, always working things out between warring parties, "any way we can roll up this rug and get some dancing started?"

Of course there was a way; we always danced at my parties. I do not have a record collection that stretches from Cab Calloway to the Grass Roots to Sheryl Crow for listening purposes only. And so we danced. At least, most of us did. Others found different amusements.

Even though Betty Ford is practically his home away from home, our director, Paul Drake, sent his sobriety away for the evening, singing Irish dirges in the bathtub. Gail Wendt, of They Wendt That-a-Way PR, went home with the bartender, who was a moonlighting actor and was probably attracted more to what Gail could do for his career than to Gail herself. Harry Howe, a painter who lives in my building, spilled red wine all over Faith Bennet *and* my couch (I was amused by the former and pissed off at the latter). It was a typical Manhattan show-biz party, and while I enjoyed myself, my favorite part was handing people their coats at the door, collecting air kisses, best wishes, and reiterations of what a nice thing I was doing for my sister.

"Well, you know me," I said, shoving the last group through the door, "St. Geneva."

Hearing a small chuckle after I'd closed the door, I jumped.

"St. Geneva," said Claire, shaking her head. "And what parallel universe do *we* live in?"

"Oh, are you helping with the cleanup?" I asked sweetly. I put my finger to my chin. "Okay, then, why don't you start with the dishes and finish up with the bathroom? The toilet cleaner's in the closet, and there's an old toothbrush in the cabinet."

Claire laughed. "A saint always keeps the lowly jobs for herself," she said, putting on her coat. "Now come on, Gen, be nice and give your agent a good-bye kiss."

"I'll give you ten percent of a kiss," I said, "That's all you deserve."

The catering crew took care of the cleanup, so there wasn't anything left for me to do besides hit the hay.

And what a hayloft I've created for myself; a California king bed, the fluffiest duvet this side of meringue, Porthault sheets—nothin' but the finest for my visits to slumberland. But . . . I couldn't sleep.

My flight had been booked, I had packed my bags (three; a record low for me, but it wasn't as if I would be needing clothes for any Minneapolis high life). My housekeeper would be coming in every other day to check on things, and all necessary arrangements had been made, except the big nagging one, the one that pulsed through my head in Roy Dale's nasal voice: How *was* I going to entertain a thirteen-year-old boy in the sticks? Actually, the sticks had nothing to do with it; how was I going to entertain a thirteen-year-old boy like my nephew?

From the framed school pictures I hung in my guest room, anyone could see that Rich had Down syndrome, but no one mentioned it much (probably because few people had cause to go into my guest room unless they were sleeping over). If they did, their concern was very furrowed-brow and earnest, yet they always seemed grateful when I'd answer a question or two and then change the subject. I would like to chalk up their discomfort to their general shallowness . . . but then, what explains my own?

I had spent time with Rich on brief visits, but always under the supervision of Ann or Riley, and Auntie Gennie could excuse herself for a bath or some "beauty rest" when the demands of family togetherness got to be too much.

The more I thought about what I had gotten myself into, the more I thought I needed psychiatric help. Surely I had been crazy when I agreed to do this. How *would* I be able to handle him? What would we do all day—or at least the part of the day when we were together? I tossed and turned in my premium-cotton-and-satin haven, trying to find answers that weren't there. I finally got up near dawn, and although I was tempted to pour myself a big drink, I didn't need a headache along with my insomnia, so I put on the coffee instead.

*T*he night before I left for Minneapolis, I treated myself to dinner and a show. I was going to treat Benny too, but then he had to suddenly fly to LA to do Mora Maynard's hair.

"What are they going to wheel her out for?" I asked of the nearly one-hundred-year-old silent-movie star. "Another film preservation benefit?"

"She died, Geneva," said Benny as curtly as he'd ever said anything to me. "I did her hair for that *TV Guide* cover, and she liked it so much, the family asked me to do her hair for the funeral."

"Oh, well . . . let me get my foot out of my mouth so I can apologize," I said before hanging up.

I'm not the sort of person who's mortified at spending a night out alone—I *like* my own company—and so I had dinner at this French/Peruvian place I had heard so much about. The room is painted turquoise blue ("like the South American sky," read the menu), and everyone sits on chairs shaped like llamas, eating food that's a blend of rich sauces and rice and beans. If I were a critic, I would have panned it; a gimmick does not a restaurant make.

The same thing could be said for the musical I saw, which could have just as well be titled *Gimmick Girl*. Of course, I wasn't expecting much of a show based upon a hairstyle, which, when you got down to it, was what this show was about.

No, I didn't come for the insightful story, I came to watch Ellie Armstrong. I sat in the back row (I was curious to hear how she projected), arms crossed over my chest, teeth clenched like a lockjaw victim, and didn't take my eyes off her.

She was pretty, but she had the kind of kewpie-doll looks that won't age well; she'll start to look soft and blurry before she hits forty. She was petite, but her breasts had been store-bought, no doubt about it. She had to be no taller than five foot three and couldn't weigh more than ninety-eight pounds, yet there she was, hoisting a double D cup—a *perky* double D cup.

The producers made full use of Miss Armstrong's (silicone) assets. She wore a high-necked shirtwaist with leg-o'-mutton sleeves in the first few scenes, but by the middle of act one she was prancing around in her corset and didn't see fit to get dressed again until the last musical number.

I admit she did have a voice, if you like that quavery kind of soprano that sounds as if its owner is so near tears you want to take her aside and tell her to get a grip.

Several people approached me at intermission, asking me to sign their programs, and didn't I think *Gibson Girl* was just the *best*?

"Absolutely *fab*," I said, my smile as fake and glittery as fool's gold.

There were three curtain calls, but I didn't add my applause to any of them, clearing out of the theater and tossing my program in a wastebasket in the nearly empty lobby.

I was going to walk a few blocks to clear my head and calm down. Seeing Trevor's latest had left me feeling anxious and angry, and as I passed a light pole, I almost kicked it.

Instead, a better target came into view.

"Geneva!"

Hearing that familiar, honeyed voice was like being too close to an electrical current: I felt a jolt, and the hair on the back of my neck stood up.

I turned toward this human lightning bolt, trying to approximate a look of bemused boredom.

He smiled, and I wanted to smile back—wanted to jump into his arms and slather him with kisses—but instead, continuing on in the bemused-and-bored theme, I said, "Trevor. What a surprise."

His smile wasn't going anywhere, and I wished it would—it's his best feature. Well, his smile *and* the two dimples that show up on each side like loyal bodyguards.

"Out for a stroll?" he asked.

"Actually, I just saw *Gibson Girl*."

The bodyguards made their presence known even more strongly as Trevor's smile widened. "You did? Oh, Ellie will be so pleased. She's a big fan of yours."

"I'll bet," I said coolly.

"I'm on my way to meet her now," he said, and then, after briefly touching his fingers to his lips (he had a whole repertoire of these thoughtful gestures), he added, "Come and join us for a drink?"

Trevor looked surprised that he had extended the invitation, and I'm sure the look on my face mirrored his own. I have never mastered the art of the civilized breakup; I take the end of a relationship as hard as I did in the twelfth grade, when Brad Norlund (the big dumb lug) asked for his letter jacket back. When my heart is broken, I carry on appropriately; I cry, I eat too much chocolate, and I consider taking up retaliatory voodoo. I do *not* go out for drinks with the heartbreaker and his new girlfriend.

And yet I found myself rearranging the surprise on my face to an expression of mild amusement and said, "Fine," as blithely as if my doorman had asked me how I was.

We chatted aimlessly those few minutes it took us to reach the bar.

"So how's the show going?"

"Great. Of course, Faith Bennet doesn't have your pipes, but she does have all those fans from her old sitcom. We had a full house tonight."

A flare of jealousy ignited. *A full house?*

"And it's great for me and Ellie—I mean, working right across the street from each other."

My smile was as thin as rice paper.

"Of course, for convenience, you couldn't beat our setup, working in the same show."

"I'm glad our setup was convenient for you, Trevor."

He cupped my elbow as we walked into Shay's Bar, a favorite hangout of Broadway actors.

"It was a lot more than convenient," he said, and as was often the case with Trevor, I had no idea what he meant.

There were some people from *Mona!* and from *The Fieldstone Papers*; there was also Ronnie Jax, who'd just opened his one-man show. It was a regular party, and I immediately joined it, ordering a double martini and letting Ronnie pull me onto his lap.

"So when are you going to write a two-person show with me as your costar?" I asked.

"Right now," said Ronnie, who was known to millions of TV viewers as the villain on the soap *Time to Love.* "Let's go to my apartment after we get good and soused and start rehearsing."

Laughing, as if I were somehow amused by the old lech, I peeled his arms off me and sat at a small table next to Trevor. My timing was perfect, because at that moment in walked Miss Ellie Armstrong.

The look on her face was a thing to behold. The blood drained out of it, and I thought she might faint from the lack of oxygen to her brain. Instead, she plastered a smile across her white face and, throwing back her shoulders, strode to the table, her breasts like headlights, guiding her.

"Darling!" said Trevor, and in standing up, he nearly knocked me out of my chair. "Darling, look who I brought along!"

He sounded like a pet owner delighted to have smuggled his bichon frise into a ritzy restaurant, and I resisted the urge to bark.

"Geneva," said Miss Ellie, her poise returning, "Geneva Jordan. I've admired your work ever since I was a little girl."

"Well, you still are," I said, shaking the hand she offered. "A little girl, I mean." I looked pointedly at her chest. "But then there are parts of you that are all grown up."

"Geneva," said Trevor in that tone that let me know I had gone too far.

"Oh, Trevvie," said Ellie, sitting in my chair, so that I had to pull up another. "Don't worry about me. I don't know why, but lots of women—especially flat-chested ones—are threatened by the size of my chest. It's something I've had to deal with since I was twelve."

Conversation had quieted; this was an after-theater show everyone wanted to watch.

"Your parents let you have surgical implants when you were *twelve?*" I asked like an outraged social worker.

A blush brought the color back to Miss Ellie's pasty pallor.

"I have *never* had surgical implants," she said, her voice as deliberate as if she were on the witness stand.

"Oh, you mean they can put them in some other way?"

"Why don't we go?" said Trevor, rising.

"No, no, I'm fine." The ingenue smiled her ingenuous smile. "My parents would never forgive me if I walked away from an opportunity to meet with *Geneva Jordan*. They've loved her since they were kids too."

"I trust Trevor gets the benefit of your witty age jokes. We are, after all, the same age."

Miss Ellie looked at Trevor, her mouth an O of surprise.

"Oh, darling," she said to him, "you mean you're sixty-five too?"

"Meow," said Ronnie at the next table. I laughed with the others to show I wasn't really low enough to participate in a cat fight and this was all in fun. (Although I was *livid* over that flat-chested crack—since when does 34B qualify as that?)

"I ran into Geneva outside the theater," said Trevor, signaling the waiter. "She'd just seen your play."

"Really?" said Miss Ellie, unable to hide a flicker of pleasure. She was too proud to ask me how I liked it, but I told her anyway.

"You made me remember why I love the theater."

Miss Ellie looked at me expectantly. Nothing commands an actor's attention more than the possibility of praise.

The waiter served the drinks, replacing my empty martini glass with a full one.

"So," said Trevor after the waiter left, "you were saying?"

I took a sip of my drink and smiled.

"Oh, yes—why I love the theater. I guess it just appeals to my blood lust. I love watching someone die onstage."

Miss Ellie made the sound of a mouse getting its tail stepped on. Then she picked up her glass and threw her drink at me. It was a clichéd gesture but an effective one.

There was no noise in the bar as I wiped my face carefully with my cocktail napkin, as if I were blotting makeup. I then took out my lipstick and looking into my compact, carefully reapplied it, obviously getting ready to go someplace better.

Still no one made a sound.

I stood up, tossing my Red Flame hair over my shoulder, and it was only then that I bothered to turn my gaze to Miss Ellie Armstrong.

"Don't always go for the obvious," I said pleasantly. "I know you like to make those sort of choices in your acting, but in real life try to be a tad more original."

Ronnie Jax let out a hoot, and with my head held high, I made yet another grand exit.

It was only after I'd walked a block (punting a crumpled McDonald's bag over the curb and pushing aside a drunk who veered toward me like an out-of-control semi) that my regal bearing became slightly less regal and tears wet my eyes.

As blasé as my response to having a drink thrown in my face had been, the truth was that *I had had a drink thrown in my face.* The tears gathering in my eyes were a result not only of the humiliation I felt (which I had desperately tried to hide in the bar), but of the nagging voice that whispered in my head, *Well, maybe you deserved it.*

Well, she started it! I answered back, but the voice only asked, in a tone of extreme boredom, *Oh, really?*

"Spare me some change, miss?" asked a shadow in a doorway.

That the panhandler called me "miss" might have merited him at least a quarter under usual circumstances, but on the verge of a major tear fest, I ignored him, increasing my usual fast pace. I must have been walking *really* fast, because suddenly I was back in Minneapolis, in my Grandma Hjordis's living room.

She was dabbing at her eyes as she helped me fold the blanket that had been used as the curtain for my one-woman show.

"Oh, Geneva," she said, shaking her head, "I laughed so hard I almost you-know-what."

"What?" I asked, my eleven-year-old self wanting to hear her say the words.

"*Uffda,* you know. Wet myself."

"Wet your what?"

"Oh, Geneva," said my grandma, laughing again. "Wet my pants."

"It *was* funny," said Ann, putting the various scarves and hats I'd used back in the dress-up bag. "You could be on TV."

"Thanks," I said. What prevented pride from almost but not quite filling my chest was a tiny sliver of guilt. "My" show had originally started out being "our" show, but when Ann forgot the lines we'd written a half hour earlier and didn't have the presence of mind to improvise any, I had banished her from the rag rug in front of the fireplace that served as our stage.

Holding my arm out, finger pointing to the dining room, I cried, "And don't come back until you know your lines!" Then the same hand lowered, and with it I tapped an imaginary cigar, adding, à la Groucho Marx, "I wanted Chico, not Harpo."

This had gotten a big laugh out of my easy audience (Mother, Father, Grandma, and Grandpa), and Ann, even though her face was beet red, laughed too as she sat on the couch next to Grandma.

Later, when our mother and father had crossed the lawn to our house and Grandpa went upstairs to bed ("Gotta get up early and put those storm windows in"), Grandma and Ann and I cleaned up the living room theater, chuckling now and then as we remembered funny parts of the show.

"I love when you do that Clem Kadiddlehopper," said Grandma in her Norwegian accent. "You do it just as good as that Red Skelton."

"Thanks," I said, making my Clem Kadiddlehopper face.

It was at this time that Ann said it looked as though everything was cleaned up and she was going home. Grandma set down a blanket she'd been folding (and which had served as a king's robe in one of my sketches) and went to my sister, enveloping her in her arms. I saw her whisper something into Ann's ear, saw Ann nod her head and kiss Grandma's cheek. When they pulled away from their hug, there was a strange look on Ann's face—a combination of victory and resignation.

"Don't forget to make a bed angel," I said as I opened the front door. We slept in the same double bed, and it was the job of whoever got there first to warm it up for the other by lying in the middle and moving her arms and legs the same way kids lie in the snow and make angels.

"What'd you say to Ann?" I asked casually after my sister left and Grandma and I finished the last of the cleanup.

"What if I said it was a secret?"

"Then I'd say it's not nice to have secrets," I said, annoyed. "You say that yourself, Grandma."

She sort of collapsed on the couch, as if someone had gently pushed her, and then looked inside one of the cups on the coffee table (even at night, coffee was the beverage of choice in my grandparents' house). Finding some cold brew remaining, she took a swig of it.

"Oh, Tweedledee," said my grandma with a sigh. "I just told Ann that she was a star too."

Star was a word that had entered her vernacular because of my frequent use of it—"When I grow up I'm going to be a star!" et cetera.

"Why'd you say that?" I asked as a funny feeling, like a hunger pang, crawled into my stomach.

Grandma laughed, but I remember thinking I'd heard happier laughs.

"Geneva." There was a bit of scold to her voice. "Geneva, come sit by me." She patted the couch cushions, and I sat down next to her, crossing my arms in front of my chest.

She laughed again, this time with more cheer.

"It's not enough for you to have all the attention, hmm, little *flicka*? It's not enough that all night we were happy to watch you, happy to laugh out loud at you, clap for you?"

"But it was my show!" I said, feeling myself irrationally close to tears. "I'm the star!"

Grandma put her arm around me—I could feel the soft flesh of her upper arm squish against my back—and squeezed my shoulder. "You are a star, but so is your sister. Good heavens, the way you made her leave the stage—" Grandma shook her head at the memory. "That wasn't very nice, you know."

"But she didn't know her lines! She was ruining the show!"

Grandma shook her head again. "Maybe she was ruining *your* show, but wasn't it supposed to be a show the two of you put on? What would you have done if she had told you to leave the stage?"

"She never would!" I said, feeling hot. "I'd know my lines!"

"But what if you didn't?"

"I would!" I tightened my arms around my chest even more, feeling my fists dig into my rib cage.

We sat there for a while without talking, Grandma letting me stew in my stubbornness. I knew she knew that I *never* would have let Ann kick me off the stage, and if she ever did, my exit would not be a graceful one—I certainly wouldn't stick around to watch *her* continue her solo act. Thinking about this, my heart hammered under my crossed arms, my constant blinking a dam against the tears that were ready to fall.

Finally Grandma picked up a cup and saucer from the coffee table.

"Just remember, Geneva, there are all kinds of stars in God's skies. Some are so bright and twinkly they take your breath away; and others don't shine so brightly but they're still there. Their light's just a little softer, that's all."

Standing up, she told me to help her take the dishes to the kitchen and then to run on home; it was getting late.

I remember my dash across her front yard to ours next door and how cold the night air was. Even though we lived in a time and neighborhood when no one locked their doors, I remember feeling scared, almost panicky, the familiar yards and shrubs and trees suddenly unfamiliar, suddenly threatening. I bounded up the brick front steps of my parents' home, missing Ann, with whom I usually made the across-the-lawn trek, the two of us holding hands, our shield against all bogeymen.

A sudden blast of a horn brought me back to the streets of Manhattan and I started, realizing that I had begun to cross an intersection on a red light, and that when I was alone at night, different bogeymen were out to get me.

Chapter 4

o me a plane ride isn't a plane ride unless there's some turbulence, and this one was a doozy. We dipped and lurched and shuddered, and the man next to me— a perfume salesman going to a beauty products convention—bowed his head through one particularly bumpy session, silently mouthing the words "Stay up, stay up, stay up."

I, in turn, looked out the window, smiling like a kid on a midway ride. Like all air travelers, I want to get where I'm going; unlike most of them, I don't mind a few thrills along the way.

On this particular trip, I doubly appreciated the distraction of an acrobatic 727 and a praying perfume salesman. I did not want to think about what I was headed toward and what I had left behind.

Joyce Dean, with her antennae that somehow can pick up a lover's tryst at the Plaza and a contract squabble at William Morris, had of course heard of Miss Ellie's and my spat and happily found space for it in her column in the *New York Post*: "Fireworks fly—and drinks too—at Broadway eatery Shay's as current lover of a handsome Brit actor douses the former lover with her drink. Seems some actresses who leave their hit musicals have nothing better to do than go out looking for trouble. . . ."

I don't have anything against gossip—as long as I'm not the one being gossiped about. After all these years, I still find it unsettling to read about my private life in a syndicated newspaper column.

My brother-in-law, Riley, believes it comes with the territory. "You're a public figure. People want to know about you."

"I'm an actor, Riley. If they want to know about me, let them come to the theater and see me work."

"You didn't seem to mind when we didn't have to stand in line at the restaurant last night."

This conversation took place years ago when Riley and Ann had flown up (my treat) to see me in *Dixieland Detectives* and I was getting all the attention attendant on the star of a hit musical.

"Hey, if someone wants to treat me special, I'm not going to stop him. *But* it's my choice whether I do or not. You don't have that choice with the media—they don't ask your permission. 'Oh, do you mind if we print this unflattering picture of you getting out of a limo?' Or 'Will it bother you if we speculate about a wild affair you're having with a South American contortionist?' "

Riley had laughed then and in a very professorial gesture stroked his beard.

"The trouble with you, Geneva, is you want to have your cake and eat it too."

"Isn't that what cake is for? To eat?"

I then asked Riley how he would like it if *his* love life was written about in the local paper.

"It wouldn't be. I'm an English professor, not a Broadway star."

I rolled my eyes. "Riley, I hope that same lack of imagination doesn't show up in your classroom. How would you *feel?*"

Riley had looked down my apartment hallway then, probably wondering what was taking Ann so long in the bathroom.

"I imagine it would be pretty . . . interesting," he said finally. "I imagine it would make me feel pretty important. Then, after a while, I imagine it would get pretty tiresome."

"Bingo," I said.

*T*he perfume salesman fished some tiny tester bottles out of his pocket and gave them to me as the plane was taxiing to the gate.

"I know you don't need any more Star Power," he said, making a pun, "but I'd like to give this to you anyway, Miss Jordan."

"Why, thank you." I uncapped the tiny bottle and sniffed. It was a pretty scent, floral and woodsy. "Mmm."

"You like it?" he asked, pleased. "Do you think it smells like star power?"

"Just as much as Joy smells like joy," I said, waving my wrist in front of my face. "As much as Obsession smells like obsession— although if you could really bottle obsession, it would probably smell pretty rank."

The salesman smiled. "It does seem like sort of a silly business I'm in, but my God, right now I'm thrilled to still be in it." He wagged his head as he pushed at the knot of his tie. "For a while there I was sure we were going down."

"Planes are built to handle turbulence," I said, sounding like an airline spokesperson. "The wing tips could actually touch each other"—I held my arms up to demonstrate—"and the plane still wouldn't come apart."

"No kidding," said the salesman. "Still, who'd want the wings of a plane to do that?"

A chime sounded when the plane stopped at the gate, and the salesman jumped up as if his seat had been spring-loaded. I, on the other hand, took my time, fussing with my purse and the buckle on my boot, waiting until everyone had gotten off. Finally, when it looked as if the perturbed flight attendant might call security to remove me, I got up, not in any great hurry to face the music, let alone dance.

They were at the gate, the anxiousness on their faces dissolving into relief when they saw that I had come after all.

"Geneva!" cried Ann, rushing toward me, her arms outstretched like an emigrant on Ellis Island welcoming the first relative from the old country.

She hugged me so hard that I had to push her back just to get a breath.

"Ann, please. I need air."

"Sorry," said my sister, her grin stretched to its maximum. "I'm just so glad to see you."

"Me too," said Riley.

"Me too," said a voice and then, with some prodding, Rich stepped out from behind Riley.

Dressed in a plaid shirt and khakis (just like his father, I noticed), he was taller than when I'd last seen him in New York three years ago, taller and heavier. He nudged his glasses up his nose with a blunt finger and smiled a smile that pushed out his lower jaw.

"Hi, Aunt Gennie." His adolescent voice cracked a little.

"Hi yourself," I said, and, holding my arms out, I added, "Come here."

Rich didn't need a second invitation; he was in my arms in a flash. Enveloped in his hug, I felt even more breathless than when I'd been held captive by his mother. It's not that he hugged me tighter; his arms were around me carefully, almost as if he were holding on to something he didn't want to break. Still, in that embrace, I felt a tremendous, smothering squeeze of responsibility.

"Well," I said, pulling free, "let's go get my bags, shall we? I might have a present in one of them for a certain thirteen-year-old boy."

Rich's underbite was again evident as he grinned. "She means

me," he told his parents. "She means me she has a present for."
Keeping his eyes on the floor, he said, "Here's a joke: I'm Rich. But
I don't have a lot of money. Get it?"

"You're rich but you don't have a lot of money . . ." I said, as if
puzzling out a riddle.

He laughed. "I'm Rich! Rich is my name!"

I slapped the side of my head. "Of course it is. Of course you're
Rich!"

He took his mother's and father's hands as we began walking
toward the baggage claim area.

"You look wonderful, Geneva," said Ann, slipping her free hand
in the crook of my arm. "Why is it that you never look your age
and I always do?"

"Because I don't believe makeup is an extravagance," I said,
looking at my sister's plain and unadorned face.

Ann laughed. "And I was hoping you were going to say something like, 'Oh, Ann, you look ravishing too.' "

"I was. Honest to God, that's what I was going to say next."

"Did you have a nice flight?" asked Riley, ducking his head in my
direction.

I nodded. "There was a lot of turbulence."

"Geneva likes her flights the way she likes her martinis," said
Ann. "Well shaken."

"Good line," I said.

"It should be, it's yours. You said that very thing to me last year
when you were telling about the plane ride you and Trevor took to
the Keys."

"Right," I said, feeling a little pang as I remembered the three-
day trip Trevor and I had been able to take during the electricians'
strike. When we weren't lying on the beach soaking up the sun,
we were lying in bed soaking up each other.

"Hey, pal."

For the third or fourth time I was aware of Rich's voice underneath my own conversation and/or morbid reminiscences of Trevor the Terrible.

"Hi there," answered a pilot, pulling his leashed luggage behind him like a black dog.

On our way through the terminal, the boy kept up his cheery greeting.

After he said, "Hey, pal," to a sour-looking woman who ignored him, I asked him what he was doing.

"You don't even know these people," I teased. "They're not your *pals*."

"Might be," he said, smiling at me. "Might be my pals someday." To a man waiting for his next shoeshine customer, Rich said, "Hey, pal," and when the man said, "Hey, pal," back, Rich looked at me triumphantly.

"He sounds like those little candy hearts we used to get on Valentine's Day," I said to Ann. "Remember, the ones with the little messages that read You're Cute or Be Mine?"

A flight attendant passed, and Rich said, "Hey, pal. Be mine?"

Startled, she nevertheless recovered quickly and, smiling, said hello.

Laughing, Riley ruffled Rich's sandy blond hair. "It's okay to greet people, Rich, but you don't want to overdo it."

"Boy," I said to my sister, "he picks up things quick, doesn't he?"

"He keeps us on our toes," said Ann, and the look on her face was so mischievous, so delighted, that I drew in my breath in surprise.

"*I*t's been the mildest fall we've had in years," said Ann as I looked out the window of Riley's big Delta 88.

"You should have seen the colors last week," said Riley. "Unbelievable."

"Still looks pretty good to me," I said, a little miffed that Riley felt it necessary to let me know what I'd missed.

Of all the four seasons in Minnesota, I relate most to autumn. It's such a show-off. The trees, dressed in gaudy reds and maroons and golds, stand there like a chorus line costumed by Roy Dale, lifting their skirts when the wind passes by.

I settled into the big old backseat, looking forward to a relaxing, scenic ride, but apparently Rich didn't read my body language that said Aunt Gennie wanted a little quiet time now.

"We got a hamster at school," he said, as sly as a convict informing his cellmate that the contraband had come in.

"No kidding." I looked out the window, hoping he would get the hint that I wasn't in a chatty mood. He didn't.

"Funny little guy," he said, shaking his head back and forth. "Got this little wheel"—this he pronounced "wee-o"—"and he runs inside it. Run, run, run inside that little wheel, all day long. Run, run, run."

"Run, run, run," I murmured, looking back out the window. We were just passing the Mendota Bridge, and I craned my neck, looking at the colored trees on the bluff above the river.

"Yup. That funny little guy sure likes to run."

There was a long silence, and I gratefully relaxed into it, looking at all the old landmarks and the new changes of my hometown.

"Don't you like me, Aunt Gennie?"

Ann turned around in the front seat as I, startled, looked at my nephew.

"Of course she likes you," said Ann, reaching over to pat Rich on the knee. "Aunt Gennie's just having fun looking out the window. She hasn't been here in a while."

"That's right," I said. "A long while."

Rich's bottom lip was pushed up, his eyes focused on his folded hands.

"Still," I continued, "I was acting kind of rude, wasn't I?"

How, I wondered, was I supposed to take care of this kid? We hadn't been on the freeway for five minutes and already I'd hurt his feelings.

"Kinda rude," said Rich, nodding. A little smile played on his lips. "Yeah, kinda rude."

Ann winked at me, and I winked back, feeling I was off the hook, at least for now.

*A*fter Rich had gone to bed, Ann and Riley and I sat in front of the fireplace, drinking wine that wasn't half bad and enjoying the cedarwood fire that was throwing off the greatest smell.

"Just think," said Riley, "in two days we'll be sitting in front of a fireplace in Tuscany."

"You think it'll be cold enough to have a fire in Tuscany?" asked Ann.

"Sure," said Riley. "Not cold as we know it, but cold enough."

"And I'll have to be content admiring this view," I said, looking out the picture window. Even though I was looking out into darkness, I remembered the view that had been offered in daylight. "It's really pretty here."

Riley and Ann lived outside Minneapolis along the shore of Deep Lake, which rested in what used to be a sleepy little town of the same name but was now getting to be quite a snazzy bedroom community. *Too snazzy,* I had thought earlier as we passed huge houses whose tennis courts and square footage screamed money, *for Riley and Ann's income, unless Minnesota has started paying its teachers a whole lot more than other states.*

"Well, you've moved up in the world, haven't you?" I had asked on the drive home as we passed a virtual castle, turrets and all.

"We got the deal of the century," said Riley. "It was the old farmstead of one of my students' grandparents. They could have sold it for a lot more because it's lakefront, but they were old Swedes who liked the idea of selling it to a teacher."

"Not just any teacher," said Ann. "Their granddaughter's all-time favorite teacher." She turned to face me. "She writes for *Newsweek* now. She says Riley inspired her to be a writer."

"She didn't need much inspiration," said Riley. "She was very talented."

"We're right by the water," Rich had piped in. " 'Course, it's too cold to swim."

"We do have a hot tub, though," said Ann. "Although the pump motor's broken."

The disabled hot tub, the back deck, and the view were the fanciest things about the old farmhouse. Older than the neighboring split-levels and castles by nearly a century, it was a white clapboard two-story whose rooms were small verging on cramped.

But in the dark that was softened only by firelight, small verging on cramped was utterly cozy.

"We put that picture window in last summer," said Ann, topping off my wineglass. "I think it's one of the smartest things we ever did."

"Besides getting married," said Riley.

"Oh, brother," I said. "I was wondering when your usual lovey-dovey crap was going to start."

"Lovey-dovey crap?" said Riley. "Geneva, you're a real romantic. Right up there with Keats."

"Give me a break, Riley. I just came out of the worst breakup since me and the Frenchman split up."

"The Frenchman and *I*."

"You are not allowed to correct my grammar," I said, hitting him with a couch pillow. "Ann, tell him what bad manners it is to correct someone's grammar."

My sister laughed. "I think you just did."

The phone rang, and Ann and I looked at Riley.

"All right, all right," he said, standing up, "I'll get it."

We watched him go into the hallway, and then Ann, with urgency in her voice, asked, "So how are you, Gen? Are you really over Trevor?"

"I think so," I said with a sigh. "I mean, I should be . . . because he is definitely over me."

"His loss."

"Mine too," I said, and spontaneously, we reached out, clamping our arms around each other. It didn't matter how long we had been separated—when we were reunited, Ann and I always found ourselves falling into each other's safe and open arms.

"Gen, you're crying."

"No, I'm not," I said, wiping away the evidence.

My twin pulled away from me and looked at me like a lawyer trying to figure out her client's innocence. "Tell me what's wrong."

I was happy to oblige; I could fool Ann on the phone with my usual let's-forge-on cheer, but it was a relief to be with her in person, where everything and anything could be said. "Well," I began, "I didn't think breaking up with Trevor would—"

"That was Jerod Schmitz," said Riley, entering the room. "He's taking over my classes while we're gone." Shaking his head, he sat next to Ann. "No matter how much reassurance I offer, he still wants more."

"Don't we all," I said. I was sad Ann's and my moment was lost; an interrupted confessional felt as abrupt and incomplete as interrupted sex. You were left longing for more.

Ann gave me a little wink, a signal for *We'll talk later*, and refilled everyone's wineglasses.

"So," said Riley, "I suppose you've been hammering out all the household details. Anything you're especially concerned about as far as Rich is concerned?"

I sighed. "How much time do you have?"

"C'mon, Geneva," said Ann. "It won't be that hard. On Monday, Wednesday, and Friday he takes the bus home; on Tuesday and Thursday he's got after-school activities, but with carpooling you'll hardly ever have to drive."

"Carpooling?" I asked, as if I didn't understand the term. "I have to *carpool*?"

"Only on Thursdays. Here, I'll show you."

She got up and, after turning on a light, took a three-ring notebook off a little secretary in the hallway.

"She's got everything written down," said Riley.

"In here and on the kitchen calendar," said Ann, sitting next to me. She opened the notebook. "See, everything's laid out for you, day by day. Rich's schedule, menu plans—"

"Menu plans?"

"Rich is kind of funny about what he eats. For instance, Monday is pizza day. Wednesdays he likes chow mein from our local Chinese restaurant. Here's the number, and here's what he likes to order."

I took the book and riffled through a couple of pages.

"What's 'Wake-up—seven o'clock'?"

"Oh, Geneva," said Ann, laughing at a joke I hadn't told. "That's what time you need to wake up Rich. At seven o'clock."

"*Seven o'clock?* Ann, I haven't gotten up at seven since . . . well, since I discovered noon."

"It's only on the weekdays. Saturdays you can sleep in."

"Saturdays? What about Sundays?"

"Well," said Riley, "on Sunday Rich likes to go to church. To Sunday school."

"You don't have to go," said Ann. "Barb—that's his friend Conrad's mom—will pick him up. But you'll have to wake him."

"Can't he use an alarm?"

Ann looked at her husband for help.

"Rich is a pretty deep sleeper," Riley explained. "For him to wake up, he needs a little physical persuasion."

"Physical persuasion?" I did not like how this conversation was going, not at all.

"You know," said Riley, "a shake or two of the shoulder. Some fairly loud announcements: 'Rich, it's time to get up!' "

"Anyway," said Ann, ignoring the appalled look on my face, "he'll get dressed and ready for school on his own, but he likes a bowl of hot cereal in the morning now that it's getting colder."

"A bowl of hot cereal," I whined. "And I suppose I have to make it?"

This time Ann's laughter sounded genuinely amused rather than desperate.

"No, just have it ready in the microwave the night before. He knows how to turn it on. He likes company when he eats, though."

"But I don't eat breakfast. At least not that early."

"Then make yourself a cup of latte. Riley gave me an espresso machine for Christmas."

"So you're not totally uncouth," I told my brother-in-law. "But I like to read *The New York Times* with my coffee. I don't suppose you subscribe?"

"We get the Minneapolis paper," said Ann hopefully. "And the neighborhood weekly."

"Swell. I can't wait to read all the news that's fit to print in Deep Lake."

"You'd be surprised," said Riley.

"Okay," said Ann, getting back to the schedule. "At eight-twenty Rich has to catch his bus. It stops right in front of the house."

I looked at the next notation on the paper, which read "3:15—Rich gets off bus."

"So what happens between eight-twenty and three-fifteen?"

Ann wiggled her eyebrows. "Whatever you want to happen. It's your free time."

It took us nearly a half hour to go page by page through the book, and when we closed its covers I was, to say the least, somewhat daunted. I had hired myself out as a baby-sitter, and lo and behold, there were all these other attendant jobs I hadn't really considered: cook, chauffeur, maid, laundress, and alarm clock. I was already exhausted from the *thought* of all my labors and was ready to whine about not understanding the job description when Ann, holding the book to her chest, began to cry.

"We can't go, Riley," she said. "It's too much for Geneva."

Now, I happened to be in complete agreement with her, but I wasn't going to let my sister decide what was too much for me. It was the principle of the thing.

"Ann," I said like a queen addressing one of her dimmer chambermaids, "you insult me. It's laughable that you think this might be too much for me. It'll be different, but it's certainly not too much. I'm a Broadway star, after all."

"A Broadway star," blubbered Ann. "What does that have to do with anything?"

Riley gave her shoulder a little squeeze. "I think what she's trying to say is that if she can conquer Broadway, she can conquer anything."

"Sort of like that 'New York, New York' song?" asked Ann with a sniff.

"Exactly." I hummed a few bars and then for the "make it anywhere" line got up and belted it out.

"Shhh," said Ann, wiping the tears off her face as she laughed. "You'll wake up Rich."

"And if I did," I said with a bravura I didn't feel, "I'd get him right back to sleep."

"How would you do that?" asked Ann, and I could tell she desperately wanted me to come up with a good answer—with the right answer.

"I'd sing him a lullaby," I said, and then, offering them the thrill thousands have paid big money for, I proceeded to give them a concert. I sang my way through a repertoire of ballads and lullabies. By the time I'd finished "Hush Little Baby," Riley, his head tilted back against the top of the couch, was softly snoring, and my twin sister was looking at me the way she used to when we played explorer in Grandma Hjordis's backyard: as if she were Thor Heyerdahl and I was Roald Amundsen and we had just discovered a utopia not on any map.

Chapter 5

 spent the next morning driving around with my sister, getting acquainted with her neighborhood.

"What do all these people *do?*" I asked as we drove past another single-family home that had room for both sides of in-laws *plus* a visiting UN delegation.

"Oh, you know. Doctors, lawyers, bankers, professional athletes. That's Maury Rungston's house right there." She pointed to a series of cubes with windows.

"Who's Maury Rungston?"

"The Vikings football coach. I always see him at the grocery store. He buys a lot of Healthy Choice."

I drove a few more blocks and then matched a house with an address on the hand-drawn map on my lap.

"So this is where I drop off Rich's friend on Thursdays?"

Ann nodded. "Rich's *best* friend lives here. Conrad—I've told you about him. Barb, his mother, is out shopping, I think, otherwise we could run in and you could meet her."

A woman in a fancy jogging suit passed us, looking in the car windows suspiciously, as if trying to discern whether we were two matrons out for a drive or cat burglars casing a joint.

"Connie's been a godsend for Rich, and Barb has been one for me. In fact, she's the one who really convinced Riley and me to take this trip."

"You needed convincing? I thought you were so excited about it."

"Well, I am, Geneva—but that doesn't mean I'm not scared to death. But Barb said it was about time Riley and I did something special for ourselves."

"What is she, a marriage counselor?"

Ann smiled. "No, just someone who understands. Conrad's got cerebral palsy. Anyway, she said a month was a long time to be away from Rich—but it wasn't *too* long. She even offered to take care of him while we were away."

"She did?" I said out loud, while silently I shouted, *You mean I really didn't have to do this?*

"Her husband vetoed the idea. Barb could have easily overridden that veto—I mean, she's the one who would have taken care of Rich; George hardly lifts a finger around the house—but I didn't want to cause a big rift." She flipped down the windshield visor. "You better start driving again. That jogger's giving us funny looks."

We drove past a few more landmarks, and when we were finished, Ann sat in the passenger seat, nodding.

"You always were good with a map," she said.

"Thank you." It was a skill I was proud of; if there was ever an opportunity to navigate, I always volunteered. "Now what do you say we find a coffee shop? I could use a double latte." What I really wanted was to take a break from all these instructions and sit and talk to Ann about, well, me.

"Coffee's the last thing I need," said Ann. "I'm so nervous I'm afraid I'm going to throw up."

"Well, kindly aim it outside," I said, opening her window with the automatic control on the driver's side. Inwardly I sighed, realizing how wound up Ann was and that she did not need the additional burden of knowing I was taking menopause and my romantic breakup hard and that the same loneliness Ann thought I'd long ago shooed away was making regular, forceful visits.

I sighed again—it was hard for me to give up the spotlight in any situation—and asked the question I already knew the answer to.

"Nervous about what?"

"Oh, Geneva. About leaving Rich. About you taking care of Rich."

"I can understand the first part," I said, "but not the second. In fact, your lack of trust wounds me deeply." It didn't, really; in fact, I totally understood her lack of trust, but I couldn't let her know that. And I must have delivered the line as the Tony award–winning actress I am, because she was immediately apologetic.

"I'm sorry, Geneva. I could have T. Berry Brazelton for a baby-sitter and I'd still be nervous."

"Teaberry who?"

"He's a pediatrician, writer, and all-around child expert." Ann rolled up her window. "Speaking of pediatricians, we didn't drive by Rich's."

"Don't worry," I said. "If it's on the map, I'll find it."

*R*ich chose not to go to the airport to see his parents off.

"Don't want to say good-bye there," he said, sitting on the couch, his arms folded across his chest. "Want to say good-bye here."

"If you go to the airport with us," said Ann, putting her arm around him, "we'll have a little more time together."

Rich shook his head.

"But Rich," said Riley, who was checking the tickets for the five hundredth time, "your Aunt Gennie is driving us to the airport, so you'll have to go with us. You can't stay here alone."

Rich pushed out his lower lip and refolded his arms. "Can't go to the airport."

Ann looked helplessly at Riley.

"Yes, you can," said Riley, his voice stern. "Now come on, son, we don't have time to argue about this."

"Not *going*."

Ann, her face peaked, as our grandma used to say, walked like a zombie to the phone.

"Hi, Barb? This is Ann. Listen, Barb, we've kind of got a problem here. Rich doesn't want to go to the airport, and Geneva can't leave him here, and . . . oh, would you? Oh, we'd be so grateful." She looked at her watch. "I don't know—ten minutes?"

She hung up the phone. "Rich, Conrad's mother is going to—"

She was tackled on her way back to the couch.

"Good-bye, Mommy! Good-bye!"

If Ann had looked peaked, now her face looked like that of someone in a newspaper photograph whose horrible caption read "Fire destroys family home" or "Relief efforts too late for many."

Riley joined his wife and son's embrace, and I stood there, swallowing hard, feeling nervous and scared, and wishing more than anything that I had a stand-in for this part.

I answered the door when the bell rang.

"Hi," said a tall woman with a frizzy permanent my hairdresser would never have allowed to leave his shop. "I'm Barb Torgerson, taxi driver."

"Geneva Jordan," I said, shaking her hand. "Baby-sitter."

She looked over my shoulder and waved at the threesome huddled on the couch.

"Listen," she said softly, "you need any help at all, you call me. Day or night."

"Thanks," I said, and didn't know if the tears that came to my eyes were because of the kindness of this virtual stranger or because Riley had started gathering up the luggage in preparation to go.

Outside Barb's Land Rover, I hugged Riley and Ann and in a buoyant voice wished them bon voyage. Then, remembering the Italian version (I had been to Italy twice), offered a *"Buon viaggio."*

Rich hugged his father so hard that a little "oof " popped out of him. Ann hugged me almost as hard and whispered, "You take care of him, Dee."

"On my honor, Dum."

When she held out her arms for a final hug from Rich, he clamped on to his mother.

This, I thought, was going to be a hug that would make them late for the airplane, that would derail their travel plans, but then Rich broke free, surprising me, and I think Ann too.

"Bye," he said, looking at the ground.

"Bye," said Ann, her voice quavering.

Then suddenly they were in the Land Rover, and Rich and I stood in the driveway waving at them like hopped-up Miss Americas.

When we could no longer see them, Rich put his arm down, but he didn't move. He just stood there, looking past the trees on the other side of the road.

"What do you say we go inside and have some hot chocolate?" I said finally. I was getting a little chilly standing there.

My words seemed to flip the control switch to his emotions. "Mommy! Daddy!" he wailed.

As he cried I patted his back, feeling utterly, totally ineffective.

When it seemed he had sniffed his last sniff and wiped away his last tear, I asked brightly (and, I realized immediately, inanely), "So, what shall we do?"

Rich shrugged listlessly. Taking him by his arm, I led him into the house. Fortunately we had already eaten dinner, so I didn't have to bother with that.

Rich plopped on the couch, where he resumed his folded-arm pose.

I sat next to him. "Good idea. Let's just enjoy the view."

What sunset colors were left looked like a healing bruise, a fading purple tinged with yellowish orange. I put my feet up on the coffee table and settled back, forgetting how much I enjoyed a lake view, how calming it was, how familiar.

"No feet on the coffee table. Mom doesn't like feet on the coffee table."

"She doesn't?" My sister was neat but not obsessive, and somehow I couldn't see her enforcing a rule that sided against comfort.

Rich shook his head. "She says no muddy shoes on the furniture."

I wiggled my toes. "But I'm stocking-footed, see?"

"Oh, yeah. Then that's okay." He put his own stocking feet up next to mine. "So how 'bout that hot chocolate?"

I laughed. Certainly there was nothing wrong with Rich's memory. "You got it. Just lead me to the kitchen."

"Lead you?"

"Sure," I said, and suddenly I got on all fours, panting and barking like a dog.

Puzzlement puckered Rich's forehead.

"Here," I said, handing him an invisible leash. "Lead me to the kitchen."

A smile burst across his face. "Oh, okay. Okay." He stood and then patting his thigh, he said. "Come on, doggie. Come on."

I barked again, and he laughed and that's how we made our way to the kitchen, master and canine. What the hell.

*T*here was a canister of instant cocoa, but I'm more a fan of the old-fashioned kind, and besides, it would give us something to do. I found a can of cocoa powder, some sugar, and the milk.

"You want to help me?"

Rich pushed his glasses up and nodded.

He concentrated as he followed my instructions, his eyebrows squinched down and his tongue sticking out of his mouth as he measured the cocoa and sugar. I poured in the milk and we both stood by the stove, taking turns stirring.

"The secret is not to let it boil."

"Not to let it boil," Rich repeated, pronouncing *boil* "boy-o."

When I poured two cups, I asked him if he liked marshmallows or whipped cream.

"Both."

"You're my kind of guy."

There was some Cool Whip in the fridge and a bag of marshmallows in the cupboard, and with them we added about two hundred calories to our drinks. Rich reached for the old-fashioned cookie jar shaped like a woman who'd eaten a few too many cookies herself. He took off the lid (the upper half of the woman's rotund body) and pushed the lower half toward me.

"Cookie?" he said, as courtly as a butler.

"Why, thank you," I said, reaching into the jar. "Don't mind if I do."

We sat for at least twenty minutes, dipping our shortbread cookies into our cocoa and offering each another occasional smiles. I was pleased at how well the evening was progressing, but then the phone rang. Rich jumped up to answer.

"Hello?" Joy washed over his face. "Mommy! Daddy!" He cupped the phone and looked at me. "It's my mom and dad."

I nodded.

He held the receiver with both hands. "Are you in Italy?"

Their conversation lasted a few minutes, and then Rich handed me the phone. "My mom wants to talk to you. They're not in Italy—not even on the plane yet."

I told Ann what Rich had already told her: that we were having hot chocolate, that we were fine.

"I'm a basket case," said Ann. "I cried all the way to the airport."

"Did you really?" I asked brightly, glancing at Rich, who watched me like a private eye. "Well, we're having a great time too."

"Geneva, I don't know if I can stand this. I mean, being away from him."

"Sure you can," I said, as jovial as a Shriner. "Now you send us a postcard as soon as you get there, and we'll send one back."

After Rich said his good-byes one more time, I hung up the phone.

"That was my mom and dad," he reminded me. "They're not even on the plane to Italy yet."

"No, they aren't," I said, and then Rich sighed. It was a sigh so big it seemed a caricature of a sigh, and I almost laughed.

"What are Italy people like?" he asked.

I drank the last of my cocoa. "Italy people are called Italians. They live by the Mediterranean and have a rich tradition in the arts and—" I cleared my throat, deciding to exit the lecture mode. "And most of them have dark hair and dark eyes and are on the handsome side."

"What's the handsome side?"

"That's the side we're on, bucko. Along with the rest of the good-looking people."

Rich frowned, thinking this through. "I'm on the handsome side?" he said finally, hope in his voice.

"Absolutely. The *extra*-handsome side."

"You're fooling me," he said, giggling.

"No, I'm not—you're on the extra-*extra*-handsome side!"

This struck my nephew as hilarious, and he slapped his knee, laughing.

"Extra-extra-handsome. That's funny."

He got up then and took a pencil off the telephone stand. "Better start that postcard now." He sat down. "Do we have a postcard?"

"No," I said, and then as his face began to crumple, I added, "But we could make one."

And so we did, out of stiff construction paper. Rich drew a picture of himself, big blue tears spilling out of his eyes.

"That's so they know I'm sad," he said.

He wrote out the message slowly, his tongue poking out of his mouth again: "Miss you. Sad Rich." After he licked the stamp and pounded it on with his fist, he started to cry. This went on all evening—bouts of crying between blustery attempts by me to entertain him.

Rich went to bed at his usual time ("Oops, nine o'clock," he said, looking at the kitchen clock and walking away from our slapjack game), and even though I heard him crying in his bed, I couldn't go in there and comfort him. I was too exhausted. Besides, I thought I might be an intrusion; maybe he just *wanted* to cry, needed to cry.

I stood outside his room for a moment, thinking one minute that I should respect his privacy and then the next minute thinking that he needed me. That's why I was exhausted: I had been playing this mental tennis all night, trying to decide what was the right thing to do.

Finally I just tiptoed to my bedroom with plans to bury myself under Grandma Hjordis's homemade quilt.

Our mother had saved all of the things Grandma had made, and allowed us, on our twenty-first birthday, to divide up all the spoils that she herself hadn't claimed. Ann got three quilts; I got two, but I also got the fancy crocheted tablecloth that Grandma had used only for company. We each got half of the matching outfits she had made for us every Christmas; precious little red velvet dresses we wore for our very first Christmas, the mod little Carnaby Street numbers that had been her last creation for us.

"You made the girls *miniskirts?*" our mother had asked when we modeled them for her.

Grandma Hjordis had winked at us and then, as if she were explaining television to one of the original Globe Theatre actors, said, "You've got to keep up with the times."

Nestled under that patchwork quilt, I invited those sweet memories in, but they were mowed down by present worries.

Sighing, I turned under Grandma's quilt, convinced that my mind wouldn't shut itself down long enough for me to sleep so I was more than surprised that in my next conscious moment, Rich was shaking my foot, shouting loudly what sounded like the name of a Swiss accountant: "Wisenshyne!" It took me a moment to realize he was urging me to get up, to rise and shine.

"I thought you were supposed to be a deep sleeper," I mumbled.

"Today—*bam!*" He slapped his palms together. "Today I wake up like that!"

"Great," I said, squinting at the alarm clock until the numbers focused. "It's only six-thirty."

"Is that bad?"

"No, Rich," I said, pushing back my wild hair. "No, that's just early."

*T*hat first morning was comparable to a terrible opening night—I was so afraid of a misstep, of screwing up my lines, of giving the wrong cues to my costar, that I was nearly paralyzed. My stomach was tied up in nervous knots from the moment I got Rich breakfast (after I managed to scorch his oatmeal, he reminded me he cooked it himself in the microwave if I premixed it) and got him dressed (well, stood outside his bedroom door asking if he needed any help, to which he pointedly replied, "I know how to put my clothes on, Aunt Geneva") to the time he finally got on the school bus. I studied the schedule and instructions Ann left for me like a senior cramming for SATs; everything I did was checked and double-checked. I don't suffer from migraines, but I had an ache in my head that certainly mimicked one, and it didn't go away until we got through the second day relatively unscathed. It was then my shriveled confidence suddenly expanded in my headacheless head and I was convinced I was that Teaberry guy's successor. Not to brag, but I had this child-care stuff *down*.

Not only was I able to get Rich up, fed, and to the bus stop, I also managed to be there waiting for him after school, just like June Cleaver minus the shirtwaist dress and heels. All my opening-night jitters were gone, and I was ready to settle in for a long, successful run.

I know I sometimes overdo the acting analogies, but in this case it was apt—I didn't so much feel like Aunt Gennie, caretaker, as I felt like I was playing the *part* of Aunt Gennie, caretaker. It's a hazard (and a help, I guess) of the trade: When in doubt, act. Of course, if I was acting, then Rich was too—he was as polite as an undertaker, *not* my idea of a thirteen-year-old kid. But, faking or not, we were doing swell. Then Thursday came.

According to my detailed schedule, on Tuesdays Rich and his friend Conrad were band aides (whatever those were) and Barb Torgerson picked them up; on Thursdays they were in swim club, and I picked them up.

I had come from a day spa Ann had recommended (I doubt my sister had ever been inside, but, knowing my needs, she had compiled a list of shops and services she knew I'd enjoy) where I'd spent the afternoon lying on a massage table getting pummeled by a lithe blonde whose size belied her strength. I had been ready to cry uncle half a dozen times, and when she was finished I wanted to sue her for battery—until I realized how utterly rejuvenated I felt. Making an appointment for the next week, I tipped her generously and asked how she got such strong hands.

"My mother taught me how to bake bread when I was a little girl," she said. "I've been kneading all my life." Here she wiggled her fingers. "Now I just work with flesh instead of dough."

"Oh, I'll bet sometimes the consistency is pretty close," I said—not speaking of my own thighs, of course.

All she would afford me was a tight little smile, as if by laughing at my little joke she was somehow breaching the protocol of the client-masseuse relationship.

I drove to Rich's school as unknotted as a stream, singing as loudly as I could to an oldies station. (Oldies—who'd ever have thought the music of the Beatles and the Rolling Stones and the Who, for crying out loud, would be called oldies?) I parked the big old Delta in the lot by the main entrance and proceeded to wait, and with every minute that passed without Rich's appearance, all the tension that the lithe blonde had pounded out began to creep back. Where was he? Five minutes passed, then ten. I looked at my watch, then at the entrance.

"Rich always gets picked up at the main entrance," Ann had said when we had taken the Rich tour. "See, the one with the school's name over the door."

Yup, the name was still over the door, etched in stone.

"Rich's after-school activities always get out at four-thirty," I said to myself, having memorized much of Ann's directions like the quick study I am.

I looked at my watch again: four forty-five. A wind had kicked up too, reminding me that winter was always closer in Minnesota than the calendar might say. My stomach started churning; I could imagine the call I'd have to make to Italy. *Hi, Ann? There's been a slight problem. I seem to have misplaced Rich.*

Zipping my jacket up, I walked to the front door, hoping of course that he was waiting inside. Or maybe the coach or whoever it was who was in charge of the swim club had rewarded them with a free swim, or maybe Rich was still in the locker room, fooling around with the hair dryer or something. Or maybe . . . I didn't even dare think of the alternatives. My heart was beating harder than I like it to, and when I tried to open the door, I thought it would go into arrhythmia. The door was locked. I yanked at it again and again, as if brute force would open it, and just when I was about to reach for my cellular phone to dial 911, I saw a folded piece of paper on the ground.

I unfolded it, my fingers trembling. It was a bank deposit slip belonging to George and Barbara Torgerson. Scrawled on it were the words "Rich is at my house."

"What a stupid place to put a note," I muttered, thinking that now that I had her account number, maybe I should abscond with some of her funds and teach her a lesson. Then I jogged to the car, relief pulsing through my veins.

I slammed the car door after I'd parked in the Torgersons' driveway, and it was a good enough slam to announce my arrival. Barb Torgerson met me at the doorway, all smiles, and I suddenly realized I had something in common with her perm: my mood. Both were bad.

"We were wondering when you'd—"

"Please," I said, cutting her off. "Next time when plans change, do you mind letting me know ahead of time? I was half sick wondering

where Rich was, and then I find your little note on the ground—
which, by the way, isn't the smartest place to put a note."

"Why don't you come in," said Barb, her smile gone, and no
sooner had I stepped inside her small foyer than Rich was on me
like a scab.

"Where were you?" he bellowed, fury pinching his features.
"Me and Connie waited for hours and hours and you never
came!"

Just as suddenly as he had been on top of me, he whirled around,
his back toward me, his arms folded across his chest.

"Not hours and hours, Rich," said a boy who stood on the staircase. Dark curly hair poked out from under a Twins baseball cap. "If
we'd waited for hours and hours, we'd still be at school."

One of his arms flailed and his head tipped back as he spoke.
His mouth was fixed somewhere between a grin and a grimace,
and his head shook slightly.

"You know what I mean, Conrad!" shouted Rich.

"I think you guys need to calm down a little," said Barb. "Why
don't you finish your game while Rich's aunt and I talk?"

"I'm calm," said Conrad, and squinched his neck down in a
shrug. "I just think it's pretty shitty that—"

"Watch your mouth, Conrad," said Barb, making a shooing
movement with her hands. "Now, both of you—come on, out."

As she led me into the kitchen a sinking feeling began to de-
scend upon me.

"It was *four* o'clock, wasn't it? It's usually four-thirty, but they
were cleaning the pool today." I could see Ann's face as she gave
me that special instruction. "Why didn't I remember they were
cleaning the pool today?"

Barb shrugged and then, nodding toward a swivel chair at the
counter, said, "Take a load off."

I sat down, shaking my head. "I'm really shocked. Shocked because I've memorized practically everything Ann's written down and I don't know how I could have mixed up the time."

"For your information," she said, peeling a carrot, "after I left a message on your answering machine, I stuck the note in the crack between the doors, for backup. I never would have left a note on the ground. That *would* have been stupid."

"I'm glad I didn't get a chance to say all the other things I was going to say."

Barb, bless her, laughed. "I can imagine. Ann told me you can be quite . . . uncensored."

"I feel like such a fool. I'm so sorry."

She tucked the carrot into a nest of vegetables on which a roast was perched, and put the pan in the oven.

"Who doesn't screw up?" she said, wiping her hands on a towel. "But it's those things that affect our boys' security that Ann and I try hard *not* to screw up. Not that we always succeed." She made a moue. "You want a cup of coffee?"

"You wouldn't have anything stronger, would you?"

"I guess a little wine might be called for. Or we have beer."

"Wine would be great."

We sat in that warm kitchen, savoring a glass of chardonnay, and as the minutes ticked away, the aroma of dinner cooking deepened, and I was filled with a sense that, at least for now, all was right with the world. I felt so at home, so at ease with this woman, even though her hair went against all the principles of style I hold dear.

"So Conrad," I ventured, "has cerebral palsy?"

"We have a correct answer!" said Barb, throwing her arms up. "So what'll it be, the curtain or what's behind door number one?"

She startled me so, my hands went to my chest in a clichéd but very sincere gesture and my mouth dropped open.

"I'm sorry," said Barb, laughing. "It's just that you sounded so *concerned.*"

"I apologize, I just—"

Barb waved her hand. "You should be flattered I feel comfortable enough with you to say something so outrageous. Most people would never get that kind of answer out of me."

"I don't know if I should be flattered or insulted."

"Definitely flattered." She took a big gulp of wine, and I followed her lead. "Yes," she said, drying her lower lip with her finger, "Connie has cerebral palsy, caused by a lack of oxygen at a very premature birth. He's seen the inside of a hospital more times than a boy his age should, but it's gotten a lot better lately. Mentally he has a very slight retardation, but I'd have to say he seems quite a bit smarter to me than a lot of people, and yes, there certainly are challenges to raising him."

"So you get asked the same questions a lot, huh?"

"I know people are curious. I don't know why I'm taking everything out on you."

"Because you feel comfortable with me, remember?"

Barb laughed again. "Right. Anyway, about today. Connie's starting to rebel against routine—right now he's on this very pleasant *swearing* kick—but Rich *loves* his, and he gets scared when things change unexpectedly. Plus Rich was worried that something had happened to you."

"I feel like such a nitwit," I said, my head automatically resuming its shaking. "And things were going so well."

"Things still *are* going well. Ann and Riley are getting a well-deserved vacation, and you've given up your life for a month to come out here and take care of Rich."

Normally I would have enjoyed her acknowledgment of my

great humanitarianism, but I didn't want to BS a woman like Barb Torgerson.

"I didn't give up much," I said. "I wasn't working, and the only plans I had were to indulge myself in . . . oh, just about everything."

"Well, see, then? That was a lot to give up—all those indulgences." She held up the wine bottle, offering me more. When I shook my head, she put the cork back in and placed the bottle back in the refrigerator. "You know, I think it's a good sign that Rich got so upset with you. He's been so concerned that you like him—but I think now he's feeling comfortable enough with you to show you how he really feels."

"*How* many more days until Ann and Riley get back?"

Barb smiled. "Don't worry, you're doing fine." She got up to check on the roast. "Now, I'd love to have you stay for dinner, but unfortunately George is bringing some people over."

"I take it that's a hint that I leave?"

"I'd say it's a little bolder than a hint."

I laughed, and genuinely hoped that I would have dinner with her soon.

"Rich!" she hollered through cupped hands. "Time to go home!"

*A*pparently my nephew was *really* feeling comfortable with me, because all the politeness of the past few days was abandoned. Despite my profuse apologies, he sulked on the way home, and then in the house, when I asked him, purely for conversation's sake, what he wanted for dinner, he screamed, "Do you even care? Do you even care?"

My instinct was to call a cab for the airport, but I knew now it was time for some action—if not the parental kind, then the *auntal* kind.

"Rich," I said, "please don't yell at me. I have told you over and over how sorry I am about getting the time mixed up. I don't want to tell you again. Now it's your turn either to accept my apology or . . . actually, you don't have a choice here. You have to accept an apology when someone's truly sorry. And I am."

With his eyes squinted, his nostrils flaring with each expulsion of breath, Rich stared at me a good ten seconds before he burst into tears.

I took him in my arms, because I didn't know what else to do. We stood there, and when I thought I'd fall over from supporting his weight, I led him over to the couch.

"I'm sorry, Auntie Gennie!" he said, taking his glasses off and wiping his eyes with the heels of his hands. "But I was so scared! Thought you left me! Thought you left me and went to Italy!"

My heartbeat, my breath, eye blinks—everything stopped for a moment. "Oh, Rich," I finally managed to say, "I'm not going to Italy. I'm here to stay with you."

"I miss my mom and dad!" he sobbed. "Miss them so much!"

"Then let's call them," I said, wiping my nephew's wet cheeks. "But first you have to stop crying. They'll be upset if you're crying."

Rich's features stretched into a gargoyle's as he dragged his hands across his face. "Okay," he said after a moment. "Okay, all done."

It was as if his conversation with his parents was balm on a wound; I saw his face relax, his smile come back.

"I am, *am* being good in school," he said. He nodded a few times, giggled, and then asked the $64,000 question. "Guess who forgot to pick me and Conrad up after swim club?"

I should have known it was coming, but still, I wanted to smack the little Benedict Arnold. Rich went on and on, relaying every tiny little detail. "And then me and Connie finally decided to call

Connie's mom to come and get us, because we sure weren't going to stay overnight at school! I don't even know if they got lights at night in the school—and where would we have slept, Mom, on a desk?" He giggled again and then, quick as a switchblade, his arm shot out, almost cracking me on the head with the receiver.

"Mom wants to talk to you."

During Sunday-evening phone calls to her sister Helen, our mother occasionally gave Ann and me the phone so we could talk to our cousin Belinda. The connection was only between Minneapolis and Chicago, but the telephone reception was as staticky as that between NASA and orbiting astronauts.

Now Ann sounded as if she were in the next room. And she didn't sound happy.

"Geneva, what the—"

"Everything's fine, Ann. It won't happen again. You don't have anything to worry about. How're things in Tuscany?"

"Things are late in Tuscany. You got us out of a dead sleep."

"Sorry. But Rich was really lonesome and—"

"Oh, Geneva, he's all right, isn't he?"

"Great," I said, looking at my nephew's expectant face, wondering if he could see the uncertainty in mine. "We're all great."

*T*here are many ways to spend a Friday night; Rich and I happened to spend it by building a model of the Alamo for his history assignment. Our quiet concentration was interrupted only by the occasional joke or conversation. But suddenly a wave of yearning washed over me, and the sensation was so vivid, so physical, that I almost gasped for air.

"What's wrong, Aunt Gennie?" asked Rich, looking up from his pile of Popsicle sticks.

"Nothing," I said, taking one of the sticks and trimming one end of it into a blunted point. (It was my job to make the fort's fence posts.)

"Then why'd you go like this?" He made a horrible sound, like someone who'd just been shot in the stomach.

So I *had* gasped.

"Well," I said, wondering if I should blow off his question or answer it. I decided to blow it off. "It was just a hiccup."

Rich squinted, looking at me the way a truant officer looks at a kid whose excuse for why he's on a street corner in the middle of a school day is that he's on independent study.

I swallowed, ashamed of myself.

"Okay, it wasn't a hiccup. I was just thinking of my grandma— my and your mom's grandma—and how she used to help us with our homework."

"Grandma Hjordis?" Rich asked, his eyes bright.

I nodded. "Does your mom talk about her much?"

"Lots!" said Rich. "Especially since we got the memory box!"

"Memory box? What memory box?"

"Come on," said Rich, pushing himself away from the table. "I'll show you."

I followed him to the small room that served as the laundry room, cleaning supply room, and miscellaneous storage room.

"Grandma Ruth sent it to us," said Rich, pointing to a big cardboard box. "Mommy only looked through it a little bit—she said she was too busy packing her stuff for the trip to unpack other stuff—but she said it looked like it had lots of memories inside. A memory box."

I remembered my mother phoning before she and Dad left for Arizona and telling me she was cleaning out their condo and did I want any of their old stuff. I had assumed "old stuff" meant knick-knacks or potholders or threadbare kitchen towels, so I politely answered, "No, thanks."

Now I opened the top of the box to see a photo album inside, and curiosity flared up in me.

"Come on," I said, pulling at the box. "Let's take a look through this."

With me pulling and Rich pushing, we maneuvered the box into the living room, where we plopped ourselves on the couch and began to look through the yellowing leather photo album.

"These sure are old," said Rich, squinting at the pictures. "Old, old, old."

Tears sprang to my eyes. "That's my grandma," I said softly. "Mine and your mom's." In a square, serrated-edged black-and-white photograph was dear Grandma Hjordis, standing in her kitchen, holding in her gingham oven mitt one of her gingerbread men.

"She made the best gingerbread," I said. "Your mom and I hated to eat them, because she'd decorate them with little frosting pants and shirts with candy buttons, but we couldn't help ourselves."

"Is that her? Is that you and Mom when you were little?"

I nodded, words lost to me. The photograph Rich pointed to showed Ann and me—we were both about five—sitting on Grandma's lap holding up the twin dolls dressed in twin clothes she had made us for Christmas. All three of us, sitting in front of the tree, looked the way people should look on Christmas—absolutely gleeful.

"She was such a good grandma," I whispered.

"I got a good grandma too," said Rich, a note of challenge in his voice. "My grandma Ruth in Aiwyzona. My other grandma died once, though."

Each photograph featuring Grandma, and occasionally Grandpa, took me for an exquisite stroll down memory lane. There was Grandma at her brand-new Kenmore sewing machine ("I don't have to work the treadle anymore!"); there were the two of them inspecting our snow fort; there was Grandpa proudly showing off his new Ford Falcon; there was Grandma braiding my hair.

"I have got to get copies of these," I kept muttering until, again, my words were frozen by emotion.

There was Grandma and me and Ann, spread out on her living-room floor, working on our model of a Viking ship for seventh-grade geography. It wasn't a photograph depicting the memory I'd had while I was helping Rich build the Alamo (that was of Grandma helping us make a pioneer diorama)—in fact; I had forgotten all about the hours we'd spent littering her floor with slivers of balsa wood and fabric, making what we named the *Mighty Helga*. I remembered we got an A on it and it was displayed on the teacher's desk during conference week.

"Good heavenly days," I said, mouthing the words Grandma used to express everything from impatience to fear to awe. "She taught us all about rigging and jibs and masts as we cut and pasted and sewed." I closed my eyes, not only to see those memories in my mind, but to stop the next generation of tears.

"I remember my grandma told my mom—that's your grandma Ruth, Rich—to grab the Instamatic and record the making of the *Mighty Helga*, and our mom asked her why she made such a big fuss with our school projects. Do you know what our grandma said then, Rich?"

"What?" asked Rich softly.

My eyes were still shut, and I saw my mother standing under the arch that separated the dining room from the living room, pointing the camera at us and scolding me to uncross my eyes and smile.

My voice was quavery. "She said, 'Making things with my favorite girls isn't a big fuss—it's big fun.' "

I remember how Ann and I had looked at each other then, and I could tell by her face that she felt, as I did, that we'd both been awarded blue ribbons in a category we couldn't quite explain.

"And I remembered," I continued, "imagining that I would be the type of mother who thought making things with her children would be big fun, too."

My chest rose in a big sigh, and I was ready to dive into a big cold pool of sadness and longing until Rich, rummaging through the box, pulled out what looked like two pieces of cardboard tied together with a faded ribbon.

"What's this?" he asked, holding it two inches from his face. "It's tied up like a present."

"Let me see it," I said lightly, restraining myself from grabbing it out of his hands.

"Can't read the writing," said Rich. "The writing's too hard to read." His arm shot out, and a corner of the scrapbook or whatever it was nearly clipped me on the chin.

"Here," he said. "You read it."

"Be glad to," I said through a clenched-teeth smile.

The faded purple satin ribbon bisected the flimsy cardboard cover, and on the top half, in fading blue ink and loopy penmanship, were the words *The Great Mysterious.*

"Oh, my God," I said softly.

"What?" asked Rich. "What is it?"

"It's a book your mom and I put together," I said, fingering the twine tied through three holes in the book's left margin. "A book we made a long time ago."

That fabulous, wondrous thing called memory again took me to a place I hadn't been in years: the lakeside cabin of my great-uncle, Carl Hillstrom, Grandma Hjordis's brother. We spent one week each summer up at the lake, and they were usually vacations filled with swimming and fishing and sleeping out on the porch as my mother and grandmother harmonized to the accompaniment of Great-uncle Carl's violin.

There was no sleeping on the porch during this vacation, however; when it wasn't windy and overcast, it was raining. One night sheet lightning filled the cabin windows with rectangles of eerie greenish light. Ann and I were sitting in the opposite corners of the main room, blatantly ignoring each other. We were crabby from being cooped up all day, and finally, to stop our bickering, our mother had separated us.

The adults were seated around the pine table, and when I wasn't looking up to stick my tongue out at Ann, I was paging through an *Archie* comic book I had already read at least a dozen times. Ann was sketching in a Red Chief tablet; somehow sensing that I was dying to see what she was drawing, she held the tablet up. The room was small enough so I could see easily the picture of a girl with horns and crossed eyes and snaggle teeth, entitled "Geneva." She smirked, I stuck out my tongue, and the minutes moved like hours.

"Well," said Grandma Hjordis, refilling the adults' coffee cups from the blue speckled pot with the burned bottom, "whatever happened to richer or poorer, through sickness and in health?"

There was anger in her voice, and as Grandma didn't often speak in anger, I closed my comic book, grateful for the unexpected entertainment.

"But Hjordis, it's not as if he planned this," said Great-uncle Carl. "I'll bet he's sick about hurting Marianne."

"That's right," added Grandpa Ole, "but does that mean he should deny what's in his heart?"

"Yes!" said my grandma and my great-aunt Tove.

"He should just forget about her!" continued Tove. "He's acting like a schoolboy when he needs to act like a husband and father!"

The conversation, which was escalating into an argument, continued, and I felt Ann nudge me. I moved over, making room for her in the battered cowboy-print easy chair. It was unusual that the adults in our family ever raised their voices, and Ann and I, our own argument forgotten, sat wedged together, fascinated.

"Who are they talking about?" I whispered, and Ann, who somehow always managed to hear more things than I did, whispered back, "Uncle Rolf."

Apparently Uncle Rolf, my mother's brother, had fallen in love with another woman and was planning to leave his wife and children. I hardly knew my uncle and his family—they lived in Colorado, and I could remember getting together only once at a family reunion.

It seemed an evenly matched argument—three opposed to his divorce ("The only one in the family!" said Grandma Hjordis, shaking her head) and three who thought it might be for the best. It wasn't women versus men, either; while Grandma and Great-aunt Tove argued against Grandpa and Great-uncle Carl, our father surprised us by siding with the older women, and even more surprising, our mother sided with the older men.

"He's been unhappy for a long time," she was saying. "Don't you remember how Marianne picked at him at the reunion? Constantly making snide comments about his job, his clothes, even the way he started the fire in the grill?"

"Maybe she knew he was seeing someone," said Great-aunt Tove.

"He only met this woman last year!" said Mother.

"Still," said Dad, "he should figure a way to work it out. A man shouldn't turn his back on his responsibilities."

"Should he turn his back on a chance at real happiness?" asked my mother. "Where's the responsibility there?"

"That's what I say," said Great-uncle Carl.

A crack of thunder so loud that it rattled the panes of the window halted all conversation. Startled, Grandma looked at Ann and me.

"Look who's been listening to all of this," she said.

"Ann, Geneva," said Dad, disappointment in his voice, "I thought you two were in bed long ago."

Not knowing why adults thought the things they did, my sister and I shrugged.

"So what do you think Uncle Rolf should do?" asked Mother.

"Good heavens, Ruth," scolded Great-aunt Tove, "that's not a thing you ask little girls."

"We're not so little," I said.

"We're almost teenagers," said Ann, even though our twelfth birthday was months away.

"I think they should get a divorce," I said, enjoying the attention the grown-ups fixed on us. "I know I couldn't be married to someone who didn't love me."

"Me neither," said Ann. "Although anyone I marry will always be madly in love with me."

Once in a while Ann said something that sounded exactly like something *I* would say, *wished* I had said, and it delighted me, making me feel our twinhood. We laughed and then, fueled on by the adults' reactions, laughed even harder.

"*Uffda*," said Great-aunt Tove. "That's an awfully cocky answer to a big question."

"Well, if you ask these two," explained Grandma, with both affection and irritation in her voice, "they have an answer for everything."

"Doesn't mean they're the right ones," sniffed Great-aunt Tove.

"They may be right answers for them," said Mom, "and isn't that how it should be? Isn't that what we've been talking about as far as Rolf's marriage is concerned?" Nodding, she looked around the table as if inviting us to agree or disagree. "Life has many big questions, and just as many answers."

"She's got you there, Tove," said Great-uncle Carl. Then Dad winked at us, and I remember feeling so accepted, so grown-up, and giddy with the sense of possibility that lies therein.

The thunder and lightning raged on that night, and after the older couples retired to the two tiny bedrooms and our parents to the sleeping loft, Ann and I stayed up, as energized as the charged, stormy air.

I don't know whose idea it was, but after a long discussion about life's big questions, we decided to make a book dedicated to their answers.

With the black-handled scissors and glue we found in the junk drawer, we cut and folded paper pockets, gluing them to the pages we tore out of Ann's tablet. On each page, above the pocket, we wrote a question and then, with the scissors tip, we punched (in a fashion) three holes into the left-hand margin of the pages and through the cardboard cover we made out of a disassembled Cheerios box.

"Ta-da!" said Ann, threading the final piece of twine into the third hole and tying it. "Now, what should we call it?"

The book lay under a cone of light shed by the old table lamp whose shade was hand-painted with bass and sunfish, and Ann and I, chins resting on curled fists, sat staring at it. We couldn't have just any old title for such an important book; its name needed to have weight, depth, allure.

"*The Great Mysterious,*" I said finally.

Looking at me, her eyes shiny, Ann said, "Perfect."

We had been to a birthday party a couple of years earlier of a friend whose parents hired a magician to entertain a dining room full of nine-year-olds. He was a frail old magician whose black suit had a green cast to it and smelled of mothballs, but he was good at sleight of hand. Lolly Patchet (who wasn't called Loudmouth Lolly for nothing) kept saying, "How do you do that?" to which the magician, in a sonorous voice, replied, "Ah . . . the great mysterious."

Ann and I had tried to bring the phrase into our own vernacular, but we soon dropped it, sensing that the words described too deep a thing to be made light of (this was odd considering that my sister and I—well, especially I—felt little compunction about making fun of strange people and the strange way they talked).

With a fumey-smelling felt-tip marker, Ann wrote the words on the thin cardboard. We then cut up strips of lined notepaper and, after pondering the first question, wrote our answers, tucking them into the page's pocket.

"Should we sign our names?" asked Ann.

"No. I think people feel more free to be deep when they don't have to say who they are."

Ann nodded. "We can probably figure out who writes what by the handwriting, anyway."

With instructions to please answer the first question, we left the book and the strips of paper on the kitchen table and went to bed, hopeful and excited that the adults would play along.

"Aunt Geneva, *open* it!"

I looked at my nephew and blinked as the door to the past slammed shut and the one to the present swung open.

"All right," I said, untying the ribbon. (When had that been added?)

"Cheerios!" said Rich, reading the fancy script of the cereal box that was the book's inside cover. "I love Cheerios!"

I drew in a breath, looking at the faded tablet paper and Ann's handwriting (we had alternated writing on each page, even though she had the better penmanship).

Rich elbowed me. "Read!"

" 'All ye who enter in,' " I read, surprised by the tears forming in my eyes, "welcome to the Great Mysterious, the Great Mysterious which is life, which is living. Please . . . do not be afraid of these big questions, these big questions that have been asked through the ages, even though it is true, bigger minds than yours have pondered them.' " I smiled, remembering how proud I'd been when I dictated that line to Ann. " 'Remember, if there is no such thing as a stupid question, there should be no such thing as a stupid answer. So please, put on your thinking caps and help us find answers to the Great Mysterious. Sincerely, Ann and Geneva Jordan. P.S. If you have a big question of your own, feel free to write it on the blank pages at the back. Thank you.' "

I turned the page.

"You're shaking," said Rich.

"I know. I'm excited."

My nephew snuggled closer to me. "Me too."

I read the question at the top of the page. " 'What is true love?' "

"What's in there?" asked Rich, pointing to the pocket we'd made by folding a pleat in the center of a square of paper and then gluing its side and bottom edges to the page.

"The answers," I said, shivering even more. "Take one."

Sensing a need to be careful, Rich gently slipped two of his pudgy fingers inside the pocket and drew out a slip of paper.

"Oh, my gosh," he said, as excited as me. "Oh, my gosh." He unfolded the strip of paper and held it to his eyes, squinting. "I can't read this handwriting, Aunt Gennie."

I took the paper from him, immediately recognizing the handwriting.

"This is Grandma Hjordis's answer," I said.

"Read!" pleaded Rich.

And so I did. " 'There are many kinds of love, and many kinds of true love. Above all, of course, and what should be the truest love, is the love of God. Next in truth is the love a mother feels for a child. This love is stronger than any other kind of love (except for that of God) because it is a love she would die for. This is not to say true love between a man and a woman is a weaker love; it is only different. There is more choice involved, more free will. A mother has no choice when it comes to her children; she loves them no matter what. The love one feels for a brother or sister, for parents or a friend, can also be true, true in that the feeling of affection and kindheartedness and goodwill and a wish for the best is no lie.' "

"Wow," said Rich after I finished. "I'm not exactly sure what she means, but wow."

I smiled, happy that at least Rich seemed impressed by Grandma Hjordis's answer. Hearing it now, I felt the same disappointment I did hearing it as a girl; she was so much fun, and yet none of that seemed to come through in her answers.

"My turn," I said, drawing out another slip of paper.

" 'Girls your age have years to go before you need to worry about things like true love.' "

"Who wrote that?" asked Rich as I laughed.

"My great-aunt Tove. More than once she told Ann and me we were too big for our britches."

"This one," said Rich, handing me another slip of paper.

I read them all. Grandpa Ole wrote, "I had a dog named Bly once, half Lab and half golden retriever. Once I fell into a creek with a strong current and Bly jumped in and pulled me out. He slept at the foot of my bed and woke me up in the morning with one lick to the face. He walked me to school and was there waiting for me when the dismissal bell rang. I told him everything and he seemed to understand. That dog was my best friend and I guess my first true love. Hjordis is a close second . . . ha ha."

Barney, my dad, did not joke about his wife but rather was inspired to write poetry: "Ruth, Ruth / She's the truth / Is my truth about love." Great-uncle Carl's was more philosophical, asking if any of us have the capacity for *true* love, "for ego inevitably has to taint true love—will I get this love back?" Mother's read, "You think you know true love when it hits you—it's a feeling of surprise and wonder and giggles and luck and you can't possibly believe that this one man feels the same way about you, but then you realize that's not true love, that's just the spark. True love, the real fire, is made through years of living together, of laughing and crying and sharing together, of seeing your daughters grow together." And then, feeling poetic, she added, "There are many branches to love, but true love is the tree."

My answer made me miss the eleven-year-old I was. "True love is *not* Annette Funicello and Frankie Avalon movies, true love is *not* Archie and Veronica, but it could be Archie and Betty, if he'd just wise up. True love *might* have been Romeo and Juliet, but maybe it just seems so because they killed themselves over it. I don't think I've felt true love yet, but I know I will, probably at least a couple of times."

Ann's answer made me miss the eleven-year-old she was. "I don't think I can quite imagine what true love is, but it must be something if so many people talk about it, sing about it, and write about it. I know it's something special, like a ballet or chocolate or the kind of laughter that almost makes you sick. Of course, to someone who doesn't like ballet or chocolate or laughing, true love is not like this."

"Well, that's it," I said, closing the book.

"Aren't you going to read more?"

"Maybe tomorrow. Look at the time."

Rich leaned over on the side of the couch until he could see the clock in the kitchen.

"Almost nine," he said. "Wow." He looked at the coffee table then, and at our unfinished Alamo that had sparked conversation about Grandma Hjordis and the discovery of the treasure I held in my lap. "Not done with my project, though."

"When's it due?"

Furrowing his brow, Rich looked up at the ceiling. "Not till after Halloween. Teacher said not till after Halloween."

"Then we've got plenty of time," I said. "Now give your old aunt a kiss and get to bed."

"Don't see an old aunt," he said with a sly smile. "Just see you."

With that gallant compliment, he pecked my cheek and gave me a hug that practically realigned my spine.

I took a long bubble bath (knowing my fondness for luxurious bathing, Ann had thoughtfully stocked the bathroom with pink, green, and blue bottles whose labels promised to either soothe and condition, energize and revitalize, or relax and pamper. I chose the last of these—I respond to anything that includes the word *pamper*.

Dressed in a flannel nightgown, my nearly dry hair pinned to the top of my head, I made a pot of tea and carried it upstairs. Setting the tray on the nightstand, I carefully folded back the bed linen, fluffed the pillows, and climbed in. Everything was done slowly and deliberately, almost ceremonially. I felt like a novitiate entering the convent: hopeful and honored and excited. I wanted to tear into *The Great Mysterious*, but instead I climbed into bed, settled the covers over me, and untied the ribbon carefully, as if I were unwrapping a box I knew contained the most delicate bone china.

I unfolded and reread what I had earlier read to Rich, remembering how Ann and I had rushed to the table the next morning.

"Where is it?"

"Where's what?" asked Grandma, who stood at the sink washing the breakfast dishes of those who rose earlier than Ann and me.

"You know, Grandma," said Ann. "Our book."

"Book?" said our mother, dish towel in hand. "What book?"

"You know what book," I said, and something in my voice convinced them that this was not the time to tease.

"Uncle Carl's working on it," said mother. "Out on the porch."

"And then it's Grandpa's turn," said Grandma. "You girls have got everyone thinking."

For the few remaining days we stayed at the cabin, we left the book on the kitchen table so that those coming to breakfast would see it open to a new question. If anyone was gone for any length of time, the assumption used to be that they were in the outhouse; now people disappeared for chunks of time to work on their answers, although Great-uncle Carl liked to work on his answers *in* the outhouse. After the supper dishes were washed, we would gather by the fire, where we would each randomly select one and read it aloud.

In bed now, pampered and relaxed, I replaced the answers that proposed to explain true love and opened the book to the second page: "What is the meaning of life?"

Again, I found myself shivering as I reached into the page's pocket.

"What is the big idea of this?" wrote Great-aunt Tove. "Who can know these answers? Girls your age should be asking questions like 'What is the capital of Denmark?' or 'Can you teach me how to bake a good pie crust?' This is all silliness. The meaning of life, of course, is to be found by following God."

Ah, yes, give me some of that old-time Norwegian Lutheranism that I balked against as a child because it made me feel joyless.

"Everyone has their own idea of what life means, and the wonder is how those ideas match up—even when they seem totally different—with others'." Not quite recognizing the handwriting or understanding the sentiment, I read the sentence again, until the meaning and the writer's identity (my dad) became clear to me. "Think of it—most often people say things like love and family and meaningful work, that's what's important. My brother Glen has never been married and has traveled the world over, and I know if I asked him this question, he would say, 'Adventure. Exploring everything there is to explore—that is the meaning of life.' Now, hearing this, you may say, 'Well, his ideas are a lot different from yours,' but think about it: They are not. He finds his adventure in far-off countries, I find mine in the city I have lived in since I was a boy. Why does a person want to explore? To know that which he explores better. Glen is not the only explorer—I go to work and discover new things about telephone installation. I talk to my wife and discover something new about her and my daughters! I discover all sorts of things from my daughters! So that's my answer. There are many things to love, many ways of having a family (Glen once said his family is every man and woman in every tribe on earth!—Ma practically fainted), and many ways to make a living. Just make sure you find things that matter. Things you want to explore."

My dad, Barney Jordan—you'd be hard pressed to meet a more solid citizen. I would have never thought he'd use words like *adventure* when talking about the meaning of life. I tucked my father's slip of paper back into the pocket and held the book against my chest, a shield over my hammering heart. After several moments I tied the ribbon over its flimsy cover made from a cereal box and carefully set it in the drawer of the bedside table, knowing that what was inside its covers was precious gold, gold I wanted to mine slowly.

*T*he next morning I took Rich to the library and we loaded up on books about Italy. Since he talked about the place so much, I thought he might as well learn a little bit about it.

It was the perfect Saturday afternoon, mild and blue-skied, and when we got home we sat out on the deck in our jackets, paging through the books.

"See, Rich," I said, pointing to a picture of some young women in a café, "aren't they pretty?" I turned the page to a picture of Michelangelo's statue of David. "And look at this guy. Wouldn't you say this guy is handsome?"

Rich cupped his hand over his mouth and giggled. "Guy's *naked.*"

It was a picture in the last book that really caught his imagination.

"What kind of boat is *that?*" His stubby finger jabbed at a glossy photograph.

I looked away from the vocabulary page of an Italian-for-beginners' book.

"Oh, that's a gondola."

"A gon-do-la?"

"Yes, a gondola. They use them on the canals in Venice." I decided this was a perfect place to stick in a little out-of-school learning. "Do you know what a canal is?"

Rich nodded.

"What?"

He stuck out his chin and scratched it. "A canal is . . . a canal!"

I reached across my chair to poke him in the ribs. "What kind of answer is that?"

"A good answer," he said, laughing, trying to bat away my tormenting fingers.

"A canal is like a street," I said, back to business. "A street made of water. Gondoliers are sort of like taxi drivers, except instead of cabs, they drive gondolas."

"That guy's a gon-do-leah?" Rich's attention was once more on the photograph. "That's what I want to be."

"You want to be a gondolier?" I asked. "You mean when you grow up?"

Rich's smile was like a beam of sunshine splashed across his face, the kind you couldn't help but smile back at.

"No," he said, waving his hand dismissively. "Wanna be a race car driver when I grow up. Wanna be a gondolier for *Halloween*."

"I thought you wanted to be a cowboy for Halloween," I said, remembering Ann's notes about the upcoming holiday and what I should use for a costume.

"Not a *cowboy*," said Rich derisively. "A *cattle rancher*. Cowboys are for babies. But now I'm gonna be a gondolier."

With great exaggeration I studied the photograph and then Rich's face. "Oh, yes," I said, "you're going to make a *buono* gondolier."

*L*ater that afternoon we got a little silly in the grocery store.

"Pasta, pasta," I said in my best Sophia Loren accent. "We gotta hava some pasta."

"And spaghetti," said Rich. "Spaghetti's Italian."

As he wheeled the cart down the aisles I stopped at the dairy section and picked up a chunk of Swiss cheese.

"Too bad it's not Italian cheese," I said. "Then we could buy it."

In the produce section I picked up an orange.

"What kind of orange is this?"

Rich peered at the stamp on the peel. "A Flo—Flo—"

"A Florida orange," I said, tossing it back onto its pyramid. "Too bad it's a Florida orange. If it were an Italian orange, we could buy it."

Gradually Rich caught on, and together we mourned that Texas chili wasn't Italian chili; that French bread wasn't Italian (although we did find bread labeled Italian, which thrilled Rich); that English toffee wasn't Italian toffee.

We giggled and filled our cart with ingredients for our Italian dinner (if Ragu can be considered Italian), and when we passed a stock boy and Rich greeted him with his usual, "Hey, pal," I corrected him.

"No, it's *'Ciao, amico.'* "

"What?"

"That's how you say 'Hey, pal' in Italian. *'Ciao, amico.'* "

Rich gave me his delighted smile. "Chow, ameeco," he said, his mouth moving as if he were chewing the words.

A dressed-up woman flipped through the shrink-wrapped flank steaks as briskly as a secretary going through her Rolodex.

"Ciao, amico," said Rich.

Annoyance flashed across her powdered face; then, when she saw the greeter, it changed to sympathy or whatever it was that people feel when they first see Rich.

"What's that you said, dear?" she asked, holding a steak to her chest as if she thought we might steal it.

"I said, *'Ciao, amico.'* "

The woman smiled, relinquishing her tight hold on the steak. "Oh, your son speaks Italian."

"My nephew," I corrected. "Come on, Rich," I said, giving the cart a little yank. "Let's go."

He half ran, half walked trying to keep up with me, and he laughed as if I were playing a game.

"Hey, pal," he said to an elderly woman standing in line at the next register. He then amended it to, *"Ciao, amico,"* but she either didn't hear or didn't want to.

I began setting the groceries on the conveyor belt.

"*Ciao, amico,*" he said to the cashier.

"Huh?" she asked, raising the remnants of her overly tweezed eyebrows.

"He's saying hello," I said, watching Rich as he wandered over to the drinking fountain by the store exit. "He's saying hello in Italian."

"In Italian?" said the cashier, drawing out the second syllable. Her earrings were glass fish that swam back and forth as she moved her head to look in Rich's direction. "Well, isn't he the smart one." She scanned a few items and then added, "It's amazing what they can teach those kids these days. I mean, learning English must be hard enough for them—and then to learn Italian!"

She sounded as chirpy as a parakeet, and I realized that more than anything, I'd have liked to grow claws and take a swipe at her.

"A friend of mine's got a son who's autistic," she went on, "and believe me, I'd take what he's got"—she nodded in Rich's direction—"any day of the week."

"Is that right," I said through clenched teeth.

"Oh, yes." The glass fish hanging from her ears bobbed as she nodded. "My friend's son just sits there rocking back and forth, back and forth. I mean, he's really in another world." She looked at the grocery tape. "That'll be thirty-eight dollars and fifty-three cents."

My anger was dry tinder that needed only a match to flare up, and the cashier threw that match in after she processed my bill and handed me back my card, saying, "Thank you, Mrs. Jorgen."

"So you can't read either?"

The cashier raised her thin eyebrows, so they looked like two circumflexes.

"First of all, it's not Mrs.—my God, don't be so presumptuous—and second, it's Jordan. J-o-r-d-a-n. As in *Geneva Jordan?*" Even as I enunciated my name, I was shocked at myself; I don't have that pitiful sort of insecurity that needs everyone to know who I am.

"I'm sorry, I . . . I don't know you." The fish earrings swam quick laps as the cashier shook her head in confusion.

"And why would a person like you know me? If ignorance is bliss, you must be high all the time."

Her face was a dark, embarrassed pink; it gave me pleasure that I had made her face turn that color.

An old man appeared to bag my groceries.

"I'll bet you learn a lot from this one," I said to him, tossing my head dismissively at the cashier, who now, near tears, was concentrating on ringing up the groceries of another customer. "I'll bet you have deep discussions about politics and the economy and—"

Looking past the confused face of the grocery bagger, I suddenly noticed that in my harangue I had lost sight of Rich, who was no longer by the drinking fountain.

"Rich?" I hollered, dodging a shopping cart as I raced toward the exit. Panic was rising up in me, dank as basement floodwaters. "Rich!"

I ran down the length of the grocery store—"Rich?"—past the pharmacy counter and the in-store floral shop. "Rich?"

Shoppers and employees stood watching me, and then someone yelled out, "What's he look like?" and I yelled back, "He's thirteen years old. He's got Down syndrome."

I was by the exit now, panting from my mad sprint across the floor. Anxiety gripped me in its tight, smothering full nelson, and I struggled for air, wondering if I should sit down so I wouldn't hurt myself when I passed out.

I was going to make another announcement—cashiers and customers were still going about their business, and I thought everyone should be involved in the search party—when the old man who had bagged my groceries tapped me on the shoulder and said, "That him?"

He nodded toward the window, and there, outside, bouncing on a kiddie ride—a mechanical horse that wasn't moving—was Rich.

I flew out of the automatic doors as if I'd been pushed.

"Rich!" I cried.

"Howdy, pardner," he said, tipping an imaginary hat.

"Rich, why didn't you tell me where you'd gone? I was half crazy looking for you. I thought—I thought—"

"Just went for a ride, Aunt Gennie," he said, patting the horse's chipped mane. "Just went for a ride on my bucking bronco."

"Would you like me to take your groceries to your car?" asked the grocery bagger.

"Sure. Come on, Rich."

"Gotta vamoose," he said, mimicking the words we'd heard a cowboy use just the other night in a Roy Rogers movie. He slid off the horse. "Gotta vamoose."

I lost it on the way home.

"Don't you ever pull something like that again! I was worried sick. When we go someplace you are to stay with me, do you understand?"

I looked away from the road to my nephew, who looked back at me with a little smile on his face.

"I'm glad you find this funny, Rich, because I sure don't. Do you understand what I'm telling you?"

The smile disappeared—it probably dawned on him that I wasn't kidding—and Rich nodded.

"All you had to say was, 'Aunt Gennie, I'm going outside to sit on a horse.' "

"Wasn't sitting on it, was *riding* it."

"All right, all you had to say was, 'Aunt Gennie, I'm going out-side to *ride* a horse.' Then I'd have known where you were and I wouldn't have had to run all around the store like some nut—"

"Okay, okay!" Rich crossed his arms. "Okay! Don't have to say any more!"

After changing lanes to get away from a slow-moving pickup truck, I looked at my nephew. "I do have to say more. I have to say more to make sure you understand how important—"

"I do understand!" said Rich, practically screaming. "Do under-stand you! *You* can forget about picking me up—"

"Rich, that was a mistake that will never happen again."

"—but when *we* go somewhere, I'm s'posed to stay with you! Not go outside and ride a horse!"

"Or go outside and ride anything! Just stay with me!"

When I pulled up into the driveway, I had barely put the car in park when Rich jumped out, slamming the door with a dramatic flair that had to please his old aunt, mad as I was. I thought about making him come back and help me carry the groceries, but really, why prolong the agony? It was clear that both of us would be happier with a little distance between us, and when I brought the groceries into the kitchen and heard Rich stomping around in his room, I thought, *Good. Stay up there all night.*

But my nephew did not receive my telepathic message; I was unpacking the last bag when I was nearly tackled from behind. I fell to the floor in the throes of cardiac arrest. Okay, I didn't *really*, but I was scared enough to, and I would have given Rich holy hell if he hadn't been crying so hard.

"So sorry, Auntie Gennie," he blubbered. "Don't be mad at me, please don't be mad."

"Rich," I said, feeling breathless in his grip, "I'm not mad at you. I was just scared." I peeled his arms off me—he was a solid, heavy boy, and when he was clinging to me, his sheer mass made me uncomfortable, trapped—and led him by the hand to the couch.

"Hate being so dumb," he said before we even sat down. "Hate having Down syndrome."

My heart might have staved off an attack when Rich scared me, but now it threatened to break in another way. I settled next to my nephew, still holding his hand. I wanted to offer sage words of wisdom, but even if I had had some, they wouldn't have been able to get past the lump in my throat.

"Hate that I like riding horses that aren't even real. Just like a little kid."

"Oh, Rich," I said finally, pushing the words past that lump (what's it made of, anyway?). "A lot of people would like to get on a ride like that."

"They would?"

I nodded. "Sure they would. But most people are too inhibited."

"What's in-hit-i-bed?"

"*Inhibited* is—" I looked at Rich, whose face held such trust that I had to look away. "*Inhibited* is," I began again, clearing my throat, "when you feel like singing a song but you don't because you think everyone will shush you."

"Shush you," said Rich, smiling, for some reason getting a kick out of the words.

"Or when you want to dance but you're afraid people will tell you to sit down. It's being afraid to do something because you're worried someone else might think it's stupid or silly."

Rich's forehead puckered in thought. "Wasn't in-hit-i-bed," he said slowly. "Not on the horse. On the horse, it was fun. Only now . . . only now it seems dumb."

"Do you know how many people would love to get on that horse and ride it?"

"How many?"

"Lots—everyone who can remember how fun a ride is. But most people are more inhibited than you."

Rich's jaw jutted out as he smiled. "I'm not very in-hit-i-bed."

I smiled back. "No, you're not."

"Still, wish I didn't have Down syndrome." He shook his head. "Know what Conrad says we should have?"

I shook my head and his eyes squinted as his smile grew wider.

"*Up* syndrome."

He was so delighted with his joke that I had to laugh with him.

"Know what up syndrome is?" he asked. I shook my head. "Up syndrome is when you're not the dumbest kid in the class but the smartest. So smart you're even smarter than the teacher. So smart that the teacher says, 'Hey, Rich, why don't you teach class today?' Connie's smart, but he can't run so good. With up syndrome, he'd run so fast they don't even have stopwatches to tell how fast he can run." He chuckled. "That's fast, isn't it?"

"That's very fast."

"Everyone would want to have up syndrome, 'cause when you have it, you do everything better. Every single little thing." Rich's smile was wistful now. "Everyone would want to be like me and Conrad."

I saw that I had two choices—dissolve into bitter tears or dissolve into tears of sadness. However, Rich did not need a dissolved aunt at the moment; he needed a fun one.

"Hey, Richie," I said in my Gina Lollobrigida accent (not to be confused with my Sophia Loren one), "you hungry, or what? Weren't we gonna cook uppa some pasta?"

Rich nodded, his eyes gleaming. "Yeah, we were gonna. We were gonna cook uppa some pasta."

In Ann and Riley's record collection I found not only Dean Martin, Frank Sinatra, *and* Pavarotti but at least a dozen operas.

We could have gone highbrow with some Puccini, but I thought the evening was crying out for Dino (not that he's lowbrow—just a different kind of brow altogether), and so as he crooned about *amore* and about being nobody until somebody loved you, we tied dish towels around our waists and tore up salad greens and slathered bread with butter and garlic and had an impromptu sword fight with handfuls of uncooked spaghetti.

"Take-a that!" I said, lunging at Rich.

"No, you take-a that!"

His accent wouldn't fool any Romans, but I'd heard worse.

We lit candles, and Dino sang, and we toasted each other with wineglasses filled with grape juice.

"*Salute!*"

"*Salute!*"

The garlic bread was a little burned, the spaghetti a tad over-cooked, but at that moment I wouldn't have traded the best table at Sardi's or Le Cirque 2000 for the one I was at now.

I lay in bed that night, propped up on pillows, looking at the starry night through the uncurtained window. I was exhausted— a day with Rich wasn't just like riding a roller coaster, it was like riding the highest, fastest, most-full-of-dips roller coaster—and yet I was so satisfied with how the night had turned out, I wanted to play it back in my mind. I can't say I felt as flushed with success as I did when I took a bow at the end of a show, but I felt *good*, as if I'd completed some obstacle course I never would have thought myself in shape for. I wondered if this was how Ann went to bed, replaying the highlights of her day in motherhood, and then, of course, I got all choked up, as I will sometimes when I think about what I've missed by never having a child.

"Consider yourself *lucky*," Trevor had told me one night after we'd watched *Cheaper by the Dozen* on the late show. As the credits

rolled I found myself bawling, not so much at the death of the father, played by a snappish Clifton Webb, but because Myrna Loy,
the mother, still had a part of him in all those children.

"And they all love her so much," I sobbed. "Who'll ever love me
like that?"

"Geneva, *believe* me," said Trevor, handing me a Kleenex box,
"there are plenty of mothers who'd change lives with you in an instant. My ex-wife, for one. Byron's completely done her in."

Byron was Trevor's seventeen-year-old son, who had been
kicked out of Eton because of drug use.

"*You* were taking acid when you were his age," I said, reminding
him of stories he'd told me.

"Yes, but that was in the sixties, when everyone was doing it—
when it was a . . . a *political* act."

"Still, you turned out all right. And Byron probably will, too."

Trevor sighed. "One can only hope." He pushed a tendril of hair
behind my ear. "But really, Geneva, you don't know how lucky
you are. The best stage is when they're cute and cuddly babies. After that it's one worry after another."

I had snuggled deep under the covers then, just as I did now. I
wouldn't have minded the worries; I knew the good parts—the
hugs and kisses, the bedtime stories and games of I Spy—would
balance them out.

I had sobbed when my doctor told me I was entering
menopause—I had rationalized that my hot flashes (I had my first
one this past summer onstage, a doozy that made me think the
audience was going to get an extra bonus in watching an actor
spontaneously combust, and in between acts Trevor had asked,
"What's the matter, luv—Your face is red as a tomato") were
allergic reactions to food and that my periods would return to
a regular cycle once I switched to a lower-dosage birth control pill.

"Geneva, please," my gynecologist had said. "Let's get you on some estrogen. It'll help relieve your symptoms."

"I don't want to relieve my symptoms," I said, sniffling into a Kleenex. That was not exactly true—I certainly wasn't *enjoying* my hot flashes, but I was in complete denial. Logically I might have been able to accept that I would never give birth to a child, but it was a harder thing to accept emotionally, and my doctor was worried enough to ask me if she should call anyone to help me get home.

"No, no, I'm fine," I said, tossing the drenched tissue into the wastebasket. "I'll get a cab and I'll be fine."

Leaving her office, I stared at the chart that diagrammed the female reproductive organs, feeling as if it were a flag of a country not my own.

But today had been one of worries and good parts, and the good parts had won out. My smile turned into a yawn, and it was with some sense of contentment that I closed my eyes to the dark night sky. But they didn't stay closed for long.

"Rich!" I said, wondering why he was such a fan of the surprise attack. "What are you doing here?"

He had padded across the floor and was getting into my bed.

"I'm scared, Aunt Gennie," he said. "Had a bad dream. A real bad dream."

He snuggled close to me, putting his arm around me, and for a second my impulse was to scream.

"What was it about?" I asked, wriggling out of his grasp to sit up and turn on the nightstand lamp.

He sat up too and looked at me, fear in his eyes. "I was lost. Lost, and nobody even cared."

"Where were you lost?"

Rich sniffed. "Don't remember."

"Well, let's see," I said, intercepting the arm that he tried to put around me. "If you had to be lost, where would it be?"

"No place. Wouldn't want to be lost no place."

"Hmm . . . if I were you and I were lost, I wouldn't mind being lost in a toy store."

"A toy store?" asked Rich, and I heard some of the fear leak out of his voice.

"Sure, a big, huge one. And how would you get home from a big, huge toy store?"

"Tell someone who worked there I was lost?" asked Rich hopefully.

"Yup," I said. "Or you could just go over to the cars and trucks department and drive yourself home."

"Drive myself home?"

"Sure."

"You're funny, Aunt Gennie. Don't have a license."

I kissed him quickly on the top of the head and then, pushing down the covers, got out of bed, inviting him to do the same.

"Come on, I'll walk you back to your room."

"Can't I stay here?"

"Nope. People sleep better in their own beds."

He didn't question this logic, but followed me. And when I'd tucked him into his own bed, he thanked me for making him feel better.

"You're welcome," I said brightly. I tousled his hair, which for some reason felt like a false gesture. "Good night," I said, walking out the door. "And pleasant dreams. No more nightmares."

"No more nightmares," he murmured.

It was only after I'd climbed into my own bed that I realized I was shaking. It had unnerved me when Rich came into my bed and clung to me. No, it was a stage beyond unnerving—it *scared* me.

I knew that if there was ever a poster boy for innocence, it would be Rich, but still, he was a *teenage* boy, and there had to be some hormonal havoc going on in his body. Did he know how to control it? Did he even know what it was that he was supposed to control?

Feeling like a nut for thinking these thoughts, I tried to hide from them by burrowing deeper under the quilt. No such luck. I desperately wanted to talk to my sister, but how could I give voice to the terrible things I was thinking? *Hey, Ann, I got a little scared when your son came into bed with me—there was something icky and sexual about the whole thing. And you know what else? I'm embarrassed by him sometimes in public, and I always make sure that everyone knows he's my nephew and not my son. And if you think that's bad, sometimes the sight of him makes me a little queasy. The back of his head is so flat, and his shoulders are so sloped, and his fingers are fat and stubby, and he sticks out his tongue a lot when he's thinking . . .*

Yes, I certainly wanted to call up my sister in Tuscany and reveal to her just what a pathetic caretaker I was to her son *Sì, operatore,* let's place that call right now!

My heart pounded. The night's darkness seemed more a shape than an absence of light, a shape that threatened to envelop me, entomb me.

"Hello, Petunia," I whispered feebly to the black loneliness that knew who I really was, knew that I was a fraud who even in real life had trouble coming off the stage. *Oh, God, what was happening to me? Why couldn't I connect with Rich? Why did I yell at grocery clerks? Who did I think I was?*

The room was too small. I opened the door so that I could pace the hallway. I needed to move, move, move.

Petunia was relentless, pounding my head with thoughts of why I deserved her. Tasting tears I hadn't even known were falling, I came to recognize the strongest of her taunts, and it was shame.

Shame that my heart, still banging away, might be a little too small, a little too closed off, to meet the demands that were being made of it.

I can't imagine the mileage I racked up as I walked back and forth in that hallway. I was like a drunk trying to walk off the effects of alcohol, only shame was not so easily shaken off. When I remembered *The Great Mysterious*, I gasped with relief and ran to the bedroom as fast as an emergency room doctor who'd just heard the word *stat*.

Chapter 6

he meaning of life is too big a question for me to answer, but I'll break it down to a question I can answer: What is the meaning of *my* life? I will tell you: When I fall into a warm bed after a day's hard work, when my belly is filled with the good food Hjordis made for me, when I've done something nice for someone else and heard a good story that's made me laugh—well, that's a good day, a day that's had meaning."

That was my Grandpa Ole's, and I laid the strip of paper he wrote on almost forty years ago on my lap, not wanting to put it away yet.

"Maybe there is no meaning to life but the one we decide to give it." Although this was in my mother's handwriting, I would have never thought this came from her. "That sounds a little frightening; after all, it's comforting to think that there is one true meaning out there for anyone willing to look for it. Too much choice, too much free will is scary. I do think most of us are like children who'd rather be told what to believe than find it out for ourselves. I know a Westerner won't find much meaning in reincarnation, and a Jew won't find much meaning in Jesus, and Mohammed means nothing to a Christian, and yet whole wars are started because one faction's dearest beliefs are dismissed by another. And writing that makes me think I want to change my first sentence—I guess that is how most people live, believing the meaning of life is the one we decide to give it. Maybe that's *wrong*. because as soon as you state a certainty, you're setting yourself up for disagreement. Maybe we should dismantle all churches, all governments, all armies, all borders and start over, with no intent to find meaning. Maybe then it would come."

I used to think that the most radical thing about Ruth Jordan was that she had a full-time job (she was a legal secretary) when all of my friends had stay-at-home moms. Now I'd found out she was an anarchist.

Ann and I were close to our parents, I suppose, but it was that fifties sort of closeness; we loved each other because that's what families were supposed to do, but the kids didn't really know the parents and the parents didn't really know the kids. But Grandma, we really *knew* our Grandma Hjordis. She was on our level, our compatriot, our comrade; it was her goal to have as much fun as Ann and I wanted. Now reading my mother's words made me want to *know* her.

I don't know what was churning around in my subconciousness (thoughts that my mother would have rather bombed the PTA than chaired its bake sale?), but my sleep was so fitful that when the alarm clock rang, I wanted to throw it against the wall. Instead, I swore at it like I was a sailor and it was Captain Queeg, and then I trudged into Rich's room to wake him up.

"Are you going to church with me?" he asked, groggy, and still groggy myself, I answered, "Sure."

I was barely dressed when we heard the little toot signaling that our ride had arrived.

"Well, hey," said Barb as Rich and I piled into the Land Rover. "From what Ann said, I didn't think you'd be joining us."

"Because I don't like to get up in the morning or because she thinks I'm an atheist?"

Barb returned my laugh. "She didn't elaborate. Are you going to help me teach Sunday school?"

"Barbara," I said, looking out at the sunny morning, "I wouldn't know what to teach."

I admired Ann's tenacity in continuing to go to church even after we'd moved out of our parents' house and weren't being forced to, but as I sat in the blond wood pew, next to some woman who apparently wasn't familiar with the concept of mouthwash, it was easy to remember why I myself did not follow suit. I tried to listen to the church member who read the lesson, but I found myself more interested in his toupee and its seemingly precarious perch on his head than his halting, nervous recitation. I found myself getting angry as the Nicene Creed was read (my own mouth was clamped shut, of course); did everyone believe what they were saying, or were they just saying everything by rote? I found myself bored into stupor by the minister, whose sermon was, I think, about justice (justice for the congregation would have been him leaving the public speaking to someone else).

The service was chintzy on the hymns too (I did love singing hymns, and the people in front of me had to sneak a peek at who belonged to the professional voice); the only mildly interesting moment came when the choir rose and the director gestured to a man who vigorously shook his head. The choir director raised his eyebrows in a look that asked, *You sure?* to which the man, red-faced, again shook his head. Later, near the end of the whole long hour, I handed the collection plate that had been passed down the pew to the usher, who was the same man who had had that mysterious exchange with the choir director. He was dressed in a dark blue suit that was obviously tailor-made, and without a trace of the embarrassment he'd earlier worn on his face, he flashed a boy-ish, chipmunk-cheeked smile at me, as if all the money in the shal-low wooden bowl I had personally given him.

*I*magine my surprise when on Halloween day the same man asked me to sign for a registered letter.

"Well," he said when I answered the door. "Ahoy, matey."

I had been rummaging through Ann's and Riley's closets, trying on pieces I thought might work for Rich's costume.

"I'm not a pirate, I'm a gondolier." I looked at him carefully. "And you're not the mailman—you're the usher at church."

"Actually, I'm both," he said as I handed him back the pen. "And by the way, I thought you were spectacular in *The Wench of Wellsmore*."

"You saw *The Wench of Wellsmore?*"

The mailman-usher nodded. "We went to Manhattan for a long weekend. We saw three plays, drank espresso in the Village, shopped at Bloomingdale's, and went to the top of the Empire State Building *and* the Statue of Liberty."

"Wow. That was some vacation." I regarded the man, who had worn his snazzy suit in church so well. I guess clothes did make the man; he was still cute in his uniform, but in a less compelling way. "What other plays did you see?"

"*Cats* and . . ." He paused, frowning. "You know, I can't even re-member what the third one was. Must be that your artistry in *The Wench of Wellsmore* erased all memory of it."

"Good answer," I said, smiling. "Although my artistry wasn't good enough to make you forget *Cats*, hmm?"

He shrugged. "One-word title. How can you forget a one-word title?" He readjusted the shoulder strap on his mailbag. "Well, I've got electric bills and love letters to deliver, and you've got pirate costumes you need to turn into gondolier outfits. Nice talking to you. Say hi to Ann and Riley when you talk to them."

He flicked the brim of his cap with his finger, and I watched him as he walked down the driveway.

Oh, so he knew Ann and Riley too. I smiled at the small-townness of it all; he knew my sister and brother-in-law, delivered my mail, *and* collected my offering (which had been one stingy don't-you-send-this-to-some-colonialist-mission dollar). No wonder he wasn't more surprised that Geneva Jordan, star of *The Wench of Wellsmore*, was accepting registered letters in a refurbished farmhouse in Deep Lake, Minnesota.

Oh, the letter. The return address was Claire's agency. What was she sending me that was so important? A big check? A contract for Scorsese's next movie?

Claire must have know the drama I'd automatically pin onto such a delivery, because this was her note:

"Dear Geneva—
Sorry this isn't a packet of residual checks, but news like this deserves to be sent by registered mail. Not only did it make Joyce Dean's column, but Liz mentioned it too. After you read them, call me for even *more* news.

Love,
Claire.

Two strips of newspaper were attached, and I read the circled item in Joyce Dean's column first: "What young ingenue has ditched her older Brit actor beau for a flashy long-haired novelist closer to her age? Tell me, Miss A., is the writer's pen mightier than the actor's sword?"

Liz wasn't so coy and named names: "The flame has apparently gone out for actor Trevor Waite and Ellie Armstrong. The star of *Gibson Girl* was seen at the recent New York Literacy Gala on the arm (and on the lap!) of hot new novelist Garret Paxton."

For several minutes I sat facing the picture window, looking out at the lake and the V of geese that honked their way across the clear, open sky.

I couldn't deny feeling a little thrill—I hadn't thought Trevor's affair with Miss Ellie was going to last long, but I'd thought it would last longer than it did. I wondered whose idea it was to break up, and how Trevor was taking it if it wasn't his.

I ground some coffee beans and made a fresh pot, proud that I didn't feel driven to *immediately* call Claire. I even drank half a cup before dialing.

"Oh, Miss Jordan!" The receptionist greeted me with the brownnosing awe that would take her far in life. "I'll transfer you right now."

A moment later Claire was on the line, sounding thrilled to hear from me.

"Geneva! I am so glad to hear from you—I've missed you! How's it going out there in Iowa? You got my little package, huh?"

"*Minnesota.* I've missed you too, it's going swell, and yes, I got your package. What's up?"

"Well, a lot, as a matter of fact. I just got off the phone with Norman Alexander—he's just about finished writing a musical based on Samson and Delilah, and guess who he has in mind for Delilah? You!" She let out a little laugh. "Isn't that great? He's planning a reading early next year and—"

"So what else about Trevor?" I asked. Norman Alexander was Broadway's latest sensation, having written the wildly successful *Fables* based on Aesop, but news about him could wait. News about Trevor couldn't.

"Well," she said, "he came to see me."

I was reclining, my feet on the coffee table, but this information made me sit up.

"Trevor did? When? Why?" Claire wasn't Trevor's agent, so the only reason he'd see her was because of me.

"He wanted to know how you were doing, and he was wondering if he could call you."

I drew in a quick breath. "He was wondering if he could call me? Did he say that?"

"Uh-huh. But I wouldn't give him your sister's number. So then he asked me to ask you to call him."

"He wants *me* to call him?"

"Yes, but the more I think about it, Geneva, the more I think you should just wait until you get back to New York and can talk to him face-to-face. So that you'll remember just what a snake he is."

"Yes, Mother."

We chatted for a few more minutes; she filled me in on other theater gossip, and I told her about the costume I was in the midst of making. Then I was put on hold as she took a call from a client who was threatening to quit the show he was in.

"I gotta go, Geneva," she said, getting back to me. "You know these temperamental actors."

"Do I ever."

"So I can tell Norman Alexander you're interested?"

"Sure. See you. Happy Halloween."

*I*t had started to snow lightly by the time Rich's school bus dropped him off.

"Who ever heard of such a thing?" he asked, stomping his feet on the rug as he came inside. "Snow on Halloween!"

"Actually, it snowed once when your mom and I went trick-or-treating," I said. "We hardly got any candy because we were having so much fun throwing snowballs at everybody."

"Last year it rained," said Rich. "Some of my candy got wet. Didn't like that."

I had to hand it to myself—I had transformed Rich into a gondolier. I had modified the costume so it didn't look so Long John Silverish, taking in the billowy shirtsleeves and replacing the bandanna I was going to tie around his head with a wide-brimmed felt hat I vaguely remembered giving Ann years before. (From its position in the closet, I doubted she ever wore it.) I painted on a thin mustache and goatee and stood back to survey my work.

"*Magnifico,*" I said, kissing the tips of my fingers.

Rich ran to the hallway mirror.

"Oh, Aunt Gennie," he said, "it's the best costume ever!"

He hugged me then, and it crossed my mind what a nice world it would be if everyone had such big reactions to small favors.

When he finally released me he asked, "Where's your costume?"

He had me stumped; I hadn't planned to dress up at all.

"Let's eat our supper first, then I'll figure out something."

We made one last search through Ann's drawers and closet, but the wide-brimmed hat I'd found for Rich was about the most flamboyant thing she had. There was an evening dress ("She wears that to weddings," Rich told me), but as soon as I pulled it over my shoulders, I could tell it was a size or two too small.

"No, I don't like this," I said, shrugging it off, not wanting to take the dress down the ego-deflating southerly journey past my hips.

I finally decided to wear some of Riley's things—an old sports coat, an ugly wide tie, and a beat-up porkpie hat, which I tucked all my hair into. With my eyebrow pencil, I added a little facial hair—big sideburns and a bushy, ungondolierlike mustache.

"Who *are* you?" Rich asked after I'd completed my transformation.

I extended my hand. "Bob," I said with a big Texas drawl. "I'm an American tourist. You know where I can find a gondola? I got me a hankering to ride one."

Rich waved his hand as if he wanted to answer a teacher's question. "I'm a gondolier! I give rides on gondolas!"

"Well, ain't that a convenient turn of luck."

The doorbell rang then, and Rich froze, his eyes wide.

"Trick-or-treaters!" he said.

We doled out Three Musketeers bars to an angel, a dinosaur, and a box of crayons.

"Good costume," I said to the mother of the crayons.

"I was up until three o'clock in the morning making that thing," said the mother. "And now it's getting wrecked in this darn snow."

Another round of trick-or-treaters came by, and then Conrad and his mother drove up.

"I am a robot," announced Conrad, walking stiffly like a robot for a moment before one of his arms jerked toward the sky.

"Are you guys dressed warm enough?" asked Barb, who wore regular clothes but had painted her face to look like a cat . . . or a mouse.

"Rich has got a sweater underneath his shirt," I said. "Do you think he needs to wear a jacket?"

Barb held her arms out in the falling snow. "Couldn't hurt."

It took a bit of negotiating to get Rich into a jacket and gloves, until Barb had the good sense to tell him that a lot of gondoliers wore jackets and gloves because the winds off the canals could get pretty nippy.

"And look, Rich," said Conrad, tapping his cardboard head. "I couldn't even wear my Twins cap under this—Mom made me wear a stocking cap." He then held up his mittened hands. "And have you ever seen a robot wear mittens?"

We stood by the door as Barb took our picture, and then left a bowl of candy out on the front steps, hoping kids would follow the honor system and take only their share.

"We usually do most of the trick-or-treating in my subdivision," said Barb, "because the houses are spaced closer together than here."

"You should have told me that," I said. "You wouldn't have had to pick us up—I could have driven to your house."

"Oh, it's our tradition, isn't it, boys?" she said as we piled into the Land Rover.

"Yeah!" chorused Rich and Conrad.

"Plus she doesn't want to miss the pumpkin house," added Conrad.

"What's the pumpkin house?" I asked.

Barb wiggled her cat-or-mouse eyebrows. "You'll see in a minute."

The snow splotching against the windshield was quickly pushed aside by the wipers. As the boys chattered in the back Barb asked me just exactly who I was.

"Name's Bob, ma'am. I'm from Texas."

"Of course. That would explain the porkpie hat."

"Hey," I said, laughing, "the pickings in Riley's closet were pretty slim." I looked at Barb, squinting. "But to tell you the truth, I can't figure out if you're Tom or Jerry."

This time it was Barb's time to laugh. "Tom's the cat, right? So I'm Tom. Face painting's not exactly my forte."

"There it is!" said Conrad.

"There it is, Aunt Gennie!"

An outline of a pumpkin fashioned from orange lights rose

from the bottom of the house to its roofline, but that was the opening act compared to the headliner, which was the parade of candlelit jack-o'-lanterns that lined the driveway. These pumpkins weren't carved with the usual triangular eyes and fangy grins, but with elaborate, true-to-life faces, all of recognizable people.

"Oh, my gosh," I said, "there's Beethoven. And Elvis!"

"For a long time, the man who carves them used to do only people who had died within the year," said Barb, "but lately he's bringing back old favorites."

"There's Marilyn Monroe—and Franklin Roosevelt!"

We got out of the vehicle and wandered up the driveway, looking at the pumpkins. They were exquisite; there was not one that wasn't immediately identifiable, that didn't look *exactly* like its model, and that wasn't a lively rendition to boot.

"Aunt Gennie," said Rich, pulling me by the hand, "look! John Lemon!"

Riley was an avid Beatles fan who had been playing their music for his son since Rich was a baby. Ann had told me that Rich's insistence on calling John Lennon "John Lemon" drove Riley nuts.

I had heard this exchange between Riley and Rich myself: "Lennon! It's Lennon, John Lennon." "Lemon," answered Rich with a sly grin. "Lemon, John Lemon."

"We better move on," said Barb as we passed a pumpkin whose face was a rakish Clark Gable. "This snow's really coming down."

*R*ich lumbered to each house in his heavy-footed way, occasionally stopping to wait for Conrad, who had an odd gait, lurching yet graceful, like a dancer who'd made too many trips to the bar. As the boys stood on the steps of each house they accepted their candy like Salvation Army bell ringers into whose pails were dropped hundred-dollar bills.

"Thanks!" they'd gush, thrilled over everything from a skimpy handout of penny candy to big Hershey bars.

Barb and I walked across the lawns with them (we couldn't stand back on the sidewalks—in the suburbs, there are no sidewalks), smiling.

"Haven't they ever heard of ingratitude?" I asked.

"No, thank God," said Barb. "I get enough of that from my other kids."

"How many more do you have?"

Barb pulled her jacket collar up and pushed her chin into it. "Two. Madeline's twenty—she's a sophomore at Grinnell—and Joel's twenty-four. He's going to law school."

"You must be very proud of them."

"I am," said Barb, nodding, "but it's Conrad I save the big pride for." She took my arm. "I know I wouldn't win any mothering awards for saying something like that, but what the hell. Maddy and Joel are great kids, but everything's come pretty easy for them. *Nothing's* come easy for Connie, and he's *still* a great kid."

"We got popcorn balls!" announced Conrad as he and Rich bounded by us.

"And who are you going to share that with?" said Barb, snapping their picture.

"My wonderful mother!"

"Don't I have him trained well?" she asked, smiling.

"I sure admire you."

"You admire me?" she asked, surprised. "Why?"

I was somewhat surprised myself; I wasn't a miser with expressions of admiration, but I wasn't exactly a geyser, either. But even though the words had popped out of my mouth, I still meant them.

"You're . . . you're such a good mother to Conrad," I said. "You make such a hard job look easy."

A fairy princess brushed past us, the hem of her glittery skirt wet and sodden from the accumulating snow.

"It's not that hard," she said, and to my derisive "Yeah, right!" she added, "No, really. Ann and I have talked a lot about this. The hardest part is at the beginning, the first huge shock: 'Your child's not normal.' "

"So you didn't know anything ahead of time either?"

My sister, who had waited so long to have a baby, had refused all tests—even ultrasound—as too intrusive. ("Besides," Ann had told me blithely, "everything is going to be fine.")

Barb shook her head. "I knew a healthy baby was inside me— until I went into labor eight weeks early. The doctors didn't come right out and say so—it took them a while to make a for- mal diagnosis—but he was so tiny and blue when he came out that I knew if he wasn't dead, he was going to be in trouble."

"How awful," I said, shaking my head.

"It was at the time," Barb agreed, "but I finally figured out it's not this horrible sentence you're given; you're *not* being punished."

"Good 'N Plenties!" Rich informed us of their latest collection.

"I mean, your heart breaks at least once a day," continued Barb, "because of all the challenges your child faces, but for just as many times it breaks, that same child helps it heal. And you start to feel lucky."

"Lucky?"

Barb nodded. "Lucky that you were singled out to have a spe- cial child."

"*Lucky?*"

Barb laughed. "It's every parent's prayer to have healthy chil- dren, but once you accept that that particular prayer isn't going to be answered, you find that other ones are." She laughed again. "I think the snow's getting the best of your mustache."

"Like what?" I asked, repositioning my porkpie hat. "Like what other prayers?"

For a moment Barb watched the boys follow another group of trick-or-treaters up to a house. "Like Connie and Rich finding each other. I prayed that Connie wouldn't be so lonely—and along comes the best friend he's ever had."

"Baby Ruth bars *and* Butterfingers!" announced the boys.

"Oh, come here, Connie," said Barb. "You're starting to become unglued."

His robot's head, which was sort of a cardboard hat, was all wet and coming apart at its seams.

"Mom, don't worry about it!" said Conrad, breaking free of his mother's ministrations. "I don't care if I'm coming unglued!"

"Yeah, he don't care!" added Rich, and the two boys, laughing, ran in their fashion toward the next house.

I pulled down the brim of my hat even further. The falling snow could no longer be described as *graceful* or *peaceful*—*aggressive* would be the more appropriate word.

"Now this is *snow*," said Barb. "What do you say we let them finish the other side of the block and then head back to your neighborhood?"

"Fine with me, ma'am," I said, getting back into character. "Ain't used to precipitation like this where I come from."

We drove back slowly, Barb sitting forward in her seat, gripping the steering wheel in the classic ten-o'clock-two-o'clock position.

"Conrad, we're going to have to go home, buddy," she said when she pulled up in front of the house. "We're in the middle of a blizzard."

"Well, that sucks!"

"I'm sorry, honey, but the driving's only going to get worse."

She turned to me. "We always finish up doing a few houses along the lake and then have hot cider at Ann's."

"I could make hot chocolate," I suggested.

Looking out the windshield, Barb shook her head. "No, I should get home."

Rich and I stood in the driveway watching them go.

"Wow," said Rich, holding out his arms. "Wow, it's *snowing*."

"Yes, it is," I said, and tipped my head back to let the snow whip at my face. "Now let's get inside before we get buried in a drift."

"But the Johnsons!"

"The who?"

Rich pointed toward what I presumed was a house. It was hard to see anything in this moving white curtain. The snow was full of motion, moving fast and in furious swirls, the way things move under a microscope.

"The Johnsons! They always take a picture of me and Conrad in our costumes!"

"Rich, Barb already took your picture. Besides, we're in the middle of a blizzard."

"I want my picture took!"

"Oh, all right," I said, taking him by the hand. Let the weather rage—I was not going to be accused of being a dud.

Three houses could have been set in the huge lot that separated Ann's house from their next-door neighbor's, and as we approached it, our shoulders hunched against the snow, I asked Rich if he wasn't going to trick-or-treat there.

"On the way back from the Johnsons'," he said. "Come on, only one more house."

Again we trudged across what seemed the length of two football fields. The snow was now ankle-high, and if you looked up at the streetlights, you could see the force with which it fell.

"Rich, maybe we should go back."

"Here's the house!" he said, clutching his pillowcase of candy like a baby.

"Oh, my goodness, two snowmen!" said a smiling older woman as she let us inside. "Stan, come and look at the two snowmen!"

"Not snowmen," said Rich with a laugh. "I'm a gondolier. Aunt Gennie is Bob the Texas guy!"

"Pleased to meet you," I said, tipping my hat and sending a small avalanche of snow onto the floor of their foyer. "Oh," I said, surprised at how much of the white stuff I'd been carrying on my head. "Sorry."

"Ann told us you were coming to baby-sit," said Mrs. Johnson as her husband appeared with a camera. "She's so proud of you— the big Broadway star."

"How nice of you to say," I said, even though it seemed from her tone that she didn't exactly approve.

"Where's your friend Conway?" asked Mr. Johnson, aiming the Polaroid camera at Rich.

"Conrad," said Rich. "Conrad had to go home. 'Cause of the blizzard."

"That's what happens when you've got no more ozone layer left," said Mr. Johnson.

"Oh, for Pete's sake, Stan, what about the Armistice Day blizzard way back when? We had plenty of ozone layers then."

"Winnie doesn't like to admit the world's going to hell in a handbasket," Mr. Johnson said in a stage whisper, and then, lifting his camera to his eye, he said, "Okay—one, two, three, cheese!"

"Cheese!" said Rich as Mr. Johnson took his Polaroid. After it developed, he gave it to me.

"Thanks," I said, putting it in my pocket.

"And thanks for coming by," said Mrs. Johnson, opening the front door.

Apparently Rich didn't take Mrs. Johnson's rather rude hint; he didn't move.

"Rich, come on," I said. "It's back to the tundra for us."

Rich held open his pillowcase. "Trick-or-treat, money or eats."

"Oh, yes, your candy," said Mrs. Johnson, and she carefully took out a miniature Kit Kat bar from a nearly full bowl.

"Thanks!" said Rich, watching her drop it into his bag.

"Winnie, don't be so stingy," said her husband, taking a handful of candy and dropping it into Rich's bag. "Pony up!"

I was shocked when we got back outside: In the short time we had spent in the Johnsons' home, the storm had picked up even more power.

"Wow!" said Rich, or at least I think he said that, so muffled was his voice by a wind that had picked up not only speed but sound.

"Rich, hold on to my arm!" I said, and together we pushed against the white, moving world toward home.

"We are going in the right direction, aren't we?"

Rich laughed, or at least I think he laughed. "Hope so, Aunt Gennie."

We trudged on, across white drifts of snow that only hours earlier had been lawns.

"The Byerlys'!" said Rich, pointing to a house that appeared out of the snowstorm like a mirage. "Our last stop!"

"Rich, we can't stop, we've got to get home."

"But they always give chocolate-covered peanuts!"

I pulled his arm as he moved toward the house.

"No, Rich, we've got to get home."

"But I love chocolate-covered peanuts!" He broke free of my grip and began to run toward the house. It's easy to see why blizzard running is not a commonly practiced sport: It's hard. Hard to maneuver through snow on the ground and snow flying through the air. Nevertheless, I chased Rich, but I didn't need to stop him, as he stopped himself by falling. He fell flat on his chest, his limbs splayed, like a baseball player sliding into home plate.

His howl was loud enough to be heard over the wind, and my heart banged against my chest as I wondered how I'd get him to emergency to set whatever bone had been broken.

I stumbled toward him. "Rich! Rich, what's the matter?"

"My candy!" he cried. "Dropped my candy!"

"Are you hurt?"

"No, but my *candy!*"

If running in a blizzard is hard, try picking up spilled Halloween candy. It's true, the white offered some contrast to the brightly colored wrappers, but it became a game of beat the snow—could we pick all of it up before it was buried?

"Can't find my popcorn ball!" yelled Rich.

"Don't stop to look for anything—just pick up what you see."

"But I love popcorn balls! *Love* popcorn balls!"

It was cold and windy and hard to see, and I had an impulse to throttle my screaming, whining kin, but fortunately it was stifled by a male voice asking, "Can we help?"

"Sure," I said, not knowing who was doing the asking, but ready to take help from any source. "We're trying to pick up my nephew's candy."

The figure bent down; my view of him was obscured not only by the swirling snow, but by the hooded parka he wore.

"Oh, you've got a flashlight!" I said as he shone the beam of light on the snow.

"I never leave home on Halloween night without it," he said, and then I saw that bent down next to him was a child.

"My popcorn ball!" said Rich, plucking the cellophane-wrapped orb out of the snow. "Found my popcorn ball!"

The four of us worked a few more moments.

"That's it, I think," said the man, searching the ground one last time for any candy we might have missed. "You'd better get home now."

"Hey," I said, finally recognizing him, "you're the mailman-usher."

"None other. Can you get home all right?"

"Are you stalking me?"

"What?"

"Nothing—it's just that you're always turning up."

"Turning what?"

"Never mind. I was just trying to make a joke."

We were both shouting, trying to be heard over the storm.

"Daddy, I have to go to the bathroom!"

This statement was loud and clear, its urgency cutting through the howling wind.

"Come on," I shouted, "she can use ours."

The mailman's little girl stumbled, and then I did, and after that we all linked arms, a huddled mass inching our way to the house. The wind pushed up snow from the ground and flung that which was falling from the sky everywhere, including into our faces. I had a brief moment of panic, remembering the stories of people stranded in snowstorms who were found frozen the next day, twenty yards away from the farmhouse they almost but couldn't quite reach.

"Where is it?" I yelled, unable to see anything except the dizzying swirls of white.

"We're almost there," said the mailman.

I could hardly make out the house until we were almost on its front steps.

"Hallelujah," I said.

"Hallelujah," echoed Rich, and if my voice was grateful, his was truly reverential.

Inside we all laughed, stomping our boots and clapping the snow off our hands.

"Dad," said the little girl, "the bathroom?"

"Oh, it's right down the hall," I said, pointing, and before she had taken her coat off, she was running toward it.

Rich hung up his jacket very carefully, brushing the snow off its sleeves, and then, remembering an earlier suggestion of mine, asked, "Aunt Gennie, how about that hot chocolate?"

"Sure," I said. Then to the mailman I said, "Would you and your daughter like some?"

"Sure, Natalie and I love hot chocolate." He stuck out his hand. "And I'm James. No nickname, just James."

I shook his hand. "Pleased to meet you, no-nickname-just-James."

The snow had done a pretty good job of washing off my mustache and sideburns, but I finished the job in the bathroom, and then Rich helped me with the hot chocolate while Natalie kneeled by her father as he built a fire.

"Well, here's to snowy Halloweens," I said, putting the tray down on the coffee table.

"And here's to candy," said Rich, clinking his mug against mine. Then, as if being reminded of something, he said, "Candy!"

He set down his mug and raced to the kitchen, returning with his wet pillowcase and a section of newspaper, which he spread out in front of the fireplace.

"Gotta sort the candy!" he said, dumping out his goodies. He sat for a moment, happily surveying his take, seemingly oblivious to its sodden appearance. "Oh," he said, looking at Natalie. "Wanna sort your candy, too?"

Natalie pulled at her dark fringe of bangs and shook her head. Then, as if embarrassed, she burrowed her head in her dad's shoulder.

"Don't want to sort your candy?" asked Rich, and the little girl shook her head. He sat on his haunches for a moment, regarding her. Then he said, "You're a shy guy, huh? I seen you at church. You seen me there?"

The girl nodded but didn't speak.

"You're afraid of me, aren't you?" said Rich after a moment. "Conrad says people get afraid 'cause I look funny."

This was said not as an accusation, but with a sort of resigned knowledge. The mailman and I exchanged looks, but neither of us said a word.

"That's okay," said Rich, and he began digging through his pile. "*Do* look funny—*am* funny. I can make you laugh before you say 'No, you can't.' "

The little girl moved enough from the shelter of her father's arm to peek at Rich.

"No, you can't," she said softly.

"Then I can make you laugh before you say 'toy boat' ten times fast."

"Toy boat ten times fast."

"No," said Rich, and he laughed himself. "Say the words 'toy boat' ten times. Just those words—'toy boat.' Ten times, and say them fast."

"Toy boat, toy boat, toy boyte—" The tongue twister proved too much for her, and true to Rich's promise, she laughed.

"Isn't that a hard one?" he asked. "Nobody can say that one."

The mailman-usher took the challenge. "Toy boat, toy boat, toy boat, toy boat, toy boat, toy boat, toy boat, toy boat, toy boat, toy boat."

"*Wow!*" said Rich. "You're the only one in the world who's ever done that!"

"Rich, please," I said with mock insult. "Let a real pro try." I stood, posing, as if about to deliver a sonnet. "Toy boat, toy boat, toy boat, toy boat, toy boyte—"

Rich screamed in delight. "You said 'boyte,' Aunt Gennie, you said 'boyte'!"

"That was just practice." I cleared my throat. "Toy boat, toy boat, toe boyte——"

"Did it again!" said Rich.

"Only this time you said 'toe boyte'!" added Natalie.

"Toe boyte," repeated Rich, shaking his head.

Slumping in defeat, I reached over to shake my contender's hand.

"You put up a good fight," he offered.

The kids laughed again, and then Natalie ran to get her Halloween bag. She dumped her loot out on newspaper next to Rich, and together they counted packets of M&Ms and rolls of Smarties and Mars bars.

"So why do you look so funny?" she asked.

"I got Down syndrome. That's the way I was born."

"Oh," said the little girl. "I have a birthmark on my tummy I was born with."

"Is it big?" asked Rich.

"Not very." She pulled at the top of her goblin costume. "See?" she said, pointing to a small mark to the left of her belly button.

Rich moved his head closer to see better. "Looks like a penny. A penny without writing on it."

The little girl looked down, regarding it for a moment, before she agreed. "Yeah, it does."

"How old are you?" Rich asked.

"Seven and a half. How old are you?"

"I'm a teenager."

"Wow," said Natalie, impressed.

"Can I get you more hot chocolate, James?" I asked, forcing myself to refer to him by his name and not as the mailman or usher.

"What?" he asked, turning away from the children.

I held up my empty cup. "More hot chocolate?"

"Oh . . . no." He looked at his watch. "In fact, I think it's time we hit the road, Natalie."

"Daddy, I'm not done yet."

She was sorting her candy in little piles, with no discernible pattern as far as I could tell. Neither could Rich.

"That Butterfinger goes over there," he said, pointing to an identical candy bar.

The girl shook her head. "No, Stella likes them too."

"Who's Stella?" asked Rich.

"Stella is one of my dolls. None of them could go trick-or-treating, so I'm making up little Halloween bags for all of them."

"Dolls can't eat."

Natalie raised her eyebrows. "Mine can."

I turned to see what her father thought of this exchange, but he was gone.

I found him standing in the darkened hallway, looking through the storm door. I looked out too.

"Good heavenly days," I said, scared and awed.

It was a virtual whiteout. There was no telling what was ground and what was sky—even the motion of the falling snow was hard to detect in the vast whiteness.

"May I use your phone?"

"Sure," I said, switching on the light and gesturing toward the little desk in the hallway.

I went back to the couch, pretending to look on with interest as the candy sorting continued, but my concentration was really on the telephone conversation. Who was he talking to? Triple A? The National Weather Service? His wife?

Bingo—it was door number three.

"How am I supposed to do that, Karin? Well, how was I to know? . . ."

There were other murmurings, other mentions of the name Karin, but the kids were talking and laughing too loudly for me to hear properly.

"What are you doing?" I asked, finally noticing their activity.

"We're drying out some of my candy," said Natalie. "Lots of it got wet."

They were setting miniature candy bars on top of the ledge of the fireplace screen.

"Rich, just the wrappers are wet," I said. "We'll put them on the countertop and let them dry out there. They'll melt up there on that screen."

"Natalie, get away from there," said her father, coming into the room. "You know you're not supposed to play by the fire."

"We weren't playing," the little girl protested. "We were drying off candy."

"Either way, stay away from that fire screen." His voice sounded not so much gruff as perturbed.

"Everything all right?" I asked sweetly, always willing to stir up whatever drama there may be in a situation.

James shook his head. "I hope you don't mind if we spend the night."

"What?" I am pretty unflappable, but at this request, I must admit, I was flapped.

Noticing this, James laughed. "You saw it out there—I can't get home. The plows can't even get out."

"But I . . . I thought neither rain nor sleet nor snow stopped you guys."

"I'm not delivering mail," he said, laughing again. "And even if I were, believe me, this weather would stop me."

"It's still snowing out?" asked Rich.

"And how," I said. "Just look." I turned off the two table lamps so that the light no longer reflected in the picture window. "See?"

"Wow!" said Rich.

"Wow!" echoed Natalie, and then coming to her father, she asked, "Did you talk to Mommy, Daddy?"

"Yup." He pulled her up on his lap. "And she said you should save her a Hershey bar."

"She did not," said the girl. "Mom doesn't eat candy."

I formed an immediate judgment about a woman I'd never met: I didn't like her. She was probably the type who counted her calories on a calculator and had buns of steel and thighs of granite.

"So," said the mailman to his daughter, "it looks as if we're going to camp out here."

"Camp out," said Rich. "Yippee!"

I told James and Natalie that they could have the spare bedroom, but Rich vetoed that idea, saying if they were going to camp out, they should *camp out* and could he too, "oh please, please, please, Aunt Geneva, *please?*" And that's how, after popcorn and one mild ghost story, the little campers wound up in Batman and Robin sleeping bags, snoring softly while the adults in charge enjoyed a second glass of wine.

"So your wife really expected you to get home in this storm?"

James nodded, then shook his head. "She expected me to get *Natalie* home. Me, well, she couldn't care less if I were buried in a snowbank. In fact, she'd probably prefer it."

I whistled softly. "Sounds like you and the missus aren't getting along so well."

James copied my whistle. "You're right about that—except the missus is no longer the missus."

"You're divorced?"

"For a year now."

"I've been divorced for—" Was it twenty-three years? Twenty-four? It had been so long I couldn't even remember. "For a long time." I looked past the little mounds of sleeping children into the fire. "He was French, and apparently he wanted a green card more than a wife."

James sighed. "Karin—oh, by the way, when I told her where I was, she said, 'Make sure you tell Miss Jordan how much I enjoyed her performance.' "

I laughed at his tight-lipped impression of his ex-wife, but, not wanting to lose track of the conversation, asked, "So you were saying?"

"Huh?" James bit his lip and then said, "Oh, yeah. I was saying how Karin wanted something different too."

"And what was that?"

He looked away from the fire and at me. His features weren't classic like Trevor's, but he had nice wavy brown hair (never mind that his hairline was heading south) and warm hazel eyes in a friendly face. And he had a cute smile that bunched up his cheeks, making a person want to say something funny just to bring it out.

"She wanted me to be a vice president of marketing at Amalgamated Mills."

"That's pretty specific. Any reason she wanted you to be a vice president at Amalgamated Mills rather than, oh, say, a vice president at Pillsbury?"

He shrugged. "Probably because that was going to be my next promotion."

I looked at him for a moment, waiting for that flash of white teeth, but there was no smile, no indication that he was kidding,

"I wasn't always a mailman," he said. "I had to become sane first."

I gave him one of my trademark cocked-brow looks—the ones that, when used judiciously, always get a huge laugh onstage. It did the trick for my audience of one too; he laughed.

"I think you have some 'splainin' to do," I said, à la Ricky Ricardo.

Natalie mumbled something in her sleep, and James went to her, drawing the sleeping bag up over her shoulders. When he returned, he took a sip of wine and told me the story of his life, or at least a recent chapter.

It was a semifamiliar one to me. I had several friends who had, in their midlife questioning, abandoned their careers for another, but usually it was a switch you could understand—a lawyer giving up his practice to write the great American novel, a banker moving up to rural Maine to make pottery. *Artistic* choices. I knew of no one who'd sacrifice a big career to *carry mail*, for God's sake. I told James as much.

"That's exactly what my ex-wife said. She thought I was having a mental breakdown or something."

"Were you?" I asked.

James shook his head.

"I would have if I'd stayed there. I didn't have a life, Geneva— it was all work. Karin and I were making a lot of money, but we had no time to spend it. We had a beautiful baby girl and no time to spend with her. We'd drop her off at day care on the way to work and pick her up after a client dinner or a late meeting, and she'd already be asleep for the night. When she started kindergarten, she'd go to day care right after school, and I was driving home one night with her sleeping in her little booster seat, thinking that I didn't know anything about her life—how she liked her teacher, who her friends were. All I was to her was a chauffeur. My job was to take her places where other people took care of her."

"So you quit your job?"

"The next day. Karin even asked the psychologist from human services to see me in my office as I was packing up my stuff—she really thought I was flipping out. Everyone did."

"So are things better now that you're a . . . mailman?"

Smiling, James scratched his cheek. "You say that word exactly the same way Karin says it—as if you're saying 'career criminal.' "

I pulled the afghan off the back of the couch and put it over my lap.

"To tell you the truth, it does seem to be sort of, well, below your station."

"Below my station," he said, shaking his head. "And what exactly is my station?"

"Oh, come on, you know what I'm talking about. Carrying mail isn't exactly a *fulfilling* profession."

He took a sip of wine and stared into the fire long enough so that I thought the conversation was definitely over and maybe I should just go to bed.

"There were other things that needed to be fulfilled." He took another sip of wine and then, putting down his glass, turned toward me. "Somehow I thought you'd get it."

"You hardly know me," I said, feeling defensive and a little miffed at his intimacy. "Why would you presume to know what I get or don't get?"

"Now you sound like the Geneva Jordan I expected."

I laughed in spite of myself. "And what exactly did you expect?"

He got up and went to the picture window.

"See that big house across the lake? Well, you can't see it now because of the storm, but it's gray fieldstone—"

"With maroon trim?" I said, stepping over Rich to join James at the window. "Sure, I've seen that house. It's huge."

"It's mine."

"You're kidding." I looked out into the white, as if I could somehow see the behemoth through the blizzard.

"Well, it was mine. Mine and Karin's. Now she just lives there. With Natalie—well, with Natalie every other week."

"You share custody?"

James nodded. "She didn't fight me on that, thank God. As it is, I have Natalie even more than Karin does. She travels a lot."

"So you're seeing your daughter more now?"

James's wonderful smile came back, filling his whole face. "Are you kidding? I'm spending more time with her in one day than I used to in a whole week."

I had to laugh, he sounded so thrilled. And it must have been some kind of potent laugh, because it ignited all sorts of other strong emotions, and before I could say "special delivery," the mailman and I were in each other's arms, kissing with the passion of teenagers but the expertise of a man and woman all grown up.

Chapter 7

woke up the next morning—stiff and sore from sleeping on the couch—to cheers from Natalie and Rich as they watched the list of school closings scroll down the television screen.

"Snow day!" Rich said, and I remembered from my own school days how exciting those two words were.

As the kids chattered about spending the day sledding and building snow forts, I went into the kitchen, looking for James.

Whatever had inspired our teenagers' kiss the night before—had watching the blizzard rage outside triggered a wild instinct?—it had broken apart quickly, almost as if a chaperone had barged into the room, clapping her hands and scolding our naughty behavior. We had, however, returned to the couch holding hands, and then we launched into a talk marathon.

At first we quizzed each other like a couple on their first date, and I learned all sorts of things in this q&a. I asked what his sign was, not because I was a big believer in astrology but because I wanted to know his birthday, and subsequently learned that I was four and a half years older than he. I also learned he had had his tonsils out but not his appendix (exactly the opposite of me) and that we both had taken piano lessons, although I quit in the eighth grade (I hated the practice) and James took them all the way through high school.

After we ended the volley of childhood snippets, we each spoke in monologues.

I told him about Trevor, about my feelings of inadequacy as far as taking care of Rich went, about the thrill of opening night in a brand-new play, about my favorite family recipe (a chocolate sauce that hardened as soon as it was poured on ice cream), about what it was like to be a fraternal twin.

James told me he'd been so relieved when the Vietnam War ended the year he graduated from high school that he celebrated for three straight years in an around-the-world party—hitchhiking through Europe, working for a boat charter service in Tahiti, washing dishes in a hotel in Rio de Janeiro.

"When I got back I took an accelerated course load so that I could catch up with my friends and then . . . I don't know. I just couldn't stop. I went from being the Happy Wanderer to"—he lowered his voice—"A Man of Ambition. Amalgamated hired me right out of college, and work became my whole life—my own boss used to joke that climbing the corporate ladder was the only exercise I got. It seemed my whole reason for being was to make money. Karin and I would sit at our kitchen table charting our projected salary increases on a graph. We'd actually cackle as we wrote the numbers down."

When I asked him if he saw himself remaining a mailman for the rest of his life, he shrugged and said, "Who knows? I've been doing it for a year and a half and I still like it."

"Well, don't you . . . don't you ever miss the action? Miss the excitement, the decision making, the creativity of your old job?"

"Oh, yeah," said James dryly. "I really miss making those decisions about the typeface on a box of instant potatoes or figuring out if a frozen dinner should be Olé Chicken or Chicken Olé. Besides," he added, smiling, "I'm far more creative as a mailman than I ever was as a marketing exec."

"But how creative can a mailman be?"

"Do you honestly think figuring out slogans or packaging is creative, Geneva? Figuring out ways to make people *buy* things?"

"Yes, I do," I said. "I think there's an art to product packaging—it may not be a profound art, but at least you're using your imagination."

"I use my imagination all day, Geneva! That's what I love about my job—all day I'm given the luxury of just walking and thinking."

"So what do you think about?" I asked, watching as he got up and added a log to the fire.

He positioned the logs with a poker and then turned around. "Well, sometimes I think of plays."

"Plays?" I asked, surprised. "Like *A Streetcar Named Desire* or *Our Town*?"

James laughed. "No, hockey plays." He must have seen the confusion in my face, because he mimed holding a stick. "You know, moves a hockey player can make on the ice. See, I coach girls' hockey—Natalie's team. They're a little young for moves—most of them are just getting comfortable on skates—but I spend a lot of time thinking of plays and drills and how I can convince Shannon Mason to stay our goalie instead of playing with her Barbies."

"She's got to make a choice, huh?"

"Apparently. She's a great little goalie—very aggressive—but her mother took me aside the other day and said Shannon thinks hockey might take too much time away from her Barbies."

"So you're happy to carry mail and think of girls' hockey strategy."

James nodded. "Yup. Although I'll occasionally let my mind wander to other topics."

"Topics such as?"

"Such as today's." This he said as if he were recalling a sweet memory. "Today I was thinking about the Commandments."

"The *Commandments*?"

He sat back on the couch. "Yeah, as in the Ten."

"I wasn't saying the word as if I didn't understand what it meant. I was repeating the word in surprise."

James smiled. "In surprise, huh?"

"Yes, surprise. I mean it's not every day that people go around thinking about the Ten Commandments, unless they're clergymen or real religious or something." I looked at him. "Are you real religious? I mean, I know you go to church, but are you some kind of *zealot*?"

"You like to know what's what, don't you, Geneva Jordan?" said James. "And no, I'm not 'some kind of zealot,' but I do think about God a lot. I think about everything a lot." He smiled his winsome smile. "That's the beauty of my job."

"So what were you thinking about the Ten Commandments?"

"How hard they are to keep."

I nodded. "Especially that one about loving your neighbor as yourself."

James was quiet for a moment. "Jesus gave that advice, but that's not a commandment per se."

"Really? Well, that's good. I mean, who could?"

"Who could what?"

"Who could love her neighbor as herself? A person would go nuts."

"How do you mean?"

"Well," I said, "you know how when you read a story about a terrible accident and you feel that flash of pain for the victims?"

James nodded.

"But it's just a flash, right? You turn the page, and by the time you've read the comics you've forgotten all about it. Now imagine if you knew those victims, if you loved them as yourself. How could you bear their pain when it's hard enough to bear your own?"

"Well, you couldn't," James agreed. "But I think that message means to want the best for another person, to treat everybody as you'd like to be treated."

"That's the Golden Rule," I said, like a kid who gets to raise her hand because she finally knows an answer. "And that's no fun."

Again I was rewarded with James's cheek-bunching smile.

"It isn't. Just think, if you stuck to the Golden Rule, you couldn't gossip or make fun of anyone or . . ." I laughed, too, hearing myself. "So I'm shallow. But it's true. I'd feel a real loss if I couldn't ever talk behind someone's back." I felt myself blush and, wanting to turn the attention away from my *un*–Mother Teresa–like self, I asked, "So which Commandments are hard for you to keep?"

"I was thinking of the first one. About honoring your father and your mother."

"You mean we're *still* supposed to do that—even when we're all grown up?"

James smiled at my little joke. "Mine side with Karin—not only are they mad I gave up a career to carry mail, they think I'm purposely trying to embarrass her by carrying it in *her* neighborhood."

"Are you?" I asked.

"I'm not that devious. It was a fluke—the guy who had this route retired and I had a transfer request in, so here I am, delivering mail to the same houses where I used to go to cocktail parties. Funny, I haven't gotten many of those invitations lately." He covered his mouth, yawning. "Today on the phone my mother said I'm worse than a black sheep—I'm a black sheep in *public*."

I couldn't believe this woman; she was making my own mother sound like a paragon of understanding.

"So what'd you say back?" I asked.

"The obvious," said James. "Baaa."

As the night wore on, there had been longer pauses between our words, and finally, as I was waiting for James to tell me his favorite movie as a kid, I heard him snoring. I was relieved—I was bushed, too, but there is something in my personality that demands I always be the last one to go to sleep. I guess I just don't like to miss anything.

*N*ow I was looking for my slumber party guest in a house bright with winter light. It really was amazing—the sky was as blue as turquoise jewelry, and under it the snow was so dazzling that I had to squint at the sun that sparkled on it.

There was a pot of coffee already made and a note on the counter.

Thanks for the hospitality. I woke up to the sound of the plows and figured I'd better shovel out your driveway so you're not housebound. I hope you don't mind that I left Natalie here, but I thought I should shovel Karin out too. Who knows, maybe I'll be back before you wake up.

James.

"Chivalry is not dead," I said out loud, folding the note and putting it in my robe pocket. Then, as if responding to my cue, the phone rang. However, it was not Sir James the Gentleman but Sir Trevor the Snake.

Still, my voice went up about nine octaves. "Trevor?"

"I just saw on CNN how you got twenty feet of snow."

"Two," I said, smiling. "But what are you doing up so early watching TV?" Even allowing for the time difference, Trevor was usually asleep at this time.

"It's a new me—I'm up and to the gym every morning by eight."

"You're kidding."

"Nope. One drink after the show and I'm home by midnight."

"Alone?" I couldn't help myself—as much as I didn't want to know, I wanted to know.

"Alone with my memories . . . of you."

Oh, brother. Here came the Trevor Waite charm, like a train speeding down the tracks, ready to flatten me. I was so unnerved I could do nothing but giggle like the sap I was.

"Oh, Geneva," said Trevor, "can't we have another go at it? I miss you so much, miss a real woman in my life."

"As opposed to a plastic one?"

He chuckled the way people will do when they want to score points with you by laughing at your jokes, however mean-spirited they may be.

"Oh, Geneva," he said again. "Don't you miss me, too? The times we had together? Our song?" He started humming the duet we sang in *Mona!* We had often sung the ballad to each other offstage.

I squelched the temptation to join in; this was all way too fast.

"Hey," I said, thinking a little diversion just then wouldn't hurt, "how'd you get this number, anyway?"

"I haf my vays," he said in a bad German impersonation. "Actually, all it took was opening up the Christmas present your sister gave me last year. That biography of Yeats? Well, it was inscribed, 'Best wishes from Ann and Riley Wahlstrom,' so all I did was ring information."

"Pretty smart," I conceded, silently cursing my sister and brother-in-law for providing Trevor with such an important clue. Why did they always have to be so damn thoughtful and give whatever man I was seeing at the time a Christmas gift?

I took a deep breath. "Trevor, I, uh—I have to go."

"So what do you think of what I've just said? Should I call again? Do I have a chance?"

I was glad he was on the phone; if he'd been speaking to me in the same room, I'd have flung myself into his arms sentences earlier.

"I . . . I don't know, Trevor. This is just sort of sudden. . . . Uh, I've got to go."

After hanging up the phone I stood there gulping in air like a beginning yoga student. Could I—should I?—risk getting back together with Trevor Waite, a man who not only had broken my heart, but seemed to take pleasure in stepping on the pieces? I was near hyperventilation as I considered my next course of action, but fortunately it was decided for me.

"Aunt Gennie, we're hungry!" announced Rich.

"Really hungry," said Natalie. Her bright eyes scanned the kitchen. "Where's my dad?"

"Shoveling your mother's walk," I said, opening a cupboard. "So what'll it be? Oatmeal, cornflakes, or—"

"French toast!" screamed Rich.

"French toast!" came his little echo.

I immersed myself in the business of getting breakfast together, keeping up a steady stream of chatter with the kids so that I wouldn't have to think about Trevor's phone call.

"Rich, can you get me the eggs?"

"Just don't beat them," said Natalie. " 'Cause you're too nice." She grinned. "Get it? *Beat?* Too nice to beat?"

Rich's eyes widened as she explained the pun, and then he burst out laughing.

"Too nice to beat! Too nice to beat!"

I took a carton out of the refrigerator. "And I suppose you're too polite to *whip* the cream?"

"Whip the cream!" they squealed. *"Whip the cream!"*

They delighted in the kitchen-sadist puns they were able to come up with themselves—"crack the eggs," "chop the onion," "slice the pie"—but it was my suggestion of "cut the cheese" that sent them into hysterics.

"Cut the cheese!" gasped Rich. "That's another way you say *fart!*"

"Fart!" said Natalie, laughing maniacally. "My mom won't even let me say that word!" There was a moment when she looked like a sailor who was considering mutiny versus staying on the ship. Mutiny won. "Fart, fart, fart, fart, fart!"

Soon they were running around the room in a two-person conga line, saying the word *fart* and making with their mouths the sound the word referred to. I was right behind them, adding to the percussion with a soup ladle against a pot and the occasional "Hey!" It was into this noisy household that James returned.

We had rounded the kitchen table when we saw James standing there, nodding to our crazy beat.

"Daddy!" said Natalie, rushing to him. "We were singing a special song about *farts!*"

"So I heard," he said, smiling. He kissed his daughter's head and then looked at me. "Great lyrics, good beat. I'll give it a ninety."

"Thanks," I said, taking a little bow. "Next we're going to have a burping contest."

"A burping contest," said Rich. "Yay!"

"Just kidding," I said, making my way to the coffeepot. "So how's it look out there?"

"I'm just glad it's my day off. It'd probably take me an extra three hours to wade through all of this snow." He accepted the cup of coffee I handed him. "But they've plowed Lake Road, so if you need to go out for anything, you can."

"Can we stay here all day, Daddy?" asked Natalie, jumping up and down. "Me and Rich want to go sledding and make snowmen and snow forts!"

"Your mom wants me to bring you home," he said, putting his hands on her shoulders to stop her bouncing. "She doesn't have to go into work because of the snow, and she wants to spend the day with you."

"But I want to go sledding and make snowmen and snow forts!"

"I know, honey, but you'll have to take a rain check."

"What's a rain check?"

James looked at me with his warm hazel eyes. "It's something I hope *I'll* get."

"*I* feel sorry for people who don't have a twin. Geneva and I aren't like the McDermotts, who trick everybody into thinking they're Lowell when they're really Lance and vice versa. We don't even look that much alike and our personalities are really different but still, I came into the world with her! When Mom explained sex to us (ick!) the only thing that didn't make me want to vomit was thinking about the miracle of the two of us being made on the same day. And growing inside our mother—we always had company! I remember once last year up here at the cabin when Geneva and I slept outside and we just couldn't believe all the stars that were in the sky and I was kind of in a funny (funny sad not funny ha-ha) mood and said that looking at such a big starry sky made me feel so small and lonesome and Geneva said, 'Well, then turn your head and look at me,' and I did and she asked, 'Do you still feel so small and lonesome?' and I said, 'Yes,' and then she put her face right up to mine, so that our noses were touching, and she said, 'Well, to me you look really big,' and she looked cross-eyed in that way you do when your face is right up to someone else's and I guess I must have too because we both started laughing and to me that is the meaning of life, having someone who makes you feel not so small and lonesome."

It was funny—after supper everyone sitting around that cabin table would randomly choose a slip of paper and read it aloud, and I can't remember anyone acting embarrassed or self-conscious. Never was a disclaimer made ("I don't agree with this at all!") or a judgment ("Come on, Ole, couldn't you have dug a little deeper?"); it was such an intense sharing experience that I think all of us, even Great-aunt Tove (who was the type of woman who *never* lingered in a hug and seemed to like to avoid them altogether) felt honored to be a part of it. I can still hear Great-uncle Carl reading what Ann had written, and I remember the flush of pride I felt hearing how important I was to my sister.

Now I sat on the bed all these years later, marveling that *I* had been able to comfort Ann in her loneliness when usually it was she who was called upon to comfort *me*.

"Hey, I've been wondering where that question book went."

I started. "Rich, you scared me."

"Didn't mean to," said Rich, bounding into the bedroom. "I was calling and calling you." He jumped on the bed with such force that I was afraid it was going to break.

"You said we were going to read this tomorrow," said Rich as he settled into the slope of pillows that rested on the headboard. "Then tomorrow came and you never did. Let's read some now."

"I was just coming downstairs to make some hot chocolate."

"We just ate!" It was true. James and Natalie had left after breakfast, less than a half hour before. "Whose is this?" he asked, gently tugging at the slip of paper I had closed my fingers around. "What's the question? What's the answer?"

"Rich, don't rip it!" Anger welled up in me, and my hand clutched the paper more tightly.

"Just read it, then! Tell me the question and read me the answer!"

"Not now," I said, feeling all vestiges of calm blow away.

With both hands Rich was trying to pry my hand open.

"Stop that!"

"But you said we were going to read them together!!"

"Well, I changed my mind!"

As if he was stunned by not only what I said but the volume with which I said it, Rich stared slack-jawed at me before he burst into tears. Then he scrambled off the bed and ran across the room, down the hallway, and to his own bedroom. I heard the door slam and I sat there for a moment, slack-jawed myself, listening to my nephew's muffled sobs, my sister's version of the meaning of life still grasped in my hand.

"Rich," I said, knocking at his door. "Rich, may I come in?"

There was no response, so I opened the door, wishing I was doing anything but going into my nephew's room to apologize.

He was a mound under the covers, an inch or so of his hair sprouting out from the edge of the comforter like dark blond grass.

"Rich?"

He didn't answer, but a shudder rippled through him, and the feelings of shame and chicken-heartedness almost sent me running out the door.

I sat on the edge of the bed and patted the highest point of the mound.

"Rich, I am so sorry. Will you forgive me?"

The mound moved again in another shudder.

"Rich, please, I am so—"

"It's my book too!" he said suddenly, sitting up, his tear-streaked face contorted. "Grandma sent it to us, and my mom helped make it! My mom would say it's not just yours, but all of ours!"

Done in by his speech, he became a mound under the covers again and sobbed.

"I know, honey," I said, feeling as low and stupid as a person can feel without turning into an amoeba. "It's just that . . . I don't know, the book was bringing back such wonderful memories that I . . . well, I just didn't want to share them yet."

"Well, you better learn to share!" His words rode a high-pitched squeal.

"I know. I know. I *want* to share them now." I patted what I hoped was his hip. "I'll go get the book now and we'll read together, okay?"

"Don't want to."

"Come on, Rich, we'll read all the questions and answers you want to, and I'll tell you all about Great-uncle Carl and Great-aunt Tove and your great—"

"Don't want to."

I sat there for a long time, certain he'd change his mind, but he didn't. When I realized from his even breathing that he had fallen asleep, I left the room.

*J*ames got double value for his rain check. On Monday he and Natalie joined us for pizza; on Wednesday, after Chinese takeout, Rich and I went with them to hockey practice.

It was cold in the rink, and Rich and I huddled on the bleachers with our shoulders pressed together. In front of us sat a trio of women who, even bundled up, looked chic in a suburban sort of way. Somehow they managed to carry on a conversation while yelling encouragement at their daughters on the ice.

"Way to skate, Emily! Hey, did you know Lori and Dave Donaldson split up?"

"You're kidding. I was at their anniversary party last year. Looking good, Jessica!"

"I heard Lori's the one who asked for it. Nice shot, Ashley! She gets her Realtor's license and suddenly she wants to be Miss Independent."

James and a tall man with a mustache were out on the ice, and their different styles of coaching were readily apparent.

"Come on, girls—faster! Faster!" barked the guy with the mustache as the girls skated around half the rink. "This is a *speed* drill! Come on, Natalie. Hurry up, Samantha—*move!*"

James, on the other hand, just watched the girls, and when they were done with the drill he congratulated them on their improved skating.

"Geez, what's with Phil?" asked one of the mothers as the girls began to take shots and the mustached guy began yelling at the girls to "aim for the net, not the boards!"

"I think he's taking too much Viagra," said another mother, and as they all laughed, Rich asked me, "What's Viagra?"

I shook my head as if I didn't want to be disturbed, while the first mother said, "As if he needs any more testosterone. The guy's worse than a drill sergeant."

"I said watch the net, girls!" he yelled.

"I don't know," said the third mother. "I think these girls need a little discipline. They need to know they're not out there just for fun and games."

What are *they out there for, then?* I wondered.

"I don't know. Emily's afraid of him," said the first mother.

"Jessica too," said the second. "Although she *loves* James."

"James," said the third mother with a little scoff in her voice. "James is too easy on them. It's as if his only goal is that they have fun."

"Well, what's wrong with that?" asked the first mother.

"Nothing, I guess," said mother number three. "But Ashley likes to win, and I want her to be coached by someone who thinks winning is as important as having fun."

I rolled my eyes at Rich, but he apparently wasn't eavesdropping, busy as he was pulling at a loose thread.

"Hey, look, Aunt Gennie," he said as his jacket button popped off. "If you pull on this string long enough, the button comes off."

*A*s we drove home, the kids decided we should continue the evening by going sledding.

"It's getting pretty late for a school night," I said, very momlike.

"Oh, come on, please!" begged Rich. "Please, please?"

"Yeah," chirped Natalie. "Sledding in the night is so much more fun than sledding in the day! It's like getting two desserts instead of one."

"Yeah, two desserts," said Rich, his eyes wide.

"How can anybody say no to two desserts?" asked James.

"Be pretty hard," I admitted.

"But Dad, I need my snow pants!" said Natalie. "I can't go sledding without my snow pants!"

"You could wear your breezers."

"Dad, those are for hockey, not for sledding!"

James looked at me and, willing to let the evening go on, I shrugged my assent.

"Okay," he said. "We'll go home and get them."

Soon we were in front of the big "living large" house that belonged to James's ex-wife. Rich tumbled out of the car after Natalie.

"Rich, get back here," I said. "We'll sit in the car and wait for them."

"But I want to see her Beanie Babies!"

"Yeah," said Natalie, "I've got seventy-eight."

"Come on in," said James, opening the passenger door.

"Well, what about . . ."

"Karin? She's gone. To Tokyo. She left this morning."

"Tokyo," I said, getting out of the car. "For how long?"

"A couple of days. Then she goes to Bangkok and Shanghai."

"That's a pretty exotic itinerary."

James hefted the equipment bags and hockey sticks out of the back. "Amalgamated's not sending her there to be a tourist. I believe she said"—here his voice changed to a robotic monotone—" 'Our goal is to increase our Asian customer base.' "

"Still," I said, laughing, "she'll probably have *some* time during the day to do a little sightseeing."

"You don't know Amalgamated," he said, shaking his head. "You don't know Karin."

"Wow!" said Rich as we stepped into the house's foyer. "A castle!"

"My sentiments exactly," I mumbled.

"Come on, Rich," said Natalie, "I'll show you my room."

We watched the children bound up the massive staircase.

The architecture was of the look-at-me sort. There was enough marble to make you think you were in a quarry, enough stained glass to make you want to genuflect, and ceilings of such height that a person could pole-vault under them.

"You actually lived here?"

"What's worse, I helped design it."

"*No.*"

James shook his head and made an expression like that of a criminal unable to believe his sordid past.

"Well, I was more like an enabler, I guess. When the architect showed us the latest plans, I never said, 'Are you nuts?' Every time he came up with another fifteen-foot window or a balcony, I just sat there saying 'Fine' or 'Looks good.' " We walked into the formal living room, which boasted a wall-sized fireplace on one end and a grand piano that looked more a showpiece than a used instrument.

"It's pretty awful, isn't it?"

Don't get me wrong—I'm not against wealth. Heaven knows I'm not exactly a pauper. Still, there are things a person should flaunt, such as brains, good looks, and talent (to name some I'm personally familiar with), and some things a person shouldn't flaunt, including money, surgery scars, and genitalia. If you're absolutely *compelled* to flaunt your money, at least do it with a little style: a Fifth Avenue penthouse, a weather-beaten shack in the Hamptons. But this was a house that said nothing about its owner except *I have lots of money and not a lot of taste.*

"I take it you don't want the grand tour?"

"God, no," I said, plopping myself down on a white leather couch whose cushions, under my weight, yielded not an inch.

"What a relief," said James, setting down the sticks and equipment and dropping down next to me. "Although I could show you my room."

I don't know what my expression was, but he laughed. "Not for *that* reason. I just wanted to show you because it's the smallest room in the house. Karin uses it as her sewing room, only she never sews."

"Why do you have a room here at all? I mean, it's not your house anymore."

James smile was hard to read. "Karin points that out to me quite often, thank you." He stretched his arms over his head, and for a minute I thought he was going to pull that old now-I'll-put-this-arm-around-you trick. But he didn't. "She travels so much that it's convenient for her to have me stay here with Natalie and keep an eye on the house, too. But believe me, after a week here, my one-bedroom in Minnetonka seems like Eden."

"And why wouldn't you show me your room for *that* reason?"

"What?" His eyes widened then, and he nodded, understanding. "Well," he said, clearing his throat, "because I didn't think you'd want to see it for *that* reason."

There had been no follow-up to our teenage-impulse kiss the night of the Halloween storm, and yet right then I wanted nothing more than to feel his mouth on mine.

"You never know if you don't try."

"Okay," he said, and then his face got bigger and bigger as it zeroed in on mine and our lips met.

Just as there is such a thing as like minds, we shared like lips— our mouths were completely in sync, like old friends who knew exactly what the other liked. Putting my arms around James's neck, I had happily settled into what I hoped would be a long necking session when we heard a thump and then, a beat later, Rich's faint "Help!"

James and I scrambled up as if the couch was on fire and raced up the polished wood staircase. We ran past several doors and then through an open one.

Natalie was sitting on the floor, pale as flour. She was cradling her arm to her chest, and when she saw us, an expression of sheepishness washed over her face, followed by a wail.

"Natalie!" said James, rushing toward her. "Did you hurt your arm?"

"I heard it!" said Rich. "She fell and I heard a little snap!"

"Let me see," said James, but he hadn't even touched her before Natalie wailed again.

"Don't touch it, Daddy, it hurts too much!"

"Looks like we're going to the hospital," he said, carefully lifting her up. To me he asked, "Can you drive us?"

"Sure."

"I heard it!" Rich said again. "Heard a little snap!" He was jumping up and down like a poster boy for Ritalin.

"Come on, Rich," I said, putting my arm around him, trying to calm him. "We've got to take Natalie and James to the hospital."

"I dint do anything!" Rich said. "We were jumping off the bed, but I dint do anything!"

"It was my idea to jump off the bed," said Natalie, her face poking out from behind her father's shoulder, "not Rich's."

I smiled at the brave little girl. Then, feeling Rich's shoulders relax under my arm, I squeezed them.

"So you guys were jumping off the top bunk?"

Rich nodded, and his eyes filled with tears. "Rescuing Beanie Babies," he said. One of the tears welling in his eyes rolled down his flat cheek, and he rested his head on my chest. "But it's my fault. I know better. I shoulda said, 'No, not supposed to do this.' Shoulda said no."

With one arm still supporting his daughter, James turned. "Hey, buddy," he said, cupping Rich's chin with his free hand, "accidents happen." He looked at the toys scattered across the floor. "If anybody's at fault, it's these darn Beanie Babies. I've never met bigger troublemakers."

"Oh, *Daddy*," said Natalie, laughing weakly.

"Bigger troublemakers," said Rich, chuckling. "Oh, *James*."

I answered the doorbell the next day to find James on the front steps.

"I can only stay a minute," he said as I held the door open for him. He patted his mail sack. "I've got miles to go before I sleep."

"And I've got some coffee," I said, running to get him a cup. It wasn't that cold out—just a little below freezing—but I thought he could use a nice warm-up.

"Thanks," he said, holding the cup in his gloved hands.

"So how'd Natalie do last night?"

"I think the Tylenol must have knocked her out," James said, sitting at the counter. "She slept through the whole night, and this morning she couldn't wait to get to school to show off her cast."

"Good for her," I said. "She's a brave little girl."

James nodded. "She's a little bummed out about hockey—and so am I—but the doctor says she should be back on the ice by Christmas." He sipped the coffee I'd served him. "I also got through to Karin. She is, in her own words, *livid*."

"It's not your fault!"

"It happened under my watch. Karin would have made sure Natalie wasn't jumping on the bed."

"She said that?"

James nodded. "And a lot more. But at least I was able to convince her that she didn't need to fly back—that it was a clean break, and it wasn't as if Nat needed surgery."

"What'd she say to that?"

James shrugged. "She said, 'Oh, so a *clean break's* no big deal, is that it?' And then she spent about ten minutes scolding me for entertaining guests in her house while she was away."

I personally think the word *bitch* is demeaning to women, but this woman deserved to be demeaned. In fact, she wasn't just a bitch, she was Superbitch, Miss World Bitch, *über*-bitch.

"I don't even know the woman and I can't stand her."

James laughed. "She's got her good qualities."

I waited a few moments for him to elaborate, and when he didn't I said, "Well?"

He laughed again. "I'm thinking, I'm thinking."

Chapter 8

he CIA lost a valuable employee when they failed to recruit Barb Torgerson. She was a subtle, masterful persuader, an expert in mind control, capable of getting anyone to do what they were certain they never would, be it revealing secrets, breaking codes, or volunteering to help in a Sunday school class.

"Will you stop grimacing?" she said. "They're not going to hurt you."

"Why did I ever let you talk me into this?"

"Because Brenda Albert has the flu," she said as Rich and Conrad took off to their class and we hung up our coats on pegs attached to the church basement wall. "And you knew I needed help."

"I'll bet she's faking," I said of the absent Sunday school teacher, whom I had never met. "She's probably at some bar right now, drinking an early-bird special with someone else's husband."

"You're terrible," said Barb, laughing. "Besides, the strongest thing Brenda Albert drinks is communion wine."

"She *says*."

James, in a dapper gray pinstripe, was standing at the end of the hallway, waiting for us.

"Don't tell me she's recruited you too," I said.

"Bribed is more like it," said James. "She invited me to brunch afterward."

"You too," said Barb, laughing at the mildly exaggerated wounded expression on my face. "You're invited too."

When we opened the door to the classroom, we were greeted with bedlam, just as I had suspected. Kids were chasing one another, scribbling on the little easel chalkboard, and flying paper airplanes. But upon seeing us adults they stopped their shenanigans and sat down quickly, and for a moment I was transported on the memorymobile to classrooms of my past where we had done exactly the same thing.

The chairs were arranged in a circle on the highly polished linoleum floor, and Barb motioned James and me to sit next to her.

"Hi, kids. Most of you know James—he's been here before."

After they exchanged greetings, Barb put her hand on my shoulder.

"And this is Geneva. She's Rich's aunt."

"Hi, Geneva," sang the chorus of about a dozen adolescent voices.

I winked at Rich, who was shyly waving at me.

"I'm Megan," said a girl whose mouth was aglint with metal. "Rich says you're a famous singer."

"Well, I—"

"What kind of singer?" asked a chubby girl. "Are you, like, in a *band?*"

"She's too old to be in a band," said a boy whom I immediately wanted to send out into the hall.

"She is not," said Megan. "Look at the Rolling Stones. I'll bet she's younger than them."

"Oh, *much* younger," I said.

"What do you sing?" asked another boy. "Like, opera or something?"

"Opera sucks," said the boy who accused me of being too old to rock and roll. Now I *really* wanted to punish him.

"Wait a minute, guys, wait a minute," said Rich, waving his arms to get everyone's attention. "My aunt Geneva sings on *Broadway*."

"What's Broadway?" asked the mouthy boy, who with this question proved his ignorance too.

"Broadway is . . . Broadway is . . ." Rich looked at me helplessly. "You tell 'em, Aunt Gennie."

"With pleasure," I said. "Broadway is a series of theaters in a certain district of New York City where the best plays in the country—in the world—are presented."

"Better than the West End in London?" asked a worldly show-off.

"In my opinion, yes. Broadway is the capital of plays and musicals just like Hollywood is the capital of movies."

"That sounds a bit nationalistic," said Little Miss West End.

"What's nationalistic mean, Holly?" asked Conrad.

"Excessive patriotism. A belief that anything your country does is best."

"Well, everything America does *is* best," said the lippy boy.

"You would say that, Chad. You've got the world view of a toad."

"And you've got the face of one."

"Okay, kids, that's enough," said Barb as they all laughed at Chad the comedian. "We're straying from our topic."

"What *is* our topic, Mom?" asked Conrad.

"Our topic today is gifts. You know, because Thanksgiving is coming up."

"Thanksgiving," said Megan. "What about *Christmas*?"

"I already made up my Christmas list," said a pretty girl whose shiny hair wasn't just blond but different stripes of blond.

"I made mine up too," said Conrad, "and you're on it."

The pretty girl blushed.

"What do you mean, Hannah's on your list?" asked Barb.

Conrad's head wavered as he smiled.

"It means I want Hannah for Christmas. For a girlfriend. And if she can't be my girlfriend, then I'll take a kiss."

"Sorry, Connie, I already have a boyfriend," she said. Then, surprising me with her poise, Hannah with the striped blond hair walked over to Conrad. "So here's your kiss."

The class whooped and applauded after she pecked him on the cheek.

"Oh, that's a good one," said Rich, slapping his knee. "That's a good one."

Cupping his cheek as if he wanted to preserve the kiss, Conrad smiled and said, "Sure was."

"So Hannah just gave Conrad a gift," said Barb to the class. "Why do you think she gave it to him?"

"Because she likes me!" said Conrad, one curled fist waving uncontrollably. "Because I'm irresistible!" This was rewarded with more laughter, especially from Rich, who once again slapped his knee.

"That's right," said Barb. "Sometimes people give other people gifts out of a sense of obligation or good manners, but most often a person gives another person a gift because he or she likes that person. And because God loves us, he gave us lots of gifts."

Oh, no, I thought, *here comes the sermonizing.*

"Like what kind?" asked Megan.

"Like good looks," said Chad, striking a pose. "He happened to give me good looks."

"And *She* happened to give me a brain," said Holly.

"That's right," said Barb, overriding whatever smart remark Chad made back. "Good looks and intelligence could be considered gifts. What else?"

Megan raised her hand. "Bryce is a really good hockey player."

A boy with the biggest Adam's apple I'd ever seen stared at his lap, while a flame red blush crawled up his face and ears.

"Athletic ability—yup, that's a gift too. What else?"

What ensued then was a spirited discussion of gifts with all sorts of questions and comments: "If talents are gifts, then are personality traits like being funny or always knowing what to say gifts too? And if they are, why would God give one person more of these gifts than others—does that mean he likes them better?" "Maybe we all get the same amount but some of us use ours more." "Aren't all these gifts really just a result of whatever genes we inherited?" (This last question, of course, came from Holly the brain.)

I was impressed by the enthusiastic participation. In the Sunday school classes of my youth, children were expected to speak only when called on, and when they couldn't wait for permission they were met with a curt "Shhh!" And my teachers would have decried some of the questions these kids asked as pure blasphemy: "What if God gives you something you don't want, like a disease or something—can you give it back?" (Barb told me later that the mother of the boy who asked this question had just been diagnosed with breast cancer.) Or "I think it's mean of God to give someone a pretty face and popularity when he gives someone else a weight problem and acne." (This was said by a plump, pimply girl who stared openly at Hannah as she spoke.)

Finally Barb suggested that we go around the circle and tell everyone the gift we had that we were happiest with.

Her suggestion was met with a few groans, but Barb prevailed. "No one has to say anything if they don't want to, but sharing your thoughts and feelings with people is a gift as well. Just remember the rules: You're not allowed to judge what someone shares."

"I'll start," said chipper Megan. "I think my greatest gift is that I'm a people person."

I expected more groans (or at least a smart remark from Chad), but they were apparently following Barb's rule.

"I just love people!" Megan said. "I think it's so cool that we're all here on this planet together!"

Barb smiled and nodded but said only, "Next?"

Bryce the hockey player, still staring at his lap, shook his head. "Pass."

"I'd say my greatest gift is my ability at math," said another boy, whose deep chin dimple could have held his lunch money. "I'm in advanced algebra and I'll be in geometry next year."

Again Barb smiled and nodded. "Hannah?"

"Hmm," said the pretty girl. "I sort of want to pass because it's kind of embarrassing, but I do think it's brave to share."

I looked surreptitiously at the hockey player, who was bright red again.

"So," she continued, "I guess I think my greatest gift"—here I expected her to say "my face" or "my ribbons of blond hair" or "my tall and slender body," but she surprised me again—"is that I'm kind." Her cheeks grew pink—the blushes were running fast and furious through this room. "At least that's what people tell me."

As we went around the circle I found I was holding my breath as each person spoke; I didn't want to miss a word of what any of these kids said. It was all so fascinating, so touching, so completely different from my Sunday school recitations of Bible verses.

"Rich, how about you?"

My nephew, sitting on his hands, was leaning forward as if examining his shoes. When he looked up, his lip was pushed up, his forehead furrowed in concentration. He mumbled something.

"What was that, Rich?" asked Barb.

"My biggest gift, I said, is my best friend." He leaned over and put his arm around Conrad. "Is my best friend, Conrad Joseph Torgerson."

Conrad's arm swung widely before he put it around Rich. "Thanks, Richard Allen Wahlstrom."

"You're welcome." The two of them sat there for a moment, smiling at each other.

Finally Conrad pulled away and, smiling at the other kids, said, " 'Course, everybody knows what my gift is." He stood up, turned his Twins cap around, and said, à la James Brown, "I can *move!*"

With that announcement, he began to dance, rolling his fists around in a circle and flailing his arms from side to side. The whole room erupted into laughter and rhythmic clapping, and Connie milked it like an old pro, shimmying his shoulders (or trying to), spastically hopping and dipping until he was panting and Barb said, laughing, "Okay, okay, Conrad, give someone else a turn."

The gaiety Conrad's dance had brought to the room was brought down when a girl named Linnea said her greatest gift was her dad's sobriety and another girl said her greatest gift was that her parents weren't divorcing—at least for the time being. When they got to me, I thought I'd chicken out like Bryce and take a pass, but if I couldn't set an example, who could?

"I guess my biggest gift is my voice," I said. "It's given me a career I love and—" I couldn't believe it—I was getting choked up. "And I really love to sing."

"Oh, would you sing for us?" asked Megan.

"Yeah, sing for us, Auntie Gen!" said Rich, and then the rest of the room picked up his chorus. Of course, I couldn't deny a roomful of thirteen-year-olds chanting my name.

"Well, usually I have an accompanist," I said as I stood up.

Then James said, "I'll play for you."

"*You?*" I don't know why I was so surprised—I knew he had taken piano lessons—but I was.

James sat down at the piano and, after playing a glissando, he asked, "What would you like to sing?"

" 'Someone to Watch over Me'?" I blurted. "Key of G?"

As he played an introduction I took a deep breath and tried to collect myself, knowing that if ever there was a tough crowd, it was teenagers.

I began singing, and he followed me as if we had rehearsed. He threw me a little wink, and I turned away, suddenly as shy and awkward as the kids I was singing for. I closed my eyes, trying to center myself, and let James's fingers on the keys take me to those places music has passport to. I sang the song as if I really were a lamb who was lost in the woods, and when I was finished, the whole room burst into applause. I even saw Megan, the cheerleader of humanity, wipe tears from her eyes. Then everyone rushed over to James and me: "I don't even like music like that, but I sure liked that!" "I play trumpet—could you tell me the name of that song again so I could get the sheet music?" "Wow, you guys should make a CD!"

"You're *good*," I said, leaning over the top of the piano.

"I return the compliment," said James.

Looking at the clock, Barb clapped her hands once and said, "Time to put the chairs away."

"But you and James haven't told us what your greatest gifts are!" said Megan.

"Yeah, tell us!" echoed the others.

Barb smiled and pointed to Conrad. "That's my biggest gift," she said, "Connie and his brother and sister."

"She has to say that," said Connie to the group, "she's my mom."

"So what's yours?" asked Chad to James, who still sat at the piano.

"And don't say your kid," said Holly the brain. "That's the obvious answer."

Smiling, James played a major chord, then a minor one. "Yes, that is the obvious answer, but it's also the true one." He played the first few bars of "A Foggy Day." "But if I had to pick my second-best gift, I'd have to say it's——" Here he played another few bars. "Well, it's my legs. I don't mean to brag, but I have got one set of shapely legs."

"Shapely legs!" said Rich, and everyone laughed. Then Barb said, "Come on, kids, grab a chair so we can get out of here," and for the first time in my life, I was sad Sunday school was over.

"Why didn't you tell me what a good piano player you are?" I said to James as he took off his gray pinstripe suit jacket and laid it across a bar stool.

"James isn't the bragging kind," said Barb. "Haven't you noticed?"

"What other secrets are you hiding from me?" I asked, watching him roll up his shirtsleeves.

James wiggled his eyebrows. "Stick around, kid, and maybe I'll show ya."

He took a cue off the wall holder and began to chalk it as Barb racked the balls.

We had all enjoyed the delicious brunch of waffles and fresh fruit Barb had whipped up, and now with Rich, Conrad, and Natalie upstairs playing a video game called Dr. Techo-Wizard or something like that, we were playing pool for money in the basement rec room. Actually, James and Barb were playing. I sat at the bar, swiveling on a vinyl bar stool, stacking the quarters I had bet on Barb's victory.

"Three in the corner pocket," she said, and true to her declaration, she sank the three ball in the corner pocket.

"Six in the side," said James, but his ball didn't obey his command, instead smacking against the table's edge and then bumping into a cluster of other balls.

"Don't laugh," he admonished me. "You cannot laugh at me *and* bet against me. It's too demoralizing."

I swiveled in my seat, turning my attention to the wall behind the bar. It wasn't decorated with the usual plastic beer signs and mounted fish, but with George's college and law school diplomas, golf trophies, and photographs of men holding golf clubs.

"Which one is George?" I asked.

Barb didn't look up from her study of the pool table. "The tall guy with glasses. Number seven in the corner."

The ball clicked against the cue and then plunked into its target.

"At least now I know he exists."

Barb laughed even as she protested I'd messed up her shot. Then she asked, "What do you mean by that?"

"Well, he's never home when I come here."

"Geneva, you've been here only twice."

"No. Remember when I stopped in for coffee last week?"

"Now this is a tricky shot," said James, "but I think I've got it."

"Okay, three times. Twice he was at work—today he's out of town."

"Where'd he go?"

"Now and then he likes to spend weekends up at the cabin. If I make this, James, game's over."

"In the winter?"

Poised to take her shot, Barb looked up at me. "Mind if I take this shot in relative quiet?"

"Oh, please, please. Don't let me get in your way."

She won the game—and five dollars—and then said she was going to check on the kids, but James told her to take a load off; he'd do it.

"Besides, maybe they'll let me play their video game. *They'd* probably have manners enough to let me *win*."

"Just don't bet them any money," said Barb over her shoulder as she joined me at the bar. Then she asked me, "You want a Coke or something?"

I shook my head. "That's all I need—more caffeine." I turned my attention to the wall. "How come there're no family pictures up there?"

"Geneva, this is George's little clubhouse. It's where he puts his trophies and pictures of his influential friends. Is that so wrong?"

I shrugged elaborately. Then, surprising me, Barb said, "You've got everything sized up, don't you? You think George is a neglectful husband and father—off to the cabin alone on weekends, spending as much time as possible at the office so he doesn't have to come home, and when he does, making sure he's got a business associate or friend with him—"

"Barb, really, I—"

"No, no, you think he's only staying in the marriage because he doesn't want the hassle of getting out." Her voice cracked. "I know that's what you think—and you'd be right."

"Oh, Barb," I said, putting my arm around my slumped-over friend. "I had no idea. I just thought . . . I just thought he was your basic, standard selfish prick."

Her shoulders shook and I tightened my grip, but when she pulled away from me I realized she wasn't crying but laughing.

"Geneva," she said, patting her frizzy permed hair back into place (wherever that was), "I love how you tell it like it is."

And then *she* told me how it was—how George had been a good ("not great—he was too busy making money") father to his other children, but Conrad was a challenge he wasn't up to.

"I can't say he hasn't tried," said Barb, staring at a Governor's

Invitational trophy as if it had hypnotized her, "but he hasn't tried enough. Every time he and Connie would make some strides, he'd step back. It's as if he's never accepted Connie's disabilities, and therefore he's never accepted Connie."

"It must be very hard for you."

Barb's mouth turned down as she shrugged. "I'm used to it." She turned to me, crinkling her nose as if she smelled something bad. "Could be a lot worse, I guess." She sighed. "It just could be so much better. For him, for us."

Both of us sat staring at George Torgerson's self-congratulatory wall until I, to break what could be descending gloom, said, "What do you say we have those Cokes after all? And any other sugar concentrate you've got back there."

"You got it," said Barb, going behind the bar. She began to straighten one of George's diplomas but thought better of it, tipping it even more. "So what's the story with you and James?"

"Where *is* James?"

"Probably getting beaten at whatever game the kids are playing. But don't change the subject. What's going on?"

"Could you believe him on the piano? I had no clue he could play the piano like that."

"He can, but he never chooses to. I was floored when he offered to play today."

"Floored, why? What do you mean?"

"Hasn't he told you?"

"Told me what?" I asked, accepting the little bottle of Coke she handed me.

"Well, apparently James is a first-rate musician, but no one ever gets to hear him."

"Why not?"

Barb took a long draw of pop and then let out a long and deep belch.

"Barb!" I said, laughing.

"Sorry. My son Joel tried to teach Connie how to burp, and he worked so hard trying to master it—I guess I picked up a few lessons along the way."

"I *guess*. Now why doesn't anyone get to hear James play?"

"Stage fright. He's got a terrible case of stage fright. He's been scheduled to play several times at church but always backs out at the last minute."

The picture of James shaking his head at the choir director flashed in my head.

"But why would someone be afraid to play in *church*? I mean, I can't think of a more forgiving audience."

Barb smirked at my unintentional pun. "You'll have to ask James." She set down her half-empty Coke bottle. "Now what I want to get back to is the subject we changed. What's going on with you two?"

"I honestly don't know," I said, my fingers playing in the little dip above my collarbone. "It's the oddest thing—like a teenage romance."

"You mean you haven't slept together?"

"Barb! A Christian woman like you asking such questions?"

"Christians have sex. How about you?"

"Not with him. There just have been . . . complications."

"Such as?"

"I don't know. . . . I'm attracted to him, but more as a friend. Granted, a friend I like to *neck* with, but that's about it." Suddenly thirsty, I took a sip of Coke. "Besides, the timing for . . . for anything further never seems to be right. Either Rich needs something or Natalie does or . . . or maybe we're both just shell-shocked and afraid to get back into battle."

"Battle is right." She opened a cupboard and foraged around in it. "Boy, you sure can tell a man stocks this thing—there's half a bag of potato chips and some peanuts, but not so much as an M&M."

"Those kids are merciless with those joysticks," said James, coming down the stairs, "but at least I was able to wrestle these away from them." Holding up a bag of Oreos, our savior smiled.

*T*he perfect day continued. Barb thought a walk around Deep Lake was called for—"We need to burn off some of these cookie calories"—but ours was an ambling stroll in which we led the kids in rousing renditions of "On Top of Old Smokey" and "Ninety-Nine Bottles of Beer on the Wall," and I doubt if our calorie burning was significant. (Later I asked Barb if it was appropriate to teach children lyrics like "Take one down, pass it around, ninety-eight bottles of beer on the wall," and she laughed, saying that sometimes you had to forgo what was appropriate for what was fun.)

I told James how much I had enjoyed singing to his accompaniment, hoping that the topic of stage fright would organically arise out of the conversation (I knew some sufferers who were perfectly fine talking about their problem and others who wouldn't admit it to anyone, and I was assuming that since James had never mentioned it, he was in the second camp), but the kids were relentless in their demands to watch this or watch that or play tag.

Everyone's cheeks were red from the cold, but there was no wind, and we could have easily made it around the whole lake except for some less-than-hearty bladders.

"Daddy, I've gotta go to the bathroom!" said Natalie, sidling up to James.

"Me too," said Rich.

"Me three," said Connie.

"How many bottles of pop did you kids have?" Barb asked.

"Not pop, Mom," said Connie with a crooked smile. "Beer. And we had ninety-nine bottles."

"Well, it's a good thing we are where we are, then," I said, pointing up the sloped hill that led to Ann and Riley's house. "We can use the phone to call the cops on you underage boozers."

"Oh, yeah?" said Connie. "I got all the cops around here in my back pocket."

Barb laughed. "We watched an old James Cagney movie last night."

"First one to the back door gets to use the bathroom!" shouted Rich, and we all raced up the hill and to the deck.

Inside, after everyone had relieved themselves, we gathered in the kitchen, debating whether we should continue our walk or get out some board games.

"Hey, what's this?" asked Connie. Picking up a strip of paper off the kitchen table, he read, " 'Ruth, Ruth / She's the truth / Is my truth about love.' " Looking as confused as a foreign dignitary in need of translation at a peace summit, he asked, "What's that supposed to mean?"

"That's an answer," said Rich. "That's an answer to a big question."

This answer, of course, generated even more questions, and so Rich and I told everyone about the book and the people long ago who wrote in it and how we were trying to figure out exactly what to do with it.

We didn't tell them about the big fight we'd had over it on the snow day, or our painful reconciliation. (After having cried himself to sleep, Rich slept for hours; then, finding me in front of the fireplace, he threw his arms around me, begging my forgiveness. That's where the painful part of the reconciliation came in. I was mad at myself for letting a thirteen-year-old boy make the apology I owed *him*. I felt small and petty and *flawed*.) We had spent that evening reading the rest of *The Great Mysterious* and since then had occasionally talked of adding to it, or restoring it, or doing *something* with it. We just hadn't figured out what.

"I wish my family had done something like this," said Barb, sitting down at the table, and opening the book. "I mean, it's just such a piece of history." She read, " 'If you couldn't be a person, what would you be?' " Then, looking up at me, she asked, "Do you mind?"

"Be my guest," I said, and she reached into the paper pocket and withdrew a slip of the old tablet paper.

" 'My first thought was that I'd like to be a bird,' " she read aloud. " 'But then I thought, no. Even though they can fly, they are so little so I think I'd like to be something more substantial, like a tree. A big oak tree in the backyard of a family with lots of children. I'd have a tire swing tied to one branch and, higher up, a tree house nestled into a crook of branches. I would shade that family when they had their summer picnics, and in the fall they would rake up my golden leaves into big piles and jump into them. Maybe there'd even be a little bench under me where a neighbor boy who had spent his youth climbing me would ask the family's daughter if she wanted to marry him. Maybe I'd rustle my leaves a little then in celebration, only they'd think it was just the wind.' "

"Can trees really do that?" asked Natalie. "Make their leaves rustle if they are happy or sad and we think it's just the wind?"

James smiled. "It'd be nice to think that way, wouldn't it?" He looked at me. "Who wrote that one?"

Everyone looked at me expectantly. Just as we did years ago in my great-uncle's cabin, we had all gathered around the table, eager to listen to the answers in *The Great Mysterious*.

"My dad," I said, feeling a little catch in my chest. "Barney Jordan."

"Can I read another one?" asked Conrad.

"Sure."

He reached into the page's pocket, or tried to. His hand, however, had other ideas, and flew to the left. His second attempt was more successful, however, and with a jerk he pulled out a slip of paper.

" 'I would like to be a rose,' " he read, " 'because it's both beautiful and dangerous.' "

Barb laughed. "Did you write that, Geneva?"

Feeling myself blush, I said, "I thought it sounded terribly sophisticated when I was eleven."

James took a turn. " 'I wouldn't want to be anything other than what I am, because what I am was God's plan, and who am I to go against that?' "

All faces again turned to me for clarification. "That was my grandma Hjordis," I said, feeling the same little dip of disappointment I had felt whenever I read one of her answers. I felt she came across as too pious in her writings; where was my fun-loving, playful grandma? I reminded myself that many people didn't express themselves well in writing, but nevertheless, I thought no one would know the real Grandma Hjordis if they judged her on these answers. Natalie, sitting on James's lap, asked if she could read one.

"You'll help me, won't you, Daddy?" she whispered as she reached for a slip of paper, but upon opening it, she smiled and said, "Oh, good, it's printed. 'I think I would be the earth. Then I'd be everything. I'd be mountains and oceans and gold mines and farms and jungles and bat caves and polar ice caps and big cities—everything! I'd be the thing everyone and everything lived on and I'd be a part of everything.' "

"That was a good answer," said Natalie.

"That was my mom's," said Rich proudly. "Right, Aunt Geneva?"

"Yup. Ann always gave good answers."

We took turns with the rest (after reading Grandpa Ole's answer, "I'd like to be my wife's coat because then I could always have my arms around her," Barb said, "It's not fair that you had so many romantic men in your family, Geneva"), and then Connie told his mother to go on to the next page.

"That's it," said Rich. "There aren't any more questions or answers."

"There aren't?" asked Connie, his voice disappointed, and Natalie said, "But there's still a lot of pages left."

"You're right," I said. "But my sister and I only wrote questions for the three nights we were at the cabin. We invited other people to write in more questions, but no one did."

"Then let's write one now," said Connie.

"Yeah!" said Rich. "Let's write one now!"

We were so happy and excited around that table, you'd have thought we were a bunch of Albert Einsteins asked to figure out a mathematical theorem.

We debated whether we should think of the questions as a group or individually and finally decided on the latter. The book was then passed to each person who wanted to write a question in it. It was agreed that only one would be read, and that would be the question we'd all work on.

"We won't have time to answer it now," said James, getting up from his chair. "Nat and I have hockey practice."

"Dad, I can't even skate—why do I need to go?"

"Because I'm one of the coaches," said James. "Now come on, get your jacket."

"Yeah, it's getting late," said Barb. "We've got to go too."

"Mom!" protested Conrad. "Let me write my damn answer!"

"Watch your mouth, Connie."

"We don't need to do it right now," I said. "In fact, we always took the whole next day to answer them. Let's just say the next time we get together, everyone will bring their answer."

"So what's the question?" asked Natalie, putting on her coat.

As everyone looked at me I took it upon myself to open the book to the first new question. I cleared my throat dramatically and then, wondering who had written it, I read the question: "What scares you most in the world?"

"The thought of no video games," said Conrad, and we all laughed.

When I finally went to bed, I felt a lightness of being that comes from a day well spent, so I was anticipating nothing more than sweet dreams when Petunia showed up.

"No," I whispered. "Not now." But yes, it was now. It was now that I knew that even though I had people who loved me, I was still essentially all alone in the world and would always be alone. I thought of Ann writing about how the meaning of life was having someone who could make you feel not so small and lonesome. *Maybe I should call her,* I thought, but I didn't want her worrying about the mental health of her son's caretaker. I would just have to make myself feel better.

You can't do everything, Petunia seemed to say, and I gulped in a huge breath. The oxygen content in the room seemed to be diminishing, and I took another deep breath. My heart revving like a Harley, I turned on the nightstand lamp, knocking my hand against the telephone next to it. *That's it!* I thought. I wouldn't have to pace all night. I'd call—the numbers on the digital clock read 1:08, but it didn't matter—James!

"Hello?" said James, his voice sounding more concerned than sleepy.

"James, it's me. Geneva."

"Geneva! I was just thinking of you."

"You were?" Well, this was nice. I hadn't called expecting to be flattered. "You weren't asleep?"

"Almost." There was a clunk and a pause, and then James said, "Sorry, I dropped the phone. Are you all right?"

I almost chickened out, almost stiffened my upper lip and said, *Fine, just wanted to shoot the breeze,* but instead I said in a small voice, "I'm so scared, James."

"Scared?" said James, as if that was the last thing he'd expected me to say. "Have you been thinking about that question?"

"No," I said after I realized he was talking about the most recent question in *The Great Mysterious* book. "No, it has nothing to do with that. I just get scared sometimes."

"What are you scared about, Geneva?"

And so I proceeded to tell him. Told him how I was scared of being alone, scared of being with the person who was me.

"Geneva," said James, "I *love* being with the person that's you."

My voice thickened with emotion. "You do?"

James laughed softly. "Of course I do. You're funny, fun to be with, full of fun, fun-filled—"

"Oh, James," I said, a catch in my voice. "I know you're trying to make me feel better, but that's not helping. Fun right now sounds sort of shallow." I crawled deeper under the bedcovers, hoping for *some* kind of comfort, since I wasn't getting any from James.

"You're a lot more than fun, Geneva—although that's a big thing in itself. You're kind and caring. Look at how you are with Rich. And you know how to relate to kids and, of course, you're not bad to look at."

I laughed, an on-the-verge-of-tears kind of laugh. "James, I'm not kind and caring—I just sort of fake it."

"You fake being kind and caring?"

I nodded, forgetting that he couldn't see me. "Yes." I was ashamed to admit this. "It doesn't come easy for me, taking care of Rich. I mean, it's sort of dishonest, because I really have to *work* at it and—"

James interrupted me. "Geneva, Rich doesn't care if you have to work at being good to him—all he cares is that you are. Maybe you're just worrying a little too much about this."

"Did I tell you Jean-Paul has four children?"

There was a beat, and then James said, "Jean-Paul your first husband?"

Again nodding even though he couldn't see me, I said, "I saw them last year ice-skating in Rockefeller Plaza. They weren't very good—it looked like it was their first time on skates."

"I'll bet you were a good ice-skater."

I gasped, the kind of sound you make right before you're ready to cry. It was the same noise I'm sure I made when I, who had been shopping, just happened to wander over to watch the skaters. First I had seen Jean-Paul, and then his wife (things hadn't worked out with the woman he'd left me for, but I'd heard his third marriage—to a woman twenty years his junior—was going great), and then the three laughing, wobbly-legged children, calling, "Papa!" and then the name I had been certain I'd be called: "Maman!" I had stared at them, transfixed, and my stare became something Jean-Paul felt. He looked up at me, and after a split second he smiled and then waved, but I turned my head ever so slightly, as if I'd been looking at someone else, and then turned and walked away.

"That's what I thought when I was watching them, James," I said finally, when I had stifled the tears that wanted to come. "I was thinking that those kids would be a lot better skaters if I were their mother."

"I'll have to get you out on an ice rink," said James, and after a minute he added, "Any children you might have would be very special, Geneva."

"I can't have any," I said, feeling my throat thicken. "I'm going through menopause."

"*No.* Women don't usually get that till their mid-forties, right?"

"Bless you, James."

"I didn't sneeze."

"Yeah, but you lied, and it was a good one. You know how old I am."

"Thirty-six? Thirty-seven?"

"Bless you again," I said, chuckling, and then, surprised, I added, "Hey, Petunia's gone."

"Petunia?"

"My loneliness. She's gone."

"You call your loneliness Petunia?"

I couldn't get a reading on his voice, but I thought he sounded pretty *uncertain*. "That's pretty weird, isn't it?"

There was another pause, and I squeezed my eyes shut, waiting for his laughter or his suggestion that I consider taking a long rest in a nice quiet place with staff trained to help people like me.

Instead he said, "I think it's wonderful, Geneva. Only you would have the guts to talk to your loneliness, let alone give it a name like Petunia."

Swimming in a warm bath of relief, I asked, "So you don't think I'm crazy, James?"

"I think you're wonderful."

His voice was a little too earnest, so to avoid any further declarations that I didn't quite know what to do with, I asked, "How about you, James? Have you answered your question about what scares you most? Would it be stage fright?"

"So you heard," he said, and after a long moment I said, "You don't want to talk about it?"

"It's just not that interesting."

"Okay, but if you ever do want to talk about it, maybe I can help you. I am a performer, you know."

"Really?" he said, and I heard the warmth return to his voice. "I had no idea."

I yawned and stated the obvious. "I'm so tired."

"Are you scared anymore?"

"No, just tired."

"Wait a second." I heard various noises, distant clunks, and what sounded like steps, and then James said, "Here's a song I wrote for Natalie. She makes me play it before every hockey game—she says it calms her down."

And on the grand piano that sat in his ex-wife's living room, dear James proceeded to play me the sweetest little song.

"That's lovely," I said. "What's it called?"

" 'Nat's Calm Down Song,' I guess. But tonight I'm calling it 'Melody for Geneva.' "

I don't know how many times he played it; all I know is that eventually I whispered, "Thank you," hung up the phone, and immediately fell asleep.

*T*he dazzling white snow that had been our Halloween legacy was long gone, now looking less like a spectacle of nature than piles of old gray laundry. The sun was as flirty as Scarlett O'Hara with the Tarleton twins, breaking through clouds in spectacular bursts that seemed like personal favors and then retreating for hours, days, and making us all ache for just a glimpse.

It was on one of these days when it seemed the sun Scarlett had taken an extended trip to visit relatives further south that I got a brilliant idea.

A brilliant idea was needed; it had not been a good day. Rich wanted to organize the photographs we'd taken in an album ("Wanna show Mom and Dad what we've been doing while they're gone"), and we had argued over placement of a photograph I had taken of Rich and Conrad as band aides. Curious as to what this title meant, I had called the school's bandleader, who invited me to sit in on an honor band practice.

I had been impressed on many levels: with the skill of the musicians and their ability to handle a Glenn Miller ballad as well as a rousing march; with the bandleader, who despite a nervous constitution (he paced in front of his students, a man full of facial tics and wringing hands) seemed to be doing exactly what he was meant to do in life; and especially with the kids, who not only played well, but treated Conrad and Rich in a special way, by treating them in no special way. (I couldn't help but think of the "special class" in my own elementary school, the class for children with disabilities, whose attendees were teased mercilessly on the playground or in the hallways by the majority of the student body.)

"They just love music," the fidgety Mr. Talerico told me after rehearsal, when Rich and Conrad were putting away sheet music and lugging instrument cases to their owners. "They really can't participate in band the conventional way—I've tried to teach Rich to read a couple of notes, but he gets much too frustrated, and I think Conrad can read music, but he doesn't have enough control of his body to play an instrument"—not once as he spoke did Mr. Talerico look me in the eye—"so I made them band aides. They get to sit in on rehearsals in exchange for running little errands."

Anyway, I'd taken a picture of the boys while the band played "My Way." It was one of those pictures taken at exactly the right moment. Rich was holding the sides of his face in a gesture of glee; Conrad's head was tipped back and his gummy smile was absolutely *huge*. That I thought it was a photograph worthy of its own page was what had caused an argument between me and Rich.

"Want it with other Connie pictures!" he said. "With other Connie pictures!"

I was mad at myself for getting upset in the first place (so what was the big deal where it went?), and Rich was mad at me for being so anal. He abruptly pushed the pages away, knocking over the jar of rubber cement, and I might have been a bit loud in my reminder to "watch what you're doing!"

Then upon discovering that I had made meatloaf instead of ordering Chinese, Rich freaked out—"It's Chinese night! Chinese night!"—and we were as sullen at the dinner table as a couple who'd been married for forty mostly unhappy years. After dinner Barb called and said Conrad wouldn't be going to swimming the next day because he had a cold, which sank Rich into a deeper funk. Then Trevor called during intermission to tell me he was thinking about me, and in our conversation he let me know that Dody Griggs, the movie director, was in the audience that night.

"Dody Griggs?" I whined, feeling like the only girl in the sorority who hadn't gotten an invitation to the big dance. "I'd love to work with Dody Griggs. Why couldn't he see the show when I was in it?"

To continue the downward spiral of the evening, I had to drill Rich on his spelling words, and a good time was *not* had by all. Rich was surly and would give wrong answers to easy questions, and I would correct him, raising my voice with each letter.

It was sleety out too, so I knew I could look forward to a nice coating of ice on the sidewalks and roads, just waiting to sabotage pedestrians and drivers.

Yes, my mood was foul, and so when the brilliant idea came calling, I greeted it like a nun realizing the person knocking on the door of the neglected convent was the Pope.

"Rich!" I said. "Rich!"

His eyebrows furrowed, his lower lip sticking out, Rich looked at me with such contempt *(What's she gonna do now that I'm not gonna like?)* that I had to laugh.

"Rich, how'd you like to blow this joint?"

"Huh?"

"Amscray. Beat it. Hit the road. Take a hike. How'd you like to get out of town and take a little vacation with your Aunt Gen?"

Rich's scowl relaxed, but only by a fraction. "I got school."

"I know you do, silly bean. I'm talking about next week. For Thanksgiving."

He squinted his eyes, still suspicious. "Where to?"

"To Manhattan!"

His silence was deafening, but I ignored it and continued my sales pitch. "Yes, Rich, *Manhattan*—New York City, the Big Apple, Gotham, the crossroads of the world! We'll see some shows, have Thanksgiving dinner at the Waldorf, and take a hansom cab through Central Park."

"What's a handsome cab?"

"It's one whose horses are really good-looking."

Rich considered this for a moment. "We . . . we go to Conrad's house for pie. For pie on Thanksgiving."

"Rich, you can have pie with Conrad anytime. I'm talking New York City! Where the fun never stops!"

"Fun never stops?"

"Never."

He tried to remain tight-lipped, but a smile won out. "Okay," he said, "let's go. Let's go to where the fun never stops."

"Okay!"

"New York City," he said, testing out the words. "But what if my mom and dad say I can't go?"

"They won't," I said. "Hey, that talk about pie made me hungry. Isn't it about time we have some dessert?" I opened the freezer door and saw that I hadn't been on top of the grocery shopping. "Now what'll it be: vanilla ice cream or vanilla ice cream?"

"Vanilla ice cream!" said Rich.

*A*nn wasn't thrilled with the idea of my taking Rich to New York, but she didn't veto it either.

"It's just that Manhattan's so big," she said. "What if he got lost?"

"Ann, I won't let him out of my sight. I'll make it a rule that he has to hold my hand whenever we're out of the apartment."

My sister laughed. "That's a lot of hand holding."

"Oh, Ann, it would be so much fun. I'd have so much to show him, and when will I get another opportunity like this? An opportunity to show him New York without his parents tagging along?"

"Gee, thanks, sis," said Ann. She conferred with Riley a bit and then got back on the phone. "Riley says okay."

"Actually, I think it's a *great* idea, Geneva," he said in the background.

"All right!" I enthused. "So, what kind of time are you having in Italia?"

A *molto bene* time, it turned out. Ann talked breathlessly of dinners at little trattorias, of wandering through museums and coming across paintings she had studied in school, of driving a rented Fiat to Rome and eating cheese and bread and olives while sitting on the steps of the Coliseum.

"And there's different light," she enthused. "The light in Tuscany is different from the light in Florence and different from the light in Rome."

"How so?" I asked. I've been to Italy, but I can't say I was struck by Florentine light versus Venetian light.

"It's hard to explain. In Tuscany the light is so gentle, but sort of autumnal, you know? Coppery at times. And in Rome it's as if it's color-washed—much softer than your usual blaring sunlight."

I let her go on and on; she is a teacher, after all.

*A*fter the community center's house lights came on, signaling the intermission of Natalie's dance recital, James and I sat watching as Rich and Conrad merged into the horde of people that had converged upon the refreshment table. We were debating whether to join them—did we really want punch and cupcakes with sprinkles?—when a woman standing in the doorway by the stage hissed.

"Psst! Mr. O'Neal!" she said, motioning him with her hands. "Mr. O'Neal, come here!"

"Who's *that*?" I asked.

"Miss Nancy," said James, rising. "Natalie's dance teacher. She's directing this whole shebang."

James and the woman conferred, the woman making big, fluttery gestures and shaking her head a lot.

When James returned he was pale and shaking his own head.

"What's the matter?" I asked. "Is Natalie all right?"

"Natalie's fine," he said, "but the pianist isn't. Apparently she felt sick all day but tried to live by the old the-show-must-go-on rule. She's throwing up in the bathroom right now." He wiped his upper lip "I may go join her."

"What do you mean?"

"I mean I'm going to vomit."

"When did you start feeling sick?"

"When Miss Nancy told me Natalie told her that I play piano. Now she wants me to step in."

"What did you say?"

"Well, I said no, of course. But then she went on and on about how disappointed the kids would be if they couldn't dance the rest of their program."

"She has no right to lay that on you," I said, thinking what a bully Miss Nancy was. "Tell her to find someone else—there must be someone else in the audience who can play."

James pulled at the knot in his tie. (I thought it was so sweet that he dressed up for his daughter's recital.)

"I did tell her that, but she said she doesn't want to make an announcement because"—here he made his voice shrill—" 'I don't want a bunch of starstruck housewives duking it out for the opportunity to play in public.' "

"She said *that*?" I wanted to laugh as much as I wanted to throttle the old battleax. "So what are you going to do?"

James wiped his upper lip again. "I guess I'm going to excuse myself, visit a bathroom, and then look over music."

Folding my program into thin pleats, I watched James disappear behind the curtain, admiring his bravery, praying he'd be given more.

"Geneva Jordan?"

I started, turning to look at a slim, dark-haired woman in a power suit. "Yes?"

"Karin O'Neal." She thrust a well-manicured hand at me, and I shook it, squeezing back in response to her tight grip.

"Mind if I sit here?" she asked, sitting down. "I didn't think I'd get here at all, but my meeting ended early and—"

"Oh," I said, as the light of dawn rose over my brain's hemispheres,

"You're *Kare*-in." James had told me how much she hated it when people mispronounced her name, so I don't know why I purposely did so.

"Actually, it's *Kar*-in. And you're Geneva Jordan," she said. "I can't believe I'm sitting next to Geneva Jordan."

"Well, you are," I said as she made herself comfortable in James's empty seat.

"How's Natalie been?"

"Great. She's a good dancer."

"I had my reservations about her being in the recital with her broken arm, but tap dancing really isn't the contact sport hockey is, is it?"

"No, it isn't," I said, agreeing with her statement even as every fiber of me disagreed with *her*.

"Geneva Jordan," she said as if she still didn't believe I was who I was. "I just loved *The Wench of Wellsmore*. Of course, James and I love the theater." Karin's pantyhose made a swooshing sound as she crossed her legs. "But never did I think that we'd actually get to meet one of my favorite Broadway actresses."

I offered one of my fake smiles. I felt like a butterfly whose antennae had been bent; I couldn't quite pick up her signals. Was she patronizing, teasing, or complimenting me? And why did she sound so proprietary, *we* this and *we* that?

"Where's James?" asked Rich, who, along with Conrad, was suddenly standing in front of me.

"You've got frosting all over your face," I said, wiping my nephew's chin with my thumb. "Rich, Conrad, this is Natalie's mother, Mrs.—uh, Karin."

Both boys greeted her politely and then sat down on my other side. "So where's James?" asked Rich again.

The lights flickered then, signaling the end of intermission.

"You'll find out," I said, a tease in my voice, appreciating the what's-going-on look on Karin's face.

After everyone returned to their seats, the lights dimmed, the curtains opened, and a spotlight shone on the middle of the stage.

"Hey," whispered Rich, "there's James at the piano!"

There was a percussive *klick-klack* as a line of tap dancers walked in single file into the spotlight, where they stood beaming their practiced smiles at the audience. The longer they stood there, however, the dimmer the wattage of the smiles, and as they cast furtive looks toward the pianist sitting stage left, I began to silently will James to play.

"Aunt Genny, what's the matter?" whispered Rich.

"James is afraid to play."

"Why? He played so good for us at Sunday school."

I shrugged helplessly, and then Conrad leaned toward me. "Why don't you go up there and sit by him?"

"What?"

Conrad's head waggled back. "He wasn't afraid to play when you were sitting by him."

"I can't go up there," I whispered. I loved to be onstage, but on my own terms.

"This is ridiculous," whispered Karin. "Someone should close the curtain and put him out of his misery."

That was my firing pistol, all I needed to jump out of my seat, and the concerned whispering of the audience got louder as I strode up the side steps to the stage and sat down next to James.

"Oh, God, Geneva," whispered James through clenched teeth. "Help me."

"That's what I'm planning to do," I said. "I'm here to block any tomatoes the audience throws at you."

A weak smile appeared on James's face.

"Now come on, James," I said, pressing my thigh against his. "Let's rock and roll."

He struck a tentative chord, and then another one, and then a few bars of music. The girls, hearing their cue, began to tap to "The Girl from Ipanema."

The audience rewarded that number with thunderous applause, but each number in the first act had been given an over-the-top ovation; still, to my ears it sounded louder.

"That was excellent, James," I whispered, my voice as soothing as a nurse's. "Now let's start the second number."

Making sure my thigh never lost contact with his, I turned the pages (let them think this was planned!) as James played "Jailhouse Rock" and "Yellow Bird," but it wasn't until "I'm an Old Cowhand" that I could tell he was enjoying himself, that he had set aside his fear and was giving the music free rein.

The girls (this wasn't a coed group, like Natalie's hockey team) danced to "Fever" and "If I Had a Hammer," and then James struck a chord and launched into "Splish Splash," his daughter's big number.

Natalie and three little girls, wearing pink towel turbans and pink bathrobes, emerged from behind a cardboard tub, blowing bubbles. Natalie was able to hold her bottle of soap solution in the hand of her broken arm, and with her other hand she dipped the wand in and out of the solution. A clattering line of girls in pink tutus came out tap-dancing from each side of the stage, flanking the bubble makers. The cuteness factor couldn't have been higher, especially when some of the girls, distracted by the bubbles, got the giggles. A pigtailed girl, who in my professional opinion had been trying to upstage everyone all night long, hissed at the gigglers, which did not have its desired effect.

"Stop it!" she said, clapping her hands like a crabby old teacher.

The clapping fueled the gigglers like a good joke.

The bubbles weren't flying so fast and furious either; Natalie and the other blowers, getting into the spirit of things, were giggling themselves, especially when Natalie's turban untwisted. That left one girl (obviously a cohort of the bossy spotlight hog) frantically blowing bubbles, trying to keep up the stage picture.

I looked toward the front row and saw Karin sitting with her arms crossed and looking disapprovingly at Rich and Connie, who were in the throes of laughter. James was keeping a steady beat for the distracted tappers. This was not such a special feat unless you consider that he also was laughing—not nearly as hard as some of the dancers, but hard enough so that his shoulders shook.

That's all the permission I needed, and my laughter joined James's and the rest of the audience's (except for Karin and probably the parents of the grim little do-gooders). Then, in a demonstration of poetic justice, the pigtailed girl slipped on some of the bubble solution spilled by the giggling girls and burst into tears.

"Mom!" she wailed, sinking into her slough of pink net.

The curtain closed and took a while to rise again for the dancers, who tapped and tangoed to "La Cucaracha." James performed admirably through several more numbers (no one would have suspected he wasn't the recital's regular pianist; his "Stand by Me" and "Under the Boardwalk" were especially inspired), but as far as the audience was concerned, the show could have ended with "Splish Splash"; we all recognized a grand finale when we saw it.

"You did it!" I said after Miss Nancy had dragged James to center stage to take a bow. "You did it!"

"Thanks to you," said James, hugging me.

Collecting Conrad and Rich, we joined the other parents and well-wishers in the common room. Miss Nancy stood at the door, allowing people in only after they offered their praises and congratulations. Karin was already there, talking with the mother of the pigtailed girl, who had sort of redeemed herself in a solo near the end of the show. She was no Cyd Charisse, clomping around as she did to "Fever," but you had to admit she had guts, coming out again after the bubble number debacle. One truth about show biz: In a cage match between talent and guts, guts wins more often than you'd think.

"Nat!" said James, bending down to hug his daughter. "That was great! You were the most graceful girl with a broken arm out there."

"Thanks, Dad," she said, elbowing him in the side. "And nice piano playing . . . *not*."

"Why, you. . . ," said James, pretending to lunge at her.

"I liked that 'Splash' dance," said Rich. "That was *funny*."

"*Really* funny," added Conrad.

Natalie's eyes lit up. "Wasn't it?"

As if hearing her cue line, Karin came bustling over.

"Natalie, before we go, I want you to apologize to Cassie."

"But Mom, I already did!"

"No, you apologized to Cassie's mother."

"Come on, Nat," said James. "I'll go with you."

Natalie took Rich's hand; apparently she wanted lots of support, leaving me alone with Karin.

"Listen, Geneva," said Karin, and there was something in her tone of voice that made me want to correct her: *Miss Jordan to you*. But I didn't; in some strange way the woman intimidated me.

"I don't know what your relationship with James is, but if it's anything more than good friends, let me warn you: He's a very confused man."

I looked at her, too surprised to say anything.

Karin flicked aside a shank of her pageboy. "It's been his dream to perform—certainly he's always had the talent, but never the confidence. He wanted to be a concert pianist, did he ever tell you that?"

"Well, he certainly plays beautifully."

"Yes, he's finally able to get through this stage fright thing, and where does he decide to debut? At a children's dance recital." Karin shook her head. "Isn't that just typical."

You're worse *than he says you are!* I wanted to scream, but instead I only managed a feeble "Excuse me" before walking away in search of some of the oxygen she had sucked out of the room.

"She said that?" James asked later, his breath vaporous in the cold night air.

After Rich had fallen asleep on the couch I had said, "It sure would be nice to sit out in the hot tub," and James had said, "Let's," even though it was still broken and there was no water in it. So there we were, in our coats and hats and gloves, sitting under a frosty sky in an empty hot tub.

"She said that I chose to *debut* at a children's dance recital?"

I nodded. "I think you might have made an even bigger mistake in the love department than I did."

James laughed. "She was nice . . . once."

"So, James," I said, tapping my boots together to warm up my toes. "Did you really want to be a concert pianist?"

"Why I ever told her that I'll never know." Shaking his head, he rubbed his jaw with the backs of his fingers, and I could hear by the faint scraping sound that he needed a shave. For a long time it was the only sound he made. Finally, he said, "When I was in junior high I thought about it—I had a teacher who seemed to think I had a shot at it, but I came to realize the teacher's standards weren't all that high. Anyway, in high school I got away from classical music and played keyboard in a couple of different bands, and I realized that there was a whole wide musical world I could be part of. I could be in a jazz group or a rock-and-roll band, or I could even see myself in an orchestra pit on Broadway."

"Wouldn't it have been fun if we'd been in the same show?"

A wistful look came over James's face, making him look younger. "Yup. That would have been something."

"So what happened?" I asked, taking his hand and tucking it under my arm.

The wistfulness hardened slightly into an expression of resignation.

"On my world tour that I told you about," he began, his voice soft, "Well, along with those odd jobs I told you about, I'd often persuade a club owner or bartender to let me play. I never made a lot of money, but I got to try out songs I'd been working on in my head." He filled his cheeks with air and exhaled. "Anyway, once I was playing in this little dive in Barcelona, and a woman started screaming at me, and while I was apologizing to her for not playing music she liked, she threw a bottle of wine right at my head."

"You're kidding," I said, the standard reply to a bizarre story.

James shook his head. "I woke up in the back room with a bloody towel over the goose egg I had growing on my forehead."

"You were knocked out?"

James nodded. "So when you sat by me tonight and said you'd block any tomatoes the audience threw at me, I thought, 'You don't know what a distinct possibility that is.' "

I gave a little laugh. "Did that woman say why she'd do such a thing?"

"No one ever talked to her—she ran out as soon as she launched the bottle, so I never heard whether it was because she hated my music, or I reminded her of her philandering husband, or what. The owner just spun his finger beside his temple and said she must have been *loco*. Everyone said I shouldn't take it personally, and I didn't—I played there again the next day and the next—but I was getting jumpier and jumpier. Anytime anyone moved fast, I assumed they were ready to pounce. Finally I just quit and left for Portugal the next day."

"And you never played in public again?"

James laughed. "No, as a matter of fact, I wound up in a little club in Lisbon. I stayed there for almost a month, but it was still hard to get that old ease back. I was always nervous, always wondering if I was about to be clobbered, or worse. But it wasn't until I got back to the States and a friend asked me to play at his wedding that I just froze up. Couldn't go on."

"Oh, James."

"I felt so *stupid*, like such a loser. I was sitting up there in the choir loft with the bride and groom and everyone's looking at me expectantly, and I just couldn't play. I don't know what made me feel worse—knowing how scared I was or knowing how much I was disappointing my friend."

"Oh, James," I said again.

"Every now and then I'd try to play in public—I tried to play in church the first time we met—but I just can't seem to *unfreeze*."

"But you played so well at Sunday school."

James shrugged. "I must not find thirteen-year-olds intimidating. Besides, I was only accompanying you, and you were right by me. Just like you were by me tonight."

"Have you ever tried to get help for it?"

"I took a course in self-hypnosis, but anytime I tried to put myself into a suggestible state, I fell asleep. I've read some books. . . ." James shook his head and then, sighing, leaned his head against the back of the tub. "Let's not talk about it anymore. Let's not do anything but enjoy the force of these pulsating jets."

"Right," I said, leaning back too. "And hand me my fruity tropical drink, will you?"

"You want it in the scooped-out pineapple or the scooped-out coconut?"

"Hmm . . . make it the coconut."

We indulged in our fantasy world until a wind that in no way could be mistaken for a sea breeze whipped by.

"You know," said James, sitting up and folding his arms across his chest, "someone should fix this thing. What's the matter with it anyway?"

"Ann says the pump motor's broken." I looked around the redwood shell, imagining it filled with churning, bubbling water. "Could you fix it?" I asked hopefully.

"Could I fix a simple hot tub pump?" He shook his head as if his feelings were hurt that I even had to ask. Then, looking up at the cloudy night sky, he said, "No."

I laughed. So you're not a handyman, eh, James?"

"Depends on what you mean by handyman."

I smiled at his little flirtation. Then, with thoroughly bad timing, I told him that I was planning to take Rich to New York for Thanksgiving.

"Aw, Geneva," said James after a long pause, "the end of November is coming fast enough anyway."

Ann and Riley were scheduled to come back the Saturday after Thanksgiving; I'd be heading home the next day.

"Why do you want to give us less time than we already have?"

"I just thought Rich and I could use some special time together."

"I thought we could too."

I stared at him. I consider myself an advanced student of human psychology—you have to be if you want to be a good actor—but regarding James, well, I was fairly clueless. What did this man want from me, and what did I want from this man? Except for our rogue kissing, our relationship, chaperoned as it was by Rich and Natalie, was still nineteenth-century, and I wasn't sure if either one of us wanted to push it to the present.

Well, maybe James did. In his slippery parka he had slid over to me, and now he put his arm around me.

"I don't get what we are together," I said softly.

"We're a man and woman together," he said, and after I laughed at his overtly husky voice, he asked, "Have you ever made love in a hot tub?"

"Uh . . . not in an empty one."

"Me neither."

When he kissed me his nose touched my face, and it was so cold I nearly drew back, but passion has a way of quickly thawing out the coldest of extremities. My heart raced, and so did my mind. Did I want to do this? (I thought I did.) Wasn't James just a good friend? (A good friend who happened to be a *great* kisser.) If I let things go further, would I be leading him on? (Leading him on to *where*, and did I want to go there?)

Abandoning the question-and-answer period, I gasped (I was gasping a lot) as we got our hands underneath the layers of outerwear; what an engine of warmth his body was on such a cold night! I was sure that once we got our clothes off, our bodies, like our breaths, would be throwing off steam. It was the sensuous experience that hot tubs are known for. That it was lacking water seemed totally inconsequential; we were still flowing in a mighty strong current.

But fate was still not willing to bring the two of us together, for the one time we had passed through the checkpoints and all systems were go was the one time Rich, who normally slept like a log (a *petrified* log), started screaming.

"Good heavenly days," I said, and James was just as fast as I was getting out of the empty tub, through the French doors, and into the living room.

"Rich!" I said, running to my nephew, who was sitting on the couch, clutching a pillow to his chest, his face twisted in fear, his scream a low bleat, like that of a sheep who's finally been caught by the wolf.

"Rich!" I said again, taking him in my arms. "Rich, it's all right." The bleating continued.

"I don't think he's awake," said James.

"What?"

"It used to happen to Natalie when she was little—she'd have these night terrors, and she'd scream and cry, but she's not awake. She wouldn't even remember it in the morning."

I looked at Rich's eyes, but they didn't focus back on mine. Instead they looked far off, at something I couldn't see.

My heart pounded, and my temples did too; I was tempted to put my hand over Rich's mouth to stop that horrible sound.

"What should I do?"

"There's nothing you can do," said James, sitting at the foot of the couch, where there was still room. "He'll wear himself out. For now, just hold him."

Chapter 9

ll great cities have multiple personalities, but New York City is the Sibyl of them all. Sometimes a thug, sometimes a grand dame, a romantic balladeer or a smooth con artist, New York can change moods as quickly as a person walks across its streets. (I refuse to use the feminine to describe a place or thing and am offended when anyone else does; once Trevor described a yacht we'd been invited on to as "she," and I asked, "Where's her vagina?") But when Rich and I visited, New York was on its best behavior, a cosmopolitan host welcoming its guests with open arms.

I gave him the super-deluxe let's-show-the-yahoo-from-the-sticks-the-big-city tour. We saw the Rockettes dance ("They look like scissors," Rich said of their synchronized kicking legs); we went to the Empire State Building and the Guggenheim Museum ("I'm dizzy," Rich claimed as we wound our way around the exhibits). We strolled down Fifth Avenue ("Where's everybody come from?" asked Rich, greeting practically every one of them with "Hey, pal"), browsed through FAO Schwarz, took a hansom cab through Central Park, and had late-afternoon dessert at the Algonquin.

Rich beamed anytime I was approached by a fan, offering his autograph as a bonus. Scribbling on a torn-off corner of an FAO Schwarz bag and handing it to a woman who had gushed about my performance in *Mona!*, he had said, "I'm Rich."

"My nephew," I added.

"Oh," said the woman, pocketing both autographs. "Well, young man, I hope you know how special your aunt is."

My nephew shook his head. "No, *I'm* special."

Rich loved that I got the joke, that I understood the word *special* and how many times it had been used to describe him. He laughed at my laughter, and the poor woman, not understanding anything, fled. It was at moments like these that I marveled in the relationship we were forging. Moments like these were happening more and more, when I forgot I was the baby-sitter watching the poor kid with Down syndrome and realized I was in the company of somebody I really *liked*.

After our Thanksgiving dinner at the Waldorf, we went back to the apartment, and Rich called his friend Conrad.

"Eat two pieces for me!" he said, and after hanging up the phone, he looked at me and said, "Pumpkin pie and pecan pie— my favorites."

He promptly burst into tears.

"We always have pie together on Thanksgiving!" he said when he had calmed down enough to speak. "Always. Connie always has pumpkin and I have pecan. I *love* pecan pie." He sniffed, and his eyebrows almost formed an inverted V over his eyes. He covered his face with his hands and began to cry again.

I rubbed his back, and it was only when I had to stop because my arm had gotten sore that I realized he was asleep.

There was a strange peacefulness in my apartment, which I attributed to the crackling fire and the sleeping boy on the couch. I couldn't remember being alone in my apartment with a sleeping child—Rich, of course, had slept here during past visits, but his parents were always present—and it made me sad to think of how different my life would have been if there had been a child or two to tuck in at night.

On a scale of one to ten, one being euphoria and ten being a visit from Petunia at her most dark and bleak, I was feeling about a five and a half—depressed, but sociably depressed, meaning I wanted to share it with somebody. If love shared multiplies, then depression shared shrinks . . . or at least becomes something you can make fun of. I knew that many of my friends spent Thanksgiving out of the city, including Claire, who was spending the holidays at her Connecticut house, and so I found myself dialing a number I'd dialed hundreds of times: Trevor's.

His machine answered now, and I stammered some message about being in town and just wanting to wish him a happy Thanksgiving even though he was an Englishman who thought America, as well as the rest of the world's countries, should be a British colony, and had he staged a protest dinner by eating plum pudding and a steak-and-kidney pie?

I hung up the phone, wishing immediately I could hit an erase button, embarrassed over my strained and long-winded meanderings.

Fortunately, my housekeeper hadn't stolen my entire wine reserve (not even a bottle, I noticed; I wondered if I could be that honest in the face of all that expensive nectar of the gods), and I opened a bottle of merlot.

Tiptoeing back into the living room, I sat in one of the big overstuffed chairs that, along with the couch, form my fireside conversation area and chugged down *vino* like it was water and I'd just run a marathon. The second glass I savored, taking tiny sips that I accentuated with long sighs. Rich interrupted his soft snores to murmur something about a shoe, and I got up to readjust the cashmere throw on his shoulders.

If you can't have company in your depression, the next best thing is to really feed it, to *submerge* yourself in it, so I put on a tape a friend of mine made for me, a compilation featuring Frank and

Tony and Ella and Billie singing songs that made you want to jump off a bridge, or at the very least cry like a baby. Rich stirred a bit but didn't wake up, leaving me to listen to "Good Morning Heartache" and "September Song," a line of tears dripping dramatically into my wineglass.

It was when I was at the peak of sodden, tipsy tearfulness that my buzzer rang with news from my doorman: "Trevor Waite to see you, Miss Jordan."

My first impulse was to scream. My second impulse, which is the one I followed, was to swallow and in a very controlled voice say, "Well, send him up, Charles."

Then, like Margaret Dumont being chased by the Marx Brothers, I made a mad dash to the bathroom, where I splashed cold water on my face and raked my hair with splayed fingers. As I was swiping lipstick across my mouth I heard a soft knock on the door (it was an affectation of Trevor's never to ring the bell, but to knock softly, as if it didn't matter whether anybody let him in or not).

Taking a deep breath and sucking in my stomach, I walked slowly to the door, as if it didn't matter to me whether he came in or not.

"Geneva," he said, wrapping me in his arms as soon as I'd opened the door. "Geneva, it's so good to see you."

"Good to see you," I said, wriggling out of his embrace, knowing that if I didn't grab control right off the bat, I'd run amok.

"So is the baby-sitting gig up?" he said, his voice in its booming I'm-an-actor mode.

I put my finger to my lips, nodding at the couch where imperturbable Rich slept on.

"Oh," said Trevor in a stage whisper. "So the two of you've come back, hmm?"

"Just till tomorrow," I said, leading him through the dining room and into the kitchen, where we could talk more freely.

Apparently Trevor wanted to do more than talk. No sooner had I opened the freezer to get some ice (he was a scotch-on-the-rocks man) than he pushed the door shut with the palm of his hand and swooped his arms around me.

Like I said, I was trying to maintain control, but that quickly became an exercise as futile as trying to resist a tornado. I think we would have copulated right there on the kitchen tile if, in our frenzied groping, I hadn't bashed my head against the counter edge. I am no masochist; pain does not figure into my pleasure principle.

"Ouch," I whined, rubbing the back of my head. "Am I bleeding?"

Trevor took my hand away and parted my hair. "No, but you should sit down. I'll make you a cup of tea."

He led me over to the kitchen table and then began preparing tea. He was familiar with my kitchen and knew where everything was, and despite my throbbing head, I enjoyed watching him fill the teapot and open cupboards.

"I thought we were going to have a drink."

"Alcohol's no good for a head injury. Besides, if we do anything, I don't want you to be able to use the excuse 'Well, we were drunk.' "

"Trevor," I said, my face warming, "what are you implying I'll need an excuse for?"

If blushing tells too much, so does the awkward look that people who don't blush get, and it was this look that Trevor had on his Anglican face.

He turned away, but not before I saw it.

"Well," he said, pretending that the teapot, which had not yet reached a boil, demanded his attention. "Well, you know. If I stay the night."

"Do you think I want you to stay the night?"

"One can hope."

One can hope. Laughing, I told him he sounded like a polite schoolboy being asked what he thought his chances with the young French tutor were.

"Geneva, I've missed you!"

I was taken aback by the urgency in his voice; it was as if we were playing a scene from a romantic comedy and suddenly switched to Greek tragedy.

Trevor rushed over to me then and, falling to his knees, wrapped his arms around me and proceeded to sob into my lap. My reaction fell somewhere in between flabbergasted and flummoxed. I could understand Rich falling apart, but this was very unusual behavior from a man whose personal sense of style did not include wearing his heart on his sleeve.

"Trevor," I said, extricating his head from my lap (I couldn't suck in my gut forever), "what's gotten into you?"

"You have!" He scrambled up then, making quick dabs at his nose with his wrist. He sat down on the chair across the table and looked at me, his expression hard to read, sort of a mixture of confusion and hope.

"Geneva," he said after clearing his throat. "Every girl—woman— after you has been . . . I don't know . . . not enough."

I was struck by the sentiment but also suspicious. How many girls—women—besides Li'l Miss Silicone had there been after me?

"How do you expect me to respond to that?" I said finally. I knew I sounded like a clinician, but I was trying to introduce a little rationality into this whole thing.

Trevor cleared his throat again. "Well, I'd hope you'd fling yourself into my arms and say no man after me has been enough either." He shrugged, looking more boyish by the second. "Of course, that's probably not what you had in mind, is it?"

My blush, not cutting me any slack, returned. "Trevor . . . this is all . . . such a surprise."

"Is it? Didn't you feel something when we talked?"

I shrugged, not really knowing the answer. We had had only a few telephone conversations—three, to be exact—while I was in Minnesota, and if the first one had been tentative, the last one definitely had been full of teasing and innuendo. But I *liked* to flirt; did it mean more because it was with Trevor? He was attractive, that's for sure—I mean, you don't make *People* magazine's list of the fifty sexiest people if you're some average Joe—but was it the normal attraction anyone would feel for a debonair actor with icy blue eyes and a British accent, or was it me, Geneva, feeling attraction for her old beau Trev? Because then that attraction would have to be shared with the knowledge of our history . . . nah, why spoil the moment?

I left my chair and before you could say "Have you really thought this over?" I was on his lap, laying on him one big, wet, juicy kiss.

"Oh, Geneva!" he said, breaking free. "This time it will be different!"

He kissed me back, meeting my passion, and once again it seemed as if we were going to practice an entirely different kind of culinary art when in walked Rich.

"Aunt Gennie?"

I shot up like a jack-in-the-box.

"Rich," I said, smoothing back my hair. "Rich . . . this is my friend Trevor."

My nephew's smile was sly, as if his definition of the word *friend* and mine were somewhat different.

"Hey, pal," he said, sticking out his hand.

Trevor wore a polite, slightly confused smile. "Well . . . hey." The two shook hands.

"You were kissing my aunt."

Trevor laughed. "Well, yes, I was. You don't mind, do you?"

Rich's grin increased. "Kissing's okay, I guess. What's your name again?"

"Trevor. Trevor Waite. Your aunt Geneva and I were in a play together."

"Trevor Waite," repeated Rich, and then, as if he were issuing a command, he said, "Trevor—wait!"

"Clever," said Trevor, smiling. "Now I suppose you're looking for a bedtime snack?"

Rich nodded, and that's how the three of us wound up sitting at the table on Thanksgiving night eating eggs Trevor had scrambled and telling knock-knock jokes and making quite a wholesome picture, I must say.

"It's so pretty, Auntie Gen," said Rich as the plane began its descent into the Minneapolis–St. Paul airport. I leaned forward to look out of the little oval window. Everything looked as if it were covered in bridal satin, miles and miles of bridal satin.

I patted Rich's knee and smiled. "It's beautiful, Rich."

Being on cloud nine had been an apt description of my feelings during the flight—it had been as nonturbulent as a bus ride across the prairies, but I hadn't needed physical stimulation. I was too occupied with my thoughts, replaying over and over the moment when Trevor asked me to marry him.

We had taken our cue from Rich; after he'd gone to bed, so did we. Trevor is a great technician and proud of it, but something more was brought to the bed, a tenderness and appreciation that comes with second chances. I wept afterward, not for any dramatic effect but for the release I desperately needed. I was filled with emotions—happy and sated, nervous, unsure, and scared. Trevor held me until I stopped bawling and then whispered into my ear, "Gen, will you marry me?"

His voice was soft as only a whisper can be, but his words—

always enunciated—were crystal clear. Still, out of surprise, I asked, "Huh?"

It wasn't the most romantic of responses, but at least it was honest. I was floored by the question.

"Are you serious?"

Disappointment settled into Trevor's features.

"Of course I am," he said, sitting up and brushing the top sheet with his hand, as if there were crumbs there.

I sat up too. It's always a good idea to be around the same height as the person you're having a serious discussion with—especially in bed.

"Well, Trevor, you can't really expect me to give you an answer now, can you?" My voice had that high whining, pleading pitch to it that I cannot abide in anyone else, but hey, when you get a marriage proposal from a guy you were sure you had no future with, any lack of voice control can be excused.

Trevor's jaw clenched and unclenched, but then he finally turned to me and, smiling, said, "I guess not, Geneva. But give it some thought. The offer stands until it's either accepted or declined."

I smiled back, ready to snuggle into his arms and drift off into a safe, protected sleep, but the theme of Trevor's evening seemed to be surprise, and he continued on in that theme by sliding out of bed.

"Trevor," I said, watching him get dressed, "you're not going to stay?"

"I wish I could," he said, buttoning his custom-made shirt, "but I've got an early audition tomorrow."

"For what?" I asked. Nothing piques an actor's curiosity more than hearing another speak of an audition.

Trevor cocked one black eyebrow. "Pour Deux is looking for a spokesman."

"Purdue the college or Perdue the chicken?"

He laughed, zipping up his pants. "Okay, so my French is a little off. Pour Deux," he said, this time pronouncing it correctly. " 'For two.' It's this new cologne they're planning a big campaign for, and I've got a callback—it's between me and two other actors from the coast."

"Oh. Well, good luck."

"Thank you, my dear." He blew a kiss at me. "Now go to sleep and call me when you get to Minneapolis."

*T*hat Trevor didn't spend the night saved me from making any explanations to Rich, but still, I would have preferred that he spend the night and then, after a leisurely breakfast, take Rich and me to the airport. I know, however, that even as much as I deserve it, I can't always have my way.

I had bought Rich a little electronic game that occupied him during most of the flight, leaving me to reflect on Trevor's proposal. But now that the plane had landed, I had to let go of reflection and concentrate on the business of getting our baggage and getting home.

Barb had offered to pick us up, and I was not above taking her up on her very generous offer, but when I called there was no one home. So after I left a message, Rich and I walked downstairs to the taxi stand and made one particular driver very happy by giving him such a nice beefy fare.

"*Y*ou were kissing Trevor," Rich reminded me as we did the dishes we'd dirtied making hot chocolate. Ann and Riley have a dishwasher, but washing dishes is one of the few household tasks I actually enjoy. I find it soothing, of all things, to plunge my hands into soapy dishwater, scour a pot until all the gunk is off, and then rinse it clean. And Rich was the type of wiper every washer hopes for, companionable and jokey. Plus he never handed back dishes with the taunt "You missed a spot."

Now I looked at my grinning nephew.

"So?" I said. "Is there anything wrong with kissing?"

His smile grew ever slyer. "You kiss James too." He frowned. "Does James know you were kissing Trevor?"

"No, James does not know I was kissing Trevor, because it's none of his business. Just like it's none of my business if he was kissing someone else."

"Why? Why wouldn't it be your business?"

I stopped scrubbing the skin of hot chocolate off the pan, realizing I would probably take the finish off if I scrubbed any more, and handed it to Rich.

"Because," I said finally, "James and I aren't boyfriend and girlfriend."

"Then why do you kiss him?"

Now I attacked a ladle with the abrasive side of the sponge.

"I don't know," I said, giving him a nonanswer. "And besides, you can kiss more than one person."

Rich's wink went beyond broad—his glasses tipped and one whole side of his face grimaced as he squeezed shut his eye.

"What?" I said, laughing in spite of myself. "Don't you think someone can kiss more than one person?"

"I guess," he said, and once again, quicker than you can say "mood swing," he stuck out his lower lip and frowned.

I laughed harder, not knowing what he was suddenly upset about, but figuring I could tease him out of it. "All it means, Rich," I said, rinsing some silverware and standing it up in its compartment in the corner of the drying rack, "is that you're popular. And there's nothing wrong with being popular."

Rich looked at me with such pain in his face that I drew my

breath in, and that quick blast of oxygen was all I needed to come to my senses. How could I be so obtuse?

"Rich . . ."

He shrugged away the hand I put on his shoulder.

"Hannah kissed Conrad, 'member?" he said, looping the damp towel over the oven door handle. "He got kissed at camp last year too. *I'm* going to camp this year."

"And you'll probably be kissed as well."

Rich shrugged again and left the kitchen. I followed him into the living room and sat next to him when he plopped on the couch.

"Conrad says that too. He says, 'We'll make sure you get damn well kissed.' Is that bad, Aunt Gennie, that I said that word? 'Cause that's what Connie said."

"Nah, you were just quoting."

"Connie says if his girlfriend goes to camp again, she'll have a friend for me." Rich wiped his nose with the heel of his hand and looked at me. "But what if Connie's girlfriend doesn't have a friend? Who will kiss me then?"

"Well . . . another girl. Another girl who you'll find all by yourself."

"Couldn't do that," said Rich, his eyes filling with tears. "Couldn't find a girl without Connie. He's the one girls like—even though he's a spaz."

"Rich," I scolded.

"That's what Connie says," he said defensively. "He calls himself a spaz all the time."

"But still . . ." I watched as tears began to roll down my nephew's face. "Oh, Rich." I held my arms out, and he flung himself into them.

"You think I'm a baby," he said after he'd cried for a good five minutes.

"No, I don't. I think you're wonderful." His head still rested on my chest, and I pushed his sandy blond hair off his forehead. "But I think the girls would like you just as much as Conrad."

Rich sat up, shaking his head violently. "He makes them laugh. They like that. He's not scared of them . . . like me."

He burrowed his chin into his collar, and I lifted it with my finger.

"Everybody's a little scared when it comes to liking someone."

"Are you?" asked Rich. "You scared with James?"

"With James?" I was not so much startled by the question as I was the name. "Rich, I don't like James."

"You don't like James?"

"Of course I like James. But not in *that* way. Not the way I like, say, Trevor."

"But you kiss James too!"

I cast a cool eye at my nephew, who obviously had cast some cool—and unseen—eyes in my direction.

"Well . . ." I said, stalling for time. "Well, I like James enough to kiss him, but I like Trevor more." I cringed inwardly, hearing myself sound like the sweetheart of Sigma Chi.

"Never kissed a girl once," said Rich. "Not on the lips. I'd like to kiss a girl on the lips."

"It'll happen."

"That's what Conrad says. Conrad says girls will stand in a big line waiting to kiss us."

I laughed. "He's probably right."

"Conrad says once they kiss us, they won't like kissing anybody else." His smile was huge, but it didn't have much staying power. "Do you think that's true?"

"I don't know," I said. "Could be."

Rich sat contemplating this for a moment. Through the big picture window I could see that both dusk and snow had begun to fall. I thought about starting a fire, but I was so comfortable on the couch that I didn't want to get up. When Rich spoke again, his voice was barely a whisper.

"Aunt Gen, you think I'll ever get married?"

My heart sank. "I don't know, Rich," I said, trying to keep my voice light. "What do your mom and dad say about that?"

"They say to wait and see."

I was ready to jump in with some platitude, but I knew Rich didn't need and didn't want some phony rah-rah cheer. For a long moment we sat there, shoulders touching, listening to the almost too-quiet sound of the house creaking.

"Conrad says he *definitely* is getting married," said Rich finally, pronouncing the word "defnetwy," "but I'm not sure about me. I *want* to get married, but what if no one wants to marry me? Miss Merserau—she's special ed—she says sometimes Down syndrome people aren't *mature* enough to get married."

I felt tears well in my eyes, but then Rich, surprising me, laughed.

"What's so funny?"

"Conrad said, 'Just for that, Miss Merserau, we won't invite you to Rich's wedding.' "

I chuckled now. "Conrad said that?"

Rich nodded. "Says things like that all the time. He's so funny." He folded his blunt fingers and rested his chin on top of them. "He says Miss Merserau is just an old stick-in-the-mud. Other times he's called her swear words." He laughed. "What's a stick-in-the-mud?"

I thought for a moment. "Someone without a lot of imagination." I looked at my watch. Barb probably was laying out Thanksgiving leftovers on the table about now. "How about you call him up?"

"Call Conrad up—yeah!"

I left him and went to forage in the kitchen for something that might resemble dinner.

The kitchen gods were with me; I found a container in the freezer labeled, in Ann's pretty writing, "lasagna." As I put the container in the microwave I wondered if my sister's lasagna recipe would change now that she'd been to Italy. I smiled, thinking of Ann and the delight in her voice as she described the light in our last telephone conversation. I was still smiling as I inspected a head of lettuce that was only slightly wilted, and I realized my mood at the moment was contentment: I was perfectly happy to have a warmed-up lasagna dinner and slightly wilted salad with my nephew, with nothing more exciting on the agenda than building a fire.

Obviously Barb and Conrad were not aware of my cozy plans for the evening.

"Aunt Gen, Connie's not home," said Rich, joining me in the hallway as I went to answer the persistent doorbell. "He—Connie!"

"Hi, Rich!" said Conrad as I opened the door to find him and his mother there.

"Come on, come on, get your coats. We don't want to be late."

"Be late?" I said. "Be late for what?"

Barb wagged her finger at Rich. "Did you forget to tell your aunt about tonight?"

Rich looked perplexed. "Tell my aunt about what?"

"About the game!" said Conrad. "Remember we talked about it when you called me on Thanksgiving?"

Rich slapped his palm against his forehead. "Oh, yeah." He looked at me. "I did forget."

Barb was pulling my coat from the front closet. "Come on, Geneva, we don't want to miss the first face-off."

"The first what?"

"Face-off. Of Natalie's game. Come on now, hurry up. I left my car running."

*L*ittle girls were swarming around the ice like padded, clumsy insects.

"What's the score?" asked Rich.

"I don't think they've started yet," said Barb. "I think they're just warming up. See, the coaches are skating with them."

"There's James!" said Rich, pointing.

We all waved at him, but he didn't notice us.

Natalie did, though, waving to us from the bench with the broken arm that prevented her from being on the ice.

"It's cold in here," said Conrad as his mother, holding his arm, helped him up the bleachers.

"That's why we won't be taking our jackets off," said Barb. Our timing was perfect; the players were skating back to their benches just as we sat down.

Watching them reminded me of the many winter nights Ann and I had walked down to our local park to skate on the rink they made by flooding the ball field. We were pretty good figure skaters, practicing our twirls and elaborate backward moves, but I always wanted to get into the hockey rink. It looked fun smacking that puck around, plus that was where all the boys were. The hockey rink was like a tree house, however, with a sign reading No Gurls Alowed, and the rule was strictly enforced. Now I marveled at these little girls, all suited up, their faces serious underneath the plastic cages of their face masks.

"This is so much more serious than their practice was," I said. The whole atmosphere of the rink had changed; this was a *game*.

"Makes you wish we had that opportunity when we were kids, huh?" asked Barb, reading my mind. I told her as much.

"We had after-school basketball," said Barb, "where we played our own schoolmates—juniors against seniors."

We watched as a little girl whipped across the rink with the puck, her shot just barely stopped by the goalie. Her mother—one of the three chic women I had sat by at practice—jumped up in excitement and then sat down, dejected.

"Yeah, I was hell on wheels. Even my dad said I was a better ball player than my brother." Barb scraped her upper lip with her bottom teeth. "And he went to the state championships."

"No kidding."

"No kidding," she said, shaking her head.

I looked across the rink to where James stood behind the boards, bending down to whisper in the ear of one girl, patting another on the shoulder, and then looking up at the action on the rink and encouraging the girls. He wore a maroon Deep Lake team jacket and a maroon stocking cap and one animated expression after another.

"James sure looks like he's having a good time out there," I said.

"Unlike the other guy," said Barb, nodding toward the mustached coach. "He just flung down his cap when that girl missed the net."

"He's always doing stuff like that," I said, suddenly feeling sorry for the girls.

Right before the second period began, Conrad announced he had to go to the bathroom.

"I do too," I said. "I'll walk down there with you."

After I was finished, I waited outside the men's bathroom for what seemed a longer-than-necessary amount of time.

"Sorry," Connie said sheepishly when he finally came out. "My mom says I'd never win a buttoning contest." He shook his head; more precisely, he bobbed his head. "I can't believe all the trouble one damn little button on my pants gives me."

The girls were already on the ice, and we stood behind the boards of the opposing team's goal to watch.

"Do you know how to ice-skate, Geneva?" Conrad asked.

I nodded. "When I was a kid, you couldn't get me off the ice."

"What's it like to move that fast?"

A Blaster, followed by three members of the other team, charged toward the net and took a shot.

"Oh!" Conrad and I said in unison as the goalie deflected it.

"What's it like to move that fast?" I said, repeating Connie's question. "It's . . . fun." I thought hard, wanting to give him as good a sense of what it was like as possible. "You've gone sledding down a hill, right?"

Connie bobbed his Twins-capped head.

"Well, you know how you're moving so fast and the ground is rushing under you? That's how it is on skates, except you're standing, and you get to control how fast the rushing is."

Looking out at the players on the ice, Conrad smiled a crooked smile. "I'd like that," he said. "I'd like to control the rushing."

"What's it like—" I began, then, thinking better of it, swallowed my words.

"What?"

"Nothing," I said, pretending to concentrate on what was happening on the ice.

"What's it like to be a spaz?" he asked.

I took in a sharp breath and then laughed. "Okay," I said. "I wouldn't put it quite like that, but yeah, that's what I was wondering: What's it like when your body's . . ."

"Out of control?" he asked as his hand jerked out. At my nod, he smiled his gummy smile at me. "Well, I've always had it, so it just seems kinda normal."

We turned our attention to the ice then. There was commotion down at the other end of the rink: a shot on goal, a save, and then a player taking advantage of the rebound and scoring.

"Oh!" said Connie and I, disappointed.

"We're still winning, though," said Connie, glancing at the scoreboard. Then, looking at me, he asked, "You know what else it feels like, Geneva? Sometimes I feel like a radio or a TV and I've got way too much electricity going through me. I mean, way more than I need to do the job I'm supposed to do." With his head tilted back, he looked at me. "That make any sense?"

I nodded and, hoping I wouldn't embarrass him, tucked my hand in the crook of his arm.

*B*ack up in the bleachers, Rich asked if we could get a snack.

"You gotta save your appetite," said Conrad. "We're going out for pizza afterward."

"We are?" said Rich and I.

Connie laughed. "I told you, Rich. I told you when we talked on the phone."

"Oh, yeah," said Rich, slapping his forehead. "Pizza party after the game."

The Deep Lake Blasters won, 7–4, and so it turned into a victory pizza party.

"I sure wish I could have played," said Natalie. She blew into her straw, creating a cascade of brown bubbles in her chocolate milk.

Rich's eyes lit up, and he began blowing bubbles too.

"You will," said James, patting her shoulder. "Only two more weeks and you get your cast off."

"Good, 'cause I don't want Tara to score more goals than me."

"Tara's the girl who got the hat trick tonight," explained James. "She's a tough little competitor."

"So am I, Daddy!"

James nodded. "Yes, you are, Nat." He gave her another pat and then reached across the table to pat Rich. "So, big guy, how was New York?"

"I saw the Rockets dance!"

"Rockettes," I said.

"Although it'd be pretty neat to see *rockets* dance," chirped Conrad.

As we helped ourselves to pepperoni-and-olive pizza, Rich told James all about our trip, or at least all about the touristy parts. It would be my job to tell him about the rest of it.

Out in the parking lot, Barb asked if we'd mind riding home with James and Natalie; Conrad was pretty tired, and she wanted to get him home.

"M'lady," said James as he bowed and opened his car door.

We listened to the oldies station on the ride home, singing along to thirty-year-old Beatles songs.

"That's John Lemon singing," Rich explained to Natalie.

When James pulled up in the driveway, his headlights shone on the toboggan that Rich kept parked out in a snowbank, and he was inspired to suggest, "Let's go sledding!"

"It's too late," I said, looking at my watch.

"Too late for a little walk?" asked James softly. "We can pull the kids in the sled."

"Yeah!" said Natalie. "You guys pull us in the sled!"

"All right," I said with a great sigh, as if I were doing everybody a big favor, when actually I didn't want the night to end quite yet either.

The kids scrambled onto the toboggan, and we began to walk through the snowy night, the soles of our boots making little squeaks. James pulled the rope at first, and then I did, and then the kids got the bright idea to boss us around.

"Mush!" they'd command. Obedient as sled dogs, we'd run for a few yards until our quick breaths filled the air with plumes of vapor.

"I don't think I've ever seen so much snow before December," said James during a lull in our mushing. "It's beautiful, isn't it?"

I nodded. This was not the furious snowstorm of Halloween; this was a picturesque Currier and Ives snowfall where the sky was full of floating scraps of lace and any minute a horse-drawn sleigh—with bells—might pass, carrying men with handlebar mustaches and women who got to wear fur without any political consequences.

"I'm glad you had a good time in New York," said James.

Rich was apparently still filling Natalie in on our trip, because she yelled, "Daddy, I don't want to go to Disneyland on our next vacation—I want to go to New York City and see the Rockettes!"

"I'll keep that in mind," James hollered back, and then, his voice quiet, he said, "I missed you, Geneva."

Rich, God bless him, chose this moment to order, "Mush!" and so I, who was pulling the sled at the time, had an excuse to start running instead of responding to James's statement.

But I couldn't run forever—I could hardly run at all; those kids were *heavy*—and soon James was at my panting, out-of-shape side.

"I knew I'd miss you," he continued, "I just didn't think I'd miss you as much as I did . . . which was a lot. And now you're going to leave this weekend and I don't know how I'll stand missing you so much. Who am I going to talk to? Who am I going to tell things like 'I'm thinking of coaching high-school girls hockey' to?"

"You're thinking of what?" I asked, caught off guard.

"Mush!" shouted the kids.

"Coaching Nat's team has made me realize how much I love coaching—and I'd *love* to do it on the high-school level. 'Course, I haven't figured out yet if I'll need to teach too—which I think I'd like. It shouldn't be hard to get a teaching certificate. I mean, I do have an M.A."

"Oh, James," I said, so happy to hear the excitement in his voice. I knew, though, that if I didn't say what I had to say now, I never would. "James, I—" Taking a big gulp of air, I decided to bite the bullet. "James, Trevor asked me to marry him."

We trudged on, and the only conversation was that between Natalie and Rich, who were talking about snowflakes.

"Well, how can anybody tell that no two snowflakes are alike?" asked Natalie. "Nobody's ever seen every single snowflake."

"Doesn't matter," said Rich patiently.

"I don't see how it can be. Nobody could ever tell that without looking at every single one—and how could anybody do that?"

"She's got a point there," I said, hoping to ease James out of his silence. I wasn't successful, and so after a very long and pregnant pause, I said, "Look at how many more billions of snowflakes there are than fingerprints, and if no two fingerprints are alike— which seems pretty impossible, if you ask me—doesn't it stand to reason—"

"What did you say?" interrupted James.

"Hey, can we play tic-tac-snow when we get back to Rich's?" yelled Natalie.

"We're gonna make a big tic-tac-toe board in the snow!" said Rich. "And draw X's and O's with sticks!"

"It's late, Rich. They need to get home," I said at the same time James said, "No, we're going to have to get going, Nat."

"Not too late to play tic-tac-snow!" said Rich. "Please, Aunt Gennie, it's so pretty out!"

"No!" Both James and I yelled this, and the kids, surprised at our outburst, immediately quieted, knowing a final answer when they heard it.

"So what did you tell Trevor?" James said again.

"I said I needed to think about it," I said so softly that James leaned toward me and said, "What?"

I raised my voice. "I said I needed to think about it."

"And did you?"

"Did I what?"

"Did you think about it?"

"Honestly, James, of course I thought about it. I'm still thinking about it. I don't have an answer yet."

"Maybe this'll help your answer," he said, and the nylon shells of our parkas rustled as he took me in his arms and, under millions of those one-of-a-kind snowflakes, kissed me.

This seemed to bring both relief and delight to Rich and Natalie, who erupted into giggles.

"Hey, we didn't say *kiss*," said Natalie, "We said *mush*!"

*R*ich and I tried to busy ourselves the next day until evening, when we'd pick up Ann and Riley at the airport. We washed, polished, vacuumed and revacuumed, scrubbed, and scoured.

It was in the afternoon, when I was trying to teach Rich how to play Scrabble, that my whole baby-sitting adventure was capped off by a near heart attack. That Rich chose to use made-up words was enough to raise my blood pressure, but only slightly; no, what almost caused my heart to seize up and forget about pumping was the knowledge that someone had broken into the house. Rich heard the door open too, and our eyes met in fear. I was filled with adrenaline, trying to decide if Rich and I should make a run for it or if I should arm myself with a nearby skillet and wage war. Thinking a Teflon-coated pan was no match for an Uzi or an AK-47 or whatever weapon suburban thieves used these days, I decided to run, and had pulled Rich up by his arm when Ann and Riley burst into the room.

"Surprise!" they shouted, certainly no understatement.

That's when I clutched my chest and thought I'd prematurely meet my maker. But Rich's scream was like a charge, jolting my heart back to a regular rhythm.

"Mommy! Daddy!"

Reflexively I covered my ears with my hands, hoping my hearing loss wouldn't be significant.

"Rich!" returned his parents, enveloping their son in their arms.

At least once in their lives everybody should have the kind of reunion Rich, Ann, and Riley had. It was joyous, full of laughs and hugs and kisses and then more laughter. I didn't even put a damper on it by yelling at them to never *ever* sneak in like that again and what were they trying to do, give someone a heart attack?

"You weren't supposed to get in until tonight," I said after everyone had stopped screaming and laughing and we could finally communicate with words.

"Oh, we just told you that," said Ann, her arm around her son. She smoothed his hair. "We wanted to surprise you."

Rich was beaming, his big, chin-jutting smile wide as the horizon.

"I'm glad," he said. "Glad you surprised us."

We talked and laughed and looked at a huge stack of pictures (I actually prefer slides—at least in the dark you can yawn unseen). Then we had our gift exchange, and although I loved my Florentine leather bag and Rich his boots (they looked more cowboy than Italian, which suited him just fine), the hit present, the one that received the most oohs and ahhs, was our photo album.

"Oh, Rich," said Ann, looking at the Halloween pictures, "you look *exactly* like the gondoliers we saw in Venice!"

Rich nodded, as if of course that were the case.

"Look at Conrad," said Riley, laughing. "He was one wet robot."

"That was one big snowstorm," remembered Rich.

"And who's that?" asked Ann, squinting at the photo. "Geneva, is that James?"

"None other. He and his daughter sort of rescued us on Halloween."

"I dropped all my candy," said Rich with the weighty import of a newscaster announcing the death of a dignitary.

"Here he is again," said Riley, turning the page.

I looked at the picture a waiter at a pizza parlor had taken of the four of us, and laughed.

"That's the night you ate five pieces of pizza, remember, Rich?"

"Five pieces!" said Ann, ever the concerned mother.

Rich rubbed his stomach. "Three pepperoni and two sausage-and-onion."

"So," said Riley, getting back to the picture, "it looks as if he's more than your rescuer."

I nodded. "James has become a good friend of ours, hasn't he, Rich?"

"James *and* Natalie." With his pointer finger, Rich gently touched their faces on the photograph. "Our *good* friends. And Aunt Gennie likes to kiss James."

"Ge-nee-va," said my sister, turning my name into a three-note mini-aria. "So you like to kiss James, hmm?"

I felt the dreaded telltale blush wash over my face. "I . . . uh . . . I . . ."

My incoherence delighted both Ann and Riley.

"I sense that you're a little rattled," teased my brother-in-law.

"Geneva," said Ann, "you haven't been tongue-tied over a boy since Brad Norlund."

"I am not tongue-tied," I said, betrayed by the spittle flying out of my mouth.

"Aunt Geneva, let's show them the really *big* surprise," said Rich, and I wanted to kiss him for being such an adroit subject changer.

"You won't believe this," I said, and sure enough, all conversation regarding James was forgotten.

"What is it?" asked Ann as Rich ran off to get it.

"Like I said, you won't believe it."

Ann's eyes bugged out when Rich placed the cardboard-covered book on her lap. *"The Great Mysterious!"* she squealed. "I'd forgotten all about this!"

"Do you know how hard this was to keep a secret? Every time we spoke I wanted to tell you, 'Ann, guess what I found!' "

"We found," said Rich.

"What is it?" asked Riley, leaning into Ann for a better look.

"Geneva and I put this together when we were kids," said Ann, carefully untying the ribbon. "Up at our Great-uncle Carl's cabin. We were just trying to keep ourselves from going crazy with boredom—it rained and stormed the whole time we were up there—but then it turned into this big group therapy thing."

" 'What is true love?' " Riley read.

"See, and then you take a piece of paper out of the pocket and find out," explained Rich.

We took turns reading the answers. Rich and I delighted at Ann and Riley's delight.

"Ann, this is beautiful!" said Riley after he read what she had written about the meaning of life and being a twin.

" 'If I couldn't be a person, what would I be? But God's plan is that I am a person, so if I weren't one, I'd probably be nothing.' " Ann looked at me. "That's Grandma's, isn't it? I remember when we read these at the cabin. I thought they never sounded like her."

"I know! They didn't capture her at all." I withdrew a slip and, recognizing the handwriting, chuckled. "But Great-uncle Carl's always captured *him*."

" 'If I couldn't be a person,' " I read, exaggerating our great-uncle's slight Norwegian accent, "I suppose I'd be a book, because a book, especially a great one, lives on and on and has the opportunity to change people's lives, to become a part of their lives. What book, you ask? I suppose I would choose the obvious answer—the Bible. Imagine having wars fought over you, religions formed over you, the devotion, adoration, and reverence of millions.' "

"Hey, look," said Rich, fishing his hand in the newest pocket. "There's some new answers in here."

"We decided to expand the book," I explained. "We wrote in new questions."

"Good," said Ann. "Remember how disappointed we were when we realized none of the adults had written in questions?"

I nodded, loving that these memories were shared ones.

" 'I don't have a biggest fear,' " Rich read slowly. " 'I used to, but then it did happen and my mom and dad did get divorced. I thought it would be really bad, but it's not. Kinda bad, sometimes, but not really bad. Now I try not to think about fears, because thinking about them doesn't make them go away. It just makes you think about them more.' "

"Whose is that?" asked Ann.

"Natalie's," said Rich. "I can tell because of the divorce part. Plus she printed it!"

I smiled, wondering when sneaky James had put the answers in the book.

"Any more?" I asked.

"Yup," said Rich, holding up two slips of paper. "Here, Dad," he said, handing one to his father. "Here, Mom." He gave one to Ann.

Riley unfolded his and read, " 'I would be most afraid if my mom and dad left or died or something.' "

"That's mine!" said Rich. "You read mine!"

Ann put her arm around her son. "I remember that's what I used to be afraid of when I was a girl."

"So what does yours say, Riley?"

" 'Stage fright has caused me to feel that I can't move, that I'm frozen to whatever particular spot I'm supposed to move from to get to the piano. Even worse are the occasions I've been in where I don't freeze until I'm sitting on the piano bench, which makes escape all the harder. But stage fright is nothing compared to the fear I feel over you leaving, Geneva.' "

Riley paused, looking up at me. "Should I go on? I feel like I'm reading your personal mail."

"If James put it in there, he knows everyone reads it," said Rich. "So read it."

"Yes, *sir,*" said Riley, and I shrugged as he looked to me again for approval. "Okay, then. 'I feel like I've found the woman I want to spend the rest of my life with, and I can't bear the thought that you think of me as only a friend you happen to like to kiss. It's my gut feeling that you *would* reciprocate my feelings if you were truly honest with yourself. I don't know what this is, Geneva—if it's a marriage proposal or what—but I love you, and I'd like a life together with you, a life I know we could make work despite its many complications. I am not prepared to freeze up over this, Geneva, and if you are, I will somehow find a way to thaw you out.' "

"Oh, my," said Ann.

"He *likes* you," said Rich.

"That's an understatement, son," said Riley.

I was feeling decidedly uncomfortable.

"Aunt Gennie, is Trevor gonna be mad about what James wrote?"

"*Trevor?*" said Ann. "Where does Trevor fit into this?"

"She kisses him too," piped up Rich.

"No secret's safe with you, is it, Rich? What else can you tell them about me?"

"Well," said Rich, scratching the back of his head, "you sure eat lots of ice cream." He held his hands out as if he were holding a roasting pan. "Big bowls full of ice cream."

Ann and Riley laughed at this display of treachery, and after pretending to be offended, I did too. At least we all understood that the subject had been changed and should remain changed.

And it had been, until late that evening. I was tucked in bed, reading a mystery and drinking a glass of the wine the globe-trotters had bought on a vineyard tour, when after a warning knock Ann entered the room.

"You still up?" I asked. "Aren't you jet-lagged up the wazoo?"

"I'm running completely on adrenaline," said Ann, "and gallons of coffee." She perched on the side of the bed, almost sitting on my legs. "I just read Rich to sleep. He usually doesn't let me do that anymore—says he's too big."

"So what did you read him?"

"His all-time favorite—*Treasure Island*. But he was out cold before Long John Silver even made an appearance."

As we talked I had slid over to the center of the bed and Ann had crawled under the covers. For a moment we just snuggled there next to each other, enjoying that deeply cozy sharing-a-bed-with-your-sister feeling.

"Gen," she said finally, "thank you so much for staying with Rich. It means so much that you did that for me."

"Wait'll you get the bill," I said, and then, stretching across her,

I reached for my wineglass on the nightstand. "You know, this is pretty good," I said, taking a sip. "Want some?"

She took a swallow. "We had so much fun at that vineyard. It was the day we met Doug and Susan—the antique collectors I told you about—and by two in the afternoon, we were all drunk."

"Ann," I said, mimicking our mother. "Two o'clock in the afternoon and *drunk*?"

"You wouldn't have recognized me, Geneva. Most of the time I felt like a twenty-year-old exchange student. I mean, I missed Rich, a lot. So did Riley. But then we'd remind each other how much we needed this vacation and what good hands he was in." She leaned over and kissed my cheek. "Thanks for being those good hands, Gen."

"My pleasure."

"Was it?" asked Ann eagerly. "Was it really?"

I sipped my wine, mulling over the question. "Yes," I said finally. "Yes, it was. To tell you the truth, I was scared stiff I'd screw something up, but I didn't!" We both laughed at the wonder in my voice. "I'm still surprised that I didn't."

"Rich said he had so much fun."

"Oh, Ann, I'm glad. I did too."

She snuggled closer to me. "So now is it safe to ask you what the hell is going on with your love life?"

I feigned innocence, but apparently Ann wasn't buying it.

"I wish you could see that look on your face," she said, laughing. "It's priceless. Now come on, Geneva. James has just professed his love to you, and you say Trevor's back in the picture—what's going on with all these guys?"

"All these guys?" Now it was my turn to laugh.

"Okay, okay, tell me what's going on with you and James."

"Nothing," I said after a long pause. "I mean, he's a very nice man, but . . ."

"But what?"

I shrugged. "I think . . . I think he was just a diversion. I'm sorry if he feels it was something more, but I don't know . . . it was nice to have a man paying attention to me after all that Trevor business."

"And speaking of that Trevor business," said Ann, "what were you doing kissing him?"

I shrugged again. "He asked me to marry him, Ann."

My sister's eyes widened. "No."

"Yes."

"And what did you say?"

"I'm thinking it over."

"You're thinking it over? After what he did to you?"

"Ann," I said to my ever-loyal sister, "it's not like he was a batterer or anything, he just . . . went through a bad time or something. Male menopause."

"I can't believe I'm hearing *you* defend Trevor Waite, Geneva. This was the man who, and I quote, 'can go to hell and reunite with his brother, Satan.' "

I laughed; Ann *would* remember my saying something like that.

"He's changed. He realizes he was a big jerk, Ann, and he also realizes he still loves me."

"Until the next minor with implants comes along."

"Come on, Ann." I was getting a little miffed at her failure to be persuaded. "Give him a break—he's changed. And he wants to prove it by marrying me."

"Usually it's your *love* you prove by marrying someone."

I took a final sip of wine, tapping the side of the glass to make sure I got every drop. "No offense, Ann," I said, putting the glass back on the nightstand. "But I think I hear Riley calling you."

Ann didn't need to be told anything twice. "Okay," she said, getting out of the bed, "but I'm only saying this because I love you, Gen. I want you to think things over very carefully."

"Yes, Mrs. Wahlstrom," I said in the singsong of a snotty pupil.

"Good night, Geneva," my sister answered coolly, and left the room, shutting the door behind her.

I idiotically reached for the phone, wanting to call James to talk over my problems, but then realized, of course, that he was a big part of my problems.

I punched my pillow to alter its shape and then punched it again just for the hell of it. All I wanted was to drift off to the sweet, unconscious clouds of dreamland, where a person didn't have to think at all. My thoughts were like a pack of wild dogs snarling at me, yapping, hungry for attention. When I finally surrendered to the arms of Morpheus, he didn't rock me so much as toss me around, and when Rich bounded into my room the next morning and woke me up, my first impulse was to wallop him.

"Auntie Gen, today is Sunday and today you're leaving!"

Tell me something I don't know, I said silently, *and then please leave.*

"Auntie Gen, I'm going to miss you!"

In that no-warning way of his, he flung his arms around me and hugged me, and I'd be hard pressed to tell you who held on tighter.

"*I*'ve decided to forgive you," said my sister by way of greeting when I lumbered into the kitchen.

I got a coffee cup out of the cupboard. "Forgive me for what?"

"For any bad love choices you might make in the future." She got the pot and poured me a cup of coffee. "I won't lecture you and I won't get mad at you."

"Yeah, when pigs fly." I looked around the kitchen. "Where is everybody?"

"Outside," said Ann, and she nodded toward a covered plate on the counter. "Want some pancakes? We already ate."

"You already ate? On my last day here, you went and ate without me?"

"Geneva, it's noon. We thought you'd be up when we got home from church, but you weren't, and, well, we got hungry."

"You didn't wake me up for church?"

Ann laughed. "You sound so disappointed."

"Well, I am. I liked going to your church."

My sister touched my hair. "I'm glad."

"Oh, don't get so excited; I'm not converted or anything. I helped Barb once in Sunday school, and it was . . . fun. And I don't know, I . . ." I couldn't believe my blathering. "Well, it was a nice way to start a Sunday morning."

Ann nodded, and although she probably didn't mean it as a told-you-so gesture, I took it as one.

"So where're Rich and Riley?" I asked brightly.

"Outside. Rich wanted to play a game he said he made up. Snow tic-tac-toe or something." She poured me a glass of orange juice. "Oh, Barb told me to tell you to call her before you go."

I blinked at the surprising burst of tears that collected in my eyes.

"And James said to tell you to have a safe flight."

"That's all?"

"No, he also said he hopes to see you again sometime."

I swallowed a piece of pancake, which seemed to take its time traveling down my throat.

"He seemed upset, Gen."

"Well," I said, pouring more syrup on my breakfast, "next time he brings the mail, tell him I enjoyed meeting him." I cut my pancakes and then cut them some more, the knife clattering against the plate like a discordant bell.

"Will you let me know when you learn the backstroke?"

Rich nodded, his chin jutted forward.

"And you'll send me a copy of your spelling test?"

Again Rich nodded; it was the only communication I was getting from him.

Boarding had begun, but I was holding off getting on the plane, hoping to engage in some sort of dialogue with my nephew.

"He's sad," my sister had mouthed, rotating her fists under her eyes in a bad imitation of crying.

"Duh," I mouthed back at her.

I put my arm around the boy and pulled him close. "Rich, you know I'm going to miss you."

He nodded, and a tear slid down his flat cheek.

"Now, none of that, Rich," I said, wiping his face, "or I'll be bawling like a baby. You don't want your Aunt Gen bawling like a baby, do you?"

In the annals of smiles, his was a tiny one, but I was encouraged.

"They'll make me sit in an infant seat on the plane if I'm bawling like a baby. I'm too big to sit in an infant seat."

I babbled on about all the indignities I'd have to face if I were bawling like a baby, but I was ultimately not responsible for the big smile that zipped across his face.

"Natty!" he shouted. "James!"

"We ran all the way here!" announced Natalie.

"We didn't think we'd make it," said James, panting and holding his side.

"Look at my aunt's airplane!" said Rich, taking Natalie by the hand to the window.

After greeting James, Ann and Riley discreetly moved out of conversational range.

"Nat wanted to say good-bye," said James.

"Yeah, she really seems broken up that I'm leaving," I joked, nodding toward the window, where she and Rich stood watching the runway. "I read what you wrote in *The Great Mysterious*."

James's face had a sudden look of expectation and fear. "And so now are you going to tell me you've decided to marry me?"

"No," I said, feeling a lump rise in my throat.

"In that case," said James as he made a quick bow, "I had a wonderful time with you, Geneva Jordan, and I will miss you."

I laughed to keep from crying, and then gasped as he pulled me to him and gave me one of those kisses that make people stand back and either shake their heads at its shamelessness or sigh softly, wishing for a kiss like that of their own.

Chapter 10

hat James and I had a history of explosive kisses was not lost on me, and I pondered their meaning on the plane, but ponder as I might, I couldn't figure out what they meant. Maybe some people just kiss well together and, sensing this in each other, look forward to such occasions as good-byes because they're able to indulge this extremely enjoyable but brief partnership. I supposed it was like being a great dancer and finding someone out on the floor who knew as many steps as you did.

Of course, I wondered what it would have been like if we had *really* danced. Would our lovemaking have lived up to the excellence of our kissing? I was both sad (I don't like to miss out on anything) and glad (the fact that we hadn't slept together certainly made it easier for me to know that James was just a friend and nothing more) that I hadn't found out. Still, I could hear Riley's voice reading James's words, and those words sat high in my chest like heartburn. He wasn't supposed to fall in love with me—he was just supposed to help me pass the time while I was taking care of Rich.

Believe it or not, I am not a woman who has a close personal relationship with her compact mirror; I think public viewing of oneself is, well, tacky (the truth is that my vanity is so great that I never feel the need to check on my lipstick or hair). But the first-class compartment was nearly empty, and I felt a need to look at the face James had kissed.

Well, there I was, with my dramatic tumble of red hair, my pretty little pert nose, my high color, my beautiful teeth. There I was, my jawline verging on jowly, my laugh lines deep enough to suggest that all I did in life was laugh, my skin's texture resembling the peel of a grapefruit more than that of an apple, and my neck!—my neck was positively crepey. I snapped shut the compact, reassuring myself that airplane light was almost as unflattering as that in department store dressing rooms.

When the flight attendant came by, I heard the man several rows back order a scotch and soda. It seemed a good, medicating drink, so I ordered one and then another and tried not to think of anything as I stared out the oval window to the miniature world down below.

I wasn't expecting anyone to meet me at the gate, but I must admit feeling a tiny flare of disappointment when I saw that there wasn't; it's always nice to be welcomed home. And so, unescorted, I walked to the baggage claim.

A man tapped my shoulder just as I hefted one of my bags off the carousel.

"Let me get that for you, Miss Jordan."

I muttered the cliché of the confused. "Huh?"

"I'm your driver, Miss Jordan. I've been hired to take you home."

"Ah," I said, remembering how much I enjoy preferential treatment. "It's good to be home."

I assumed Claire had hired the driver, but that assumption evaporated as soon as I got into the backseat, which, unlike most backseats I've sat on in my lifetime, was covered in rose petals.

"Oh, my," I said.

"I wasn't too sure about that," said the driver, getting into the front seat. "You know, would it wreck the upholstery, that type of thing. But your boyfriend's very persistent." He checked his rearview mirrors and then moved into traffic. "He said the oil from the rose petals would soften and condition the leather, and then he gave me a hundred-dollar bonus."

Not only could I enjoy the romance of the gesture, but lucky me, my leather coat would get free softening and conditioning to boot. I settled back in the sweet-smelling limousine, forgoing the champagne but helping myself to the box of chocolates Trevor had thoughtfully stocked. The man was batting a thousand.

I was dropped off at my building and cut short the doorman's welcome in my hurry to get up to my apartment.

Throwing the door open, I expected to be greeted by a roaring fire and Trevor's supine body on the fake bearskin, but the hearth was cold and there wasn't so much as a flea lying on the rug.

"Trevor?" My voice was high and girlish, and I hoped it would be answered by a manly, British-accented one. "In here, darling."

But there was no one in the bedroom, or the guest room or my office, or any of the rooms I searched.

There was, however, a note, weighted by a rose, on the entry-way table, which I would have seen right away had I not been playing hunt down the man.

My darling:
I'll see you after the show tonight.
                    Can't wait,
                    Your Trevor.

Well, it wasn't Lord Byron, but it told me what I needed to know: He was excited to see me, and I had time for a nice long bubble bath.

"*A*hhh," said Trevor with a contented, postcoital sigh. "I am so happy to have you in my arms again, Geneva."

"I'm happy to be in them," I murmured, my nose pressed against his shoulder, breathing him in.

"Do you suppose it'll be like this when we're married? Or even better?"

I felt myself tense up, and Trevor must have too, because he laughed.

"Oh, Geneva, I know you haven't said yes yet. I'm just hoping that with subtle reinforcement, you'll gradually come to the correct answer."

"Which is?"

He kissed me, and I heard that wonderful zip of a five o'clock shadow against my cheek. "Which is 'Of course I'll marry you, darling, how could I think otherwise?' "

I kissed him then, trapping those very words that 95 percent of me wanted to shout back at him but that 5 percent decided to withhold.

Wonders never cease, especially in the theater. *Mona!*'s producer, Angus Powell, called me the day after I returned to New York, begging me to come back to the show for a few weeks, "until we can replace that awful Bennet woman. She says she's got nodules on her vocal cords, and her doctor's backing her up—although I'm sure she's paying him a pretty penny to corroborate her story."

"What about the understudy?"

Angus's sigh was long and world-weary. "*She* just found out she's pregnant after twenty years of trying. She thinks the role is too rigorous—she doesn't want anything to jeopardize the baby."

"Well, what about the second un—"

"Geneva, please. We need you. You're the belle of Broadway."

Well, how could I deny someone smart enough to refer to me as the belle of Broadway?

It was great to be back onstage, great to run through songs and have the rehearsal pianist mouth the word "Super!" to me over and over, great to discover I hadn't forgotten any of the dance steps, great to be lifted up by the actor who played Michelangelo and who asked, "Have you lost weight, Geneva?" (I knew he was just being polite; I had gained five pounds in Minnesota eating all that ice cream with Rich, but I still appreciated the gesture.)

Then on the way to lunch the stage manager said, "We can't wait to have you back. Faith Bennet's a real bitch."

"The worst," agreed a featured dancer. "Talk about chewing up the scenery—no wonder she's got *nodules* on her vocal cords."

Could the day get any better? A seamless rehearsal *and* cast and crew bad-mouthing my replacement?

I couldn't wait for my reopening night, scheduled for December 23 (call me Santa, giving audiences the gift of my return for their Christmas present), and I was thrilled. The old excitement was back: thrilled that in my working life I was back in the arms of Leonardo da Vinci as played by Trevor Waite, thrilled that in my personal life I was back in the arms of my lover as played by Trevor Waite. It's not often in life that so many thrills coalesce and I was enjoying the coalescence to the hilt.

"If we get mugged, you have to pay me back all my money plus fifteen percent."

"You brought money?" I asked, mock horror in my voice. "Who'd be stupid enough to bring money into Central Park? I only brought my driver's license, in case they need to ID the body."

Claire laughed, a small, pathetic you-are-kidding-me-aren't-you laugh.

"Really, Claire, you're an agent. You're not supposed to be afraid of anything."

"I'm not afraid of anything," she said, her eyes darting from one side of the path to the other. "Anything but Central Park."

"But it's daytime," I reminded her. "And there are people all around us."

It was true, the park was filled with joggers and walkers and mothers and nannies pushing strollers in which were packed bundled-up babies.

I had dragged Claire out of what she thought was a lunch date to accompany me on one of the quiet, snowy walks I'd gotten used to in Deep Lake. The trouble was, it was never really quiet in Manhattan, and the snowfall had been downright puny.

"Can we go back now?" whined Claire, whose two-inch heels were not exactly hiking material. "I'm hungry. I've been thinking about lobster salad all morning."

"Big baby," I said as an accusation, and then with a great, put-upon sigh, I took her arm and turned her around. She would have none of it.

"Oh, no," she said, turning *me* around. "Far be it from me to intrude upon your newly discovered need for fresh air and exercise. I'm going to walk as long as you want to, even if it kills me."

"What about your lobster salad?"

"Agents make sacrifices for their clients all the time."

I laughed. "So noble of you and those in your profession."

A jogger passed, and both Claire and I admired the view offered by his spandex-clad glutes.

"So," said Claire, "should we take care of business first, or pleasure?"

"Pleasure."

"Let's do business. You're going to find the news pleasurable enough anyway."

"What?" I asked, my curiousity piqued.

"The read-through for *Samson and Delilah* is next Tuesday. Norman Alexander's done with the script." Claire patted her ever-present briefcase. "It's sensational, Geneva. Prepare yourself for another Tony."

I squeezed her arm. "That's great, Claire. I've always wanted to work with him."

We passed a white-faced mime dressed in thin clothes inappropriate for the weather. I put a five-dollar bill in his real hat, and as he tipped his imaginary hat, I advised, "Get a winter coat."

"So how's Trevor?" asked Claire, and I realized what it took for her to make her voice sound blithe.

"Oh, so we're on the pleasure part now." I smiled at my agent and saw her try to resist smiling back. "Come on, Claire, be happy for me. It's going to be so fun working with him again." I had a rehearsal scheduled the next day, readying myself for my unexpected return to *Mona!*

"Forget about working," said Claire. "How is it *being* with him?"

"He's changed, Claire. It's not all about him anymore. It's about *us*."

"It better be, because if he hurts you again, I swear, he'll have to answer to me."

Squeezing my agent's arm, I thanked her. "He sure wishes I'd hurry up and give him an answer, though."

"And when will you?"

"When I know the right answer. I just need more time. I'm not going to jump into anything I can't swim in."

"I don't think it matters whether you can swim or not. I think what matters is whether there are sharks in the water."

"So you think Trevor's a shark?" I asked as I moved to let a power-walker speed by.

"Well, now," said Claire, giving me her biggest smile. "You know I don't like to bad-mouth sharks."

*T*revor got the Pour Deux spot and signed a contract guaranteeing him at least two more. He was the cologne's new spokesman.

They arranged the two-day shoot around Trevor's schedule so that he wouldn't miss a show. It was to take place in an old inn outside of Bedford, New York. Always ready for a mini-vacation, I had planned to drive up with Trevor, but then I got an audition of my own.

"Geneva," Trevor pouted, "can't you cancel?"

"Yeah, right." Asking actors to cancel an audition is like asking them to give blood on a daily basis in unhygienic circumstances for the next year. "But I can drive up afterward." I put my arms around him and kissed his neck. "It's the night you want me there for anyway, right?"

His reply was the sort of growl a bear might make during mating season.

*S*easoned vet that I am, I still can't predict an audition's outcome. There have been times when I've felt I gave a flat reading and Claire will call me to say, "You're booked—they loved you!" Other times I've practically danced out of the room, certain I gave the most stirring cold reading since Moses read the Ten Commandments, only to hear that I didn't even get a callback.

This particular audition was a voice-over for *Hoedown*, an animated film (never was the word *cartoon* mentioned) about the Old West. The character I was reading and singing for was one Bronco Betsy. They laughed at the right spots during my reading, and after I sang one of the songs, you'd have thought I'd come up with the cure for cancer.

"Oh, Miss Jordan," said the lyricist, "your shading, your phrasing—" He kissed his fingertips. "—and the way you emphasized *britches* and *hitches*—oh, my God, I never laughed so hard."

"You're a national treasure," said the songwriter.

"We'll be talking to you," said the director.

Afterward I repeated the conversation to Claire over the phone.

"And how do you feel about it?" asked my agent.

"Actually, great. I don't think I could have sung better, I made 'em laugh, and best of all, now I get to spend a night up in an old romantic inn with Trevor."

"Oh, boy," said Claire, and I could just picture her shaking her head, one hand making an awning above her eyes. "Have you got it bad."

*I*t was a pretty drive up to Bedford, with falling snow that was light enough not to impede the ride but only enhance it. My car—a five-year-old Mercedes—didn't get out of the garage much, and yet every time it did, I was reminded how much I like to drive. There's that sense of being in control of powerful machinery and that even better sense of adventure. I found myself whistling and singing to the radio, and after I'd turned off the highway and toward Bedford, I realized that I was the happiest I'd been in a long, long time.

Oh, that happiness were a more steadfast companion! Excuse the bad Shakespeare imitation, but wouldn't you be driven to dramatic ranting if you discovered the love of your life in flagrante delicto? Of course, Trevor tried to convince me that there was nothing inappropriate about the Harmony Products executive being in his hotel room, enjoying a glass of wine and conversation; after all, *she* had some ideas about the direction in which the company wanted to take Pour Deux, and was there anything wrong with that?

I never said there was, but apparently Trevor could sense my anger, puzzlement, and suspicion. Not that I screamed and threw things around the suite (a suite decorated completely in a Paul-Revere-is-coming motif); no, I simply wasn't my typically high-spirited, friendly self. Okay, so I was a little cold.

After we were introduced, I let Meg (so tall and chic I'd have liked to slap her even if she *hadn't* been planning to go to bed with Trevor) know what was what by going to the bedroom door and asking them if they'd mind continuing their business discussion down in the lobby; I was a little tired.

"Geneva," said Trevor, packing a warning into every syllable.

"Oh, I really should be going," said the Madison Avenue slut. "I've got a lot of calls to make." She picked up a folder off a rustic pine table and gave a tiny wave in my direction. "So nice to meet you, Miss Jordan. I think you're an absolutely fabulous actress."

I held up my arm and flicked my wrist, more a dismissal than a wave.

When she left, Trevor looked at me as if I had lost all my marbles—past, present, and future.

"You mind telling me what that was all about?" he asked, his ice-blue eyes icier than usual.

"Oh, come on, Trevor," I said, getting out of the bed I'd made such a statement in. "What do you take me for, stupid?"

"Yes," said Trevor, nodding. "In this case, I would definitely take you for stupid."

"Oh, you expect me to believe the two of you were just talking business?"

"Damn it, Geneva, of course we were!"

He hit the pine table with his fist, and even as I was impressed by the gesture, I was skeptical of it—was it really born of fury, or was it a conscious acting choice?

"Well," I said, gathering my coat and purse, "I can see there's no reason for me to stay around here. I mean, you're certainly not starved for company."

Trevor intercepted me on the way to the door.

"Come on, Geneva. You're joking, right?"

"No, I am not joking," I said, trying to shake his hands off me.

"Geneva, what's gotten into you? This is Meg's first big campaign. She wants everything to go right and so she's pestering everyone—she'd already been to see the director before me."

"Oh, does she find him attractive too?"

"Geneva," he said, and then, surprising myself, I burst into tears.

I did stay overnight in that Paul Revere room and am happy to report that more than the British were coming.

Although really, I thought as I drove home the next day, *what's so hot about multiple orgasms when you don't know if your partner reserves them just for you?* I mean, I guess I believed Trevor, but it was the guessing that bothered me. I wanted to *know* that I could trust him; I wanted to be able to see him with another woman and not assume that they were in the process of a seduction; I wanted to know that I was enough for him.

What I really wanted to know, though, was if in this game of love, the yes I had finally said to Trevor the night before was the right answer, or if I should take what's behind the curtain.

Slowing down at a stop sign, my car fishtailed on a patch of ice, and although it was no big deal—I hadn't positioned myself in front of an oncoming semi or anything—it made me realize that I was just a bit too agitated to drive and maybe I should take a little walk or get a cup of something hot but decaffeinated.

The town was decked out for Christmas. Swags of evergreen were draped over shop windows, and bowed wreaths decorated every other door. It was a Seasons Greetings from New England postcard come to life.

I got out of the car and wandered up one side of the street and then down the other. Finally, because I felt like a vagrant, I stopped in an antiques shop.

There were some interesting pieces—some Hepplewhite chairs and an armoire in bird's-eye maple—but I was at a point in my life where shopping as an antidote to depression was a little, well, over-done. I chatted briefly with the store owner, who I could tell recognized me but had that flinty I'm-not-going-to-fuss-over-anyone attitude. I was about to leave when I spotted a little wooden figure of a gondolier standing in his boat.

"Oh, I'll take this," I said.

"Can't tell you where it's from," said the shopkeeper, ringing up the sale, "although it does look like a Glauschein."

"A Glauschein?"

"A German toy-making family. Early nineteen hundreds. Lots of wood, mostly vehicles—train cars, horse carts, ships, and what-not. Don't remember their work being so intricate, though."

I forked over an amount of money that would have bought me a *really* good pair of shoes, but it was worth it. Rich would love it.

"*D*id you know I bought you a present?" I asked when he and Ann called me that evening as I built a fire.

"You bought me a present?" came Rich's low, sweet voice. "What is it?"

"I'm not telling," I said, laughing. "You'll get it by Christmas."

"You coming here for Christmas?"

"No, Rich," I said, hating to dampen his enthusiasm. "You know I'm staying in New York for Christmas."

"Don't you want to see the Christmas pageant? I'm a wise man."

"Really?" I said, but before I could ask him more, he said, "Conrad's in the hospital."

"Conrad's in the hospital?" I closed the fire screen. "What happened?"

There was another pause, and when he spoke again, his voice seemed clogged, as if there were something caught in his throat.

"Don't know, exactly. But now it's worse than a cold . . . what he's got."

"Oh, Rich."

"He's my best pal," he said, sniffling. I heard voices in the background, and then he said, "Here—Mom wants to talk."

I was still on the phone with Ann when Trevor got home.

"I'll call you tomorrow, Ann," I said. "Give Barb my best."

"Who's Barb, and why are you giving her your best?" he asked after I hung up the phone.

"Conrad's mother," I said. "I told you about her, remember? Conrad is Rich's best friend. He's in the hospital with pneumonia."

"I had pneumonia twice as a kid," said Trevor, pouring himself a scotch. "Blasted English winters—they always find a way to climb into your lungs."

Sitting down on the couch next to me, he kicked off his shoes.

"Full house tonight," he said, "and guess who was front row center?"

"The Pope?"

"Very funny. No, someone who can do more for my career than the pope—Jake Bartholomew."

"The Jake Bartholomew who directed *Hunter's Dawn*?"

"The selfsame. And guess who came backstage to ask me if I'd be free for a film that's to begin shooting in February?"

"Uh . . . gee, I give up."

"Jake Bartholomew," gloated Trevor, ignoring my sarcasm.

I went to the bar, deciding it was time to switch to the hard stuff. "How come all these big directors are showing up when I'm not there?"

Trevor laughed. "If I didn't know you better, I'd say you had a persecution complex."

"I don't think I'm being persecuted. I just think I'm missing out."

"We're having supper together after the show tomorrow night."

"Can I come?"

"Geneva, it's a business meeting. You'd be bored to tears."

"But I've always wanted to meet Jake Bartholomew!"

Trevor took my hand and pulled me to the couch.

"Watch it," I said, trying not to spill my gin and tonic.

"Geneva," he said, crooking his black eyebrows, which signaled his earnest look, "please don't take this the wrong way, but I don't want you there."

"Thanks a lot!"

The lines on Trevor's forehead deepened as his eyebrows lowered even further. "Geneva, please. This is hard for me to admit, but I'm afraid . . . I'm afraid that if you show up, I'll be lost in your shadow. I'm afraid Jake Bartholomew will forget all about me in the glare of your starlight."

"The glare of my starlight? Oh, that's a good one, Trevor."

He moved his hand in a little circle, and the ice cubes in his drink made little clicking sounds. "Forgive the histrionics, but you understand what I mean, don't you, Geneva?"

I sat for a moment in a cold chill of dislike. Of course I understood. If I were having lunch with a big-shot director, I certainly wouldn't want another actor distracting him . . . but it was all so tiresome. At that moment I disliked—no, hated—Trevor, my profession, and the egos that in the beginning we had to cultivate because we needed the armor, egos that were now not only offensive weapons, but defensive ones as well.

"Well," I said finally, "if you talk about the project and Jake Bartholomew mentions a part for a leading lady, will you bring up my name?"

"Of course I will, darling." Trevor set his glass on the coffee table and kissed me. "I'll do more than bring you up, I'll *rave*."

We clicked glasses, perfectly understanding each other.

*A*fter rehearsal the next day (which really was only a formality; everyone could see that I knew *Mona!* backward and forward despite my two-month absence) I finished my Christmas shopping, which made me feel *extremely* efficient; after all, Christmas Eve was only a week and a half away, and I hadn't left things to the last minute. Bloomingdale's was packed—how I love the contact sport of rifling through a sales rack with chic Manhattanites who smell of good perfume, have two-hundred-dollar haircuts, and use their elbows better than hockey players—but I flashed my credit card with the authority of Joe Friday showing his badge, and the salesgirls flew to my aid.

As I left the store a light wind was whipping up. I was absolutely *laden* with presents and wondering how I'd possibly hail a cab when neither of my arms was free, but then a cab *pulled over*, and not only did the driver get out of the car and ask me if I needed a lift, he took my packages out of my arms and loaded them carefully into the backseat. Ah, the miracles of the season.

Bing Crosby and Nat King Cole lent their voices to the festive atmosphere that filled my evergreen-smelling apartment as I wrapped presents, helping myself to the huge box of fancy chocolates Faith Bennet had sent over (I tried to discern an evil motive—was she trying to make me fat?—but then I finally realized she just might be making a nice gesture) and called friends whose Christmas cards I hadn't reciprocated.

I actually talked and ate (there were some killer caramels in that candy box) more than I wrapped, so it was only after I'd swept up all the snipped tendrils of ribbon and crumpled the last scrap of wrapping paper that I realized it was past midnight.

I had stoked the fire twice and cleaned out practically the whole first tier of the candy box by the time Trevor's key turned in the lock.

"Geneva, you're still up?"

"How'd it go?" I asked, sitting up on the couch.

Trevor sat next to me and took my hands.

"The part is mine."

"Oh, Trevor, congratulations!"

"We start shooting in March—in Mexico City."

"Mexico City in March—lucky." I loosened my hug and looked at him. "What will you do about *Mona!* during shooting?"

Trevor made an airy, dismissive sound. "Did you forget whose contract happens to be up in February?"

"You're going to leave the show?"

"*You* left the show."

"I know, but . . . how can *Mona!* survive without you?"

Obviously I knew that if it could survive without me, it could survive without Trevor, but I just didn't like the idea of him leaving it. Our history was wrapped up in that show, and now that we had a future . . . well, I wanted as few things to change as possible. Trevor didn't hear any of the subtext, of course; he just heard that I thought the show would collapse without him, and he thanked me for the sentiment with a big, long kiss.

"Any word on the leading lady?" I asked, pulling away.

"Well, you can bet I nominated you for the part, but . . ."

"But what?"

"I think they're going with Kimberly Killian."

"Kimberly Killian the *TV* actress?"

Trevor nodded, concern flooding his eyes

"But she's young enough to be your daughter!"

That was a pretty lame excuse to give to a man whose last girl-friend could have called him Daddy, and Trevor's smirk expressed nonverbally exactly what he, Hollywood, and society had to say: "So?"

"Well, it just burns me up. When are they going to cast me with a twenty-two-year-old male costar? When are they going to realize—"

"Geneva," said Trevor, boredom thickening his voice, "let's not even get started on that." He stood up and stretched. "Now come on, let's go to bed. It's late."

Not for you, I thought. *You still get to play with ingenues.*

*I*n my dream I was having the time of my life, riding a unicycle up a mountain, waving to a cheering crowd of Swiss yodelers. When the phone rang, it took me a few moments to recognize that it wasn't part of the yodeling noise but part of the real world that the noise was waking me up to.

"Hello?" I said, more a challenge than a greeting.

"Geneva, it's Ann."

Her voice was so no-nonsense that I sat up, fully alert. "Ann, what's wrong?"

"It's Conrad. His heart. He's . . . he's . . ." Her strong voice cracked. "He's failing, Geneva."

"He's failing?" How I wanted her to elaborate, to finish the sentence with something like, *Yes, he's failing in English! Ha, ha, ha!*— but she didn't.

"Oh, Ann," I said, my own voice breaking. "I'll come as fast as I can."

"Will you? You don't have to, I'm not expecting you to, but . . . will you, please? Rich would love that."

"I'm calling my travel agent now," I said by way of good-bye.

"Geneva, what would I do out there?" asked Trevor as I threw things in my suitcase.

"You'd support me. You'd stand by me."

"No, I'd just get in the way." Still in bed, he leaned forward, trying to take my hand, but I waved his off. "Geneva, I don't know any of these people."

"You know my sister and my brother-in-law," I said, trying to fit the presents I'd just bought for them into the suitcase. "You know Rich."

"I've met them; you can't say I know them. And besides, I've got a show tonight. You expect me to just call in and say I need a couple of days off?"

"You do have an understudy, don't you? An understudy prepared to go on in the event of an emergency?' "

"Geneva." His voice was scolding in the way someone's is when they know the other person is right but consider that rightness irrelevant. "Geneva, we were going to go shopping for rings today, remember?"

"Of course I remember," I said, fighting the temptation to crawl back into bed with him, "but that can wait, Trevor. This can't."

"I'll be sending you good vibes," he said as we kissed good-bye.

"Thanks," I said, even as I thought, *Big deal.*

To say that I was surprised to see James at the airport gate is to say I enjoy chocolate.

He gave me a chaste little kiss on the cheek and took my bag.

"Thanks for coming," he said. "It means a lot to everybody."

"You're welcome," I finally managed to say. "But why did

you pick me up, James? Shouldn't you be on your route or
something?"

"It's my day off. When I heard you were coming, I offered to
pick you up."

"How'd you hear I was coming? I just found out that I was coming today."

"Ann called me. We've been talking a lot lately."

"You have?" I asked, sidestepping a trio of grim-looking
businessmen.

"Sure. There's this network of people who've been keeping
each other posted on Conrad and his family, and whenever Ann
and I talk, I get the extra bonus of hearing about you."

"Did she tell you I said yes to Trevor?"

Pulling me out of the foot traffic, James placed one hand on my
forehead. "You are sort of feverish."

I gave him a courtesy smile—I couldn't summon a laugh—and
then I asked him how Conrad was.

"I'm taking you to the hospital right now," he said. "Everybody's there."

"Oh, James," I said, my heart speeding up, "it's really bad,
isn't it?"

He nodded. "It's really bad."

As we entered the hospital my brain was filled with motiva-
tional directives: *Chin up! Be strong! When the going gets tough, the
tough get going! Look alive!* I thought I was doing pretty good at following them until we got off the elevator and began walking
down the hallway toward swinging doors whose sign read Inten-
sive Care Unit.

"Oh, James, I feel like I'm going to faint."

"Don't," he said, putting his arm around my waist. "Just hold on
to me."

*T*he rule that kept Christmas decorations out of Rich's classroom (Ann had read me the letter he brought home that urged parents not to send anything remotely Christmassy to school with their children, "as it's not fair to the children who don't celebrate the holiday") was not in effect in the waiting room, and I was glad. If anything needed something cheerful in it, it was a hospital waiting room. I respect anyone's religious beliefs, but Christmas trees and wreaths and reindeer cutouts are all-inclusive; everyone likes the idea of Santa Claus and presents. Of course, I can also support the argument that any offshoots of a religious celebration are still offshoots, but the Santa Christmas seems to be an entirely separate holiday from the Christian Christmas.

Anyway, there was an artificial Christmas tree in the corner of the waiting room, draped with red and silver tinsel. It was the only bright spot in a room whose vinyl wallpaper easily qualified for top honors in an ugliest wallpaper ever made contest. It was salmon with what looked like silver metallic sperm swimming through it. The two paintings on this ugly wallpaper were the kind bought in hotel ballrooms in an "Incredible Starving Artists' Sale!" and I had a good mind to speak to the hospital administrator and ask them if they purposely wanted people to feel worse or—

"Aunt Gennie!"

Once again Rich confused tackling for hugging, and I was almost knocked to the floor. Then Ann and Riley surrounded me, and we stood in a hugging, kissing huddle that gradually inched its way to the couch that was upholstered in what looked to be extremely flammable fabric.

As soon as we sat down, the happy noise of our reunion ended. They all had that drained, dazed look, particularly Rich, who looked the way a baby does after he's woken up from a too-long nap.

"Conrad's heart's not working right," he told me.

I nodded, unable to get any words out.

"He's been in the hospital before," he said, "and he always gets better."

I looked at my sister, whose grief-filled eyes were almost too painful to look at, and I was struck by how the things that let us see the world also let people see the world in us.

"Better get better this time," said Rich, and his forehead creased as he crossed his arms.

James, who had been sitting on the piano bench, stood up.

"Barb," he said, both a greeting and an announcement.

We met each other in the middle of the room, and our hug was tight and long-lasting.

"Geneva," said my friend, "thank you so much for coming."

"How could I not?" I said, trying hard to keep my voice from cracking.

"Will you go in and sit with him?" Barb asked Ann, and immediately she and Riley and Rich left the room.

"I'll go too," said James.

Not letting go of each other, Barb and I went to the couch.

"Barb, what *happened*?"

She didn't seem to take offense at my blunt question but sat for a moment shaking her head. My friend was not looking too well. There was a mark on her cheek, and her bad perm was flat on one side, as if she'd been sitting with her head resting in her hand.

"It started out with that cold, remember? I kept him out of swimming because he couldn't seem to shake it?"

I nodded, yearning for that time when it seemed all that was bothering Conrad was a simple cold.

"Well, he seemed to be better around Thanksgiving and at the beginning of December. Then I found him one morning sitting on the stairs in his pajamas."

Tears filmed her eyes. "My first reaction was to yell at him. You know, 'Hurry up, Connie, you're going to miss the bus!' But then he looked up at me and said, 'Mama, I can't breathe too good.' " Barb bowed her head. "I can't explain this feeling—this *coldness*— that came over me. I just knew it was something bad."

"Rich said he's been in the hospital before?"

Barb nodded. "His lungs were so weak when he was born. Well, he's always had these respiratory problems." The sharp breath she drew in almost sounded like a cry. "But they seemed to be getting stronger. The swimming helped, I know, and then . . ." She stared off at the Christmas tree, the thumbs of her folded hands moving back and forth.

"But it's his heart and not his lungs that's causing the problems now?"

"Both. His heart's enlarged, and his lungs have been so weakened. Each conspires to make the other worse. I'm afraid—oh, God, Geneva, I'm so afraid!"

I held her, but we were soon interrupted by her other children, who looked as if they hadn't logged many hours of sleep.

"Mom, we got you some food," said the girl, who introduced herself as Maddy. "Soup from the cafeteria—it's supposed to be good."

"Mom," said Joel, sitting next to her, "I talked to Dad. He's on his way."

Barb put her head on her son's shoulder and accepted the container of soup from her daughter, and I was struck at how capable these older children were in comforting their mother.

"Barb," I said, "do you mind if I go see Conrad now?"

"Oh, no. Please do." As if to assure me she was all right, she managed a thin, polite smile.

"I'll show you where his room is," said Joel, gently disentangling himself from his mother. "I'll be right back, Mom."

Joel was tall, like both of his parents, and he had black hair as straight as I imagined Barb's would be if she didn't perm it.

"Mom's told us a lot about you," he said as we walked down the hallway. "It means so much to her that you're here."

"Oh," I said, embarrassed at the attention I was getting just for showing up. "It's no . . . I . . . well, I got to be pretty good friends with your mother. And with Conrad."

He had the sort of erect bearing of those who think they're in charge of bigger things than they are, but when he heard my words, his head dipped, as if I'd physically struck him.

"Are you all right?" I asked as he leaned against the wall.

He shook his head, his eyes closed. "I . . . I just can't believe any of this is happening. This was *not* supposed to happen."

I joined him against the wall, watching a nurse scurry by.

"Poor Connie." He sniffed, and after a moment he added, "It's gonna destroy Dad."

"Destroy your dad?" I asked, taken aback. "How?"

Joel tipped his head against the wall and looked toward the ceiling. "He'll never get the chance to know Conrad like Mom and Maddy and I do." He produced a gurgly sound, as if he was ready to spit or cry. "And he won't forgive himself for that."

"What about your mother?" I whispered.

That gurgly sound came back in the form of a laugh. "Oh, she forgives him for everything."

"No, I mean, do you think if Conrad . . . dies, it will destroy her too?"

I was amazed at the intimacy of our conversation, seeing as we'd known each other for five minutes, but I guess hospitals are a lot like trains or planes—the people inside are on some sort of journey and want to talk about it.

Joel was standing on one leg like a flamingo or pelican or what-ever the hell bird it is that stands on one leg. His other leg was bent, the sole of his shoe against the wall. Now, instead of the ceiling, he kept his eyes on the foot that was on the floor.

"Nothing destroys Mom. My grandma—my mom's mom—likes to say that whatever Mom is dished out, she'll take."

"Still, I wonder—"

Joel pushed himself off the wall and, pointing, said, "Connie's room is right there. The one with the balloons."

With that dismissal, the tall young man with the good posture walked away, one finger trailing along the wall.

I, however, seemed rooted to the spot, not wanting to go left or right, forward or backward. I smelled coffee brewing and imagined some doctor, on duty for forty-eight hours, standing bleary-eyed by the pot, hurrying along the nurse or candy striper or whoever was making it. *I could use some coffee,* I thought, and, deciding to track down the source of the smell, I began walking in the direction opposite Conrad's room.

"Geneva, over here."

Caught, I stopped in the middle of the hallway and then slowly turned around to see Riley motioning to me from the door with the balloons.

"Oh, there you are," I said, as if I hadn't been planning to chicken out.

"I'm going to get some coffee," he said.

"I was just thinking the same thing," I said.

"We'll get you a cup," said Ann. "You'll stay with Rich and Connie?"

"Where's James?"

"I don't know; he left a couple of minutes ago."

"We thought he went back to the lounge."

I shrugged, as if to say, *Nope.* Then they moved past me in the doorway, and suddenly I was inside the hospital room. Christmas and get-well cards were strung across the walls on string, and stuffed animals sat crammed together on the window ledge. Connie's Twins cap was on the bedside table.

"Hi, Auntie Gen," said Rich, sitting at the side of Conrad's bed. I took a deep breath. "Hi, Rich."

Sitting in the chair next to my nephew's, I tried hard not to look at Connie, who was hooked up to all sorts of beeping and swishing machines. It was hard, though, like trying not to peek at a crash scene.

"How's he doing?" I asked rhetorically, taking the hand of Rich's that wasn't holding Conrad's.

"Don't like this," said Rich quietly. "Don't like this at all."

"Me neither." I squeezed my eyes shut, fighting against the panic that seemed to have shrunk every artery and vessel that had to do with my circulation.

I don't know how long I sat like that, but finally Rich asked, "Auntie Gen? Aunt Gen, wake up!"

"I wasn't sleeping," I said. "I was just thinking about the first time I picked you up at the pool."

"The time when you were late and we had to call Connie's mom?"

"No, the other time when I got to see you guys swim."

I had come into the humid, chlorine-smelling pool area early and sat on a bench against the wall as a young coach urged his swimmers to go faster. Obviously a race was on, but I couldn't tell who was who in the lanes of churning water. Everyone was able to execute somersault turns when they reached the end of the pool except the two slowest swimmers, who stopped and touched the edge before turning back. Everyone was out of the pool by the time the two slow swimmers (whom I had by then recognized as Rich and Connie) finished.

"Hey," the coach had said, holding up his stopwatch. "You guys beat your record!"

To their teammates' applause, the boys had high-fived each other before boosting themselves out of the water, and then Conrad started flapping his arms and pawing at the tiled floor with his feet. I remember my first reaction was that he must be having some sort of seizure.

"Remember when Conrad did that little chicken dance after you guys had gotten out of the pool?"

"Wet-*hen* dance," Rich corrected. " 'Cause Coach told us we would swim faster if we swam like we were mad, and he was right. When we got out of the pool, Connie said to Coach, 'I wasn't just mad in there, I was madder than a wet hen.' And then he started that crazy dance!"

It *had* been hilarious once I realized from everyone's reactions that Conrad wasn't in need of emergency care, and it had been even funnier when, in a show of unity, the entire swim club, including the coach, chicken-danced their way to the locker room.

"He dances every chance he gets," said Rich softly. He leaned closer to Conrad, but the tubes prevented him from getting too close. "You are so funny, Connie. You're the funniest best friend ever."

There was a short rap on the door, announcing a crowd of people including a doctor, a nurse, Barb and her children, and a tall man I assumed was George.

"Come on, Rich," I said, pulling my nephew's hand.

Rich stood up slowly, and then with a wagging finger admonished his best friend not to go anywhere.

*R*iley took Rich home, and Ann and I sat in the lounge drinking flavorless coffee. That it was flavorless didn't seem to diminish its caffeine power; no sooner had I tossed the Styrofoam cup into the wastebasket than I stood up, restless.

"I think I'll take a little walk," I told my sister. "Join me?"

Ann shook her head. I left that lounge so fast that I nearly collided with an orderly pushing a cart full of laundry.

Some fresh air was what I needed, something to breathe other than the slightly sweet, antiseptic stuff that was being pumped through the hospital ventilators.

I jabbed at the elevator button, and when the doors opened, I drew in my breath—not in reaction to seeing a sheeted corpse on its way to the basement morgue, but in reaction to seeing James.

"Hey!" I said, stepping into the elevator. "Where've you been?"

"All over," he said. "Outside, the cafeteria, the chapel."

"Hold the door!"

James blocked the closing door with his arm.

"Thanks," said a young man accompanying a hugely pregnant woman. "My wife and I got off on the wrong floor. I guess we're a little nervous."

"Ohhhh," moaned his wife.

"Floor?" asked James, and when the man said, "Five," James pressed the button.

The woman moaned again, and the man tightened his grip around her.

"It's all right, honey."

"No, it isn't," said the woman, her arms across her huge stomach. "I want to go home."

"It's our first," said the man, with sort of a manic grin. "Her due date's not until next week"—the elevator let out a little ding, and the door opened—"and the funny thing is, other than this, my wife is always late."

"Please," the woman pleaded as they walked toward the nurses' station, "I don't want to do this anymore."

Oh, yes, you do, I thought. *Because at the end you get a baby.*

The elevator door was about closed when I punched the open button.

"Let's stay on this floor, James," I said. "Let's go look in the nursery."

Standing in front of the glass wall, I pointed at one of the four occupied bassinets.

"Look at that one—she'll be the first female Speaker of the House."

Under her pink knit cap, the newborn's red and scrunched-up face was dominated by a huge open mouth.

"Or a Broadway star," said James.

"Thanks a lot," I said, giving him a good nudge. "And look at that one." The baby I pointed to was sleeping, his expression placid and peaceful.

"He's not going to let anything bother him," predicted James. "He'll probably be a diplomat . . . if he can stay awake long enough."

A nurse smiled at us as she set another wrapped bundle in the clear plastic bassinet.

"Now her," I said, watching as the baby stared out at the world with her unfocused eyes. "Definitely an explorer. Maybe the first astronaut on Mars."

"Now that's a sigh," said James, putting his arm around me.

"Oh," I said, unaware that I'd sighed at all. "It's just . . . it's just that I love babies so much. And I'll never have one of my own."

James's arm tightened around me.

"But maybe that's good," I said, my voice high and soft. "Because there's always that chance that they might . . ." I thought of Conrad, three floors below. "That they might die."

With our foreheads pressed to the glass, we stood staring at the babies. The smiling nurse glanced at us again and began to look concerned.

"Why does God let children die?"

This time the big sigh came from James.

"I don't know, Geneva. Why does he let children live? I don't know why He does what he does."

"Then how can you be so sure of your faith?"

"I guess because faith isn't knowing, it's believing."

"Yes, but I've believed in things"—I was thinking of my marriage to Jean-Paul here—"that haven't turned out to be true."

"But when you believe in God," said James, "as much as you're faced with evidence that he doesn't exist, you're faced with even more evidence that he does."

"I don't know that I believe God is a *he*," I said.

"I don't know that I do either," said James. "But I haven't figured out the right word to describe all that God might be."

Another laboring couple, probably looking for inspiration, stopped at the nursery window to look in.

"Let's take a walk," I said to James, suddenly overwhelmed by all this *birth*. "Why do you suppose God never gave me a baby?"

"Oh, Geneva," said James. "Why do you ask me all these big questions?"

A faint smile lifted the corners of my mouth. "Now you sound like my great-aunt Tove. And I ask them because I'd like some answers."

"Well, everyone would. It's just that sometimes when you ask me something, it's as if you're challenging me to come up with the right answer. And if I don't, you act as if I've failed you."

"Really? I don't mean to. It's just that sometimes it seems everyone else has more answers than I do."

"You strike me as the one with the answers, Geneva."

We were at the elevator bank now, and one set of doors whooshed open as soon as James pressed the button.

"Well, I don't have the answer as to why God never gave me a baby."

"I don't think God's about what he gives us and what he doesn't—I think it's about what we do with it."

He looked up at the lighted strip of numbers above the door. I stepped back a foot and inexplicably, like a child lashing out at a classmate who always knows the answers, stuck my tongue out at him.

*T*hat night I slept like a baby—a colicky, fretful baby who woke every half hour, desperately in need of comfort, warmth, a reassuring voice. My falling-back-asleep routine rarely varied; I'd fan the waistband of my pajama bottoms, which were damp with sweat (ah, sweet maladies of menopause), punch the unyielding couch pillow, and stare at the Christmas tree lights blinking on and off, on and off. It was a routine whose effects weren't immediate, but eventually I would drift back into a sleep whose dreams were the scary, being-chased kind, making it a relief to wake up. Until it took so long to get back to sleep.

Finally, after a dream about a predatory square dancer, my eyes opened and I blinked once, fully awake. I could tell by the fuzzy gray light that it was dawn, and even though I couldn't see or hear her, I knew Ann was in the room.

"I guess I should have unplugged those Christmas lights," I said, sitting up. "Remember how Mom would yell at Dad to turn them off before he went to bed?"

Getting no response, I turned to see Ann, dressed in her coat, standing under the room's archway. Her posture, so still and erect, reminded me of statues, a game we played when we were kids.

"Ann?" I said softly, going to her, and as I got close, I could see that unlike a statue, she was trembling.

I hesitated then, not wanting to step any closer, not wanting the seconds and minutes to move forward, because I didn't want to hear what she would say in them. But before I could tell her to wait, why don't we just ignore the laws of time and space, her eyes widened as if she were looking at the bright gold of a hypnotist's pendulum and she said, "Well . . . Connie died."

I squeezed my eyes shut against the blow of her words, and then after we practically pulled each other to the ground in a hug, I found myself going to the closet and putting my own coat on.

"Come on," I said, walking back to her and taking her by the arm. "Let's take a walk."

"I can't," she said, as if she were apologizing. "It's too cold out there. I'm too cold."

"Okay, then," I said, opening the door. "We'll take a drive."

In a crisis, I always obey instinct; it's like a gruff but well-intentioned tour guide who takes you by the arm, leading you to a place you might not want to think about but where nevertheless you have to go. Instinct told me now we needed movement, we needed to go somewhere different.

The Bonneville was still warm.

"Did you just come from the hospital?" I asked, taking the keys from her and putting them in the ignition.

Ann nodded.

"So he just . . . how long . . ."

"He died at four-forty-two," said Ann, understanding my babbling. "Conrad was born late at night and died early in the morning—that's what Barb said." Ann wiped condensation off the window with a gloved finger. "She kept saying that over and over—like a chant or a news announcement."

Blinking back the tears that had swarmed into my eyes, I

backed out of the driveway, obeying the need to flee. The eastern sky was pink now, and it was toward that color that I drove, swallowing down the bile that kept rising in my throat.

"He didn't say good-bye," said Ann as I turned onto Lake Road. "Barb said she was sure he'd open his eyes at the end and give her some kind of sign—a blink or a smile—but he just slipped away." She said this so calmly that I was completely unnerved when a moment later she yelped as if she'd been stung by a wasp. "He just slipped away!" she said, her voice the same piercing level as her scream. "Can you imagine Conrad leaving without some little joke? Some bon mot?" She thrashed her head back and forth like a test dummy in a simulated crash. "Oh, God, Geneva, he didn't even say good-bye!"

She was shrieking now, and when she couldn't sustain her screams anymore, they tumbled into sobs. Every muscle and every ligament in my body tightened until I felt I might crack in half, right there in the driver's seat of the Bonneville.

The frozen lake looked like depression itself, wide and gray, the trees black and bare and crab-fingered alongside it. I turned toward the freeway just to escape its view.

Her head buried in her hands, Ann cried, and I zipped back and forth across lanes yet to be clogged with rush-hour traffic. I flashed on the conversation I'd had with the perfume salesman on the plane, and I knew what a scent called Grief would smell like—it would smell of a car interior where the heat was on a little too high and old snow and the clammy sweat produced by a body that's hyperalert. Not only did I know the smell of grief, but I knew the sound: my sister's cries muffled in her gloved hands, tires slicing through slush, and my heartbeat loud as a drum played by a tribesman announcing war.

I wondered what exactly driving aimlessly (and too fast, I noticed, checking the speedometer) was going to accomplish, but then as I drove toward the skyline of downtown Minneapolis, I realized I had a destination after all.

When I parked the car and turned off the ignition, I thought Ann was asleep, but a moment later she took her hands away from her pale and tear-washed face and looked out the windshield.

"Hey," she said, her voice thick, "the old neighborhood."

We sat silently for a moment, surveying the two houses we grew up in.

"What happened to the big tree that used to be in Grandma's front yard?" I asked.

"Dutch elm disease, I'll bet," said Ann. "It took down thousands of trees."

"When was that?"

Ann sniffed. "I don't know—fifteen, twenty years ago."

"It was a nice tree. Remember the card table we used to set up under it to sell lemonade?"

"Ten cents a glass," said Ann, smiling. "We charged double what everyone else was charging, but we told our customers we used only the—"

"Choicest lemons," I said, remembering, and then we both said our old slogan together: "The choicest lemons from Lemon City, Florida."

"We always sold out," she said, squeezing my hand. I was surprised at the pressure; I hadn't even realized we'd been holding hands.

"You want to walk around the block?" I asked.

Ann nodded, opening up her door.

Arm in arm, we stood on the shoveled sidewalk, looking at our parents' and grandparents' homes.

"They restuccoed Grandma's house," said Ann.

"And look at the trim on ours. It was much prettier when it was green."

"Remember how we built that clubhouse and cut up one of the screen windows to use as our own?"

"Dad was *livid*," I said. "And Grandma asked him, 'Don't you know great architecture when you see it?' "

Ann laughed at the memory, and no doubt at my right-on Norwegian accent.

We decided we'd better start walking before someone called the police to report two middle-aged women standing there staring at houses.

"Let's go through the alley," suggested Ann, and so, under the leafless branches of the boulevard trees, we walked down the block, turned, and then turned again once we got to the alley.

In Minneapolis, if your block had a lot of children on it, the alley was a playground and meeting place. There we'd race our bikes on either side of the center crack; pat Timmy, the beloved albeit stinky old retriever who kept watch from his perch next to the garage door; and play games of kick the can or four square, calling out "Car!" whenever Mr. O'Keefe's Ford (its back window clothes hook always hung with shirts for his business trips) or Mr. Myer's wood-paneled station wagon needed to pass. Those were in the days when you'd run through yards whose clothesline were filled with rows of drying overalls and work shirts, capri pants and blouses, and, on the obese Mrs. Huffman's line, huge-cupped cotton bras and graying girdles that made you feel a little naughty and a little sad just looking at them. You could still burn your trash then, and we kids would stand on a driveway in a half circle throwing sticks and rocks into the rusty barrel that shot out sparks if your aim was good. Now by every garage stood big plastic trash containers, lidded to contain the smell, and green recycling boxes.

We walked along in silence, strengthening our grip on each other when one would start to slip on the ice. It had been decades since I'd walked down this alley, and yet it was more familiar to me than my own street in New York.

We stopped in front of the short driveway that led to our grandma's garage, and Ann said quietly, "Oh, Geneva, look."

The corner of the shoveled driveway sloped down to the alley. It had been on that corner one hot summer's day that Grandma Hjordis and Ann and I had, with twigs we'd snapped off the lilac bush, inscribed our initials in the newly poured concrete.

"God, I miss her," I said.

"Me too," said Ann. "But at least we had each other to help us get through it." She looked at me, her eyes desperate "Who will Rich have? The only person who could help him get through Connie's death is . . . was . . . Connie."

A German shepherd bounded out of the house across the alley and, barking its I'd-like-to-rip-your-throat-out bark, paced the fence along the driveway where furry, stinky, placid Timmy used to lie, thumping his matted tail when we'd stop to pat his head. Ann and I, clutching each other, simultaneously burst into tears.

Chapter 11

*T*he worst sound I ever heard in my life was the sound Rich made when Ann and Riley told him that Conrad had died. It was like a goat whose leg was caught in the jaws of a spring trap, a screaming bleat that was so terrible it was almost comical.

I had asked Ann if she wanted me there, but she had looked so confused at the question that I told her maybe it would be better if just she and Riley told him but to holler if she changed her mind. So there I sat on the guest room bed, wringing my hands like a bad actor projecting worry. When Rich's keening and bleating went on and on, I felt sick, and I clamped my hands over my ears to mute that horrible noise.

About an hour later they came down to the kitchen where I sat at the counter trying to erase a wrong answer I'd made in ink in the newspaper crossword puzzle. They were so pale that I felt the blood drain out of my own face in sympathy and in shock. Under his glasses, Rich's eyes were red-rimmed, and he seemed smaller, scrunched over as if he'd just been socked in the stomach. He stared at the floor, his chin jutted out, and after Ann asked him if he'd like some juice and Riley poured two cups of coffee, he looked up at me and said, his voice as raspy as someone with a pack-a-day habit, "I'm sure you heard the bad news."

I nodded, and projectile hugger that he was, he shot himself into my arms.

The crying started all over again; we were nearly prostrate from our tears, our bodies sagging against the counter like drunken gunfighters in the town saloon.

We let the machine pick up all the calls that were coming in, but when I heard a long pause and then my mother's voice saying, "I hate these darn machines," I took it upon myself to tear off a paper towel from the roll, wipe my face with it, and answer the phone.

"Geneva, is that you?" asked my mother. "Are you back there again? My heavens, what you must spend on airfare! Say, listen, your dad and I are going to be spending Christmas at our friends' in Scottsdale, so we thought—"

"Mom, Rich's friend Conrad died."

She gasped, hearing my words over hers. "Oh, no, Geneva. How?"

I motioned for Ann, and we all listened as she told Mom the sad details. I made another pot of coffee as Riley sat staring at a refrigerator magnet that advertised the local pizzeria.

"Rich," said Ann, cupping her hand over the receiver, "Grandma wants to talk to you."

I expected Rich to not respond, or at least to shake his head (which had been cradled in his arms on the kitchen counter), but he rose obediently and took the phone from Ann.

Watching his face, I tried to figure out what his grandmother was saying to him, but his features, usually so full of expression, were still.

Finally, after bobbing his head and saying, "Okay," he hung up.

"That was Grandma," he reminded us. "She told me Conrad is in a place where nobody is sad or can't run fast. Told me Conrad's my angel friend now, and anytime I want to talk to him—even at midnight—he can hear me."

Ann and I looked at each other. This was *our mother* giving such comforting advice? The kind of advice our own grandma had given us?

Rich stood looking up at the ceiling, his lips moving. When he looked at us, he gave a little smile, as if he'd been caught with his hands in the cookie jar.

"Just told Connie I got him blue swim goggles for Christmas. He said I could keep 'em." He smiled again, or tried to, before his face crumpled.

*I*n a church filled with holiday poinsettias, hundreds of people came to pay their last respects.

We sat in a row behind the Torgersons, Rich flanked by his parents, Ann on my left, James and Natalie on my right. My heart was hammering away as if I'd just done five hundred jumping jacks in under two minutes, and I wondered how long it could keep up this pace before I fell over dead. Then I felt guilty for making light of the word *dead* when there was a real dead person in the mahogany box not ten feet away from me. It didn't help any that I felt myself falling into a volcanic hot flash.

I let go of James's hand—I'd been gripping both his and Ann's—to fan my face with the program.

"Are you okay?" James whispered.

I shook my head, and he said, "Tolerable not okay or intolerable not okay?"

I thought about this for a moment, and as the internal lava cooled to a level that might not cook me, I said, "Tolerable not okay, I guess."

"Breathe deeply," said James. I took his counsel and tried to draw huge quantities of nourishing oxygen into my anxiety-ridden, Mount Vesuvius–like body without attracting too much attention. I began to feel calmer with each breath, but when a voice from the choir loft began to sing, all hopes of getting through the service as something other than a basket case were dashed.

I was, however, not the only one. The soprano voice was singing that Quaker or Shaker song "Simple Gifts," and by the time she got to the part that said, " 'Tis the gift to come down where we ought to be," I heard a half dozen sobs, one of them coming from Ann. I squeezed her hand, thinking of Conrad getting up to boogaloo in the circle of his Sunday school friends and announcing that one of his gifts was, "I can *move!*"

Barb turned around and Rich leaned forward, and I could tell we were sharing the same memory.

"I can *move*," I mouthed, and Barb nodded slightly, her lips drawn in—a gate trying to hold back a flood.

Rich reached across his mother's lap to pat my arm.

"He *could* move," he whispered in agreement.

It was a beautiful service. The pastor knew Conrad enough to really eulogize him, and the congregation sang "Children of the Heavenly Father" and the soloist sang Simon and Garfunkel's "Bridge over Troubled Waters." When there was about an inch of tears flowing down the center aisle, the pastor announced that it was time for us to share our stories of Conrad, and by the third one, the tears were a river, with the odd Bible and pledge card bobbing along on its current.

Okay, I exaggerate, it wasn't quite a river, it was a creek.

Two of Conrad's teachers spoke, and then nervous Mr. Talerico, the band instructor, stood up.

"When you teach music to middle-schoolers," he said, reading nervously from notes, "you can go from utter frustration to joy, and all in the space of a few bars." He cleared his throat, and I saw that his hands holding the note card trembled. "When Connie sat in on honor band practice, the joy factor was always raised. He loved music—he used to tell me he didn't hear it here"—Mr. Talerico, not looking up, touched his ears—"so much as he felt it here." I was sure the instructor was going to bring his hands to the left side of his chest, but he surprised me (and a lot of people, judging by the gasps I heard) by touching his backside. "Yes," he said, and with a twitchy smile, he finally looked up at his audience. "Connie always told me, 'Good music makes me want to shake my booty!' "

The congregation laughed.

The band instructor seemed to gain confidence from their laughter. Putting the note card in his pocket, he said, "Connie loved all music, but one of his favorite booty-shaking songs was one we played at pep rallies." He looked to the back of the room. "Kids?"

Suddenly the strains of the *Hawaii Five-0* theme filled the church as band members strode down the aisle, their tubas and trumpets flashing. Rich clapped his hands, his mouth open in surprised delight.

The church erupted in applause when they finished, and it seemed a collective sigh rose from everyone's chest, thankful as we were for the reprieve.

Conrad's brother Joel spoke next, and then Hannah of the striped blond hair stepped up. She stood staring at Conrad's coffin as she spoke.

"I liked how you could make one tiny little kiss seem like such a big deal, Conrad. Thanks for making me feel like I gave you something special." She sat down then, tossing back her hair in what seemed an arrogant gesture, but you could tell she needed to do something like that just so she wouldn't fall apart.

More kids from Sunday school spoke; Megan the zippy cheerleader enthused ("I just *loved* Connie!"), and Mensa member Holly, who I was certain was going to quote from some deep poem whose meaning I'd be too shallow to catch, said simply, "Conrad taught me a lot of things."

There was a silence then, and Ann poked me in the side with her elbow, handing me a damp and folded piece of paper.

"Will you read this?" she whispered, her voice quavery. "I helped Rich write it, but he can't read it and neither can I."

Immediately my heart responded as if I were back to doing high-speed jumping jacks.

"I . . . I . . ." I wanted to so badly, but I knew that if I stood up, I'd completely lose it, raising the level in the creek of tears.

"James?" I whispered—no, *beseeched,* handing him the paper.

He looked at me, puzzled for a moment, like a seventh-grader onto whose lap a note had been thrown. But he understood immediately when he opened it.

"Would anyone else like to speak?" asked the minister.

"You want me to read this?" James whispered.

I nodded furiously.

I watched his Adam's apple bob in his throat, but without hesitation James stood up and introduced himself.

"Connie once came to a hockey game I coached," he said, his voice strong and true, "and afterward he said, 'James, I think I'd make a good goalie.' 'Why's that?' I asked, and he said, 'Because I'd fake 'em out. I'd be moving around so much, no one would know where to shoot.' " James waited as the congregation laughed. "And now," he said, holding out the note, "I'd like to read something written by Rich Wahlstrom, Connie's very best friend in the world."

He scratched the hair above his ear and then read. " 'Dear Conrad: When I die it won't be so scary because you'll be there waiting for me. You were always there waiting for me and I hope I find out what to do now that you're not. When you were alive I sure was lucky. Love, your pal forever, Rich.' "

James stood for a moment in his well-cut suit, staring down at the paper in his hand. There was a deep silence. And then the creek of tears swelled and the whole church was under water.

*A*s children, Ann and I always opened our presents on Christmas Eve, which pretty much shot any Santa Claus myths we wanted to believe in, although we tried.

"Maybe Santa comes early to some houses," I would tell Ann hopefully, "because think of it—how could he do all those houses while everyone was sleeping?"

"You girls don't need to believe in Santa Claus," said Grandma Hjordis, whose kitchen table we were seated at, helping her make *krumkaka*, our favorite Norwegian Christmas cookie. "All you need to believe in is God. He's way bigger and gives you more than Santa ever could."

I grew up thinking that the one flaw our fun-loving grandma had was her unwillingness to let us believe in Santa—what was the matter with a little magic, a little fantasy? But to tell you the truth, the slight deprivation Ann and I felt over not being brought up to believe was *nothing* compared to the betrayal our true-believer friends felt upon finding out Santa Claus was Mom and Dad.

My hairdresser friend Benny told me that his mother even read him the "Yes, Virginia, there is a Santa Claus" letter, hoping to soften the terrible blow he felt upon learning of Santa's nonexistence.

"Did it help?" I asked him.

Benny shook his head. "I called her a liar and kicked her in the shins."

So that was our tradition, and I thought it was a sweet one. And besides, it's more dramatic to open presents at night than in the daytime.

Because I would be going back to New York the next morning, we decided to open presents *really* early (by more than a week) this year, but boy, there were no shrieks of happiness this evening, no scraps of wrapping paper flying through the air like a juggler's hankies, no modeling of sweaters or hats or gloves, no getting on the floor with Rich to figure out how to put together one of his so-called easy-assembly toys.

It was a very subdued affair; we ate a quiet dinner and afterward sampled from the tray of Christmas cookies Ann had been baking and freezing all month, and drank freely of the Christmas cheer, which in our case was red or white wine.

Rich sat in between his parents on the couch, and we all took pains to try to draw him into conversation when it seemed he had been staring at the fire too long. I asked him which he preferred, the cookies with the Hershey's Kisses in the middle or the ones shaped like candy canes. And Riley asked him if he liked the gondolier Aunt Geneva had given him.

"Do like it," he said in answer to Riley's question. He'd been holding on to the wooden figure since unwrapping it. "But he'll be lonely," he said, petting the figure's head with one finger. "Needs a robot."

I could see the confusion on Ann's and Riley's faces, and so I reminded them that Conrad had been a robot on Halloween.

" 'Member how snowy it was?" Rich asked.

"I remember."

" 'Member how that one house gave us popcorn balls?"

"I remember."

When the doorbell rang, I got up quickly to get it, happy to leave, if just for a moment, the sadness in that room.

"James said he might stop by," I said, banging into an end table in my haste.

My relief was short-lived when I opened the door and saw not James but the person who had to bear even greater sadness than ours: Barb. She held a package and an uncertain expression.

"Ann said you were going to open some presents . . ."

"Oh, Barb," I said, hugging her, and then as I pulled her inside I saw the headlights of another car turning into the driveway.

"Looks like James is here," I said.

"Good," said Barb. "I could use a party."

*T*here was a flicker of the old Rich when he opened the video games that James gave him.

"Space Expedition," he said. *"Thanks."*

He gave himself a few minutes to enjoy his bounty, but then it was as if a buzzer rang: *Enough happiness. Now it's time to get back to grief.*

"Rich?" said Barb when he returned to his fire-staring trance. "Rich, I've got a present for you too."

I really didn't know how she did it, how when her own heart had been shattered she still had enough of a piece left to even *think* of giving Rich a Christmas present.

She and Ann exchanged looks, and I could see in those looks how they were giving each other all sorts of things—courage, support, a little hope.

Rich opened the package carefully, stopping twice to adjust his glasses, which to me didn't look as if they needed adjusting.

When he had finally unwrapped the box, he sighed a deep sigh before taking the lid off. We all did; it was a fraught-with-tension unwrapping, like watching Roosevelt open a present from Stalin. (I'm not comparing Barb to Stalin, but you get my drift.)

At the moment he saw what was inside, Rich's face was one of awe—the same look I saw on his face when the Rockettes began to kick for the first time.

"Connie's hat," he breathed. "I got Connie's hat."

He lifted it out of the box as gently as you would a baby. He looked expectantly at his mother and then at Barb, who said, "You can put it on, Rich. Conrad would have wanted you to wear it."

And so Rich put on the hat that had been his best friend's signature.

"Fits perfect," he said, tugging at the brim. "Anybody got a mirror?"

We adults sat there mesmerized, as if watching a magician pull a whole herd of rabbits out of his sleeve. For one sweet moment we believed anything was possible, that Rich was going to be all right.

"Hey, I've got something for you too," said Rich, and we all watched as he ran into the kitchen, wondering what on earth he was getting.

He came out of the kitchen flushed, hugging *The Great Mysterious* to his chest. "Connie and me answered a bunch of questions one night when he slept over. One night before he went into the hospital." His forehead puckered as he looked at Barb. "You haven't already seen them, have you? Because we wanted them to be a surprise."

"No," Barb whispered, "I haven't seen them." And judging by the looks of surprise on Riley's and Ann's faces, neither had they.

Rich wedged himself in between his mother and Barb and opened the book. His tongue stuck out in concentration, he thumbed through the pages, his finger running below each question as he silently read it. Finally he stopped and with a big smile said, "This is a good one."

The question was "Who do you most admire?" and Rich dug his fingers in the pocket and extracted two slips of paper. "Do you want to read just Connie's or mine too?" We all agreed we'd like to read his as well, and so he gave James one slip of paper and me the other with orders to read.

James unfolded his. " 'I know he's not real, but I still admire Superman because he came from far away not knowing anybody and then was able to do a lot of good for people and fight off bad people. I like how he's sort of dorky as Clark Kent but then as Superman you couldn't find a dorky bone in his body.' "

"That sounds dumb, doesn't it?" asked Rich. "Sounds like some kid wrote it."

"It sounds wonderful," said Ann. "I like how he's dorky as Clark Kent but not as Superman too."

"Should I read now?" I asked, trying to still the little tremble that vibrated through my body. Barb, staring at me, nodded.

"You'll love this," said Rich, putting his head on Ann's shoulder.

" 'I would like to know who wrote this question,' " I read from Connie's inconsistent handwriting, " 'because I'd like to yell at them. How are you supposed to pick one person when there are so many people to admire like your mom, or your brother and sister, or Mr. Talerico or your swim coach or Arnold Schwarzenegger or those guys that go down the giant ski jump and twirl around in midair? If someone told me I had to pick one or they'd shoot me, I'd say, well, then, go ahead and shoot. Just kidding. Okay, if I had to pick one, it would have to be: who else but Rich? Think about it. The guy's hardly ever in a bad mood, and if he is in one, it's easy to joke him out of it. He doesn't have my looks or my brains or my way with women, but it doesn't bother him. He's not jealous of anything you might have—in fact, he's happy for you! How many people are like that? A lot of people say people like Rich and me are "disabled" and in their voices you can hear how sorry they are, but people, don't be sorry! In fact, why don't you just eat shit!' "

There was a second or so of silence, and then Barb said, "That's my boy." Then Rich whooped with laughter, and we all had to join in. Again I thought, *It's going to be all right,* but in the next moment Rich burst into tears, tore Connie's hat off his head, and held the hat to his mouth, kissing it again and again.

We all went into comfort mode, surrounding him, patting and holding him. He cried until his reservoir of tears was dry, and then he fell asleep. I felt humbled that it was against my shoulder.

"He'll cherish that hat," said Ann once Rich's snores assured us all he was asleep, and we all looked for a long time at the hat, which was balled up under Rich's hands. Finally Barb asked if she could have some wine.

"We're some hosts, huh?" said Riley, patting Ann's knee as he stood up. He returned from the kitchen with two more glasses and filled them for Barb and James.

"Would you read some more, Geneva?" asked Barb after taking a big swallow of the Italian wine.

"I'd be honored," I said, shifting my shoulder slightly; Rich's head was like an anvil on it.

Ann passed me the book, and I opened it to the back pages.

" 'What makes you happy?' " I read, and then asked, "I wonder who wrote that question?"

"I did," Barb said. "I was sort of daunted trying to think of a big question."

"That's plenty big," said Riley, and the rest of us agreed.

I dipped my hand into the pocket and unfolded the piece of paper I withdrew.

"Bingo. It's Connie's. 'Hannah makes me happy. Did you ever notice how her hair is different colors? Yellow blond, plain blond, dark blond. Her low voice makes me happy too. Girls with low voices seem like they have a secret everybody else would love to find out. What else? Let's see. PEZ, video games, the Sci-Fi Channel, and when my brother, Joel, calls from college and wants to talk to me. My mom singing in the morning makes me happy too, even though she can't sing. It just is a good start to a day, you know? Pancakes and my mom using three notes to sing "You Are the Sunshine of My Life." ' "

"Oh," said Barb softly. "Oh, he was."

What can you do in those moments when sadness is another element in the air, just as real as hydrogen and oxygen and nitrogen? What can you do but simply sit there and breathe it in, feeling it in each long and heavy breath?

"Would you like me to read more?" I asked finally.

Barb shook her head. "Although I'd love to take the book home with me, if you don't mind. I could use some answers to the great mysterious about now."

Moving carefully so I wouldn't wake up Rich, I tied up the book and set it on the coffee table.

"How's your family doing?" asked Ann, her voice soft.

Barb took a sip of wine that nearly emptied her glass. "The kids both went to bed early, and George . . . well, George is sort of incommunicado right now."

"I talked to him a little after the service," said James. "He's not doing too well, is he?"

Barb shook her head. "Actually, James, he is doing rather lousy." She let out the kind of sound a person makes when they've got whooping cough.

Rich stirred, and I took the opportunity to slide out from under him, easing him down to the couch pillow. I sat on the floor, massaging my shoulder with one hand and refilling Barb's glass with the other.

"You know what Maddy said?" asked Barb, taking the glass from me and nodding in thanks. "She's the poet of the family. Anyway, she said it's like we're in this awful storm, but at least we're in lifeboats, little boats made of all the love and memories we have of Conrad. And what she said is true for us, but George?" She took a sip, wrinkling her nose. "George doesn't have a boat. George is drowning."

"Oh, Barb," said Ann, pale as muslin.

"Well, you knew that, Ann. You knew how George was going to sink."

Ann nodded. "I did."

"What can we do to help?" asked Riley.

Barb bit her top lip. "Just what you're doing," she said. "Listen to me."

And so we did. We listened long into the night, to Barb at first, but then to the stories we all told about Conrad. As the Christmas tree lights blinked on and off and Ann replenished the cookie tray, as Riley poured more wine and I made a pot of coffee to counteract the wine, as James added another log to the fire and Rich snored, we held our own little wake for that dear boy whose baseball cap was still nestled in the shelter of his best friend's hand.

Saying good-bye to Rich the next day was torturous, not because he clung to me, sobbing, but because he didn't. He was subdued and resigned, as if departures were inevitable and maybe a person had just better accept them.

I had taken James up on his offer to take me to the airport, and so I said good-bye to my kith and kin at home.

"Thanks again, Dee," said Ann as we gave each other one last hug.

"You're welcome—for whatever it is you're thanking me for."

"For being here with us." She fluffed a strand of my hair. "And hey—good luck on opening night."

"*Re*opening night," I reminded her. "And thanks, Dum."

I went over to Rich, who stood looking out the picture window. When I put my hand on his shoulder, he flinched.

I took his hands. "You know you can call me anytime to talk. Anytime at all."

Rich stuck out his lower lip and did not meet my eyes.

"I wish I could stay, honey, but I've got to get back to New York. Big return to Broadway, you know."

Uninterested in my babble, Rich stared straight ahead.

"Maybe you can come see me during spring break. Wouldn't that be fun, Rich, to come to New York in the spring? It's really beautiful then, almost as good as—"

"Connie's never coming back, is he?" asked Rich, his voice flat.

I squeezed his hand. "No, Rich, he never is."

"Are you ever coming back?"

My breath caught in my throat. "Oh, Rich," I said, when it returned, "of course I am. I'll come back whenever I can. And when I can't . . . well, that's when you can come see me."

"I like New York," he said, nodding. Then, looking at me for the first time during our conversation, he asked, "You know what Connie said once?"

"No, what did he say?"

A shy smile played on my nephew's lips. "He said James was lucky to kiss you. He said if you were a little younger, he'd like to kiss you too. He said your red hair was foxy."

He laughed, and then I did too, because it was such a pleasure to hear his laughter.

"Maybe that's what heaven's like," said Rich, his voice soft again. "If you like kissing, maybe you get to kiss all day."

I nodded. "Sounds kind of heavenly to me."

*T*he drive to the airport began awkwardly—it was as if James and I had been set up on a blind date and already knew we weren't a good match. Bits of conversation began and then, having no weight at all, drifted off.

"So what are you doing for Christmas?" I asked.

"I don't know. Karin's taking Natalie to Hawaii, so I haven't really made any plans." James looked behind his shoulder before changing lanes. "You?"

Should I mention Trevor?

"Oh, no plans yet."

Finally we let silence take over, and James occupied himself driving and I occupied myself by staring out the window, not really seeing anything at all.

We were walking through the parking lot to the terminal, our silence still a presence, when suddenly James stopped, his head slightly cocked.

"Do you hear that?"

I stopped, cocking my head in an exaggerated manner, willing to play whatever little game he was playing. But then I did hear something besides the usual airport parking lot noises. I heard someone crying, or to be more precise, a child crying.

We both stood there for a moment, and then James began to walk in between the parked cars, calling softly, "Hello?"

I followed, echoing him. "Hello?"

He stopped when he came to an old Chevrolet with those pointy, dangerous-looking fins.

"Hello, can we help you?" he asked, poking his head into the opened window.

I sidled up to him, ready to comfort the frightened child, but there was no child in the old Chevy. What there was in the old Chevy was an old woman.

"Oh, dear," she muttered in between sniffles, shaking her head.

"Madam," said James softly, "is there any way we might assist you?"

I wondered why James suddenly sounded as if he'd slipped into a Henry James novel, but his courtliness seemed to soothe the old woman.

"Well," she said, dabbing at her eyes, "I . . . I seem to have lost my way."

"Come with us," said James, opening the door. "We'll help you find it."

The woman, wet-faced, pulled her tasseled stocking cap over her ears and smiled at James with sheer gratitude.

"Yes," I said, as she stepped out of the car, tiny and frail as only a lost old lady can be, "come on, we'll help you get where you need to go."

Mrs. Crandall—she introduced herself as soon as James grabbed the suitcase that had been perched next to her in the front seat—had a surprisingly strong gait for someone who was so stooped and frail (looking at her, I made a mental note to take my calcium). She was slightly duck-footed, and the toes of her old-lady shoes pointed outward as she walked. Her fists were clenched as if she were ready to knock down anyone who might get in her way.

"May I ask you, Mrs. Crandall," said James, "what has caused you so much distress?"

I shot him a look—why was he keeping up with this Henry James stuff?—and he understood it completely, shrugging and making a face.

"Well," said the old woman, looking straight ahead, "I was just a little confused. Confused as to how I got to be sitting in that big old car in the first place."

"It's not yours?" said James, stopping in his tracks. "If it's not your car, I'd better return these keys." Thinking he'd done the old woman a favor, he'd taken the keys she'd left in the ignition.

"Keys?" she said, stopping too. She bit her barely there bottom lip. "Keys? To the car? The big Chevy?"

We waited for a moment, expecting her to say more, and when she didn't, James said. "Yes, the big Chevy. Is that your car?"

"Of course it's my car," said Mrs. Crandall. "Has been ever since Mr. Crandall relaxed his women-shouldn't-drive policy." She chuckled. "He thought he was an old toughie, but he was really pudding inside."

"Is Mr. Crandall still living?" I asked.

The small woman stuck out her chin—some of her gestures reminded me of Rich's—and said, "The last year he saw this earth was 1975."

"Do you have any children we can call?" asked James.

"Children? Of course I have children Five of them, the last time I checked."

"Do they know where you're going?" I asked.

"I'm a grown woman," said Mrs. Crandall. "I expect I don't need my children's permission to take a little trip."

A traffic cop gestured for us to cross the intersection to the terminal. James, ever the Boy Scout, held Mrs. Crandall's elbow.

"So where are you going with such a light suitcase?" asked James as the automatic doors of the terminal opened. Raising the suitcase in one hand, he looked at me and mouthed the words, "It's empty."

"Why, I'm going to Louisiana, son. With a banjo on my knee."

The relative sanity that Mrs. Crandall had summoned up during the brief walk from the car was lost when we entered the airport. She began crying and muttering again, and tried to break free of the restraints James's and my hands offered.

"Don't be frightened, Mrs. Crandall. We're going to help you," said James.

"Everything will be all right," I lied in a reassuring voice. I looked at James with a what-now expression, which he answered with another shrug.

"How about over there?" I whispered, nodding to an information kiosk.

"Oh, it's never all right. I put the kettle on to boil, and then there's not a cookie in the house." Agitated, Mrs. Crandall's eyes darted back and forth. "All I asked for was one little tiny cookie."

"There, there," I found myself saying, patting her shoulder with the hand that didn't have a grip on her arm.

"How are you doing for time?" James asked me.

I looked at my watch, having forgotten that I was at the airport for a purpose other than assisting a confused woman. "Well, we might not be able to have that drink."

"I don't want you to miss your flight."

"And then that darn sink stopped up," said Mrs. Crandall. "If it's not one thing, it's another."

"That's for sure," I said, patting her again.

The woman at the information booth looked confused as we told her our story.

"You found her in a *car*?"

"Yes," said James. "We heard someone crying in the parking lot and found her—uh, Mrs. Crandall."

"Why was she crying?"

"We don't exactly know," said James.

"Look," I said, deciding this ignoramus needed to be given some information, since she obviously couldn't dispense it. "We don't know much more than you do, so why don't you just call the police and see if anyone's reported her missing."

James's lips pulled down and his eyes widened in an impressed expression.

"Well, all right," said the information woman, as if she were doing us a big favor.

"Tell Mabel it's not oleo," Mrs. Crandall said. "Tell her it's just pale butter."

With the telephone to one ear and a finger stuck inside the other (she was apparently the sort who didn't function well with distraction), the information lady was nodding her head.

"Well, yes, yes, they brought her here just now." She squinted at Mrs. Crandall. "No, I don't think she looks harmed." She looked at me. "Is she harmed?"

"Why don't you let me talk to them?" I said, holding my hand out.

The police officer told me that yes, a Winona Crandall had been reported missing from Field Manor, an assisted-living facility.

"I'm looking at the screen here," said the officer, "and this is the third time she's run off. Last week they found her at a casino."

"She just gets in her car and goes?"

"Gets in *a* car and goes. It says here that the last time, she 'borrowed' a resident's car."

"Was it an old Chevrolet?"

"No, ma'am. In the other incident she was reported as having confiscated a 1992 Toyota belonging to the home's receptionist. Took her purse too."

After hanging up, I relayed the conversation to James, while Mrs. Crandall muttered about her inability to find double-E-width shoes for Mr. Crandall.

"So they're sending someone to pick her up," I said. "We're supposed to wait for them by the southernmost door on the departure level." I looked at my watch. "I have time to walk up there with you, but then I'd better be going."

"I too must be going," said Mrs. Crandall in her well-modulated, sane voice. "I don't have time for all this monkey business."

"Where is it you're going again?" I asked her.

The old woman squinted her eyes and shook her head, as if she'd just heard the dumbest question ever asked.

"I told you, missy. I'm going to Kansas City. Got some crazy little women, and I'm a-gonna get me one."

James and I laughed out loud but quickly stopped ourselves, ashamed that we found humor in some poor old woman quoting song lyrics.

There was a bench by the door I had been told to wait at, and we both sat down, wedging Mrs. Crandall between us. The adventure must have tired her out, because as soon as she sat down, she closed her eyes, and in less than a minute she began snoring.

"So that's not her husband's car, huh?"

"Maybe he had one like it," I said. "But that one's definitely not his."

"Too bad," said James. "It was a nice car." He sighed and stretched his arms out in front of him, his fingers laced together. "This isn't exactly how I pictured our farewell moment."

"How did you picture it?"

"Oh," he said, looking at his hands, "we were going to have that drink—maybe some Irish coffee—and then you were going to set the glass down and say something like, 'I can't go, James. I've fallen in love with you.' "

My throat was suddenly tight, and I swallowed hard.

"And then I was going to say, 'Good. Because I've fallen in love with you too.' "

We looked at each other, and for a moment I was tempted to lean over Mrs. Crandall's tasseled stocking cap and kiss him, but I knew to do so was to invite trouble. And I'd already had enough of that.

"I'd better go, James," I said, standing up. He was ready to stand too, but Mrs. Crandall, losing one of her supports, leaned into the other, and I shook my head. "You'll wake her up."

He smiled one of those wistful Rick-from-*Casablanca* smiles, and I suppose I smiled a wistful Elsa smile back at him. I blew him a kiss, and then, seeing him with that little white-haired lady nestled against him, I couldn't help but think of the Halloween night he helped Rich and me find our way back to the house. "You know what I like about you, James O'Neal? You're always rescuing lost souls."

He drummed his fingers against Mrs. Crandall's empty suitcase. "You know what I like about you, Geneva Jordan? I thought you might be the one who'd rescue mine."

Chapter 12

got on the plane feeling sad and weepy, but one time zone and a thousand-mile distance offered their balm.

It's easy to shut a door on your doubts and problems when you open another and find an apartment full of roses waiting for you (what *was* this rose theme Trevor seemed to be working?). Ten dozen (I counted) red roses arranged in ten vases on various surfaces of my living room. Coupled with the Christmas decorations I had put up, it made for one festive atmosphere.

"Trevor?" I called, feeling a little zip of excitement—a welcome counterpoint to the sorrow that for days had been a constant emotion. "Trevor, are you here?"

I kicked off my boots as he came out of the bedroom, very James Bond–ish in his silk robe, the cordless phone wedged between his ear and shoulder. He blew me a kiss, then pointed to the phone and mouthed, "Bartholomew."

He pretended to catch the kiss I threw back before disappearing back into the bedroom and closing the door.

I would have liked to unpack my things, but I certainly didn't want to bother Trevor during his conversation with the famed director. Ha! Actually I'd have loved to bother him, would have loved to jump on the extension and scream and holler and plead my case for at least a lousy *audition*, but no, I was an adult. I made a dry martini instead.

When his big-shot telephone call was finally over, Trevor stole out of the bedroom, coming up from behind to wrap his silky arms around me.

If there were an Olympic record in the straight-up jump, I would have broken it.

"My God, Trevor—don't sneak up on people like that!"

"I didn't sneak up on people, I sneaked up on you." He kissed my neck. "I hope you don't mind the roses—you don't think they're too overpowering, do you?"

"Not at all," I said, although the scent did seem to be on the verge of florist shop overkill. "I love them. Thank you."

"So how are you?" he asked. "How's everyone back home?"

I sighed. "Not too good."

"I'm so sorry, Geneva."

We stood there for a moment, his arms around me, his chin resting on the top of my head, looking out the window at the view, which pretty much consisted of the apartment building across the street.

"Well," said Trevor finally, turning me around, "as much as I'd like to stand here, we've got more important things to do."

"Do we have time?"

Trevor laughed. "Not for what you're talking about, you saucy little tart." Taking my hand, he led me to the couch and gently pushed me down. Then out of his robe pocket he took out a box.

"Trevor, I already opened presents early at Ann's. I'd like to wait until the real Christmas before I open any more."

"It's not a Christmas present."

His smile was boyish and hopeful, and as I opened the small, pretty box, my stomach muscles tensed, as if I had just dared someone to go ahead and punch me. Inside I found what I thought would be there: a diamond ring.

"Yikes," I said, and Trevor beamed, assuming I meant *Wow!* instead of *Great God in heaven, help me!*

"It's beautiful," I cooed, because (a) it was and (b) I didn't know what else to say.

"I think it's prettier than the first ring I gave you, don't you?" I nodded dumbly.

"Well, try it on," he said. "I had it sized, but you never know."

I slipped the ring on, trying not to be blinded by the mega-carat diamond or its implications. Holding my arm out, I moved my hand from side to side, as if I were just learning how to wave.

"You like it?" he asked again, his voice sounding younger than usual.

"I love it," I said, which wasn't a lie; it was a beautiful ring. But when the word *engagement* preceded it, it seemed gaudy, out of place, *wrong* somehow.

"I'm glad," said Trevor, and he leaned toward me, giving me a quick kiss. "Now let's get to the theater—everyone's dying to see it."

I threw myself into the business of holiday cheer and getting ready for the show, although a telephone call from Claire didn't help with the former.

"Geneva, I've got some good news and some bad news."

I could tell by the sound of her voice that the bad news was worse than the good news was good.

"I'm all ears."

"They want you for *Hoedown.*"

"*Hoedown* the cartoon?"

"Honestly, Geneva, do you know of any other *Hoedown* that's being cast?"

"Is that the good news or the bad news?"

I heard a little *tsk*. "Well, the good news, of course. These animated movies have long shelf lives, Geneva, and Bronco Betsy's a good, funny part."

"So what's the bad news?"

Now I heard my agent sigh. "They don't want you for Delilah."

"What?" This was news I was *not* expecting. "How can they not want me for Delilah? You said Norman Alexander wrote the part for me!"

"He did, Geneva, and he's sick about this. It's the producers who want to go with someone else."

"Well, can they do that? What happened to what Norman Alexander wants?"

"What can I tell you, Geneva? Apparently he doesn't have cast approval."

I felt myself beginning to tear up. "Did they tell you who they do want? And please don't say Ellie Armstrong."

Claire's chuckle was grim. "No, it's not Ellie Armstrong. It's Martine Jeffries."

"Who the hell is Martine Jeffries?"

"She's the twenty-three-year-old girlfriend of one of the producers, is who she is. Any more questions?"

"No," I said, understanding everything perfectly.

*T*he announcement of "Geneva Jordan's surprise return to *Mona!*" was in both the *Times* and the *Post*. I savored both my latte and the newspaper copy, which gushed about my star power and ability to boost the box office. "Hear that, assholes?" I rhetorically asked the producers of *Samson and Delilah*.

"More than enigmatic smiles are on the faces of *Mona!* fans," wrote Joyce Dean in her column. "Tonight Geneva Jordan returns to the role she originated, and it's SRO until next year!"

I chuckled; ol' Joyce wasn't above the "next year" joke every adolescent uses when a new year is just days away. My chuckle stopped, however, at Joyce's next line: "It should be a sweet reunion for Jordan and Trevor Waite, who not only continues in his role as da Vinci but reprises his offstage role as fiancé. We shall see if the second run is more successful than the first."

I flung the paper across the kitchen—it had been a while since I'd read a gossip column, let alone a gossip column with me in it, and I really didn't have the stomach for it. Not that Joyce Dean had said anything overtly slanderous; it was just being the target of her cutesy, prying knowingness that bothered me. But bother me long it didn't, skipper. I was going to be back onstage that evening, and I couldn't wait.

The day was cooperating with my mood too; it was a bright winter morning, and if I held my hand just right, I could catch a ray of light shining through the window on my diamond. I was getting mighty fond of this little gem, and warming up to its symbolism too.

"*B*aby doll!" greeted my hairdresser when I went in that afternoon. "You're back!"

We kissed each other's cheeks—Benny was one of the few people I knew whose lips made contact with a face and not just the air around it.

"I called, and Wendy said you had a cancellation."

"I didn't really," said Benny, taking my arm and leading me to his chair. "I just told Cin Flanders I had overbooked and asked if she could come in next week."

"You bumped Cin Flanders for me?" She was a local newscaster who'd recently become a network anchor.

"I'd bump Greta Garbo for you, dearie."

"Greta Garbo's dead."

"Of course she is. You don't think I would have bumped her if she were alive, do you?"

He draped the tiger-striped smock over me and sat me down in his chair. "So how's life? Did the baby-sitting work out okay?"

I looked forward to telling Benny all that had happened—he was a great gossip but could be just as good a listener when you needed him to be, and I wanted to tell him all about Rich and James and Conrad. But before I was able to utter a simple word, he screamed, "Oh, my God, what's that?"

"What's what?" I asked, hoping the question wasn't prompted by some sewer rat skittering up the shampoo sink.

"That," said Benny, pointing. "That rock on your finger."

"This?" I said, my heart still pounding in reaction to what I thought was a rogue rodent on the premises. "Well, that's my engagement ring, of course."

"You're engaged?" said Benny, clasping his hands to his chest. "To who?"

"Geez, Benny, you can't run a salon that caters to celebrities if you don't know what's what. It was in all the columns this morning."

"*To who?*"

"I believe the correct word would be *whom*." Benny was making me nervous; I felt if I gave him the wrong answer, he'd attack me with the curling iron. "To Trevor, of course."

That the color leached from his face gave me an indication that yes, I had given him the wrong answer, but as he didn't grab any hair implement as a weapon, I stayed in the chair.

We stared at each other in the mirror, and frankly, I didn't like what I was staring at: a man shaking his head, his face wearing the shocked expression of a witness to a train wreck with many casualties.

"Geez, Benny, don't look so thrilled."

I can't remember Benny ever being speechless, but he was now, standing there gaping at me, his mouth open.

"Benny, are you all right? You're not having a stroke or anything, are you?"

He failed to laugh at my questionable joke and continued giving me the fish-eye.

"Really, Benny, if you're just going to stand there and—"

"Say it isn't so, Geneva," he finally managed to say. "Tell me you're not going to make that kind of mistake."

I didn't know if it was a hot flash or a by-product of embarrassment—either way, I felt mighty flushed.

"The last time you were in here the cad was out of your life for good, and we were glad of it, remember? And now you're going to *marry* him?"

I swallowed hard, feeling I was either going to burst into tears or a temper tantrum. "He's changed," I said quietly. "He's admitted his mistakes, and now we're going to move on."

"Until the next bimbo comes along."

The conversation was vaguely familiar, and I remembered I had had virtually the same one with Ann when she found out Trevor had proposed.

"Benny," I said loftily, "*bimbo* is a sexist term."

One of Benny's eyebrows lifted in a perfect, cynical arc.

"So what are we looking at today?" he said, suddenly business-like. "The usual trim?"

I nodded, willing away the tears that wanted to spring forth.

He snipped my hair in silence, and we both expended lots of energy making sure we never made eye contact in the mirror. I tried to eavesdrop on other conversations between stylists and clients, but nothing held my attention.

I jumped a little when Benny turned the blow dryer on me.

"Oh, sorry, dear, I didn't mean to scare you," said Benny. He turned off the dryer and put his hands on my shoulder. "Look, Geneva, I only want what's best for you. Don't you know that?"

I nodded, those damn tears disobeying what was supposed to be a long-term order and welling in my eyes.

"He has changed, Benny," I said, my voice raspy.

"I hope so." He fluffed my hair with his hands and then leaned close to my ear, his voice back to its have-I-got-a-secret-for-you mode. "Now, did I tell you what happened to Erin Michaels when she went to Palm Beach last weekend?"

*M*y dressing room was an advertisement for floral arrangements and Western Union.

From the telegrams, one would have thought best wishes were being sent to a boxing champ.

"Knock 'em dead!" read Angus Powell's, and Claire's advised that I "kill 'em!" Whatever happened to the more benign "break a leg"?

I had the kind of energy that made me want to race around the room like a pony. If my metabolism were always this jazzed up, I'd wear a size minus two instead of a size ten.

After I reglued the corners of my false eyelashes, I looked into the mirror circled with telegrams and did some vocal warm-ups. "On-ye-way-mo-oh-oh-oh, on-ye-way-mo-oh-oh-oh, on-ye-way-mo-oh-oh-oh."

The stage manager knocked on the door.

"Fifteen minutes, Miss Jordan."

"On-ye-way-mo-oh-oh-oh."

I moved my mouth with great exaggeration. "On-ye-way-mo-oh-oh-oh." My reflection reminded me of a drag queen's, but this was no great shock; in my mind, most Broadway actresses do look like drag queens. It's that stage-makeup thing.

Standing up, I walked across the room and back, breathing deeply, running song lyrics through my head—not only mine but some from Trevor's ballad: *I am an artist / Yet this could be the hardest / Face I've ever tried to capture / Can paints and oils convey rapture / The rapture of her smile?*

In costume, I held out my peasant skirt and did a little dance step. Some actors don't like to get dressed until the last minute, but I always get dressed early and then excuse my dresser, wanting to spend time alone, sitting around in full costume and makeup and settling into my character.

I danced some more, watching myself in the mirror and admiring how gracefully my hands moved. They felt light and girlish, and I realized that my left hand in particular *was* probably lighter. I had taken off my engagement ring (I could hardly go onstage as Mona Lisa wearing that rock), putting it in the pocket of my robe, which was hanging on the door hook (surely would-be thieves would never look in the pocket of a pink chenille robe). I can't say I was dying to put it back on or that my finger felt lonesome without it; no, I can't say that at all. Still, just because I hadn't bonded with my engagement ring didn't mean I hadn't bonded with my engagement.

"Oh, yeah?" I said out loud, plopping myself down in an overstuffed chair. My impulse was to spring up again, go through a few more dance steps and songs. After all, I had a show to worry about. I didn't need to sit and worry about my personal life. And yet I sat.

Ann had called me after I'd gotten back from Benny's to wish me luck.

"I saw James yesterday when he dropped off the mail, and he told me to tell you to knock their socks off."

"How was he?"

"James? Well, I didn't get to talk to him much, but he looked fine. Well, actually he looked cold. It was twenty below yesterday."

"That I do not miss," I said, and then I asked, "How's Rich?"

I could hear Ann's sigh loud and clear over the phone line. "Grief-stricken. Really, Geneva, it's as if he's been struck by grief. I understand that expression now—it's as if he's been hit by lightning, and everything's been numbed. That jolt of grief has just seared him."

"Can I talk to him?"

"Oof, this coffee's hot," said Ann, making a sucking sound. "Rich isn't here. He and Riley are taking a walk."

"In twenty-below weather?"

Ann managed a small laugh. "Oh, it warmed up. It's only eighteen below today."

We talked a little longer of Barb ("She and I are going out for dessert tonight," said Ann), and then I told my sister about my new jewelry.

"So you're officially engaged?" she asked.

"Well, if it's the ring that makes an engagement official, then I guess it's official."

There was a long pause.

"So I take it you're not willing to be my matron of honor?" I asked, and when the expected laugh didn't come, I said, "Ann, can't you at least fake it?"

"To make you feel better? No, Gen, I'm not going to fake feeling happy about news that makes me sad. You deserve better."

"You know what, Ann? I'm looking at the clock here, and I've really got to get to the theater. Give everyone my love."

"But I wanted—"

I love phone conversations in that if need be, you can end them forcefully. Hanging up on someone is like slamming a door in their face, and that is what I did to Ann.

"*I* do love Trevor," I mouthed to the mirror, gesturing broadly. "He may have his faults, but so do I."

There was a rap on the door. "Mona? It's Lennie."

Speak of the devil. He was outside my door.

"Come in."

Trevor cut a dashing figure as Leonardo da Vinci, in his leggings and flowing clothes and floppy hat. He swooped in, took me in his arms, and kissed me.

"It's show time, darling. Now let's go out there and give them what they want."

And we did. Trevor and I were electric together. When we danced, we kicked higher; when we sang, our notes were truer; and when we said our lines, it was as if we were saying and hearing them for the first time. I heard sniffles in the audience when he sang Leonardo's ballad to me, and felt my own tear snake down my face (just one very dramatic tear—don't ask me how I do it). We had the audience in our hands, and when we put them gently down after the closing number, they responded with rousing applause, standing and clapping and cheering. I took more bows than a geisha in training.

When the curtain was brought down for the final time, Trevor lifted me up in a hug.

"We were great!"

"We were, weren't we?" I said, clamping my legs around him.

He carried me past the cast, who stood backstage applauding me, past the stagehands who said, "Great show!" and "Wow!" and into the hallway that led to our dressing rooms.

"Whew." He put me down and, giving me a quick kiss, said, "See you in ten."

He opened the door to his dressing room, threw me another kiss, and shut the door. I walked down the hall, feeling mildly disappointed that he hadn't carried me all the way to my room, carried me across the threshold.

I didn't have much time to be disappointed; I only had time to put my engagement ring back on before my room was swarming with well-wishers and echoing with the sound of popping champagne corks.

"Geneva," said Claire, looking awfully chic in a white wool suit, "you just reminded me why I'm so honored to represent you."

"Claire," I said, feeling a hint of a lump rising in my throat, "that's the nicest thing you've ever said to me. Next to 'I've decided to represent you for free.' "

"You wish," she said, accepting a glass of champagne from a chorus member who was doubling as waiter.

"I've never seen you do a better first act," said Paul Drake, the show's director. "You were *on*, Geneva."

"Thanks, Paul," I said, stifling my urge to ask, *What was wrong with the second act?* Instead I took a glass of champagne and held it up in invitation, but Paul shook his head.

"On the wagon," he whispered. "*Again.*"

"Well, good for you," I said, and didn't drink from my own glass until he was on the other side of the room.

I basked in the glow of admiration, posed for pictures with the lyricist and his boyfriend, shook hands with the husbands and wives and partners of chorus members, and autographed yet another picture for the mayor's wife, who had seen the show fourteen times. I was a queen bee, buzzing around in my hive and loving every minute of it.

"Miss Jordan!" The tall, dark woman wore a big smile and a pretty scent.

I shook her outstretched hand, smiling back at her.

"I'm Meg Adams," she said, reading in my face that I didn't remember her. "I'm working on the Pour Deux account. We met up in Bedford?"

Tipping my head back in recognition, I said, "Oh, yes. I believe I was a bit of a crank that night."

"Not at all. I was just thrilled to meet you. Thrilled to finally see the show. I didn't want to see it until you were back in it."

"How kind of you to say so," I said in my best Gloria Swanson diva voice, and then I made a big deal out of needing more champagne, which I actually did. Need, I mean.

Seeing Meg made me feel a little funny in the chest, as if I had an itch there, but not quite. I sincerely doubted that she and Trevor had anything going; it's just that I didn't know how sincere my doubt was. And where was the British gift to women and theatergoers anyway? Hadn't he said, "See you in ten?" Was I wrong to presume that was minutes? The final curtain had been almost a half hour ago. Wouldn't that have given him plenty of time to shower and primp? Wouldn't you think that someone's fiancé would want to hurry up and join the party celebrating his wife-to-be's return to the show?

"Excuse me," I said, angling past a knot of people whose response to having me within earshot was to begin throwing me compliments.

"Fabulous show, Geneva!"

"I feel I saw a piece of theater history."

"They should give you another Tony for tonight's performance."

"Thank you," I said, inches from the door, "thank you so much."

I marched down the hallway, where a few revelers had escaped the crush of my dressing room.

An actress who plays one of Mona's confidantes saluted me as I passed. "You and Trevor were magic tonight, Geneva."

I nodded in thanks, and I can't say that a light went on, that I had an epiphany or an awakening, but I did finally acknowledge the truth that had been like an old mangy dog in the corner. I had tried hard to ignore it, but I had always known it was there. Trevor and I *were* magic—onstage. And that's a powerful thing, but it doesn't mean the magic is transferable. I deserved to have a leading man like Trevor onstage; conversely, I *did not* deserve to have a leading man like Trevor in my life.

I walked faster to Trevor's dressing room, giddy, feeling such love for him—as my *costar*. I wanted to break down his door and offer him the revelation *We have* real lives!"

A foot away from his door I stopped, hearing voices. My knees went weak, but not for reasons you'd suspect. I wasn't hearing the dulcet tones of Trevor as he declared his undying love and commitment to Meg and Pour Deux cologne; I was hearing a voice that, at least to my ears, was far more musical.

"Great show, Miss Jordan!"

Holding up the long skirt I still hadn't changed out of, I ran backstage.

"Quite a performance, Geneva," said the stage manager.

"Thanks," I said, confused. There was no one else on the stage except two guys pushing aside a flat painted to look like sixteenth-century Rome.

"Rich?" I said.

"Great show, Miss Jordan," repeated my nephew. I heard his throaty giggle, and as he stepped out from behind the far curtain he said, "Hi, Aunt Gennie!"

"Good heavenly days," I said, opening my arms. He ran into them to give me one of his linebacker hugs. "What's going on, Rich? I just talked to your mom today—she didn't say you were coming."

We held on to each other for a long time before he disentangled himself. "Merry Christmas, Aunt Gennie! I'm your Christmas present!"

Rich was wearing Connie's baseball cap, and I flipped up the brim.

"Oh, Aunt Gennie, you were so good in that play!"

I laughed, loving the way he said each sentence with the enthusiasm of a page asking the masses to hail the king.

"When did you get here? How did you get up there? Rich, who's with you?"

He giggled again. "Well, James is, of course."

"Hi, Geneva," said James.

I followed his voice and saw him standing in the orchestra pit.

"If you don't know these guys, I'm in big trouble," said the stage manager. "But your agent convinced me they were for real."

"They're for real, Jack," I said, walking arm in arm with Rich toward the lip of the stage.

"Hey, Aunt Gennie, are you surprised to see us?"

"To put it mildly."

"I've dreamed of playing Broadway, Geneva," said James, sitting down at the piano. "So don't wake me up."

And then, following the sheet music on the piano stand, he played my ballad from *Mona!*

> *My smile, you say, is like a country no explorer's ever seen*
> *How can I paint the mystery, the history of this exotic place?*
> *Oh, Leonardo, it's nothing more than a woman*
> *In love with a man, nothing more than that sun upon my face.*

I sang along with James, and I must have been putting my heart and soul into it, because by the time I'd finished, a nice little crowd had gathered in the wings and applauded me. I bowed deeply and gestured toward the orchestra pit. "And please, let's hear it for my accompanist."

I stood staring down at James, and he stood staring up at me, and the smile on my face felt as goofy as the one on his face looked. I thought at any moment I might paw the ground with my toe and offer a giggly *Aw, shucks.*

"Geneva?"

Uh-oh, kids—play innocent, the principal's here!

"Trevor," I said, turning, "You remember Rich."

"How you doing, buddy?" asked Trevor, holding out his hand.

"Okay, I guess," said Rich, suddenly shy.

"And the guy coming out of the orchestra pit is my friend James. James O'Neal."

James raced onto the stage, and the two men shook hands.

"Are you joining us for supper?" Trevor asked James, who looked at me, shrugging slightly.

I smiled at Rich and James. "Will you excuse me for a moment?" Taking Trevor's arm, I walked with him not to where the small crowd had gathered, but to the empty side of the stage. There was a time and place for an audience, and this was not one.

"Trevor," I said, tugging my ring off my finger, "I can't use this anymore."

Trevor looked like a soldier whose commanding officer had just told him to go flush out a sniper. "Geneva, what are you saying?"

"I'm saying, or I'm trying to say, that I don't want to marry you anymore, Trevor. I'm sorry, I don't want to hurt you, but I just can't marry you."

"Why not?" His voice carried a tone of *how dare you?*

"For the same reason you shouldn't marry me. We don't really love each other. At least not the way we deserve to be loved."

"The way we *deserve* to be loved? What exactly is that supposed to mean, Geneva?"

"I need someone I can count on, Trevor," I said quietly. "Someone I'm sure about."

Trevor, his nostrils flaring, turned around and looked at James. "It's he, isn't it?"

"Well, yes, Trevor, it is." I felt power and wonder admitting it. "It is."

More than one magazine or entertainment reporter has enthused about Trevor Waite's icy blue eyes, and it's true, they are a sight to behold, but the last time they fixed their gaze on me, they were full of anger and hurt and, I'd like to think, a teensy bit of relief. After that long stare, and without another word from either one of us, Trevor turned and then, letting me know he'd do just fine, tossed my engagement ring up in the air, catching it as casually as if he were tossing a quarter. He then walked across the stage and out of my life.

*T*he night was bright with neon and Christmas lights as we left the theater and began walking down Forty-second Street. It seemed as if the snow hadn't yet decided what it was going to do; there was the random flake falling, but it was definitely more a solo act than a big production.

"Never in my wildest dreams did I think I'd be with you two tonight. How come you didn't tell me you were coming?"

"It was sort of an impulse thing," said James.

"Yeah," said Rich.

James went on, "Not only did we not tell you *we* were coming, but—"

"Mom and Dad are here too!"

"But . . . but Ann called me from Minneapolis today."

"No," said James. "Ann called you from the hotel. Since Karin took Natalie to Hawaii, well, the rest of us decided Christmas in New York was not a bad idea."

"Still surprised, Aunt Gennie?"

I nodded, even though *surprised* was too small a word for the way I felt.

A pretzel vendor stood by his cart, rocking from side to side and slapping his hands together.

"Ooh, can I have one?" asked Rich.

"Go for it," said James, handing him a bill.

"He was *bereft*," said James as we watched Rich gallop to the vendor. "When I mentioned to Ann that I was thinking of coming to see you, well, everything just escalated. We all wanted to get away . . . to get Rich away." He buttoned the top button of a well-cut coat, obviously a holdover from his corporate days. "We can't take away his sadness, but at least we could get him away from ground zero. Give him a little reprieve."

"It seems to be working," I said, seeing Rich pat the vendor's shoulder as he accepted his pretzel. "How long are you staying?"

"Well, I think your sister's got a big Christmas celebration planned for tomorrow night and the Blasters don't have a game until the third, so . . . so I thought I'd hang around long enough to see if I could get a date for New Year's Eve."

"Hmm," I said, tapping my chin. "I might have a friend—no, she's not your type. . . . Oh, then there's—no, she's not your type either."

"No one's my type," said James pulling me to him, "except you."

"And you're mine!" said this prom queen, who finally realized it wasn't the BMOC who was for her, but the nice guy in homeroom who was always willing to help her with her homework.

And then we did what we did so well. We kissed, and my heart raced and my face flushed and I felt woozy.

"Whew," I said, turning my head, "I think I'm having a hot flash."

"Me too," said James.

"Hey, you guys were kissing," said Rich.

"Guilty," admitted James.

The three of us linked arms and sashayed down Forty-second Street like we were at the head of the Macy's Thanksgiving Day parade. Both James and I took a bite of the pretzel Rich offered, and when I saw the smear of mustard on the sleeve of my good coat, it couldn't have bothered me less.

People passed us, and as we sidestepped a group of Japanese tourists, Rich greeted one.

"Hey, pal."

The tourist nodded, smiling, and I . . . well, I was filled with a sense of bliss.

I knew that it would take Rich a long time to learn how to carry the weight of Conrad's loss so that it wouldn't drown him, but I also knew that Conrad's love, as his sister had said, would be a lifeboat too, something Rich could climb into and stay afloat. And if the loss sometimes seemed stronger than the love, if the boat tipped over, I knew Rich had people who would swim out to him and help him hold on. And he, in his unpolished but steadfast way, would dog-paddle out to the rest of us and help us hold on. *That* was my bliss, knowing that when people love each other, they know what their jobs are.

I looked at James, who was gawking at all that Times Square gives someone to gawk at, and I knew it might be hard—no, make that *extremely* hard—figuring out how a menopausal Broadway star like me and an introspective mailman like him were going to have a life together, but I thought I was up to the challenge. Better yet, I *knew* James was.

He turned toward me, and one of those random snow flakes

landed on the outside curve of his nostril, where it sparkled for a second like a diamond nose stud.

I squeezed his arm, smiling. "Hey, pal."

He nudged my hip with his own. "Hey, yourself," he said, and his cheeks bunched up in that funny chipmunk way as he smiled back.

Epilogue

nce a woman came up to me while I was lingerie shopping at Bergdorf's and said she had just seen *The Wench of Wellsmore* the night before.

Suffice it to say it's a little disconcerting to have a stranger grab your arm, especially when draped over that arm is any number of lacy (padded) bras and (control-top) panties. Plus she had that shiny-eyed zeal of what might be a dangerous fan, so I thanked her kindly, but not too kindly, and proceeded to the dressing room, where I hoped she wouldn't follow me.

She did, however, and this fact seemed to distress her as much as it did me.

"Oh, God, you want to try on lingerie and here I am following you. I'm so sorry, Miss Jordan, you must think I'm one of those rabid fans you read about."

The look on my face must have convinced her I hadn't quite abandoned that thought, and she laughed nervously.

"I'll get out of your way right now—but before I do, let me tell you what an incredible experience *The Wench of Wellsmore* was. I was so sad when the curtain closed."

"But it had a happy ending," I said, relaxing a little, my fine-tuned antenna assuring me that while this suburban matron (her chic but understated hairstyle and well-cut coat screamed Greenwich) was enthusiastic, she was hardly rabid.

"Well, sure, for a while maybe—but did their happiness last? Did the wench adapt to life as a baroness? Did the baron's mother ever apologize to her? And what about the scullery maid? Did she and the butler finally get together?"

I understood her need to know more; I'm a sucker for an epilogue, too. It's a chance to tie up all the loose ends, or at least cauterize them so they don't unravel.

Samson and Delilah was a smash, and Martine Jeffries is enjoying all the acclaim she deserves. (I saw the production and she was wonderful—a big Ethel Merman voice coming out of a Mary Martin body.) My approval of the actress, however, didn't stop me from railing on Norman Alexander when I ran into him at a benefit.

"Thanks for standing up for me, Norman."

"Damn it, I thought I was going to escape without your seeing me."

"I saw the play, Norman. It's good, and Martine's good."

A look of surprise lifted his features. "You mean it?"

"Of course I mean it. I'm not saying I wouldn't have been the Delilah to beat all Delilahs, but . . . Martine was good."

"You know I really pushed for you, Geneva."

"I know," I said, feeling teary.

"I wanted to call you, to write you, but I . . . well, there's no excuse for bad manners. What can I do to make it up to you?"

Now this was a question I'd normally toss off a smart remark to, but if Norman Alexander was asking . . .

"Well . . . I'm thinking of doing a nightclub act."

"Seriously? Have you got a writer?"

"It depends. Do you know a good one?"

Some of Norman Alexander's success had obviously gone to his teeth, because he sported blinding white dentures, and the smile he gave me was positively luminous. "Sure I do. I've always wanted to write a nightclub act."

"You have?"

He nodded. "Especially for someone like you."

So that's what I've been working on lately. I'm not saying my days on Broadway are over by any means; I'm just saying I'm not going to sit around until the next part comes along.

I have every confidence that James can accompany me, and so does he. Our little preview performances have gone swell—twice in church I've sung with him, and once in a downtown Minneapolis bar that was hosting a party for the pipefitters union, we took over the piano and regaled everyone in a two-hour song-fest. We made fifty-five dollars in tips, a house record according to the manager.

I've reminded him that Manhattan audiences are a little more sophisticated than church congregations or half-drunk plumbers in Minneapolis, to which he replied, "Your snobbery is one of your least attractive qualities, Geneva. Besides, I could play any-where, as long as you're with me."

James still carries mail; I saw him in his summer uniform for the first time, and he's right, his legs *are* shapely. I get to Min-neapolis every couple of weeks, and he visits me in New York every other month. When I recorded Bronco Betsy in Los Ange-les, he and Natalie spent a long weekend with me. It thrilled Natalie that she got to meet Nick Ralston, who does the voice of Wendell the Wonder Wizard on PBS.

At lunch with Faith Bennet the other day, she told me she was glad for me.

"When I heard you fell for some mailman in Minneapolis, I thought, oops, she's finally lost it, but seeing you now—well, I've never seen you look better."

"Thanks, Faith."

"I mean, when you were with Trevor, you always looked so—I don't know—haggard. Haggard and anxious."

My smile tightened. "*Thanks,* Faith."

"Oh, you know what I mean," she said with a laugh. "Anyway, good for you. You give me hope. Maybe I'll find my own mailman."

"Just as long as he's a nice guy."

"Is that the secret?" asked Faith, and her lower lip, which she trembled for great comic effect on her sitcom, quivered, but I don't think she was trying for a laugh now. "To find a nice guy?"

"I don't think it's a secret, Faith. For women like us, it's a revelation."

*R*ich is taking his role as best man very seriously. Yesterday I found him standing in front of his bedroom mirror, fumbling in his pocket and asked him what he was doing.

"Practicing," he said. "I'm practicing getting the ring out of my pocket."

Today the men (with Ann and me exercising the power to veto) are going to pick out the tuxedos. Ann and Barb and Claire are going to be my bridesmaids, but I've told them just to wear something pretty because I refuse to dress grown women in bridesmaids' dresses.

Claire is trying to be enthusiastic for me—she really seems to like James—but ours is a union that she believes is destined to fail.

"This is my last shot at trying to get you to reconsider," she said over the phone, "and then I'll shut up."

"Why don't you skip the first part and jump to the last?"

"I just don't want you to get hurt, Geneva."

"Believe me, Claire, that's the last thing I want to get."

"Well, then, look at how rife the situation is for it! You haven't worked out where you're going to live, and I sincerely doubt you'd be happy living in Wide Lake—"

"Deep Lake, Claire. It's Deep Lake. And who says we're going to live there?"

"You mean you'll stay in New York?"

"We'll probably be commuters for a while, but eventually we'll live together. It might be in Manhattan, it might be in Minneapolis."

My agent scoffed. "And what about Natalie? If you choose New York, how will James bear to be away from his daughter?"

"We've been talking to Karin. She seems willing to give James more custody—especially since she travels so much."

"So you've got it all worked out, hmm?"

I laughed. "Good heavens, no! I don't know if we'll ever have it all worked out. But the point is, we want to *try*."

I didn't dare tell her about the calls we'd recently made to American and overseas adoption agencies—it was still James's and my beautiful little secret, and it would send her to prescription medication.

I heard nothing on the phone for a while except a noise I often hear Claire make when she was deep in thought: the tapping of her pen against her desk blotter.

"What if a great part for you comes up?"

"Then I'll audition for it."

"What if James doesn't want you to?"

"Claire, James wants me to be happy. If a great part'll make me happy, he'll be cheering me on on opening night."

"You sound so confident."

"I am," I said, "I'm confident in his love. Like a person in love should be."

Waiting for Ann and Riley to get home so that we could look at tuxedos, Rich and James and I sat on the couch in front of the big picture window that now offered a summer view. We would have sat out on the deck, but it was too muggy, and marauding mosquitoes were out patrolling for warm-blooded victims.

"Hey," I said, lifting *The Great Mysterious* off the coffee table. "I think I'll bring this to the wedding reception. It'll be our guest book—only people have to write in their answers instead of their names."

"Let's all read an answer," said Rich, and he plucked a slip of paper out of one of the pockets.

"The question is," he said, " 'What is your greatest fear?' " He opened the paper and furrowing his eyebrows read, " 'Pe-tun-ia.' "

James took my hand.

"What's it mean?" asked Rich. "Why would anyone be afraid of a petunia?"

"Not just any petunia, Rich, but a big, bad Petunia."

"So that's *your* answer, Aunt Gennie? Your greatest fear is a big bad flower?"

I smiled. "No, my Petunia was more like a big bad wolf. Only now I'm not so scared anymore."

"Why's that?"

I looked at my husband-to-be. "Because I've got someone to help me chase it away."

Rich looked at me and at James. Then, shaking his head, muttered, "Weird." He turned a page. "You pick one now, Auntie Gen."

My hand reached into the pocket underneath the question "What's the best piece of advice you could give to someone?"

" 'The best piece of advice I could give someone,' " I read, " 'is to not pay attention to advice if it doesn't sound like it would work for you.' "

Rich leaned into me, excited. "That's Connie's, isn't it?"

Nodding, I continued. " 'People are always giving me advice

like "Be careful," 'cause they think I'll fall or do something to hurt myself. If I took everyone's advice to be careful, I'd never have any fun! My swim coach never tells me to be careful—he tells me, "You won't know if you don't try." The first time I ever swam across the pool I thought I was going to drown, but I didn't and I felt great afterwards, like I could do anything! If I had been careful, I'd never have gotten out of the shallow end, never would have known that feeling of feeling great. So remember, some people give advice that would actually hurt you if you followed it—you be the judge of what's right for you and tell everyone else to go eat shit!' "

"That's pretty good advice, isn't it?" asked Rich after a moment. "Except for that swearing part."

"It's *very* good advice," I said, and I could picture Connie writing it, his hand flailing out, his head tipped back, smiling his gummy smile as he penned the last words.

"I'm going to wear his hat to the wedding," Rich said, and then, his voice softening, he asked, "Is that okay? Okay for the best man to wear Connie's baseball cap?"

"It's more than okay," said James. "It's perfect."

*I*t was a noisy car ride to the tuxedo rental store, with everyone jabbering away except for me. I was content to look out the window and watch the passing landscape and think of the nightclub act we were set to open in September (heavy on the love songs, wouldn't you know), of how positive the woman at the agency that finds homes for South American infants sounded, of all the people who'd be gathering in a few days to see me and James get married in the church where I was now a member (officially that meant I paid a pledge, unofficially it meant I felt I belonged there). I was excited to see my parents and share *The Great Mysterious* with them, knowing that we all had some pretty good answers to those big questions, and if we didn't, we could get them from someone else. I thought of Grandma Hjordis and Grandpa Ole, of Great-uncle Carl and Great-aunt Tove, and hoped they'd all squeeze into some choice seat to watch the nuptials. If they did, I know they'd invite Conrad to join them, but only after Great-aunt Tove laid down the law: *No swearing. There'll be no swearing in church.*

I could see the twinkle in Connie's eyes as he considered this advice he might or might not take, and, shutting my own eyes, I said a silent prayer of thanks to the boy who knew the really important stuff: when it paid to be careful and when it paid not to.

About the Author

LORNA LANDVIK is the author of *Patty Jane's House of Curl*, the bestselling *Your Oasis on Flame Lake*, and *The Tall Pine Polka*. She is also an actor, playwright, and proud hockey mom.